A FIRE in THEIR HEARTS

A FIRE in THEIR HEARTS

PHILIP PARIS

Black&White

Black&White

First published in the UK in 2025 by
Black & White Publishing
An imprint of Bonnier Books UK
5th Floor, HYLO, 105 Bunhill Row,
London, EC1Y 8LZ

Copyright © Philip Paris 2025

All rights reserved.
No part of this publication may be reproduced,
stored or transmitted in any form by any means, electronic,
mechanical, photocopying or otherwise, without the
prior written permission of the publisher.

The right of Philip Paris to be identified as Author of this
work has been asserted by him in accordance with the
Copyright, Designs and Patents Act, 1988.
This is a work of fiction. Names, places, events and
incidents are either the products of the author's
imagination or used fictitiously. Any resemblance to
actual persons, living or dead, or actual
events is purely coincidental.

A CIP catalogue record for this book is available from the British Library.

ISBN (HBK): 978 1 78530 774 4
ISBN (TPBK): 978 1 78530 863 5

1 3 5 7 9 10 8 6 4 2

Typeset by IDSUK (Data Connection) Ltd
Printed and bound in Great Britain by Clays Ltd, Elcograf S.p.A.

The authorised representative in the EEA is Bonnier Books
UK (Ireland) Limited.
Registered office address: Floor 3, Block 3, Miesian Plaza,
Dublin 2, D02 Y754, Ireland
compliance@bonnierbooks.ie
www.blackandwhitepublishing.com

for Catherine

Prologue

10 December 1679 the Crown of London, *rocks off Deerness, Orkney*

MEN CRY OUT FOR LOVED ones, but there are no mothers, sisters or sweethearts to reply, only the creaking and cracking of huge oak planks as the doomed ship breaks up. They beg for the Lord's mercy, but the hungry sea screams louder and it will have all our souls before this night is over, for while Captain Teddico and his crew rowed to the safety of the shore, we were kept locked in the hold – left to die.

Two hundred and fifty-seven of us are crammed together with our filth and fear while the *Crown of London*, driven onto rocks off the coast of Orkney, is battered by a storm that will soon reduce everything to broken pieces of wood, canvas and bodies. Despite the desperate efforts of those heaving against the hatch, it remains fast.

And so the end of our long, hard fight has come to this, when we began with such hope and certainty. We who have been falsely accused, beaten, starved, tortured, forced to watch friends and family executed . . . all for daring to claim a freedom that is every Scotsman's right.

Amongst the madness and mayhem, I clutch to my chest my darling wife Violet, disguised as a man so that we would not be separated – now about to die for her love.

'I'm sorry,' I whisper, wishing desperately there was a way I could go back, undo what's done and save her from a watery grave.

Somehow she hears me above the howls of misery and despair, or perhaps it's simply that she knows what's in my heart. Her instincts were always so astute you could rely upon them even if they contradicted what your own eyes told you. I loosen my grip as Violet pulls back to look at me.

'Samuel, I would rather die than continue alone. I have no regrets.'

The few remaining lanterns that have not smashed on the floor swing wildly from their hooks, briefly illuminating the terrified faces around us before they are plunged back into darkness and making what is seen, then unseen, even more frightening.

'Better that we end this very night than be banished to a strange land.' She speaks so calmly, with such conviction and certainty; not at all as if she is standing on the edge of life itself. 'We've kept true to what is right, and for all his wealth and power the king is merely a man who'll eventually die and be replaced by another. Never doubt that others will continue our fight. We might not see it, but the time will come when Scotsmen don't have such hate in their hearts that they murder countrymen on sight for carrying a Bible.'

The ship lurches and we're pushed painfully by the crush of bodies, only staying upright because there is no space to fall down.

'Violet, if you get the chance, you must swim for the shore,' I beg her.

'Not without you.'

'Please! I'll try to keep us together—'

As if suddenly picked up by some giant, the vessel shifts upon the rocks, then a grating noise so loud it feels as though it is inside my head is followed immediately by icy water rushing into the hold. Within seconds, it is up to my waist. Men scream as we're engulfed by the sea, then moments later Violet is wrenched from my arms as we're sucked violently out of the broken hull – into the waiting blackness.

Part I

Covenanters and Kings

1

Violet
19 August 1662, Coylton, Ayrshire

We're thirteen years old and I've loved Samuel since that day when we were six and he presented me with five violets tied together with a blade of grass. And Samuel loves me, although, being a boy, he hasn't grasped this fact yet, even though we spend every single minute we can together. Our parents simply expect that we'll be married one day. So do I. When Samuel's a bit older, I'll let him know.

We're surrounded by heather on a hill that's halfway between our two homes. There's a depression on the top that allows us to be out of sight of anyone below and this is our usual meeting place. As so often happens, I'm lying on the ground while he sits and draws. I watch as his hand makes quick, precise movements across the paper, stopping occasionally to glance up before continuing. I know this scene well, yet I'm still fascinated by Samuel being so totally lost in concentration as he sketches in minute detail whatever has captured his interest. He must have dozens of similar drawings.

'Don't you tire of having me as your subject?' I ask him.

'Of course not. Each time is new … the light, your face, your hair.'

'How can my face be new? It's the same one I've always had.'

He looks up briefly to cast me an amused look. 'Violet, you obviously change with every year that passes. And you'd be surprised how much you give away. You're so . . .' He searches for the right word, trying to sound more grown up than he is. '. . . brilliantly expressive,' he finally says, flashing me a quick smile.

Well, I don't know about my face being 'brilliantly expressive'. I do know that it's unlikely anyone would ever consider me attractive, yet that's strangely never bothered me. I'm tall and strong and, despite Samuel's enthusiasm, I've always considered my face to be . . . sturdy.

'Now your father—'

'Careful.' I cut him off in case he says something inappropriate, for no one is allowed to criticise Father in my company. 'And don't forget who pays for all your painting materials.'

'Well, of course he's very generous, but you have to admit he's a bit dour. His expression is nearly always the same, whatever he feels inside. I think a single sketch of him would capture his personality.'

'What about *your* father!'

'He's meant to be dour. He's a Church of Scotland minister. There . . .'

Samuel turns around the papers on his knee so that I can see what he has created with nothing but a small piece of graphite held within a brass holder. I can't help a small gasp; he has such skill, such an eye for the hidden wonder in this world.

'See,' he says, 'because your head is propped on your elbow, your long black hair falls towards the ground in a certain way, and it's moved by the breeze in a certain way. No matter how often you lie again in that same position, your hair will never fall exactly the way it just has. Nor will the sun shine on the curves of your nose and chin in the way it has this morning.'

He carefully puts the papers and the brass holder into a canvas case then lies down, curling up into my side with his head on my chest. My breasts are small mounds, and despite Samuel's artist's eye, I doubt he's even noticed those particular changes in me. He's intelligent and sensitive, yet maddeningly naive and impulsive. I'm not certain who takes care of whom at times.

For a while, I hold him tightly against my body. His beautiful wavy ginger hair is only inches from my face. It seems to grow at the speed of a galloping horse, and I often tease him that if he had been a girl such a striking colour would see him accused of being a witch.

I just ... love him so much. Sometimes it feels frightening.

'If you weren't meant to become a minister, you would be good enough to be an artist.'

'And you would like to follow your father into medicine,' he says.

My father sailed around the world as a ship's surgeon and returned to Scotland with ideas and knowledge that he takes great pleasure in secretly passing on to me. We spend hours together in his study during the evenings. My twin brother, Hamish, and Mother are wary of this private tuition and insist that I never mention such unnatural activity outside of the house. As if I would be stupid enough to do so.

'Well, that would never be allowed,' I say, angry at the unfairness of it.

Samuel lies on his back, staring at the clouds above with a frown between his brows. It's always a sign that he's about to say something serious.

'You know the minister over at Maybole was forcibly thrown out of his manse last week?' he says. 'Then beaten up while he was merely trying to gather his few possessions off the ground.'

'That's awful!'

'My parents can barely sleep for worry at the moment. Every day there are more stories about the growing violence towards Covenanters from the king's army. And it's getting closer.'

Despite the heat of the day, I'm suddenly chilled by the thought of our families being in danger. 'My father,' I tell him, my voice thick with concern, 'says Scotland is heading towards a civil war the likes of which no one has ever seen.'

'A throne can never be for more than one,' adds Samuel, whose life as a minister may be stopped before it's even started. 'I'm frightened neighbours will end up fighting neighbours and even families will turn against one another.'

'It can't get that bad?'

In my heart I believe it can, but I just want to hear him say everything will be all right.

'Kirks will be split like logs on the cutting block. Many parishioners will stay loyal to their minister, like my father, because he's always been there for them, christening their babies, burying their dead and providing spiritual guidance and help when they most need it. Ordinary folk who are completely loyal to the monarch will still be in danger of his Royalist army.'

I stroke his hair. Samuel is strong and brave, but sometimes he's so vulnerable, although I would never say that to him.

I'm suddenly aware of shouting in the distance.

'Listen!'

We're silent for a few moments before picking up the frantic calls of Samuel's eight-year-old brother, Calum. We jump up, gather our things, and run towards the sound. We soon meet the boy, who's so out of breath we have to wait for him to recover enough to speak.

My Samuel is handsome, but his brother is the image of an angel, even with his face red from exertion and with snot running from his nose. His long blond hair is the envy of all the local girls and any one of them would willingly lose an eye for the chance to marry him when he's older. His mother says the angels take care of Calum because he looks like them. He's so innocent – and I hope he may remain so for as long as possible.

'Soldiers, Sam! Soldiers at the house threatening Father.'

Samuel starts forward but I grab him by the elbow. Just because he is already as tall as many grown men does not mean he's capable of fighting them.

'Don't even think about doing something foolish,' I tell him. 'How many soldiers, Calum?'

'Four plus a sergeant.'

'Run and get my father.'

'What can your father do?' asks Samuel, agitated at our delay.

'He's a man of high standing in the community. I think soldiers are less likely to start a fight if he's there.'

At least, I hope so.

Samuel nods his agreement, then the three of us set off as if the Devil himself is at our backs.

There are two soldiers outside the manse looking after five horses, which means the other three must be inside. We're panting hard and I take Samuel's hand to make him slow down so that we're walking by the time we pass the men. One of them makes a lewd comment about me and I feel Samuel tense, but I tighten my grip to prevent him from responding.

When we enter, I go with Samuel to stand beside his mother. The Reverend Colvil is in a fierce argument with the sergeant.

'I'll have you know, sergeant,' says Samuel's father, 'that I've been the minister here for more than ten years.' The reverend is a tall, powerfully built man, not easily intimidated, and yet I sense the situation is fast slipping from his grasp.

'I don't care how long you've been minister,' sneers the sergeant, 'we'll return at noon tomorrow, and if you've not left by then, you'll be forcibly thrown out. And that won't be all!'

Samuel's mother is shaking. We press in a little closer to her but dare not speak.

'This is a disgrace!' protests the reverend.

'Take it up with the king!'

The two men are locked in a tense stare when outside, the sound of a galloping horse approaches. Moments later, my father strides through the open doorway. He takes in the room with a sweep of his gaze, pausing on me, no doubt making sure that I appear all right.

'Andrew, are you all safe?' he asks Reverend Colvil.

'Douglas, thank you for coming. We're unhurt but have to leave the parish by noon tomorrow.'

'That's a ridiculously short time. What are your orders, sergeant?'

'Who the hell are you?' the man barks at Father.

'I'm Doctor Milligan, and you'll mind your tone when speaking to me.'

'This traitor is being thrown out of the parish because of his disloyalty to the king – and he's lucky to be alive if you ask me.'

'Well, if you've delivered the king's instructions, there's no reason to remain. The minister and his family can hardly pack their belongings with you lot standing in the way.'

The sergeant glares at my father. 'We'll be back at noon,' he shouts as he storms out, followed by his men.

When the soldiers ride away in a thunder of hooves, the tension in the room finally breaks and we all sigh with relief. Mrs Colvil goes to her husband and he puts his arms around her. Samuel hugs me. At that moment, Calum comes rushing into the house. He goes straight into his mother's embrace and bursts into tears.

'Where will you go, Andrew?' asks Father.

'I'm waiting for God's guidance on that.'

'Stay with us.'

Father says what I'm already hoping. In so many ways, we're like one big family. Hamish and Samuel are close friends and I treat Calum as a young brother.

'I appreciate the offer, Douglas,' says Reverend Colvil, 'but helping us would put you at risk and I won't allow that. We need to stay hidden for a while, at least until those particular soldiers have left the area. Then we'll see who wins between God and king.'

I catch Father's eye, and I see in his face the fear he has spoken out loud so often recently: war is brewing in Scotland.

And for us, it begins here, right now.

2

Violet
22 August 1662, near Coylton, Ayrshire

A NEARBY FARMER HAS OFFERED TO let the Reverend Colvil and his family stay in his large barn, which is currently free of animals. Although it's not ideal, it solves the immediate problem of where to spend their nights. This evening, they join us for our meal and we sit around the heavy oak table, as we've done on many occasions, for the minister and my father have been close friends for years.

'The barn is big enough to hold my sermons in, and this new law only prevents me from preaching in the kirk,' says Samuel's father, his face animated as he explains his plan to us.

'It also resulted in us being thrown out of the manse,' remarks Samuel's mother, who is stoic, practical and loyal, a combination of characteristics I'm beginning to think all wives need to have amongst a huge list of other requirements.

'Yes, my dear, that is true. I'm sorry.'

'Oh, it's not your fault, Andrew. I blame King Charles ... only within these walls, of course.'

'I believe most of the congregation will follow us,' he says.

'That will leave the kirk rather empty,' adds my own father, 'which is a situation the authorities won't allow to continue.

I assume they'll appoint a minister willing to obey the new bishop and everyone will be expected to attend his Sunday services.'

'I gather they've already named my replacement,' says Reverend Colvil. 'Some curate I've not heard of, who's been brought in from outside the area.'

'There'll be more conflict ahead over this,' says my mother. 'Don't hog the game pie, Hamish.'

'I wasn't.'

'Pass it around.'

'It just happens to be in front of me!'

With rather bad grace, Hamish pushes the large dish along the table.

'Why has the king thrown us out?' asks Calum, who has grown up in the manse and known no other home. 'Does he hate us?'

'The king doesn't actually know us,' says Hamish.

The Reverend Colvil nods gravely. 'That's true, though it doesn't stop him from hating us.'

'Why?' asks Calum.

There is a brief pause. It's only right that the minister answers the question, and I can almost see a long explanation forming in his mind.

'Don't give the boy a sermon, Andrew,' warns Samuel's mother quietly.

His kindly smile reveals he was indeed about to do that very thing, and in that brief gesture I see something of the younger man, before he was 'meant to be dour'.

'The Church of Scotland is Presbyterian, which means we have little hierarchy: there are no people above the ministers, elders or the congregation telling them how to worship. We believe that the head of the Kirk is Jesus, and we follow those teachings as given to us in the Scriptures.'

He waits for young Calum to nod that he understands before continuing. Around the table, all is quiet as the reverend speaks; even sounds of chewing and cutlery scraping against plates are dulled as his voice fills the room.

'King Charles, and his father before him, believes that he should be the head of the Church of Scotland and that he has the right to reintroduce a hierarchy of bishops with wider powers who can order everyone to worship in a way that is not our tradition. It's the way of Episcopalians or Anglicans in England.'

'He wants to make things simple for himself, with a similar styled church throughout the entire kingdom,' adds Mrs Colvil. 'That's what lay behind the introduction of Archbishop Laud's *Book of Common Prayer* all those many years ago, trying to force English ways of worship on Scottish people without our General Assembly having any say in the matter whatsoever!'

'Now the king insists that ministers have to be approved by the local laird and the bishop,' says Samuel. 'Isn't that right, Father?'

'And they have to swear an oath,' chimes in Hamish, keen to demonstrate his own understanding of the situation.

'You're both correct. Calum, it's important to understand it was only with the help of Covenanters that Oliver Cromwell won against King Charles I, and later on it was only with the aid of Covenanters that King Charles II won back his crown.'

'We fought on both sides?' asks Calum in surprise.

The reverend nods sombrely. 'Yes, and they both betrayed us, promising to make Presbyterianism the recognised religion when they needed fighting men, only to break their promises once they were in power.'

'Sadly it's so often the case that power and honour are strangers,' agrees my father.

'Is the king going to send more bad men?' asks Calum, his voice quivering.

As I'm sitting next to him, I gently take his arm and move him onto my knee, hugging him close. I could not bear it if anything happened to him.

'I can't promise you that, son. He's given orders to his army to evict ... throw out ... Scottish ministers who will not agree to his demands, even those who are happy to swear loyalty to him as the monarch.'

'As we are,' adds my father. 'That's never been an issue with the majority of Covenanters. During my travels around the world, I've encountered many different cultures and religions and have enjoyed conversations with extremely learned men about their beliefs.

'Some were pretty lively discussions, yet in every instance we each respected the other's right to hold that alternative view. In fact, I was often shown the greatest hospitality by those I had just had the greatest theological arguments with. It's when I come home to Scotland that I end up fearing for my safety, and that of my family.'

'There is only one God and one way to worship Him, Douglas,' says the Reverend Colvil. 'And these new bishops don't even pretend to be pious. They're powerful men who will use their position in the Church to their own advantage.'

'Of course, Andrew. I was only pointing out how I've encountered tolerance amongst religions completely at odds with our own.'

'State and Kirk should remain separate.'

'We're in complete agreement on this, yet we surely cannot take away from others their right to worship as they wish when freedom from oppression is the very thing that Covenanters are fighting for.'

An uncomfortable silence descends around the table. Father has raised an important issue for which there doesn't seem to be an answer. I love the Reverend Colvil like a second father, but if given the chance he would have the entire world Presbyterian, regardless of cultures and religions. He probably thinks the Pope should be converted and would no doubt be off to Italy on the first ship available if he thought there was a possibility. He'll accept no middle ground on which those with different opinions could meet to debate.

The old friends are entrenched in their views and stare at each other across the game pie, which might as well be a mountain of rock, such is the division between them on this point.

Eventually, it's my mother who breaks the deadlock. Without me realising, Calum has fallen asleep in my arms.

'You have a tired boy there, Violet. You're welcome to leave Calum here, Ellen. His presence overnight will not put anyone at risk.'

'Thank you, Isabel. I think that would be most helpful.'

It wouldn't be the first time that Calum has remained in our house rather than the Reverend Colvil having to carry him home. If soldiers come knocking on our door in the morning, no one will bother about a small boy, but the truth is that if Samuel and his parents stayed, they might put us in danger.

The suggestion is agreed upon and our meal brought to an early end by the tension in the room. As some of us clear away and others get ready to leave, Samuel and I offer to check that the animals and hens are all right. I suspect nobody believes for an instant this is why we're going outside.

'That was awful,' I say, once we're out of hearing.

Samuel exhales loudly. 'You can say that again. Of course, my father is right.'

'Well ...'

'What?'

'I would say that my father is right, but I'm not going to fall out with you on this, Samuel.'

'But this is not a point for debate, Violet! You either believe in God or you don't, and if you do then you acknowledge there is only one God and one way to worship Him.'

He's frowning, which is normally a bad sign, but I'm not backing down in my opinion or my own right to hold an opinion, despite being a girl and what others think, including my twin brother.

'What about people with different beliefs, like all of those that my father met on his travels?'

'They're wrong!'

'All of them!' I say, raising my eyebrows at him. 'Everyone in the entire world?'

'Yes.'

I take a huge breath to release some of the tension I can feel building up inside me. 'All right. As I believe in God as you do, I'll agree with you that they're wrong, but they still have a *right* to be wrong. That's their choice.'

'That just doesn't make sense.'

'Didn't the Lord Himself give us choice?'

'They need to be shown the correct way and if you don't agree with that then I don't see how you can truly—'

'Be careful what you say, Samuel.'

We fall silent as he paces around angrily, before coming back to face me. He's still frowning.

'Don't mutter, Samuel, it's annoying.'

'You either believe or you don't believe.'

'I believe as much as you do, as well as in the Covenanters' fight to free the Kirk from the king's control, and don't you ever dare imply otherwise. And stop frowning!'

'Well, if I'm frowning, your eyebrows look like ...'

'What?'

'Like ... caterpillars!'

'Caterpillars!'

'Yes, black, bushy ones that have almost disappeared under your hair.'

I'm on the verge of ... well, I don't know what, when Samuel bends over, suddenly helpless with laughter. I try to hold on to my anger, but it evaporates like a thin mist under a hot sun. I never could stay angry with him for long.

'I'll give you caterpillars,' I threaten.

'No, don't, they tickle.'

He takes me in his arms and for a few moments I stand stiffly, but I soon put my arms around his waist. He kisses my eyebrows.

'Sorry,' he says quietly.

I pretend not to have heard properly. 'What did you say?'

'SORRY.'

'I'm sorry too.' We pull apart to gaze at each other. 'Samuel, we must never let anything come between us. Promise?'

'I promise.'

'Then so do I.'

We hold each other again, tightly. I have no concerns about us. But when I think of dinner and the rift that so easily raised its ugly head across the table between old friends, a seed of fear plants itself in my heart and immediately begins to grow.

3

Violet
24 August 1662, near Coylton, Ayrshire

Word spreads like fire on a moor that is tinderbox dry and the Reverend Colvil's service in the barn this Sunday is attended by almost the entire congregation from his previous kirk. He's beaming with pride and I can't deny the feelings of hope and commitment that fill the building, which we spent all of yesterday cleaning out. It's an impressive victory for him, yet a tiny part of me is fearful. Fires can so easily get out of control.

'God is everywhere and He is no less in our hearts while we stand in this barn than He is when we're in the kirk. We have no disloyalty to King Charles as the monarch of Scotland, but the Scriptures are clear that the head of our Church is Jesus Christ, and no man, even the king, can replace him.'

The congregation hums in agreement. Samuel's father is a good preacher; for more than an hour he holds everyone's attention so tightly that we are like one large family. I too am swept up in the swell of hope and kinship that washes through the barn, proud that he is the father of the man I'll marry.

There is only one person amongst us who has loudly displayed his displeasure at being here.

'Today is a special occasion,' announces the reverend, 'for our congregation has a new addition.'

A young couple moves to the front, the woman holding a restless baby who has been crying throughout most of the sermon. Folk nod and smile and mutter quiet prayers for the baby's good health. The Reverend Colvil speaks softly to the parents while we watch on in silence. He's good at dealing with people of different ages and backgrounds, dispensing tenderness or severity depending upon what's required. Lifting up a small pewter flask of water, he speaks once more so that all can hear.

'For you, little child, Jesus Christ has come, he has fought, he has suffered. For you he entered the shadow of Gethsemane and the horror of Calvary. For you he uttered the cry, "It is finished!" For you he rose from the dead and ascended into heaven and there he intercedes – for you, little child, even though you do not know it. But in this way the word of the Gospel becomes true. We love him, because he first loved us.'

Then he lets a trickle of water fall onto the head of the baby in its mother's arms. 'I now baptise you Fraser Young, in the name of the Father and of the Son and of the Holy Ghost. Amen.'

* * *

It's strange to be outside by a barn rather than our familiar kirk, but there are still certain things expected of a minister's son and while Samuel speaks to members of the congregation, I walk to the area where horses belonging to the wealthier folk are tied up.

'I knew you would be here,' I say.

Hamish smiles back at me. 'Where else is there to be? I suppose Sam is stuck having to speak to people?'

'He sees it as good training.'

'I would rather speak to the horses.'

I stroke the neck of the nearest animal. 'Do they speak back?'

'Of course, you just have to know how to listen. Don't go near the bay, he's angry.'

'He told you?'

'If you go near him, he'll tell you as well!'

I watch my twin, so much more at ease with animals than people. He would never make a minister. Eventually, Samuel joins us and the two of us slip away, walking up a hill that doesn't particularly lead anywhere as we want to have some time alone and out of sight of others. He takes my hand and I smile.

'If everyone was as happy as I am now, then there would be no fighting anywhere,' I say. 'Maybe that's what's wrong with the king.'

'He needs to hold someone's hand?'

'Perhaps he doesn't have anyone.'

'There's probably an official, dressed in gold, called the king's hand-holder, and every time the king feels lonely this person rushes over and takes his hand!' Samuel stops walking. 'There might be others.'

'Like who?' I say, laughing and wondering what foolish ideas he's going to suggest.

'There could be an official ... mover of the king's hair,' he says, gently moving a strand of hair from my face. 'Or an official kisser of the king's eyebrows.'

'You said they looked like caterpillars!'

'Very nice caterpillars,' he says, kissing them tenderly.

'Maybe, there should just be an official kisser.'

'What would they do?' he asks, trying to sound innocent.

'This,' I reply.

It's a long while later before we continue our walk.

'I hope that one day I can give sermons as well as my father,' he says, when we've covered some distance in silence.

'I'm worried,' I reply. The fear that has been growing inside me nudges aside my happiness of earlier. 'The names of those who do not attend Sunday services in the kirk will gradually be gathered by the new curate and handed to the local garrison. Then everyone, including us, will be visited by soldiers demanding the payment of a fine or implementing some other punishment.'

'Well, what's my father supposed to do? He's a minister, and despite the king declaring that the Church of Scotland is now Episcopalian, my father's congregation wishes to listen to him rather than some poorly trained curate nobody knows. Is he meant to abandon his flock?'

He's too proud of his father. We're both too proud of our fathers to talk about them without emotion.

'No, of course not. Ministers throughout Scotland will hold similar events in barns and houses. They have no choice, and Parliament will have no choice but to react with violence, and at some point ordinary people will rise up with violence and there will be slaughter amongst innocent Scotsmen and women and we'll be caught up in it, Samuel, because we will have no choice, then you and Calum and others I love—'

Samuel takes me in his arms, for I'm crying uncontrollably as I relate with growing upset the words that I've heard my father say and which have gone around inside my head for days and nights, giving me hardly a moment's peace of mind.

'Shhh. It's all right, Violet. I've got you. You're safe.'

'We can't live on this hill to avoid people, and so we won't be safe! Those I love will die. I know it, Samuel. I feel this more strongly than ever.'

'We can't alter what is God's will.'

'But what is His will, Samuel? What *is* His will?'

4

Samuel
6 November 1666, near Coylton, Ayrshire

Hamish and I glance at each other nervously across the table. We've been planning this in secret for weeks but now we're about to announce it to our families my mouth is almost too dry to speak. Everyone has finished their meal so it's now or never. I stand up, in my haste knocking over my chair, which clatters loudly on the stone floor. It certainly gets everyone's attention.

'Samuel?' says Father.

'Hamish and I intend to help the Covenanter cause, to stop the king forcing Presbyterians to worship in ways that go against the Scriptures.' I had expected comments, but everyone remains silent. Violet's silence is almost thunderous. She doesn't know any of this. 'So we've decided to leave in a few days' time and let God guide our feet to a destination where we can make a difference.'

'Hamish,' says his father. 'Are you set on this course of action?'

Hamish stands, visibly bridling at the implication, which in truth is often made, that he always follows my decisions.

'Yes, Father. Sam and I are equally determined.'

Everyone turns to my father – everyone except Violet, who continues to stare at me. I pluck up the courage to give her a quick smile. The gesture is not returned.

'If Samuel and Hamish feel that they will be doing the work of God by making this journey, then it is not for us to hold these boys back,' he says.

With that simple statement, we are free to leave. But I'm quaking inside at having to face the girl I love.

* * *

'You could have discussed this with me!'

Our meeting is not going well. Violet and I have left everyone and come to the barn, where she's pacing around with increasing agitation.

'It wouldn't have been proper to do that before speaking to my parents.'

'Just what do you think you and my brother can do?'

'I don't know! I just know that I can't stay here and do nothing except listen to stories of violence against innocent people who can't protect themselves.'

'And you'll fight?'

'If I have to.'

'What about Hamish? He's doing this because you are, Samuel. You know that. It's not in his nature to fight.'

I don't reply because what she says is true. Violet's twin would be happier tending to animals and working the land.

'Please stop pacing around. Hamish has the right to make his own decision. Violet, stop!'

She faces me, panting hard with emotion.

'I'm sorry I didn't tell you, but I have to do this, Violet. I have to stand up to the tyranny of the king, the injustice of bishops telling us how to pray, the violence of the Royalist army killing people where they work in the field without any sort of trial. Even a witch could expect a court case.'

She's crying now. I take her in my arms.

'What sort of man would I be if I didn't do something? What sort of minister could I hope to become in the future? I'm not even sure I want to be a minister in the Church that we'll end up with if we don't make a stand to prevent these changes.'

'If you or Hamish are hurt ...'

'I promise I'll watch out for him. And I want you to look at me with pride ... on our wedding day.'

She pulls back. 'Our wedding day!'

'Of course, didn't I say? Once Hamish and I have returned, we'll get married. We're not going to be away for ever.'

'Samuel, that's about the most unromantic proposal a girl could get!'

'But you'll say yes?'

She doesn't. Instead, she buries her head in my chest and bursts into tears.

* * *

13 November 1666, Kirkcudbrightshire

Parting from our families had been a great deal more upsetting than Hamish and I had imagined. We weren't allowed to leave until we had as much food as we could sensibly carry, spare warm clothing plus some coins in our pockets. The most astonishing gift for me was from my father, who handed into my keeping the Colvil family dirk, the weapon made long ago by a skilled ancestor.

With nothing to guide our feet except the belief that God will take us in the right direction, we've headed south-east. Finding shelter has so far been easy with so many sympathetic to our journey and our spirits are high as we approach the outskirts of a village.

'What's this place?' says Hamish, as if I am somehow to know.

I ask the first person we meet, an elderly man carrying an armful of whins and twigs, no doubt for the fire from which smoke drifts reluctantly through the thatched roof of his tiny dwelling.

'It's the clachan of Dalry,' he replies, stopping to study us with an amused expression that instinctively makes me like him.

'Do you need a hand around your cottage?' I ask.

'Ha, I suppose you two want food.'

'We'll help for the pleasure of helping, though we wouldn't want to insult you by refusing your kind offer.'

'I haven't offered.'

'My mother says I'm too optimistic for my own good!'

This sets him off cackling, which turns into a coughing fit. We have to wait for him to recover.

'Well, ginger head, you can bring in the rest of those logs, and you,' he says to Hamish, 'chop up that wood over there.'

'Don't let him eat everything,' says Hamish, happily going off to complete his given task.

The cottage is similar to what can be found throughout Scotland, with one room to eat, sleep and live in. The small fire in the centre gives out little heat. There's a flimsy wooden partition that separates this area from a place where animals would live throughout the winter. I can tell straight away by the smell that there has been no livestock for a long while. Despite his age, the occupier is sharp-eyed.

'I've known too many seasons to keep animals, so it's easier to obtain milk or whatever I need from others who have some to spare. We look out for each other around here.'

'We don't want to take any food that you need yourself, sir.'

'I don't often get called that. You're heading east?'

'Yes, with no particular destination other than where God guides us.'

He goes quiet for a while and when he speaks again there is no humour in his voice. 'You carry a Bible?'

'No.'

'Good. You don't want to be caught around here with one. The king's—'

His sentence is interrupted by shouting. When we go to investigate we're faced with four soldiers and a corporal. Two of the soldiers step forward, roughly taking hold of the old man and tying his hands behind his back with rope they have ready for the task. Hamish and I are so stunned at this sudden aggression that we've no idea what to do.

'Keep out of this, lads,' the old man instructs us. 'Don't get into trouble because of me.'

In silence, we follow the group as it heads further into the centre of the village. People join us and soon there's a noisy crowd clamouring for the old man's release. As we near the alehouse, four men emerge on to the street. Although they appear extremely unkempt, as if they've been sleeping rough for a considerable time, the way they stand so erect and look about them with an air of confidence conveys a sense of privilege that immediately sets them apart from the ordinary villagers.

'Why have you bound this man?' asks one, stepping into the path of the corporal.

The two soldiers holding their victim continue to head towards the nearby blacksmith's forge. Hamish and I go with them, though we can clearly hear the angry exchange behind us.

'Don't you dare challenge my authority here,' replies the corporal. 'That filthy traitor has been fined for not attending the kirk and he's refusing to pay. He's about to find out that you can't defy the king.'

The blacksmith looks up in surprise as our small group enters his enclosure and I glance back to see the corporal, flanked by the remaining two soldiers, striding quickly towards us. If they're attempting to leave everyone else behind, it's certainly not working as more folk join the mass of bodies headed by the four men from the alehouse.

'Get on with it!' shouts the corporal as he reaches us.

One soldier pulls down the old man's jerkin to bare his thin, hairy chest, while from a knapsack another produces a short branding iron, the sort of implement used to mark the ownership of cattle. He thrusts the end into the glowing coals.

'What's the meaning of this?' asks the blacksmith, a huge man who, I suspect, is not intimidated by many.

'This man will be marked for his disloyalty and if he's got any crops they'll be destroyed as well.'

'You'll not use my forge to brand a man.'

'Swords!' shouts the corporal.

Everything that happens next is driven by instinct, with no thought to consequences, at least not on our part. As the men from the alehouse tackle the corporal and three of the soldiers, Hamish and I grab the one nearest to us. Several villagers immediately join in the scuffle, dragging the soldiers into the street and tying them up. Hamish and I are left by the forge, so I untie the old man and help pull up his jerkin.

'Thanks, ginger head,' he says quietly to me. 'Let's see what the Wanderers are going to do after this.'

Now I understand who the four men are. Wanderers – nonconformists who are usually forced to live as vagrants, hiding in the hills and depending upon food and aid from others. Some forgo their inheritance, including substantial estates and fortune, because of their belief in the Covenanter cause.

'Who's the one in charge?' I whisper.

'John Maclellan of Barscobe Castle,' he says. 'He's been avoiding the military for quite some while.'

'Well, they've certainly met each other today,' I reply.

With an expression of disgust, the blacksmith pulls the branding iron from his forge and throws it on the ground. We step out with him into the street. By the large number of people who have gathered, the entire village must be present. Maclellan is taking control; most folk must know who he is, because everyone listens with respect to what he says.

'Preventing an innocent Scotsman from being tortured was the right thing to do. How can honest men be considered so low that we're treated worse than beasts in the field? How can men like this –' He points at the corporal – 'treat us so?'

There is much nodding and a growing buzz of agreement amongst the villagers.

'What's happened will not go unpunished. More soldiers will come and anyone found here will be in danger. You can scatter to other places, taking your possessions. There should be sufficient time to get away safely ... Or we can raise such a noise that the king has to hear us!'

So many shouts and exclamations erupt from the crowd that it's difficult to gauge the overall mood, which seems a boiling cauldron of anger, fear and uncertainty. Maclellan lets them have a few moments before holding up a hand for silence.

'We can't win by ourselves but we know that people throughout the area, throughout Scotland, believe it's time for us to have the religious freedom that is our right. There are a dozen soldiers staying at Balmaclellan and extorting fines from the local population. I say we start by capturing them.'

'We don't have enough fighting men or weapons,' says the blacksmith.

'Do you speak for the village, hammerman?' asks Maclellan.

'Sometimes . . . yes.'

'Good. Send out messengers. Put men on horseback to take the news farther afield. We gather at Dalry and in the morning we capture some more of the king's soldiers.'

* * *

Around seventy of us walk the few miles south-east to the village of Balmaclellan. More men had arrived at Dalry before we left, but John Maclellan didn't want to take them all for so few soldiers. We're hoping there's enough of us to make them surrender without a fight. Hamish carries one of the blacksmith's hammers while I've picked up the branding iron. We've become friendly with some men from Ayr – Cornelius, Alexander and George. They're much older yet make no reference to our age or inexperience, and for that we're grateful.

'I think we've set a boulder rolling down the hill and it's already grown too big to stop,' says George, who's as short and stout as his friend Cornelius is tall and thin.

'Let's hope we don't get crushed by it,' adds Cornelius.

'John Maclellan seems a good leader,' says Hamish, who's keen to be involved in the conversation, keen to be viewed as an equal.

'Seems so,' replies George, 'although we don't know him. We were on our way to Dumfries looking for work when we heard the call. What about you two?'

'We arrived in Dalry as the trouble broke out,' says Hamish.

'Seeking work?' asks Cornelius.

Hamish looks to me to reply.

'Just seeking,' I say.

'We're all doing that, lad,' says George quietly.

When we get near to our destination, Maclellan orders a halt and then speaks to the three men he was with in the alehouse. We're soon split into groups. Maclellan comes over as if specifically seeking us out.

'Leave your weapons, lads. You can pick them up on the way back.'

'Why don't we keep them?' asks Hamish.

'Because you're fresh-faced and don't look threatening, not like these ugly bastards.'

This gets the Ayr men laughing loudly, and they appear to take no offence at the comment.

'Aren't we going to fight them?' asks Hamish.

'I don't want to fight them, I want to capture them, and the way of doing that without anyone getting hurt is to put them off their guard. So you two stay close to me.'

And so we follow in a group of fewer than twenty while the others head in different directions. The soldiers have taken over the largest house in the area and we stop a short distance away.

'They've not even set a watch,' says a man behind us.

'That's because they're confident,' replies Maclellan. 'Who have they to fear around here?' He raises his voice. 'The king's soldiers! We wish to speak to the king's soldiers!'

It's several minutes before figures stumble out of the front door, obviously having just grabbed muskets. Some men aren't even fully dressed and nearly all of them are blowing on the lit cords that are needed to ignite the black powder in their weapons.

'We're sorry indeed to interrupt you while breaking your fast, but we need to talk.'

Maclellan speaks as if we're all friends and his expression doesn't change, even when he's facing the muzzles of twelve muskets.

'What do you want here?' shouts the corporal. 'We're on the king's business and if you don't disperse immediately, I'll order my men to fire.'

I didn't understand Maclellan's strategy but realise now that he's got the soldiers exactly where he wants them. If they had seen a mass of seventy armed strangers, they would have barricaded themselves inside and the task of capturing them would have been much more dangerous.

'We don't wish to fight and there's no reason for anyone to get hurt,' says Maclellan, raising his arms as if to surrender. In reality, it's a signal. Scores of figures creep quietly around both sides of the building and form up behind the soldiers.

'All we want is for the king to listen to our demands. We've always confirmed our loyalty to the monarch, but we have a right to speak and be heard.'

The corporal and his men look around nervously, realising they're trapped and hopelessly outnumbered. Some of our men carry muskets, and these are raised almost casually.

I can see that the plan is to do everything slowly and without any sudden indication of a threat that might result in unnecessary violence.

'Lay down your weapons. You have my word that no one will be hurt.'

'Hah! The word of a traitor,' sneers the corporal.

One of the soldiers taken at Dalry is pushed forward. I hadn't even realised he was amongst us.

'Speak,' commands Maclellan.

'We were captured yesterday and have been treated well,' says the man miserably. 'I don't believe they mean to harm us.'

Several soldiers lower their muskets and a couple lay them gently on the ground.

'Retrieve your weapons!'

The corporal seems set on a pointless confrontation and as he aims at Maclellan, there is something about his stance and expression that makes my heart miss a beat. He intends to fire. The next moment there's the crack of a musket. People look around in surprise before the corporal sinks slowly to the ground.

'Damn,' says Maclellan, taking another step forward. 'There was no need for anyone to be hurt. Lay down your weapons. Bind them. Check him and if he's dead, see that he's buried appropriately nearby.'

He shouts these orders without even waiting for everyone to obey, his obvious status meaning that men simply obey his commands.

'This is bad,' says Hamish quietly to me. 'I think that one tiny ball of lead is about to result in a great deal of violence.'

I lay a hand on his shoulder protectively, but, of course, he's right. A soldier in the king's army has just been killed and the revenge upon us all will be terrible.

* * *

Within an hour of the events at Balmaclellan, most of us head east, while the captured soldiers are escorted to Dalry, where they'll be held with the others. We leave behind a freshly dug grave. As we move through the countryside, word spreads that Covenanters are to gather about six miles north-west of Dumfries at the kirk in Irongray. The plan is to capture Sir James Turner, an important figure in the Royalist army who's been responsible for much of the harsh treatment handed out to nonconformist Presbyterians.

Many in the group believe the entire Scottish nation is about to rise up and our actions will ignite the touchpaper that starts the rebellion, while plenty of others think we're on our own. We're filled with so many contrasting emotions and expectations no one actually knows where our apparently insane actions will end.

'What are you thinking?' I ask Hamish.

We're walking through a pasture. The startled farmer watches from a safe distance, probably unsure whether to run away or to welcome so many Scotsmen trudging through his land.

'I think if we had met the king himself and poked a willow up his arse, we probably couldn't cause more trouble for ourselves than what we're about to do.'

The comment is so unlike what I'm used to hearing from the usually reserved Hamish that I burst out laughing, which sets him off as well. George asks the cause of our amusement and when I explain several of the men join in the fun, with voices shouting out around us.

'We need to find a willow.'

'We need to find the king's arse.'

'I expect he knows where it is.'

'Willows! Willows!'

We're weary but in good spirits when we arrive at Irongray kirk, which is currently without a minister. Fortunately, there have been opportunities to obtain food along the way and plenty of streams to drink from. Scores of men join us during the evening and in the gloom it's impossible to know how many we now number. Hamish and I sit around a fire with some of the men from Ayr, discussing the various officers in charge of us.

'They do come in all shapes and sizes,' says Alexander, who is of such average build that he is a complete contrast to his friends George and Cornelius. 'Maybe you two could apply.'

We all laugh, including those at the butt of his joke.

'Well, I hope whoever leads us tomorrow on our assault on Dumfries knows what they're doing,' says George.

'Assault!' says Hamish, sounding alarmed. 'I thought we were only going to capture one man?'

'One man who happens to be in charge of an awful lot of soldiers,' says Alexander.

'The rumour is that most of them are spread around the countryside,' says Cornelius.

George winks at Hamish. 'You might yet get to use that hammer, lad.'

'Aye, just don't forget,' says Alexander, 'hit them with the fat end!'

People soon settle down for the night as best they can in the kirk or nearby. Hamish and I are lucky enough to find floor space under a pew. However, despite my tiredness, sleep evades me for a long while and I sense that Hamish is also awake. I can't stop worrying that, in a few hours' time, we're going to poke that willow.

* * *

The only sounds from Dumfries at daybreak are the occasional barking of dogs and the call of a lone cockerel.

'There doesn't even seem to be a watch,' says Alexander, expressing everyone's surprise.

Most of the men on foot remain behind, but Hamish and I are amongst a small group ordered to accompany those on horses and we approach the town from the Galloway side, walking over the ancient bridge without any warnings being raised.

'This is unbelievable,' exclaims Alexander. 'We're not being challenged at all.'

Most of those on horses set off towards the garrison as quietly as they can, although the clipping of hooves seems to us to echo along the street like cannon shot.

'People will hear them,' says Hamish warily. 'There'll be trouble.'

'Could you hit someone with that if it came to a fight?' I ask.

He looks at the hammer as if it might inspire an answer. 'I don't know. Am I doing God's work by hitting a man on the head?'

Hamish is so physically like a male version of Violet that he reminds me of her every time I look at him. I think that's why I try to watch out for him so much.

'If someone's coming at you with a weapon, then hit him – don't hesitate.'

We end up in front of a large house along with a handful of horsemen led by a man called Neilson of Corsack. We've obviously been heard by the occupant, for a few moments later an upstairs window opens and a rather dishevelled figure, still in his nightdress, peers down upon us in a state of alarm.

'Quarter! I ask for quarter.'

'This snivelling turd is the man behind so much suffering?' says George.

'Come down without resistance,' Neilson orders, 'and on my word as a gentleman you shall have quarter.'

And as easy as that, we capture the head of the local army, who appears at the front door just as a messenger arrives to announce that the small garrison of soldiers has been disarmed and bound without anyone being injured.

I don't know whose idea it is, but Turner is put on a mule and paraded through the streets, accompanied by jeering residents along the way. However, he isn't harmed and when we get to the market cross we're soon joined by most of the other Covenanters on horseback, a few of them absent because they're guarding the soldiers.

'I bet you lads won't forget this morning!' says George to Hamish and me.

'Yes, but what happens now?' asks Hamish.

As if in reply, several local men appear from the nearby tavern carrying trays with cups of ale which are handed out, including one to Turner, who's still in his nightdress on the mule. Then, to make this utterly unimaginable morning even more unreal, we demonstrate our loyalty to King Charles as Scotland's monarch by raising our cups and enthusiastically toasting his health.

5

Samuel
20 November 1666, Bridge of Doon, near Ayr

THE EDGE OF THE SWORD whistles past my head. With a sinking heart, it dawns on me that my opponent could cleave open my skull anytime he wants and there's little I can do to stop him. Violet's father, who learnt how to handle the weapon from a ship's officer, drilled Hamish and me in using one when we were younger. However, the man circling me slowly is an expert, and for all the good I'm doing I might as well pick up a rock and throw it.

'You've had some training,' says Captain Arnot. He speaks loudly so that the dozens of men watching can hear.

'Yes, sir,' I reply clearly, without lowering my sword, and mighty glad that he's on my side.

'In a battle, you're unlikely to have the luxury of walking around an enemy having a conversation or enjoying an ale together.'

Those nearby laugh. We're all caught up in a mad fever of excitement and hope, which has been our constant companion ever since leaving Dumfries with the various captured soldiers and Sir James Turner, who had at least been allowed to dress properly beforehand.

Now we have experienced officers under the leadership of Colonel James Wallace, a devout Christian and a soldier of such renowned bravery that even his enemies speak of him as a man of honour. He may be past his prime, having lived quietly for many years, but such is his loyalty to the Covenanter cause that he has come out of retirement.

There's a belief that we're going to be part of an important advancement in this fight for religious freedom, despite the fact that the entire venture has had little planning behind it. We've ended up here because an old man in the village of Dalry was being mistreated by a handful of soldiers.

Captain Arnot suddenly sheaths his sword and greets someone behind me. 'Colonel Wallace, sir.'

I lower my sword and turn to show my respect. The next moment I'm hurled roughly to the ground. When I've regained my wits, there's the point of a sword at my throat. The men give a great cheer at my folly.

'Never turn your back on an opponent, even one as good-looking as me.'

The officer sheaths his sword again and holds out a hand to help me up. I'm impressed by the strength in his arm when he easily pulls me to my feet. He claps me heartily on the shoulder and speaks so that everyone nearby can hear.

'Well done ...'

'Samuel, sir.'

'Well done, Samuel. You'll do us proud. Most of you won't be fighting with a sword. That's probably just as well as you're more likely to cut off your own bollocks than hurt the enemy and I don't want to be surrounded by a bunch of castratos singing in my ear!'

This results in much laughter and I realise that the captain understands how to handle men. I'm learning fast that there's much more to being an officer than knowing how to fight.

'Those with pikes or similar, form up over there and I'll speak to you shortly. Those with other weapons should go with Captain Paton, who will instruct you how best to use whatever you have.'

Men disperse while I stand alone, still catching my breath and trying not to rub my throbbing shoulder. There's enthusiasm, commitment and courage in abundance, but time to practice, and the weapons themselves, are in terribly short supply. Some of the pikes, halberds and spears look as though they were made in the last century.

The majority of the five hundred or so men on foot have something home-made such as a scythe fixed firmly to the end of a wooden pole, or a hayfork with sharpened prongs. Amongst our hastily assembled army, there are almost as many men with horses and they're better armed, mainly with pistol and sword.

'You did well against Captain Arnot,' says Hamish, who's come up beside me with George, Cornelius and Alexander. 'I wouldn't have wanted to face him.'

'It was more of an exercise in humiliation.' I'm trying to appear calm but I'm still breathing hard from the exertion and the experience, which was more than a little frightening.

'Well, I wouldn't have fared any better against Arnot,' says Cornelius.

'You wouldn't fare well against anyone,' jokes Alexander. With good humour, he fends off some half-hearted punches from Cornelius.

'You can't expect to have done better than you did, Samuel,' George tells me. 'Captain Arnot has had years of fighting experience.'

'What's going to happen when we come up against experienced soldiers?' asks Hamish.

I can't bring myself to admit it out loud, but this is the very fear in my own heart.

'We fight,' says George simply. 'That's all we can do.'

But Hamish isn't quite reassured. 'Is it true that there's hardly any powder for the muskets or pistols?'

'Don't worry about powder,' says George, slapping Hamish on the shoulder. 'We haven't got that many muskets and pistols to fire anyway! God is our weapon against the enemies of the Kirk. Looks like we need to join the others.'

'Come on, Cornelius, I'll help you over,' says Alexander.

To everyone's astonishment, Alexander suddenly heaves the unsuspecting Cornelius over his shoulder as if he were a sack of grain, then casually walks away, his friend complaining loudly while everyone around laughs.

'Put me down, you great Ayrshire arse!'

They walk off, leaving Hamish and me alone, the humour of the moment dispersing like smoke in a gust of wind.

'Are you scared, Sam?'

'After that demonstration with Captain Arnot, I'm even more terrified than I was before.'

'I'm scared, though at the same time I've never felt so alive. We're finally doing something real, something that will make a difference. Perhaps we can help change Scotland's destiny, free people from the tyranny of King Charles and his Royalist army. Imagine what our fathers will say when we return. They'll not call us boys any more.'

It's his last comment that gives me the greatest concern because, compared to men like Paton and Arnot, that's exactly what we are. Besides, there are many here who are younger than us and even less able to defend themselves.

Over the years, I've met Covenanters who want to die for the cause. They seek death and entry into Heaven. Well, I'll die if that's God's will but I would rather live. To actively wish it seems contrary to anything we've been taught. I don't express my concerns, for it is best that Hamish maintains whatever enthusiasm and hope he can find.

'We've got together with some good men,' he says. 'We should stick close to them in case there's any trouble.'

'Hamish, the one thing we can be sure of is that there's going to be trouble ... lots of trouble.'

6

Samuel
28 November 1666, Collington, south-west of Edinburgh

FEELINGS OF HOPE AND DESPAIR, certainty and doubt hang about the camp as sharply as the fierce early morning frost, each competing with our hunger and cold for attention. In the end, we marched to Edinburgh not to make war but to present the Covenanters' demands to the Privy Council: the king is not the head of the Church of Scotland and cannot use his bishops to force Presbyterians to worship in ways that go against their beliefs.

It had been anticipated that our arrival would result in a great uprising of support within the city, which would force the authorities to listen. However, the three messengers sent yesterday were not even permitted entry through the gates. There's been no uprising, no hordes of volunteers rushing out to join us, no supplies of food or weapons. In fact, at first light there was a skirmish between our watchmen and a small detachment of government soldiers, who fortunately withdrew quickly.

We're alone, our company comprising mainly of the nine hundred who set out from the Bridge of Doon. Along the journey, some have added to our numbers with loud acclaim while others have slipped quietly away or simply not been able to keep up, and now the total is much the same.

To add to our distress, we've been pursued by a Royalist army believed to be headed by Sir Thomas Dalyell of the Binns, Commander-in-Chief of the king's army in Scotland and a fierce enemy to face. So far we've managed to stay ahead of them, but with no help coming from the capital, the story going around is that we're about to break camp and head west, back towards an area where there is greater support for the cause.

'What are you thinking?' asks Hamish.

'I don't know what to think,' I say. 'We've come all this way, not just in distance, only to head back to where we started and, when we get there, more than likely disperse so that there's no army for the bastards to chase.'

'Can we win if it comes to a fight?'

Hamish always expects me to have answers that I can't possibly know. He was the same when we were children, even though I'm only three months older.

'Look around us. Most of those who don't work the land are weavers, shoemakers, bakers and carpenters.'

'But we're fighting to restore Jesus to his rightful place as head of the Kirk. God must be on our side.'

'That doesn't mean God will ensure we win a battle if it comes to it. He may well want to test us more.'

Hamish falls silent, then says quietly, 'I miss Violet.'

For a moment I'm lost for words. In so many ways, Violet is like a beacon of light in our lives. Our mothers may feed and care for our families and our fathers are the heads of them, but we're drawn to Violet like moths to a candle, and she is all the brighter for not realising how her love captivates us all.

I put a hand on Hamish's shoulder. 'So do I. If events turn against us, then we must do everything we can to survive and fight another day. Don't get captured or you'll likely be transported to America or the West Indies, and I'm not brave enough to tell Violet such news.' I cuff him gently on the head. 'And don't get hurt.'

'I'll try not to,' he says, attempting to smile but failing.

George approaches, trailed by several others. 'It's time to pack up,' he says, the urgency in his voice obvious. 'We're heading home as fast as we can.'

'The Royalist army?' asks Hamish, in alarm.

'No sign of them,' says Cornelius, 'and Colonel Wallace is trying to keep it that way. Whatever you need, collect it and get moving.'

* * *

We don't make it. Our mounted scouts reported that the main Royalist army would have been directly in our path on our original route, so we've headed east and south in an attempt to use the Pentland Hills as cover to get around them. However, by late morning we had to stop for men to rest and let stragglers catch up.

Hamish and I have stayed close to the men we've befriended. Alexander knows the area, which is apparently called Rullion Green. Around noon our scouts drive off a small force of government cavalry and with our presence discovered, Colonel Wallace orders us into formations on the slopes of Turnhouse Hill, men on foot stretched out in lines in the middle and those on horseback protecting our left and right flanks.

It's not long before the enemy appears and forms up along the slope of a hill facing us, with an unoccupied glen between the two sides. Most Covenanters stand watching, although there are plenty sitting, a few eating some saved cheese or bread, perhaps thinking it might be their only chance to have it, maybe their last meal. Some men jeer and shout insults, which are returned in kind by those facing us.

How strange it is to so naturally consider fellow Scotsmen the enemy.

'What are we waiting for?' asks Hamish.

'We hold the high ground,' replies George, 'and Wallace won't want to give up that advantage. What we're seeing is only the vanguard of the king's army and they won't want to come charging up here until the main body has arrived.'

'So we wait?' I say.

'Perhaps not without some encounters,' says Alexander, who's looking over to the enemy's left.

Opposite, about fifty men on horses are moving away from the foot soldiers, heading slowly south. To our right a similar number of Covenanter horsemen mirror their position, each group riding along the side of the hill they possess.

'They're trying to turn our flank, but they won't succeed because there's not enough of them,' says Cornelius.

There's no one sitting down eating now and we gaze in a fascinated silence at the events unfolding before our eyes. When the two troupes of horsemen reach flatter ground, they spread out and fire a mixture of carabines and pistols.

'They're too far apart,' says George.

As if to confirm the accuracy of his comment, and the inaccuracy of the weapons, none of the riders appears to be hurt by this exchange, and moments later the two groups charge over the open ground, swords drawn and their shouted battle cries carrying clearly to those on the hills. Captains Paton and Arnot are there and I hope they make it safely back.

'For king and country!'

'For God in Heaven!'

The horsemen on both sides are experienced soldiers. Labourers, craftsmen and those too young to call any trade their own stare in horror at the carnage that unfolds before us. Blades clash, they bite into flesh and sear gashes across bodies while men scream in pain, fear and hate. I can barely breathe because of the tension in my body, for the truth is that Hamish and I wouldn't last a single minute against such opponents.

Men fall – dead or too injured to remain in the saddle – and in the mayhem they're trampled upon, whether friend or foe. Desperate to avoid hooves, a few crawl along the hard earth, still covered in frost where the sun hasn't reached . . . now turning red. Others ride slowly away, hanging on with their last strength in an attempt to reach the safety of their own lines. The fighting is beyond anything that the majority of us have ever witnessed. Some of the sword skill of the officers is astonishing.

'How can Scotsmen end up on such opposite sides?' says George. 'You would think we worshipped a different God.'

No one answers. Gradually there are fewer horsemen able to continue and then suddenly the government soldiers break away. A couple are injured in that brief moment of retreat when they're still close enough to their foes to be reached by the tip of a weapon. About a dozen Covenanters chase after them, but they quickly give up when they're within musket range of the enemy soldiers.

'That was the most awful sight I've ever seen,' says Hamish.

'Be prepared, lad,' says George. 'It'll be worse when we're fighting on foot.'

Whatever Hamish and I imagined we were heading towards in the early days of leaving our families, it wasn't this. We had faith and belief and perhaps a little courage, but no idea of the reality.

As the afternoon wears on, the main bulk of the government army arrives, spreading out along the flat land in front of the bottom of Turnhouse Hill. With their appearance, the soldiers who've been opposite us for several hours come down from their position.

'Sam,' says Hamish.

'I see them.'

'There are thousands.'

'I see them.'

Like most of us, they wear knee-length breeches with stockings, plus short jackets and a mixture of hats. Some groups are dressed identically, indicating that they've been raised by a particular commander who has paid for their clothing and arms. These men know what they're doing as they form up, row upon row, and begin to load their muskets with a confidence that stems from experience.

Terror creeps towards us like a mist of madness, and when it reaches the toes of the Covenanters at the front, the terror crawls up their legs and moves on to the next row. It consumes them. Up and down the lines, men hurriedly take out their cocks to piss where they stand, a few have to drop their breeches. No one comments. It's as if nobody sees what the man next to him is doing.

'Steady, lads,' says George, who's kept close to us. 'The waiting is the worst bit.'

We hear the orders from the enemy's officers loud and clear, and soldiers blow on the lighted cords used to ignite their muskets. Moments later, we're faced with a black wall of muzzles which any second will fire thousands of lead balls, each one capable of killing a man or causing terrible injury and a slow, agonising death. I've never wished more to be with Violet, surrounded by heather on our hill, so removed from all this hate.

Captain Arnot, who returned unharmed from the earlier encounter, picks his moment precisely when he screams, 'Down! Get down!'

We practised this during our few days of training and throw ourselves forward to lie with faces, limbs and bodies hugging the earth as though we want to disappear under the grass and be part of the soil. We do this in those few crucial seconds between an officer shouting 'Fire' and the inevitable delay there is before the muskets discharge. The air above my head shimmers and in my chest I feel the shock of so many weapons fired together. Something plucks at my jerkin, followed by a sharp sting down my back. Either side of me there are cries from those hit, either because they were too slow or merely unlucky.

'Up! Up!' shouts Captain Arnot.

We jump to our feet to find that the enemy has all but disappeared behind a thick haze of blue-grey smoke. It's almost impossible to see an individual figure. Our own muskets, few as they are, send their balls of lead down the hill then, orders or no orders, we're charging after them with such fierce determination it's as though we intend to catch up with every single one.

We run with the knowledge that we'll win this battle because the enemy fights for a man they've never met, who only sits on the Scottish throne because his father or uncle or brother once sat there, and so it goes back in time and will go forward in time and all of them will one day be dust. But we fight for God – and He is in our hearts and daily lives and has never been a stranger.

If I die today it will be for a freedom that is every Scotsman's right, and I will face any danger for my family and friends and those in the Kirk to have that freedom.

My long legs take me near the lead, the halberd in my hands stretching out its deadly point. The dense smoke is to our benefit, for the enemy doesn't realise we've charged until we're so close it's impossible for them to defend themselves quickly. Most of the musketeers are in the process of reloading and stare with shock as we burst into view like demons emerging from the underworld.

I aim at a particular figure but as I race the last few yards his features become clear; and he is so young, just a boy, like Calum, holding out his discharged musket towards me with unpractised, shaking hands. He hasn't even fitted the plug bayonet or turned the weapon around to use as a club.

He speaks to me in the instant before the rusty iron tip of my halberd pierces his skin with such force that the boy is thrown backwards into the man behind. My momentum carries us on. The spike goes deeper into the boy's chest. He's still speaking as I wrench it out and face the soldier behind, who has regained his balance and comes at me with a sword.

For the present, the six-foot shaft gives me an advantage and I simply lunge. His blade hits my weapon, which deflects it slightly so that the spike pierces the side of his stomach, but it's likely a killing blow and when he falls to the ground, I ignore him. Just in time. Out of the corner of my eye there is a flash of metal – I raise the halberd like a staff to take the blow intended for my head on the shaft.

The force embeds the sword into the wood, and in this brief opportunity, I kick my opponent in the knee as hard as I can. He cries out in pain as I try to headbutt him. It's a foolish mistake, for I'm too tall. We're becoming hemmed in, so I let go of my weapon and retrieve my dirk.

The exact moment he frees his sword, I stretch to my full extent, aiming for his face, by good fortune piercing his eye. It's enough to render him helpless and the blade that was hammered upon a forge by my ancestor proves its sharpness when it's driven into his stomach. I push the dying man away, grab his sword and straighten up with only a heartbeat of time to prevent my skull being split in half.

Nothing in the world could have prepared me for this. No words or training or descriptions or sermons. We are all of us in Hell and the Devil stands at our shoulders and laughs. Men cry out for their mothers. Men shit themselves. Men die. There's so much blood you can taste it in the air. Men step over bodies in order to kill some more without hesitation or mercy. My world shrinks until it's nothing beyond the face of my next opponent ... until I'm no longer Samuel Colvil.

I don't think I'm even human any more.

A hand takes hold of my arm and I'm already turning with my dirk when the figure shouts into my face.

'Samuel! It's George ... George! We have to run.'

'What! We can't retreat now.'

'We've no choice. Look!'

I follow his outstretched arm and in that instant everything changes. God is not letting us win this battle. Dalyell has sent his entire cavalry into our right flank, swamping our own horsemen. Covenanters are being cut down like wheat under the blade of a farmer's scythe. We have seconds to escape. I'm about to say I can't leave without Hamish when he appears by our side, having also seen the danger.

'Run!' I shout. 'Don't stop for anything.'

And the three of us tear back through the throng of dead bodies, dying men and those still fighting. Scores of Covenanters are scattering in all directions, some chased by soldiers, others by those on horseback.

'This way,' I shout, having made a snap decision on where to head. 'Throw away your weapons.'

Speed is our potential saviour and Hamish and I are fleet of foot, soon outpacing the older men ahead. We gradually leave behind the noise of battle and the sound of pursuit. The light is fading when we finally collapse upon the ground, unable to speak for many minutes because of our exhaustion and shock. I'm surprised to see that the Colvil family dirk is still in my hand, the intricate carvings obscured by a hideous gore. My fingers have locked and I have to prize them open to free the handle.

'What's happened to George?' asks Hamish eventually.

I look around, half expecting to see him catching up, but realise I haven't been aware of his presence since we left the battle. In fact, I think we've been alone for quite a while.

'I guess he couldn't keep up. I hope he's found shelter somewhere and gets away. There should be enough darkness for cover but sufficient moonlight for travel. Hamish, your clothes have blood on them. Are you all right?'

'Yes. Sam ... you're soaked in it. You must be hurt somewhere?'

'I can't feel anything.' I check my body and limbs but don't find any obvious injury. We are both shivering. 'We can't stay here.'

'Where do we go?'

'Most Covenanters will probably go west, heading straight for home.'

'That's where we should go.'

'No, that's what the soldiers will expect. They'll be hunting for days in that direction. We'll go north, then work our way towards Ayrshire from wherever we find ourselves.'

'Will we get back, Sam?'

'God willing.'

Hamish shakes his head, looking so utterly downcast. When he speaks it's with a bitterness I've never heard from him before.

'I killed a man, Sam. As he lay dying at my feet, he started to cry. I've never heard a sound so awful. It didn't feel that this was part of a great cause in God's name.'

I don't know what to say to him, don't even know what to say to myself.

'Come on, Hamish,' I say eventually. 'Unless we find shelter we'll have to keep moving throughout the night or the cold will finish us off.'

Our bodies, and our souls, weigh so heavily that we have to force ourselves to stand, then, walking into the approaching night and whatever fate awaits us, we head north.

7

Samuel
30 November 1666, fields near Falkirk

Hamish and I creep between the trees until we're at the edge of the woods about ten yards from a farmer working in his field. We haven't eaten in two days, and if the farmer cannot see us, he will soon know we are here by our growling stomachs. When we saw the figure a little earlier we decided to watch him closely before asking for help, although how studying a man at work will reveal his inner beliefs . . . well, it's just what we agreed to do.

We hide behind a gorse bush while he pulls up turnips and throws them into a small handcart nearby. Most will probably be used to feed livestock over the winter. It's a peaceful scene; one repeated across the length and breadth of the country. After about five minutes, Hamish taps my arm with a finger and indicates with a head tilt that he thinks we should show ourselves. I nod and he's beginning to rise when I thrust out a hand and slam his body into the earth.

'Keep down!' I hiss.

A small number of mounted soldiers have appeared at the far edge of the field and gallop towards the farmer. We're stuck, unable to move without almost certainly being discovered. The farmer stops what he's doing to wait and appears unconcerned even when the soldiers form a rather menacing semicircle.

'Were you at Rullion Green?' shouts the corporal.

'No. I've never been more than a few miles from here. There's enough work to do without travelling to places I'm not interested in visiting.'

'You know where it is, though.'

'Only because of the battle. People everywhere are talking about it.'

It's obvious that he's speaking the truth, but the truth isn't heard by those determined to be deaf to it. He takes a step back, clearly beginning to realise the danger he's in.

'Seize him!'

Two soldiers jump down and roughly grab an arm each. The corporal dismounts and faces his victim. Without any warning he starts feeling the man's pockets and with a cry of triumph pulls out a Bible.

'You carry a Bible!'

'Yes.'

'You've been to a conventicle or you're on your way to one!'

'No! I'm lifting turnips. I read a little of the Lord's good book while I have my bread and cheese midday, as any Christian might do. There's no crime in that. I've broken no law.'

'You're a filthy Covenanter!'

'I'm not, I swear it. I work the land and care for my family. We attend the kirk every Sunday and listen to the new minister. I won't raise my hand in violence against another.'

Despite what we experienced at Rullion Green, what happens next shocks me to my core. The corporal throws the Bible to the ground, pulls out his sword and rams it into the man's stomach.

'Damned lying traitor! Now there's one less.'

The farmer makes no sound as he sinks to the ground. With distaste, the corporal wipes his sword on the man's jerkin. As he's doing this, one of the soldiers dismounts.

'What are you doing?'

'I need a piss, corporal, and my cock's so big I don't want you lot to be envious.'

As the others laugh, the man walks over to where we lie and starts to relieve himself. I can't believe he doesn't see us. We're feet away and he's facing towards our hiding place; the branches might as well not be there. Hamish has buried his head in his hands. I stare in horror at the soldier.

And he stares back at me.

We're dead men.

The man gives a small cry of alarm.

'What's wrong?' asks the corporal, who has remounted and is waiting with the others.

My heart is about to burst in panic as the soldier hesitates to reply.

'Nothing, corporal. It's just that my cock's so heavy, it's difficult to hold at times.'

They laugh raucously at this, while the one in front of us fastens his breeches, staring at me for one last moment, and rejoins them. I don't know why he's given us our lives. Maybe one brutal murder is enough for this bright November day.

'Hamish, they've gone,' I whisper, when my shaking has finally reduced enough for me to speak. 'Come on.'

Our hunger is forgotten as we kneel by the side of the injured man. It's clear that he won't survive long.

'We saw what happened,' I say. 'I'm sorry we didn't help.'

'Here's your Bible,' says Hamish, putting it gently into the man's hand.

'You'll tell my wife? The cottage ... three fields away.' He points weakly in the right direction.

'We'll take you there,' says Hamish, 'in the cart.'

'Not alive ... take my body home. Tell Peggy what happened.'

'We will,' I reassure him. 'You have our word on it.'

'Perhaps ... you'll read something ... from the Scriptures?'

He's failing fast, his breathing quick and shallow while the effort to speak is almost beyond him. I take the Bible and hold his hand. His eyes are closed. I don't open the book for I know Psalm 121 by memory and this is the most appropriate I can think of.

'I will lift mine eyes unto the mountains, from whence mine help shall come. My help cometh from the Lord, which hath made the Heaven and the earth ...'

He dies while I'm reciting the psalm, but I finish it nonetheless, then we empty the handcart of turnips and do our best to be respectful as we replace them with his body. The cart's too small and no matter what we do his legs dangle over the side, denying him any sort of dignity on the journey. It takes both of us to push and we have to rest often before we see the cottage.

A woman outside watches us approach. She's joined by a boy and girl probably a couple of years younger than us. As we get nearer, the girl bursts out crying and the boy picks up a hayfork, holding it like a potential weapon, but he lays it back down following a comment from his mother.

When we reach the cottage the five of us stand around without speaking, merely staring at the body with its legs hanging over the side. The only sound is the girl weeping. It seems completely unreal, as if Hamish and I couldn't possibly have actually just brought a dead body to this family and changed their lives forever.

'I'm very sorry,' I say eventually. 'There were soldiers ...'

'Didn't you help?' asks the boy accusingly. He's trying to hold back tears and I don't blame him for the hostility.

'No,' I reply, 'and we're ashamed because of it.'

'There's no shame needed, unarmed and the pair of you looking as if you're about to collapse with exhaustion,' says the woman. 'Thank you for bringing Walter home to us. Is any of that blood yours?'

I'd forgotten that I look like a butcher who's been gutting pigs all day. 'No ... at least not enough to worry about.'

'Robert, help them get your father laid in the barn. We'll organise his burial later on. Bessie, sort out food for them.'

'Mother?'

The daughter is distraught and surprised at the order but I understand how the mother is giving her a task to help cope with the tragedy, at least for now. *'Busy hands calm the mind'* my mother is always saying. Robert is stocky and in truth we're glad of his aid in moving the body. Once we've laid his father out Hamish hands over the Bible, which he had tucked into a pocket for safety.

'Your father's Bible. Samuel read from the Scriptures. It gave comfort in his last moments.'

'Thank you.'

The tears come, so we go to the cottage to allow the son time alone. We're invited to sit at the table and I almost fall into the chair.

'Do you wish to know what happened?' I ask, appreciating that it's only proper to make this offer before we eat. Our hunger is nothing compared to their loss.

'Eat first,' says the wife, 'then we should hear what happened together.'

Afterwards, when we've had our fill and the terrible tale has been told, the five of us remain silent for a long while. So far, Walter's wife has been nothing but practical and kind; a different kind of strength from what we've seen recently. We haven't mentioned why we came to be at the edge of their field and I sense this will not go unanswered.

'Were you at Rullion Green?' she asks at last.

Hamish and I look at each other, hesitating, yet the woman's husband has just been murdered for nothing more than carrying a Bible and there's no reason for us to deny it in such company. We nod.

'Soldiers are hunting everywhere for rebels who fought there,' she says. 'They've intensified their patrols and their brutality. Could you ever have won?'

The question throws us and we consider it for quite some time. As usual, Hamish lets me answer. 'I don't believe so,' I say. 'We were swept along by events and emotions like twigs caught in a flood, but there was no real planning or preparation for the battle. We were unlikely to ever beat an army such as the one we faced.'

'So all for nothing then?' She heaves a deep sigh. 'And my husband dead because soldiers are even more obsessed with killing, whether they've found a Covenanter or not. Walter was a farmer. He loved the land, the animals and his family, with no thoughts of taking up arms. Such a violent death goes against everything he believed.'

I'm crushed by the weight of guilt. The food feels like stones in my stomach and for a moment I fear I'm about to be sick. Our actions have been partly responsible for the cruel murder of an innocent man going about the task of lifting turnips.

A madness has taken hold of men in this land, and a fearful knowledge takes root within me – it is only going to get worse.

* * *

I'm shaking and breathing hard as I try the door. It's bolted so I slap my hand several times against the wood. There's the sound of movement from inside and moments later my father stands before us, crying out that we're home. Hamish and I are bundled inside. My mother stifles a scream. Calum looks scared. In the light of candles and the fire, we must appear as if we've emerged from the bowels of Hell. It certainly feels as if that's where we've been.

'Are you hurt?' asks Mother, suddenly hugging me and taking charge.

Every single inch of my body hurts but I'm not 'hurt' in the way she means so I shake my head. She hugs Hamish and checks with him as if he was another son.

'If Andrew goes with you, can you make it back to your family? They should know as soon as possible that you've returned and will be better able to care for you.'

Hamish nods and my father fetches his coat, plus another that he puts over my friend's shoulders. Hamish looks at me in parting and I see such pain and grief in his eyes ... aged eyes. Yes, no one will call us 'boys' any more. Part of me wishes they would, that we were the lads who left home only a few weeks ago. How could we change so much in such a short time?

'Let Violet see that Hamish is all right, then bring her back here, Andrew. The girl won't rest until she's with Samuel and she'll be the best medicine he can have.'

As soon as they're gone, my mother issues a stream of orders to Calum, who so far hasn't come near me. I can't blame him for that.

'Heat water in the copper pot and get that stew reheated. Samuel, I've got to strip these wet, filthy clothes off you and check you over. You're covered in blood. Is any of it yours?'

I can't answer. Most of it belongs to men I've slaughtered. In that moment I realise what I stink of – death. That's what frightens Calum. It's the stench of death upon me. She doesn't wait for a reply and takes me nearer the fire before gently removing items until I stand as naked as the day I was born. With a cloth and some hot water Mother begins to tenderly wipe away the filth. Calum soon has to take the basin outside to empty and refill with hot water from the pot.

I'm covered in bruises, scratches and cuts. There's a gash on my back, which may have come from a musket ball. My mother's still removing soil from this when the door bursts open and Violet rushes in, out of breath and crying. She stops dead at the sight of me. There's a moment of stillness and silence until Mother takes control.

'Clean his face, Violet, then you can see more clearly the person you love.'

Violet gets a cloth and starts to wipe my cheeks and ears, my eyes and brow. She doesn't speak even as she wipes away my tears. They keep falling. Calum helps by emptying muddy water outside and refilling the basin. When the two women have done what they can, Mother wraps a blanket about my middle and sits me in a chair by the fire.

'Violet, feed him some of that stew. I want to see to this gash and a few of the cuts.'

Father hasn't yet returned. Violet feeds me. Tears continue to blur my vision. Now and again, she wipes them away with the back of a finger. Mother is behind me, applying honey on the worst of my injuries. When she's satisfied no more can be done, she carefully wraps another blanket around my shoulders.

For days the horrors of Rullion Green have been patrolling around the edges of my mind, only kept at a distance by the all-consuming need to reach safety. Now they're overwhelming my defences. I can't get the image of that boy out of my head ... his face as I drove the spike into his chest ... pushing so hard he was flung into the man behind him.

Violet quietly puts the bowl down and takes hold of one of my hands. Father's returned and stands with Calum near the door. Mother goes over to them. I can't hear what they're saying. It's about me, though. They don't want me to know.

The boy said—

'It's all right, Samuel,' says Violet. 'No one will hurt you here.'

'*Please.*' That's what he said, even before the wicked rusty metal pierced his jerkin. '*Please.*' I drove it further in, beyond skin and muscle and bone and hope. '*Please.*' He kept repeating the word, even at the end when he was almost dead. Above all of the other sounds of battle, the shouts of fury, the cries of pain, the clash of weapons, I could hear him. He's still saying it. In my head he's still saying it.

'Whatever you've done was for the glory of God,' says Violet.

How can I explain that there was no glory? That I never saw God amongst the guts, blood and waste that were so mixed up with hate and terror. It was as though our bodies and our emotions couldn't be separated ... they all sank together into the dirt to be trodden upon.

'Please.'

'What is it, my love?' says Violet. 'What can I get you?'

'PLEASE!'

Mother comes over. 'Violet, Samuel needs you more than he needs us. You'll stay the night?'

'Of course.'

'Let's get him bedded down here in front of the fire. It's all right, son. You'll be better after a while at home. It's the shock of everything that's happened to you.'

'PLEEEAASE!'

'I know, son. I know. Look, Violet will cradle you and you couldn't be safer than in her arms. Let's get you together.'

They lay me on the floor with blankets and Violet lies with me. My mother tucks us up like children as I nestle into the body I've loved for so long ... like I used to do on top of the hill, before one stranger's obsession for power affected all our lives. Why can't we be as we were then? I would draw her picture and explain how her long black hair moves in the breeze. We were so in love and happy.

I'll never know that peace of mind again.

8

Samuel
27 December 1666, Ayr

None of us wants to be recognised and the driving rain at least provides a reason to have hoods up or large hats pulled down tightly. We've split into two groups amongst the crowd to more easily blend in. Hamish and his father stand with Calum a short distance away while I'm with my own father and Violet, who refused to be left behind regardless of what anyone said. We're standing behind a man who's as tall as me so that my own height is less likely to attract attention.

'You shouldn't be here, Violet,' I say, angry that she's not stayed behind, angry at the disaster of Rullion Green, angry at everything and everyone. The real truth is that I'm scared. I've felt scared ever since returning to my family, on occasions almost overcome by fear. Every time I close my eyes, that boy is in front of me saying *please*. I haven't admitted it, though I suspect they know. You can't hide such a thing from people who love you.

After all of the fears we had about our inexperience, it was actually our youth that saved Hamish and me from the fate of many Covenanters at Rullion Green ... we simply outran those pursuing us. Several captured Covenanters have since been executed on the infamous scaffold in Edinburgh's Grassmarket, including the brave Captain Arnot. Those banished abroad are unlikely to see Scotland again. A few with the money and means have fled the country, like Colonel Wallace, who has gone to Holland.

'I'll be back soon,' says Father, interrupting my thoughts, before moving away slowly through the throng of bodies.

There are easily more than a thousand people around the scaffold that's been built to execute eight of the Covenanters captured at Rullion Green. Some of the men who sat in judgement during the court case are standing on the platform, along with a minister, the local magistrate and a couple of burly soldiers.

Amongst these men are two tall ladders that rest against a high wooden frame upon which a rope hangs, the sodden noose dancing ominously in the wind. Twelve men were tried and twelve sentenced to be executed, with two Covenanters sent to Irvine and two to Dumfries to meet their fate in the towns they came from so that local people may see justice being done. Three of the men to be hanged in Ayr come from the village of Dalry, where this all began with a handful of soldiers mistreating an old man.

I stare at the gallows. Justice, they call this.

'What?' Violet asks me.

'Sorry, I was speaking what's in my head.'

There is a pause while she casts a worried eye over me. 'Don't, Samuel. It's a dangerous habit.'

She's right – especially here and now. Armed soldiers and militia patrol around the crowd, studying people with watchful eyes. Since the six of us arrived in Ayr this morning, we've heard rumours that there are people amongst the crowd who are pretending to be sympathetic to the Covenanter cause but are secretly working for the king. We're nervous and on our guard, as well as being wet, cold, weary and despairing.

'Have you heard the news?' says Hamish, coming up behind us.

I half turn my head, which I keep bowed to better hide my face. 'What news?'

'The Ayr hangman has disappeared.'

Violet frowns. 'Disappeared?'

'Left the area as soon as it was known that the trial would take place here. No one else in Ayr is willing to carry out the executions, so they've brought in the hangman from Irvine, but he's also refused, even when threatened with torture or his own death.'

'A brave believer,' says Violet under her breath.

'The local magistrate's so angry that he's got the poor man locked up in the tolbooth, but he's unable to force him to do it.'

'What will happen?'

It's at this moment Father returns, his expression even more grim than when he left. 'I hardly know what to make of what I've heard. The authorities have offered one of the condemned eight his life and freedom if he will hang the other seven.'

'No!' Violet gasps as we all stare at him.

'Will someone do it?' asks Hamish.

Father shakes his head. 'Who knows what any man would do with a choice of life or death in such stark circumstances.'

'Neither Hamish nor I would ever agree to such a heinous act,' I say, as though stating it aloud will dispel the doubt in my heart.

Father's eyes dart to me, so quickly I almost miss it, but my stomach churns. He can see right through the false bravery in my comment.

'It's one thing to stand alongside your friends and face the enemy in battle,' he says solemnly, 'where you have the comfort of a weapon in your hands and can fight with at least a chance of surviving. But in this, a man's courage might fail him ... though the sin would be terrible.'

'But which one might accept?' wonders Hamish.

I've trained, eaten, laughed and fought with these men; all good, honest and true to the Covenanter cause. How could any of them kill the other seven? Father is wrong; no one will agree to do this wicked deed. They cannot.

'Samuel.' Violet says my name quietly, but there's a warning in her voice that I've learnt to heed over the years.

'I was at Rullion Green,' a man whispers to me.

I turn to the stranger but hesitate to reply. What if I give myself away?

'You've no business with us,' Violet tells him. 'Be on your way.'

The man blinks rapidly, as if struck, then sneers. 'Does this ... woman ... answer for you?' he asks me.

I'm certain that Violet's suspicion is correct: this man is a spy. Suddenly all that anger brewing within me boils over. I grab his jacket with both hands and yank him forward so violently that he's forced onto his toes, looking up at me from only inches away. He splutters, holding up his hands in a sign of peace.

'Hey, hey, friend! No need for that.'

'I'm no friend of yours and if you don't move away, you'll feel my fist in your face.'

'All right . . . just a misunderstanding. No need to threaten me.'

I push him away, though not too roughly as I don't want to draw attention to myself. He vanishes into the crowd.

'Something's happening,' says Violet.

I look towards the scaffold, where soldiers are escorting the condemned men. The crowd goes silent. I begin to fear that one of the eight may have given in to temptation, for why else would they be brought out? Like those around me, I count the figures and tick off their names in my head. There are seven with their hands tied in front of them. The last one doesn't.

'Cornelius!' whispers Hamish. 'I wouldn't have believed it. He fought bravely at Rullion Green.'

'Everyone fought bravely at Rullion Green,' I say quietly. 'We lost because we were hugely outnumbered.'

'I think,' says Father wearily, 'that this man will regret to his dying day what he is about to do.'

One of the judges on the platform steps forward to address the crowd. 'These men have been found guilty of treason and are condemned to be executed for their heinous crime against the king, who was anointed by God to be our monarch and as such is head of the Church of Scotland. Let no one here doubt the authority of King Charles II. Carry on, sergeant.'

George is the first to be brought up, followed several yards behind by Cornelius, who appears so drunk he can hardly stand.

'This is going to be more desperate than ever,' says Father. 'Burghs have hangmen because they know their trade. This man can barely keep himself upright.'

'I can't watch,' says Violet, who buries her head in my chest.

I wrap my cloak around her body so that she's almost hidden from sight. 'It's all right.' I try to reassure her. 'Stay there and I'll keep you safe.'

Heaven knows I don't want to watch either, but I have to be present even though I feel crushed by guilt that we left them behind at Rullion Green. I can't ignore the fear that one of them will recognise me and shout out how I betrayed their friendship.

When George reaches the platform he says something to the sergeant, who releases his grip without hesitation. As is the custom, a condemned man is entitled to speak before his execution. Some confess their guilt and ask for forgiveness from their victims. Others protest their innocence and curse their accusers. Those who have accepted their fate usually say nothing. A few have to be restrained and their executions are particularly violent. George stands serenely as if he hasn't a care in the world.

'Fellow Scotsmen ... we Covenanters are, and have always been, loyal to our monarch. We've never had treason in our hearts. We only ever wanted the head of our Kirk to be Jesus as the Scriptures tell us he should be. Too many have died and more will be killed in this unnecessary fight. It will go on until we are heard. I won't see it, at least not from this earthly body of mine.'

George pauses because his eyes have fallen upon me, despite my attempts to be unrecognised. I'm unable even to blink. We stare at each other across a distance that cannot be measured in anything manmade. His head moves slightly. It could have been a nod. I don't know. He looks once more upon the crowd.

'I hope some of you here will still be alive on that day. Now, I leave to go to a better place and I have such joy within me that I shall soon meet God. I have no fear.' He turns to face Cornelius, who staggers backwards as if struck, until the railing prevents him going any further. 'I forgive you for the deed you are about to do ... Cornelius Anderson.'

George pronounces his name like a sentence, and it is – for this name will become infamous throughout the whole of

Scotland. He then walks calmly to the ladder for the condemned and climbs slowly up to the fifth step, stopping when his head is in line with the noose.

Cornelius appears frozen in horror and it's only with prompting from the magistrate that he clumsily climbs the other ladder, this one fixed firmly at the top to the frame. When he reaches the same level as George, the two men look at each other from only feet away. The silence from the crowd is thick, like the smoke from thousands of muskets at Rullion Green. If any words are spoken between the two, no one hears them. Eventually, one of the judges loses his temper.

'Christ on the cross, get on with it!'

Cornelius reaches over and places the noose around his former friend's neck, then he returns to the platform and staggers to the foot of the ladder upon which George stands. Grasping a rung near the bottom, he heaves, losing his balance in the process and ending up sprawled at the magistrate's feet.

People rarely die quickly. Instead, their death is a hideous display of twisting and jerking as the person desperately tries to suck air into their lungs. It's instinct, even for the bravest and staunchest of men.

I can't breathe. It's as though that rope is around my own neck, the tough hemp fibres crushing my windpipe like the garrotting of a witch. I desperately try to take a breath, but I can't do it. I can't. The world around me spins. I'm falling ... falling into a void of despair and blackness.

'Samuel ... Samuel.' Violet's voice is low but urgent. 'Loosen your arms. You're hurting me. Samuel!'

Violet is still mostly hidden by my cloak and it's the fear in her voice that brings me back. I take huge gulps of air and it's only then that I realise I've been squeezing her fiercely.

'I'm all right ... I'm all right,' I say quietly. 'I'm sorry if I've hurt you.'

And so the bodies pile up ... George MacCartney, John Graham, Alexander MacMillan, James MacMillan, John Short, James Smith, John Muirhead. With every death the sympathy towards the Covenanter cause increases amongst the people present, while my hate for a man I've never met grows beyond anything I've ever experienced. He may wear a crown but he's no king of mine if he can cause such grief amongst loyal subjects because they won't accept he has the right to put himself between them and God. There is no middle ground to stand upon. I will fight against what this man represents until we win or until I'm dead.

News of these barbarous events will result in even greater numbers joining the fight. What is happening in Ayr today will stain Scotland's soul for generations to come. And if the king and his government think that this cruelty will force his subjects into submission, they don't understand the power of the desire for freedom.

9

Violet
10 July 1668, Gadgirth, Ayrshire

MY MARRIAGE TO SAMUEL OFFERS a brief moment of happiness in a world that seems to have become filled with such hate and cruelty. But I won't think of that. Today, no one is allowed to speak of anything that isn't pleasant. As if giving its approval, the sun shines brightly upon us while nearby the beautiful singing of a skylark fills the air.

'You look lovely,' says my mother. 'This is the day we've all been expecting for so very long.'

'So have I, Mother. It's almost difficult to believe it's finally happening.'

We're being married by the Reverend Colvil a few miles north of Coylton, by the side of the River Ayr, which forms the border of the parish. It's sufficiently out of the way not to draw attention from those in authority. Dozens of friends, neighbours and fellow Covenanters have gathered for this secret ceremony, while armed men keep a lookout from the surrounding higher ground. How can this be Scotland?

According to civil and ecclesiastical laws, we should have had public banns announced over three sabbaths in the nearby kirk and be married there by the new curate. Like many other couples who believe in the cause, we refuse to do this, but it means our marriage won't be registered in the parish records, nor will it be recognised officially, so there'll be difficulties ahead when we have children.

Our marriage can't even be spoken of openly because if news reaches the curate, he will inform the soldiers currently based in the nearby village of Drongan. Throughout the country, these replacement ministers regularly inform upon parishioners whom they consider have been disloyal to them. Many people we know have been threatened or fined. It's driving an ever bigger wedge of mistrust and ill-feeling between the Kirk and many ordinary people, who view the Church and military as being too close.

I'm still trying to calm my nerves when Samuel approaches, the huge smile on his face a rare thing to see these days. My mother tactfully moves away. He's obviously gone to considerable efforts to smarten his appearance, while his wavy ginger hair has been neatly cut; a task I will now take on. However, it's what he's carrying that catches my attention the most. He holds out his hand.

'Five violets, tied together with a blade of grass,' he says.

'You haven't forgotten!'

'Of course I haven't forgotten. That was a big event in the life of a six-year-old.'

'I've still got them.'

'What!'

'I took the flowers home and my mother showed me how to dry and press them. Those violets are still within the pages of a book. I even kept the blade of glass.'

'What was the book?'

I laugh but don't tell him.

'Come on. What was it?'

'I needed a big book because it had to be heavy.'
'Not the Bible!'
'I used Father's copy of *Don Quixote*.'
Samuel laughs loudly and I'm filled with joy at the sound. 'My gift rests within a story of chivalry. I love you, Violet Milligan.'

'Well, we're about to get married, so I hope you do. And I love you. I always will.'

He takes me in his arms and is still holding me when we hear a polite cough nearby.

'I believe you're meant to get married first,' says the Reverend Colvil, beaming more than I've ever seen him do. 'Perhaps we should get started.'

People have been talking quietly but everyone falls silent as Samuel and I stand in front of the Reverend Colvil. He prays for a blessing for us. His voice carries so clearly in the valley that I fancy people must hear it from miles away. I want them to hear, for everyone to know that I'm marrying the person I love, and that not even the king will prevent me. When the Reverend Colvil stops, he looks upon us with such love. It washes away the pain and fear we have held in our hearts these last few years.

'Before the great God, who searcheth all hearts ... if you, Samuel, or you, Violet, know of any cause, by precontract or otherwise, why you may not lawfully proceed to marriage, then you must own to it now.'

There's a long silence broken eventually by Calum pretending to sneeze loudly. We burst out laughing and even the usually severe Reverend Colvil smiles at his younger son's foolery.

When he is instructed, Samuel takes my hand and swears his vows to me.

'I, Samuel Colvil, do take thee, Violet Milligan, to be my married wife, and do, in the presence of God, and before this congregation, promise and covenant to be a loving and faithful husband unto thee, until God shall separate us by death.'

'Violet, take Samuel's right hand,' says the Reverend Colvil. 'I think you know the words.'

I look into the eyes of the man I love and know that no other man will touch my heart as he does. No other man will touch my body as he will.

'I, Violet Milligan, do take thee, Samuel Colvil, to be my married husband, and I do, in the presence of God, and before this congregation, promise and covenant to be a loving, faithful, and obedient wife unto thee, until God shall separate us by death.'

The Reverend Colvil places his hand upon ours. 'I now pronounce you to be husband and wife, according to God's ordinance. And let no man ... beggar or king ... try to come between you.'

* * *

We've been given a local barn for our wedding night and friends have spent a lot of time cleaning it out, laying down fresh straw in the loft while both of our mothers have made it homely with blankets and clothes, items like my hairbrush and a small looking glass. There's water and ale plus some food, which is wrapped tightly in a large cloth and hanging from a beam by a short rope.

After a long, joyful day celebrating with friends and family, Samuel and I lie down together on the blanket and I lay my head on his chest.

'Happy?' he says.

'More than I ever thought I could be. You?'

'Yes ... and proud, and ...'

'What?'

'Hopeful.'

I don't reply straight away. 'What gives you hope now that you didn't have before?'

My husband (my husband!) takes a deep breath as though this will help him collect his thoughts. 'We've always been bound together ... faced the world and its dangers as one, but with you as my wife I feel stronger, more certain and hopeful that we will one day be able to settle in peace, surrounded by at least a dozen children.'

'A dozen! I think I might have something to say about the number of children.'

He chuckles softly. 'Well, it's really in God's hands. Don't you think twelve is a good number, to start with at least? Perhaps ...'

'What?'

'Well, maybe we should make a start ...'

Samuel's attempt at humour doesn't fool me for an instant. He's more nervous than I am. We've known each other's bodies for all these years and yet never *known* them, not as a man and wife. I move my head to look at his face, so open and honest. I stroke his hair.

'I shall cut this from now on.'

He takes my hand and kisses it. 'Violet.'

I've never heard him say my name like this, never known that one word could convey such passion and urgency. We remove our clothes and look upon each other's naked body as if never seen before.

'Kiss me,' I say.

When his lips touch mine, the world outside no longer exists.

* * *

Samuel and I lie amongst the heather as we used to all those years ago as children. It was a time of such innocent joy. Now we've been married for three months and, despite the continuing conflict around the country, they've been the happiest in my life. Samuel has made money selling drawings to the local laird, who wanted a picture of his wife and was so pleased with the result that he asked for one of each member of his rather large family. Word of Samuel's skill is spreading.

Yet I've sensed there's something very important that he's been wanting to speak about. I suspect he's suggested coming to a place where we're completely alone so that we can talk freely. I wait. He remains silent, hesitating at hurting me. It's obvious to me what he wants to say, but he needs to be the one, so I wait. I'm quite good at it.

'Violet ... there's something I need to tell you.'

'You can tell me anything.'

'I want ... *need* ... to do my training as a minister.'

'I always expected that you would, Samuel.'

'But it's much more difficult to do now in Scotland, with our beliefs. There's only one place ... and it's where many go ...' He takes a deep breath before blurting out the word 'Holland'.

'Yes.'

'But it's another country, and I'll be away for years before I'm ordained.'

'Samuel, do you really think I didn't realise that you'll have to go to Holland to do your training? Your mother has often spoken to my mother and me about this.'

He twists in the heather to look at me with a frown. 'My mother's spoken about this?'

I reach over and gently rub away his frown, as if it's a mistake in a drawing. 'Yes, Samuel. We'd obviously worked it out.'

'But don't you mind?'

'Of course I mind! It'll break my heart when you leave, but it'll break both our hearts if you don't. Samuel, you must follow the path that God has shown.'

After a moment's pause, he says quietly, 'You could come with me.'

As if I hadn't considered the options a hundred times over with the counsel of my mother and his. I shake my head. 'This period in your life needs to be with your studies, your fellow students and tutors, not me. I'll be waiting. When you're ready to return, I'll be waiting.'

Samuel takes me into his arms. 'Violet, you are the most extraordinary, clever, wise, brave woman. I love you so much.'

'It's because I love you that I must let you go.'

I clutch him tight, too tight for someone who is fine with this decision I've made. Because my heart won't be breaking when Samuel leaves ... it's already breaking, right now as we lie amongst the heather.

Part II

The Price of Freedom

10

Violet
15 February 1678, Sorn, East Ayrshire

MOTHER AND I ARE PREPARING a meal when we hear Hamish cry out. We rush to the door but Mother quickly pushes me behind her so that I'm largely hidden from the dozen men who have appeared outside the house. Hamish is sprawled on the ground before them, and Father hurries over from the barn to help him before addressing the one man on a horse.

'What's the meaning of this?'

The man, who is obviously in charge, replies curtly, 'You're to provide accommodation for three men. Make sure they're fed and looked after well ... or you'll be in even more trouble.'

My stomach clenches. We've heard terrible stories of these rough men. It's rumoured there are ten thousand; Highlanders plus militiamen from the Lowlands, with orders from the Privy Council to inhabit the south-west of Scotland and hunt for rebels, collect unpaid fines and prevent conventicles taking place. No house is spared, from the meanest hovel to the grandest estate. Folk are mistreated regardless of age, health or status. Most women are terrified and husbands, fathers, brothers and those in authority, even ministers, protect them at their peril.

Without any further conversation, the men outside move off, leaving three figures behind who stare aggressively at Father and Hamish.

'Dear Lord above, are they human?' I whisper.

All wear the fèileadh-mòr, the tartan material so filthy it's difficult to see where it ends and blackened knees begin, while their wild faces are so bearded that it's doubtful their mothers would even recognise them. They look like devils. Two of them are huge, but it is the smallest one who conveys the greatest sense of evil.

'Violet,' whispers my mother. 'Leave quietly by the back door and hide in the woods until one of us comes to get you.'

'What about you, Mother?'

'They're not interested in an old woman like me.' She squeezes my hand, but I feel a tremor in her touch; a tightly leashed fear. 'I'll be fine, but you're in great danger now.'

* * *

It's been three days since the Highlanders took over the house. Samuel and I keep to the barn with my parents. Hamish has remained, sleeping on the floor by the fire. They enjoy humiliating him, but apart from a black eye he's so far been unhurt. The Reverend Colvil, his wife and Calum are living a few miles away and trying to be unnoticed by anyone in authority.

Samuel left at first light this morning on yet another Covenanter mission. Since his return from Holland two years ago, he has gone away on many occasions, usually for several weeks, helping famous field preachers like the Reverends John King and John Kidd move safely from place to place. Often I don't know what he's doing or where he's gone, much like when he was in Holland training to be a minister.

The loneliness during this period was a constant knife to my soul, even though I was with my family. We wrote, of course, and a small bundle of letters would arrive perhaps twice a year, often tattered, stained and frayed at the edges, passed on from stranger to stranger – friends, though we didn't know them. I would hide away for days reading them, weeping over them, my heart filled with joy and breaking at the same time.

Father grumbles as he, Mother and I huddle over a hunk of bread that Hamish has been able to smuggle out to us.

'The government is so desperate to prevent our religious meetings,' he says, 'that it's brought in Highlanders because they have such a long-standing hatred of those in the south-west.'

The bread is hard, old, but at least it's food. Poor Hamish – he's already been made to kill three of our chickens and endure the added humiliation of having to cook and serve them to the Highlanders, waiting upon the table as if they were lairds and he a servant.

'I'm worried that Hamish is going to strike back in anger and he'll be seriously hurt, or worse,' says Mother.

Father sighs, shaking his head. 'I fear you're right, Isabel. Tomorrow I'll take his place. They won't find me so easy to intimidate and I can put up with their abuse better than a young man.'

Samuel slips into the barn. He kisses me as he sits down and I hand him his portion of bread.

'They're searching every dwelling, hut, cave and barn, looking for named individuals, weapons and valuables,' he tells us. 'We're only just managing to keep ahead of them.'

'The Reverend Cargill?' asks Father, clearly worried.

'He's safe, Douglas. We've got people keeping watch throughout the area and we would all give our lives to protect him.'

'If the heathens caught such a leader in our cause as Donald Cargill, it would be a dark day indeed.'

'The Highlanders are beating up folk trying to get them to reveal the hiding places of those they're searching for. Old McGregor was in a very bad way after they had finished with him. He didn't tell them anything, though.'

'He's as tough as dried-up leather,' says Father. 'If they'd attacked him twenty years ago, he would have had them fleeing for their lives, the cowards. I wish I was twenty years younger and able to use a sword as I used to.'

'Any weapons they're not keeping are being broken up,' says Samuel.

'Where's your dirk?' I ask, noticing that he's not carrying it around his belt as normal.

Samuel points to a place at the back of the stall that the two of us are using, having cleaned it out once the cow had been moved into the adjoining stall. 'It's behind that plank there, out of sight but easy to reach if needed urgently. I've managed to speak to Hamish. They're smashing up furniture in the house to burn rather than use logs that are stacked and ready.'

'They're going to destroy what they can't later take,' says Mother.

'Yes,' agrees my father. 'Destroy, steal and punish us for our commitment to God.'

'You must continue to keep out of their sight, Violet,' my mother urges me. 'You hear such frightful stories.'

Samuel drapes an arm around me and draws me in protectively. 'They'll be out tomorrow searching for conventicles. We've spread a rumour that Reverend Cargill is holding a sermon about five miles east of Cronberry. Scores of people are going to head in that direction early in the morning, making sure they're seen while pretending they're trying not to be. They all have instructions on where to split up and secretly make their way home. The Highlanders shouldn't be anywhere near the real conventicle over by Failford.'

'The Reverend Peden's old site in Coilsholm Wood was well chosen for its remoteness,' says Father. 'Hidden from eyes that might otherwise betray those attending.'

'I've heard much about his preaching,' I say.

'An inspirational man,' says Father, nodding appreciatively. 'He nearly died during his captivity on the Bass Rock. Well, let's pray that there's no violence tomorrow.'

'And pray that these demons will be gone before something terrible happens to one of us,' adds Mother, 'because I fear we cannot continue for much longer without such a thing occurring.' The glance she casts in my direction makes my soul shiver.

* * *

The three Highlanders have gone along with all of the others nearby. They're like dogs on the scent of a bitch in heat, so certain they'll find a large crowd to attack and be able to capture the famous Reverend Cargill. Samuel, Hamish and my father have gone to the real one near Failford, leaving Mother and me to go through the house and see what we can salvage without it being too noticeable. Like most people, we had put our coin in a safe place, burying it in the woods well in advance of the arrival of this rabble. We just hadn't realised how destructive the Highlanders would be and now regret leaving any valuable items in the house at all.

It's late in the morning and I'm in the barn trying to find a suitable place for a small but precious painting of my grandparents. I've wrapped it carefully in a cloth. When I hear a noise behind me, I turn, expecting to find Mother with more retrieved items to hide. My blood goes cold at the sight of the smallest of the three Highlanders.

'You've been keeping out of our way, haven't you, girl? That's not friendly, is it?'

He takes a step towards me and I move back, frantically trying to work out what to do. I've never spoken to one of these men, and although I speak Gaelic, I hadn't realised how difficult their accents are to understand.

'Why are you here? Haven't you heard about the conventicle?'

'I thought we were hearing a bit too much about the conventicle. You Lowlanders think we're all stupid ... whispered comments and snatches of conversation that were always just enough for us to catch. Well, I'm a suspicious bastard and didn't believe there wasn't something going on here, so I turned back. And look what I find ... not a man in sight and you hiding your treasures. Where's the traitors' meeting really taking place?'

He'll easily catch me if I try to run around him to reach the door. The only potential weapon is the hayfork, but that's by the entrance.

The dirk!

If I move into the stall and can't reach it, then I'll be completely trapped. His curiosity about the conventicle is overcome by his greed.

'What's that you've got?'

He's not rushing me and instead is enjoying the game, like a cat with a mouse.

'It's a painting of my grandparents.'

I back away slowly, getting closer to the open gate of the stall, then decide this needs to be done quickly. I throw the bundle into the air, right at him.

'The frame is really valuable. Here.'

He's so surprised that he reaches up to catch it as I spin around and run to the plank, hoping that Samuel hasn't pushed the dirk so far along that I can't reach it. I've got hold of the handle when the Highlander slams me against the wall.

'Trying to trick me, girl! What's that you're after?'

He's far too strong for me to fight and forces my arm around to reveal the weapon in my hand.

'A very nice piece of work,' he says, bending my wrist. The dirk slips from my grasp. 'You and I are going to have some fun, and afterwards you can tell me where the conventicle is taking place.'

He moves his head towards mine and I almost gag at the stench of him. I twist my head away and in response he bends my arms so painfully I scream. Suddenly he's also screaming and I don't understand what's happening until I hear my mother's voice.

'Let go of my daughter, you heathen bastard!'

She's rammed the prongs of the hayfork into his back and for a moment the three of us are motionless, before Mother yanks out the fork and backs out of the stall. She's drawing him away from me. He turns with a roar, pulls out his sword, and staggers after her. I retrieve the dirk. Mother is blocking the way to the entrance and the long hayfork means that he can't reach her.

'You bitch. You'll die for this, you and the rest of your miserable family.'

He knows I'm there and tries to keep us in sight. We go either side of him. It's like a macabre dance, each person seeking that brief opportunity to strike. My foot kicks an old horseshoe. I pick it up and make a big show of hurling it at his head. It's enough of a distraction. Mother rushes forward, jabs him in the stomach, and jumps back out of the way.

He howls, his pain and anger making him careless, and as he slashes his sword through the air, I step in and drive the dirk into his side. I move away just in time. The tip of his sword whistles past my face, only inches away. He would kill me in an instant if it wasn't for the danger of the hayfork. The Highlander is like a wounded wild animal, enraged and terribly dangerous. His end is hideously messy as we jab and slash and stab until he lies amongst the dirt and straw, a bloody, motionless shape. No songs of glory will be written about this miserable death.

Mother and I collapse into each other's arms, crying, shaking and scared out of our wits.

'Did he hurt you?'

I'm trembling so much I can hardly speak. 'No.'

'I never knew a body could hold so much blood. It doesn't seem possible. These Highlanders aren't human,' she says, staring at the unbelievable amount of gore.

It's at this very moment that the Highlander's eyes snap open and stare back at us. We scream as if Satan has risen up from the ground at our feet.

'He's alive! He's alive! Mother, I can't stab him again. I can't! I can't!'

'God save us, neither can I! What are we going to do? I can't go near him, Violet. He's a demon.'

Our terror almost drives us insane as inch by inch the man stretches out a hand towards the entrance to drag himself forward.

* * *

We're still almost beyond the ability to speak when Samuel, Hamish and my father return, horrified at the sight that greets them. Once they've assured themselves that we're not physically harmed and the figure near the entrance is definitely dead, the three men get into a serious discussion about where to put the body.

'We can't bury him outside,' says Father. 'The ground's frozen solid, and even if it wasn't, it would be obvious that the earth has been disturbed.'

'The river's too far to get him there in the time we have,' says Samuel.

Hamish is on the verge of panic. 'The other two will be back soon. We've got to do something – quickly.'

'The stall,' says Mother, who is recovering much faster than me. 'The earth is soft enough to dig, then spread it out evenly and cover it with straw.'

Everyone is immediately frantic with activity. Mother and I clean the hayfork and dirk of blood then sweep up any signs of a fight while the men dig out the soil with a furious desperation. When they get down about four feet, they put in the body along with the bloodied straw then refill the hole and spread out the soil.

The five of us stamp around as though we've lost our senses. When we've finished, the earth appears too neat, so we cover it with fresh straw and Father moves back the cow from the adjoining stall. The animal moos loudly as if pleased to have returned. By this time, it's mid-afternoon and the light is fading as we stand around, panting with exertion and fear. So far there's no sign of the others returning. Once again, it's my mother who points out what has to be done.

'We'll say that the Highlander never showed up and stick to that story whatever happens. The other two aren't bright enough to find the body and they won't be able to prove anything. Samuel, you must take Violet away from here. It's too dangerous for her.'

'Where would we go, Mother?'

'These invaders are based throughout the entire south-west of Scotland, so go east ... east and north. Anywhere that's far enough.'

'There are Highland officers in the area and they won't be so easily fooled,' says Samuel. 'They'll be suspicious if we leave just when one of their own has disappeared.'

'Yes, I think you may be pursued but it will be worse for Violet to remain. We can't protect her.'

Slowly, Samuel nods in agreement. 'All right, we'll go and hopefully any potential blame will go with us and none of you will be harmed. We need to do it now. Hamish, will you find us whatever food we can carry and then let my parents and Calum know?'

'Of course,' says Hamish, straight away setting off for the house.

'I'll go as well,' says Mother, heading to the barn's entrance. 'I'll get you spare clothing and anything else I can think of. Douglas, they'll need money.'

'I'll dig up our coin and give you a purse. I can't believe it's come to this. I'll pray for your both.' Father rushes out with one of the spades that has so recently been used to bury someone.

'Thank you, Father. We'll need all the prayers we can get,' I reply, but he's already gone.

11

Samuel
19 April 1679, Perthshire

VIOLET IS FEVERISH AND LIES in my arms, murmuring and twitching in her troubled sleep. It's been over a year since we fled the south-west and although the Highlanders left the area after a few months, our names and descriptions have been circulated by the authorities; we are wanted for murder. The rough life we've been forced to endure, combined with the constant feeling of being hunted, has taken its toll on us. The winter has been fierce and we've survived only due to the kindness of folk who've often barely had enough food for themselves or fuel for the fire that we've sat around.

Violet mutters something I don't catch. She fell ill a few days ago, although I suspect she's been unwell for a while and hasn't said anything. We're resting in a field near a small town somewhere in the east of Perthshire. Whatever it's called, we can't stay in the open. The temperature is dropping fast as the afternoon light fades. We'll have to trust to God's protection.

'Violet ... Violet ...'

It's difficult to wake her, which worries me greatly.

'Samuel?'

'It's time to move. We'll ask for shelter in the town.'

'Can we risk it?'

'I fear we must. Come on, I'll help you.'

* * *

I don't know what makes me choose the manse; perhaps because I'm now struggling to carry Violet in my arms and it's the first substantial house we come to. Part of me screams that this is the last place we should seek help because if we're discovered to be wanted Covenanters, the minister will be duty-bound to tell the authorities. Despite this, I kick the front door and wait.

It's opened by a powerfully built man of about forty, dressed in the black clothes of a Church of Scotland minister. Before I can even form the first words of asking for aid, he steps forward and lifts Violet out of my arms as if she weighs no more than a child.

'Agnes!' he shouts, moving quickly along the corridor. 'Our help is needed.' With these last few words he disappears into a room.

I'm so astonished at Violet being taken from me in such a manner that I stand like a fool in the doorway before gathering enough wits to go inside and close the door behind me. When I enter the room, a woman I take to be the minister's wife is already removing Violet's outer clothes.

'These are soaked right through. This poor woman needs to be dried and cleaned and fed and – Bella! – kept warm and safe. Bella!'

'And prayed over,' says the minister.

'I'll leave that to you. Now out ... OUT!'

This instruction is directed towards the minister and myself as we're firmly pushed into the corridor. He takes hold of my arm and leads me to the kitchen as a young maid rushes past.

I'm physically put into a chair by the fire and it's only then I realise I have been swaying on my feet. The minister pours whisky into two goblets and hands one to me.

'Sip that while I stoke up the fire and get you some food. You looked as though you were about to collapse at my front door.'

He sets about his tasks, cheerfully humming to himself. Despite my weariness, I find myself fascinated by this extraordinary man, who moves with a grace I would expect from a gentlewoman of high birth, not someone of such bulk. I sniff the liquid and my eyes water.

'It's not a bad batch that, not bad at all. A gift from a wealthy parishioner.'

I drink a little and immediately feel the heat of it down my gullet and into my belly.

'Here, get this into you.'

I'm taken aback at how quickly he's put food together and wonder if I've actually fallen asleep. My goblet is on the table so I guess I did. The plate he puts in my lap is like a feast and for an instant I just stare at it as if frightened that moving might make it disappear. There are two cold chicken legs, plus slices of ham and a large hunk of bread thickly coated with butter. I barely manage to say 'thank you' before cramming food into my mouth. He kneels in front of me and for a moment I think he's about to pray, then to my surprise he carefully removes my sodden footwear.

'You're wet as well, my friend, and these boots are doing you more harm than good.'

The food sticks in my mouth. That I should have feared coming to the manse, and now this stranger is so tenderly taking care of me. Tears flow down my cheeks. I'm ashamed. He pats me on the knee.

'Eat your food and you can take more time. I promise no one will steal it. You're safe here. Whatever has happened in the past, nobody is going to hurt you in my house.'

'What minister are you?'

'I'm Reverend Graham, and you, I suspect, are Covenanters.'

What's the point of denying it? Violet lies in a fever in another room while I sit here with no boots, eating this man's food.

'How did you guess?'

He settles a kindly gaze on me. 'I've encountered all manner of humanity over the years, and you, I'm certain, are no criminal. However, you have a wariness of the hunted about you.'

'You'll have to inform your bishop.'

'I'll do no such thing. He's a fine enough man who lets me get on without much interference. In fact, I don't think I've seen him this side of a year. However, he would feel obliged to inform the local garrison, so it's best for everyone if we don't put him in a difficult position. We'll just keep you out of sight until your wife — it is your wife? — recovers. What's her name?'

'Violet.'

'And yours?'

'Samuel.'

'Well then, Samuel,' he says, standing, 'eat up while I fetch blankets and we'll dry your clothes.'

With that he leaves, humming his tuneless hum as though he's the most carefree man in the world.

* * *

Reverend Graham has been keen to hear our story, and although I've omitted parts, such as my involvement in Rullion Green, he probably guesses much of what I've tried to hide. This evening there's been an unusually long silence between us as we sit either side of the fire, drinking whisky while staring at the flames dancing in the hearth.

I am impressed by how much help he gives to his parishioners. He's not above chopping wood for an elderly widow or sitting up all night with someone who's ill. Yet, as I've recovered my strength, I've become tenser in his presence. The fact that he lives in a manse and preaches in the kirk means that he cannot believe in the Covenanter cause and I am uneasy, despite the fact that he has not given us away.

'You don't know what to make of me, do you, Samuel?' He observes me with keen eyes and gives me his easy smile. 'I've taken you and Violet into my home and we've cared for you both as best we can, but I suspect you view me with suspicion. Your soul is in conflict.'

'I won't deny it, for you deserve nothing but honesty. You and Agnes have proved to be caring Christians and I probably can't ever repay our debt. Are you an Episcopalian minister?'

'No, as Presbyterian as you.'

'So you've accepted the King's Indulgence and that he is the head of the Kirk?'

'I did what I had to back in sixty-two so that I could continue to care for the spiritual and physical needs of those in my parish.'

'But the Scriptures are clear—'

'Are they! Are they truly, my dear friend? We may accept that the Scriptures represent the words of God but those words have been translated from another language and then their meaning has been interpreted by men – clever, honourable and righteous, I grant – but men nonetheless, and you know as well as I do how often contrasting conclusions are reached from those same holy sentences.

'Even the famous National Covenant is a document so vague and open to different interpretations that many of the thousands of lairds, noblemen and common people who signed it believed they were agreeing to different things. The Covenanter cause has been split into various factions ever since, so how can anyone tell me that I'm wrong in my belief when you can't even agree amongst yourselves?'

We fall silent. A chasm has opened between us. I look down upon a huge void and fear that it's me who will fall into the nothingness. I'm terrified by the possibility.

'What are we here for, Samuel, as ordained Church of Scotland ministers?'

'To spread the word of God,' I reply immediately, by rote, almost.

'All right, let's consider that one point. Since you were ordained, how many sermons have you given? How often have you preached to a congregation? How have you spread the word of God?'

I open my mouth but have no defence. He knows me for the fraud I am, for I've done none of those things. Since I took up arms for the cause, I have not even helped my fellow man in the simplest of ways – not even to chop wood. I've benefitted no one, accomplished nothing outside of this never-ending conflict with the king.

'Don't punish yourself, Samuel. You've done what you believe to be right and suffered greatly for it. I have done what I believe. God knows what's in my heart and I don't accept the king as the head of the Kirk, not where it matters. As for being told what to do by a bishop, well, I hardly see him,' he says with a shrug. 'And if I baptise a baby at a font by the kirk door, is that really such an affront to God? By agreeing to such things, I'm able to continue to help the people in my parish in whatever way I can. So who's right?'

'The king shouldn't have any power over the Church of Scotland,' I reply, repeating the one argument that all Covenanters agree upon. 'No man can put himself between his fellow man and God. Only our Saviour Jesus Christ can claim that throne and I will give my life fighting for the Kirk's freedom.'

'I understand, truly I do, Samuel, yet the Kirk is equally guilty of wanting control over secular matters. Church and state both believe in their divine right to be superior to the other – and in the meantime, Scotland is ripped apart, its fields and villages washed in the blood of Scotsmen. And have you killed, Samuel? Have you taken the life of another person in this quest that you're so certain is correct?'

I can't answer for a long while, because the boy is there in front of me, saying *please* as I drive the spike of the halberd into his chest.

'At Rullion Green,' I say quietly, my voice lost somewhere on that battleground, 'I lost count of the number I killed or maimed. I tell myself it was for God. I have to believe that, otherwise I'm merely a monstrous murderer and I can't live with that thought.'

The reverend tilts his head at me, studying me with an expression I cannot fathom.

'Look at us. I would say we're decent, honest men of the Church, yet we face each other across this fire as though we're a Frenchman and an Englishman with hatred entrenched in our souls. I understand your cause, Samuel, and I'm not without sympathy for it. Yet the actions of Covenanters are tearing families apart ... and I don't see an end to the killings.'

In the deepest recesses of my heart, his words take root, and a fear kindles. I know, before long, I will be forced to kill again.

* * *

Violet and I sit in the kitchen with Agnes, enjoying a rare conversation about ordinary things, everyday events, swapping amusing stories. Violet laughs over a tale about a man whose breeches are eaten by his pig and it sounds to me like the most beautiful music I've ever heard. Our stay with the Reverend Graham and his wife has transformed her and she looks in better health than she has for a long time.

As for myself ...

We stop talking when the front door opens and the familiar footsteps of Reverend Graham echo along the corridor. When he enters the room, it's immediately apparent that something awful has happened.

'What's wrong, dear?' asks Agnes.

'Grim news. Grim news indeed,' he replies, pacing the room. 'Covenanters have murdered Archbishop Sharp!'

We cry out in shock at this. Sharp had been a Presbyterian minister and initially a staunch supporter of the Covenanter cause. To everyone's astonishment and dismay, he later accepted the position of Archbishop of St Andrews and became a hugely outspoken critic of the cause. It was an enormous betrayal – one that made him a hated figure amongst Covenanters.

But to *murder* him?

'The Devil has been at work,' continues Reverend Graham. 'The archbishop was on his way back to St Andrews and it was purely by chance that his coach was stopped on Magus Muir by a group of Covenanters who were hiding in the area with the intention of kidnapping the sheriff-depute of Fife. Apparently, they considered it providence that such a prize was handed to them. The poor archbishop was dragged from his carriage and, in plain sight of his daughter, stabbed by his assailants until he was dead!'

We're stunned. 'This is terrible,' I say. 'The persecution of Covenanters throughout Scotland will reach unknown levels because of the actions of a handful of fanatics. They've done more damage to our cause than the entire Pentland Rising.'

'We can't stay here,' says Violet. 'We'll put you at too much risk and you've already done so much for us. We can never repay your kindness.'

Reverend Graham nods sadly. 'No, we can no longer shelter you after such an evil deed, even though I know you had no part in it and condemn the actions.'

'Where will you go?' asks Agnes.

Violet looks to me to answer. They stare at me, waiting for my reply, yet in truth I have no idea ... no idea at all.

12

Violet
1 June 1679, Drumclog, Lanarkshire

W<small>E STAND IN SILENCE</small> – Samuel's parents and my own, plus Hamish and Calum – amongst thousands of Covenanters who have gathered for a conventicle in a valley a couple of miles from a village called Darvel. Many people have travelled long distances to hear the famous Reverend Thomas Douglas preach and every single one of us is committing an act of treason by simply standing here together in the countryside.

The risk of attack by Royalist soldiers is so great that there are many armed men amongst us, led by Sir Robert Hamilton of Preston, who seems to have taken on the role because of his position in society rather than any military experience.

Samuel and I were lucky after leaving the Reverend Graham and Agnes, and lived undiscovered in the large town of Perth until word reached us about today. We had to come, not least because we heard via the huge network of supporters throughout the country that our families would be here.

The Reverend Douglas is positioned part way up Harelaw Hill so that people can see and hear him more clearly. He's been speaking for over half an hour and is expected to continue for a long while yet.

'We've been forced out of our kirks, out of our houses, out of our barns and fields ... now we stand in this remote valley amongst God's creations and we are stronger than ever before. The king's army may break our bones, yet they will never break our spirit. They may crush our bodies but they will never crush our hope. They may kill us, as so many have already been killed, but they will never kill our beliefs!'

The sound of thousands of voices call out as one that we will not give up the fight. We've attended many conventicles over the years and often the preacher swaps between a religious sermon and a political speech so seamlessly that they merge into one like the white and yoke of a beaten egg.

A man nearby shouts out: 'Christ and the Covenant! Christ and the Covenant!'

The chant spreads throughout the congregation like a river in flood and soon the valley echoes to the call. The Reverend Douglas nods his approval and makes no move to instil silence.

'I feel washed clean once more by the spirit of God,' says Samuel, exhaling a deep, contented breath.

He was troubled greatly after we left Reverend Graham, although would never explain why and I did not press him for an answer because I sensed it was an inner struggle that only Samuel could calm. Being here and seeing him filled with such joy, I know that his soul is once more at peace.

'Why can't we just be left alone?' I say, although I know the answer as well as he does. 'We could find a parish where you could preach as you've always been meant to do and we could build a home to live our lives without fear of violence.'

'One day, Violet. When our work is done.'

A single shot rents the air, and the chanting stops in an instant. A musket has been fired by a watchman. On a nearby rise, a figure hurtles down towards the minister, shouting as he runs.

'Dragoons, heading in force from the east about a mile away!'

The Reverend Douglas raises his arms. 'You know the theory – now for the practice!'

Hamilton immediately takes control. 'We mustn't meet them here,' he shouts. 'Those men with arms, form lines, quickly now! Reverend Douglas, everyone else should head farther away. Go west until you hear news.'

'I'll see to it,' shouts back the minister, already coming down amongst people to organise the movement of the women, elderly and children.

'Violet, you must head west,' says Samuel.

'Don't worry about me. Keep close to the others.'

He runs off to catch up with Calum, Hamish and our fathers. There's confusion and fear amongst the congregation but also great determination to do what needs to be done and within minutes about two hundred men set off, running after the fifty Covenanters on horseback who've already galloped away. I'm not alone in what I'm considering and soon I'm one of more than thirty of the strongest women who agree that we need to provide what help we can to our menfolk, some of whom will inevitably be injured.

With no weapons to hinder us we're not far behind them and we reach the top of a hill as Hamilton is organising men into formations along the side facing the direction of the expected attack, Covenanters with muskets in front of the lines of men with improvised weapons. Those on horseback are split into two groups positioned either side. Samuel is at the end of his line nearest to me and I walk over, still trying to catch my breath after our frantic dash.

'Don't be angry,' I say in response to his expression. 'We're here to help the injured and no one can expect anything less of us.'

He nods, his chest heaving after his own run. It's only minutes later when dragoons appear, their horses brought to a stop several hundred yards away on the other side of an extremely boggy area.

'It's Claverhouse!' says Samuel, upon seeing the officer at the front. 'He'll have been hoping to catch us at our prayers, damn him.'

Since his recent return from military service on the Continent, John Graham of Claverhouse has become one of the most feared officers in the Royalist army, a man whose zeal for hunting Covenanters throughout the southwest of Scotland has made him infamous. I hear his name being spoken along the line as more people realise the danger they're facing.

'Those prisoners?' I ask, pointing to a dozen or so men who are bound and being taken over to one side of what may become the battleground. 'One's a minister.'

Samuel looks to where I'm pointing. 'That's the Reverend John King. He must have been captured on his way to our gathering. Such a famous Covenanter preacher will have been high on the authority's wanted list.'

A single officer rides slowly towards us holding up a short branch that has a white cloth tied to the top, a clear sign that our enemy wants to speak.

'Hold your fire,' shouts Hamilton. 'Let's hear what they have to say.'

The ground is so soft that the officer is forced to remain some distance away and raise his voice. 'If you lay down your weapons and hand over your leaders, the rest of you may go free, unharmed.'

There's a moment of silence before the men in the lines start jeering and calling insults. There are plenty of obscene gestures and laughter at the suggestion and also of the idea that anyone would be allowed to just walk away.

'You have your answer,' shouts Hamilton. 'Now go and tell your master that this time he's facing men who are prepared for a fight, not unarmed Christians at prayer.'

Everyone falls silent as we watch the officer ride back and speak to Claverhouse. His response carries clearly over to us, as it's meant to.

'No quarter! No quarter to be given!'

'Violet, move away now,' says Samuel.

I run back towards the other women and out of the direct line of fire. Hamilton repeats the order to the men under his command. It's a desperate thing to hear because it means neither side will spare anyone, regardless of how injured they are or even if they throw down their weapon to surrender. It will be a fight without mercy.

There are about a hundred and fifty dragoons and some fire a ragged volley from their carabines, hitting a few of our men. Covenanters return fire. It's not long before Hamilton orders those on horseback to make their way around the boggy ground and attack the enemy's flank while those on foot are ordered to move forward. I expect them to rush down the hill but instead they march in line as they sing.

'God is known in Judah; His name is great in Israel . . .'

Tears prickle in my eyes to see them so fearless, even as those dragoons who have not already discharged their weapons fire them. Carabines are extremely difficult to reload while mounted and Claverhouse orders a charge, his rasping voice carrying above all other sounds. Several women cry out in terror as the horses thunder onwards, straight towards the men on foot.

However, the heavy animals are soon floundering as they sink into the mud, and the tide of battle turns in an instant as Covenanters armed with long pitchforks, pikes and halberds, and with their determination to do God's work and free the Kirk, set about a bloody revenge on the dragoons. Moments later, Hamilton's horsemen attack from the firmer ground.

This scene of carnage roots me to the spot, until one of the women shouts out that we have to help the men left behind. Those injured have been shot, but there are only a few and after quickly checking them, I leave their care to others. Down the hill the Royalist soldiers are already fleeing, leaving many dead amongst the riderless horses that stand trembling in shock. Several mounted Covenanters chase after Claverhouse.

Samuel is easy to spot. He's talking to Calum and they appear unhurt. Hamish is there too, showing his skill with animals by calming a terrified horse. Over to the right, my father and the Reverend Colvil are helping to untie the prisoners. I breathe a deep sigh of relief; now I know they are safe, I can tend to some of the injured. I'm binding a slash wound to a man's arm when Samuel finds me.

'Our men have all returned,' he says to us. 'Some of them chased Claverhouse but our farm horses are no match for what the dragoons ride. The cowards probably won't stop running away until they reach Glasgow! How are you, friend?'

'Your wife is a natural healer and this is a great victory,' replies the man.

'Violet is a natural healer, but whether this is a great victory ...'

'But we beat them completely,' I say, surprised that he seems so wary.

'I fear what we've done,' says Samuel, 'is merely poke a willow up the king's arse.'

13

Violet
21 June 1679, Bothwell Bridge, Lanarkshire

'DAMN THEM! THEY'RE CONTINUING TO fight amongst themselves with no thought to the real enemy that we're going to face in the coming days!'

My father has rejoined us and I've never seen him so angry. We're gathered around a fire, Samuel, Calum, Hamish and me. The Reverend Colvil, I assume, is still at the meeting that my father has refused to remain at. He sits down, his expression suddenly of such despair that it's as if we've already lost. We wait in silence for him to speak.

Around us, thousands of Covenanters are spread out in similar small groups, sitting around their fires, eating and talking. Eventually, he calms down sufficiently to explain what's happening.

'They're still arguing fiercely about points of dogma and whether ministers who accepted an Indulgence to retain their position should even be amongst us. It's become so heated that certain officers are refusing to work alongside those from different factions. What's more damaging is that some ministers are preaching against their fellow ministers, which means ordinary men will have their loyalties split further.

'They're so far apart in their individual demands it's hard to believe anyone has got together at all. Sir Robert Hamilton would have the king off his throne and probably his head off his body, while the Reverend John Welsh and his moderates want to meet the king and have a bloody discussion. As if such a thing is likely after so many murders and atrocities ... I grant it, on both sides.' With this outburst, Father drops his head into his hands and falls silent.

Our success at Drumclog, where we so decisively beat Claverhouse and his dragoons, changed everything ... and yet nothing. To many it was a sign from God and thousands rose up to join the fight, yet to me our journey feels aimless and without firm leadership. Days ago we set up camp on the south side of the Clyde, only to move it several times within the same area.

There are said to be six thousand Covenanters and, in principle, we're led by Sir Robert Hamilton, who took charge successfully at Drumclog. However, not everyone supports his appointment, which appears to be largely his own decision. Sometime soon, we'll face an army of regular troops and militia led by the king's illegitimate son, the Duke of Monmouth, who has been ordered back from England because of our actions.

Father lifts his head. 'Welsh might at least get to speak to Monmouth. The duke is said to be an honourable man and may be keen to avoid mass bloodshed if possible, yet he's certain to be under strict orders from the king and I doubt he'll have much room to negotiate. How have we come to this?' The despair in his voice is heartbreaking. 'Nobody is even checking that men have sufficient powder or shot for the forthcoming battle.'

* * *

'I'm going to stretch my legs,' says Samuel, standing and looking at me.

It's about an hour since my father returned and the mood around our fire has been unbearable. There's still no sign of the Reverend Colvil. I get up without speaking and walk slowly away with Samuel in the direction of the river, passing through numerous other groups. I'm surprised to see so few around some fires and there are a couple burning down unattended.

From the top of the hill, we watch men building a sturdy barricade across this side of the large stone bridge, its four impressive archways spanning the width of the Clyde. Gangs of men carry heavy timbers, horses drag the trunks of sawn trees, wooden crates are carefully positioned and filled with stones. The activity is being repeated to the east and west of the bridge on this side to provide cover for those firing muskets.

The surrounding area of the river mainly consists of ploughed fields with some woods in the distance. The nearest village is called Bothwell. It's on the north side and, although there isn't any sign of the government's army, I assume the residents fled as soon as they heard of our arrival. Samuel and I haven't spoken since leaving the others and I can't stand the silence ... the unspoken words ... the unacknowledged fear.

'Are you thinking of Rullion Green?' I ask him.

His eyes darken at the mere mention of it. 'I'm always thinking of Rullion Green.'

'What else?'

'That the river is too wide and fast-flowing for anyone to cross other than by the bridge. If we hold it, then we keep Monmouth's army on the other side, where all they can do is fire muskets from a distance that makes the weapon so inaccurate, targets can be hit only by sheer luck.'

'You think we can't hold it? The barricade is beginning to look formidable.'

'The problem is we can't hold it *forever*. We might keep them back for a few hours ... maybe a day or two ... but eventually they'll get across.'

'And we'll lose?'

'This fight, yes. The various factions have been arguing for years. If every point of view was a colour on a painter's palette there would be sufficient variety to reproduce any picture in the world. There's almost no chance that those in charge are going to agree anything significant by tomorrow. So, like your father says, we'll be divided. Men are already slipping away.'

'What! Covenanters are leaving?'

'Men say they're going to take a piss, only they don't come back. Others are more open, walking away quietly in small groups.'

'And no one stops them?'

'People are here of their own free will. They might be condemned and cursed for leaving but they can't be compelled to remain. They don't lack courage, but when they hear that their leaders are falling out amongst themselves, they lose hope. Violet, you must leave before the fighting starts.'

There are scores of women amongst the Covenanters ... wives, sweethearts, sisters, others who believe so strongly in the cause that they're here because there is nowhere else to be. Following Drumclog, my mother and Samuel's returned to Coylton, where they have many friends and could be certain of finding a safe place to stay. It was a decision that we made together as families, agreeing they no longer had the ability to play a part in any sort of army.

'Samuel, all the men I love are here ... you and Calum, Hamish, my father and yours. We're bound together on this tiny patch of Scottish soil. Do you really think I'm going to leave? You and I have faced danger side by side these many years. It won't be any different tomorrow.'

His eyes are brimming with sorrow as he looks at me. 'My love, this will be different. The loss, brutality, violence and deaths will be on a scale we've not seen before. Men like Claverhouse will want revenge for the humiliation of Drumclog. I don't believe our family will all survive and those that do might not be free.' His voice breaks as he continues. 'It's ironic, we've fought for freedom to worship as we wish and may yet lose any freedom whatsoever. We won't even be able to take a walk in the countryside at our own choosing.'

'Oh, Samuel!'

He takes me in his arms. I can hear his heart beating wildly against my ear. Will it still be beating this time tomorrow? Am I to return to Coylton a widow?

Dread such as I have never known threatens to sweep me away like a twig thrown into the Clyde. I cling to Samuel. As long as we have each other, we have a future together and will be all right. I tell this to myself over and over, but the repetition doesn't dispel the doubt in my heart, not for a single second.

* * *

The vanguard of the government's army arrives during the night and sets up on the north side of the Clyde. Daybreak results in a few dozen shots being exchanged across the water but no Covenanters are injured. The encounter is brief with the soldiers opposite no doubt deciding to wait for the main body to arrive.

Apparently, arguments between different factions continued throughout the night with little thought given to planning for the battle. I can feel how divided we are as a force, as surely as I can smell the woodsmoke from the fires. We've become separate groups. The most noticeable are the three hundred men behind the recently constructed barricade.

Samuel and Calum are amongst them. It's easy to make out their figures near the brass cannon that has been positioned so that it can fire along the length of the bridge. Most Covenanters remain on the hill, the senior officers on horseback gathered around the Covenanters' gold and blue flag proclaiming *For Christ's Crown and Covenant*. The flag hangs limply upon its pole, the words unreadable as if they've somehow been lost.

Hamish joins me. We're still together mid-morning when the enemy arrives in force. We watch in silence as they form up on the other side of the river. Several cannons are manhandled into specific positions facing us. Our one cannon, which had seemed so formidable, now appears rather vulnerable.

'They outnumber us at least two to one,' says Hamish, who has no orders and so has simply wandered where he wants. 'I'm sorry, Violet.'

'For what?'

'Anything and everything I've ever said or done that's hurt you.'

'I can't think of any instances.'

'I've always loved and admired you ... even when you were so irritating ... my big sister.'

'By about twenty minutes, according to Father.'

'He says that bringing us into the world was the happiest moment of his life.'

I smile, recalling the many times Father has told me this story. 'I was loud and you were quiet.'

He kisses me on the forehead. 'Nothing's changed then.'

I hug him. 'Well, know that I love you and I'm proud of all you've done.'

We're silent for a while, satisfied with holding each other. Finally, he pulls back to speak.

'I should have gone with Samuel and Calum. I got into such an argument with a couple of other men that I hadn't realised they had left.'

'Look at that gap, Hamish, between the river and where we stand on the hill. That's not a distance that can be measured in yards or covered in a few minutes. It's a gap of beliefs that I fear will not be crossed this day.'

'You need to leave, Violet, before the fighting begins.'

'I feel as though I've been fighting most of my life.'

'I'll find Father and keep close to him. I'll watch his back.'

For a long while, we hug each other again in silence. Perhaps he is wondering if this will be the last time. I know I am. I don't want to let go. Then my baby twin brother kisses me once more on the forehead and walks briskly away, probably hoping I haven't noticed the tears flowing down his cheeks. He soon disappears amongst the throng of men, and I'm filled with fear; Hamish will watch Father's back, but who will watch his?

* * *

No one orders the women to be anywhere in particular and, although some have moved further away from the expected violence, a few dozen are still with the main body. Scattered around us are several groups listening intently to their ministers, for it's the Sabbath as well as a day of battle. The biggest congregation is gathered around the famous Reverend Cargill, who's now one of the most wanted men in Scotland.

A hand strokes my arm and I turn to find Father next to me. I rest my head against him and he puts an arm about my shoulder.

'Hamish has gone looking for you.'

'He found me. I'll go back to him in a while.'

Despite the presence of thousands of people there is very little sound apart from the voices of the ministers. We stand in silence listening to snatches of different sermons. We're not here long when we see three men walk down the hill towards the bridge.

'There's the Reverend Welsh,' says Father. 'He must have finally won agreement from Hamilton that he can attempt to approach the Duke of Monmouth to discuss the Covenanters' petition.'

'Petition?'

'Yes, for all the good it will do. He's going to request the creation of a General Assembly for the Church of Scotland that is free from control by the state or monarch, and that Presbyterians have the right to practise their religion without fear of punishment. Apparently he's even going to ask for a pardon for those who have gathered here under arms.'

'Would the duke consider such things?'

'Oh, he'll listen. We may yet end up trying to kill each other but there is a certain etiquette in these matters. I doubt that he'll give what Welsh says much consideration. Most of the demands are exactly what Covenanters have been fighting to achieve for years. At least there shouldn't be any attack until Welsh returns with Monmouth's reply and it may be that he has to go over again with Hamilton's answer.'

We watch as the famous minister and his two companions climb the barrier and walk slowly across the bridge, hands clearly visible to show they hold no weapons. As they reach the other end, an officer steps forward and they speak for several moments before they are taken away out of sight.

'If I don't make it home—'

'Don't say such a thing, Father.'

'Violet ... I hope that one day you'll have children of your own and then you'll understand the love I feel for you and Hamish. Promise me that before the fighting starts, you'll move to the rear. You'll still be in some danger, but I can't be worrying about where you are if I end up in the middle of it all.'

I don't want to do this, yet I don't want to disobey my father. Nor can I tell him that he should leave this to the younger men. Hamish is expected to fight, even though it's not in his nature, while I am expected to avoid it, even though I would take up arms.

'I won't promise to stay away if I think you're in trouble.'

He nods. 'We can wait together until Welsh returns. Nothing significant will happen before then.'

So we wait. I'm good at waiting.

* * *

Samuel

Like most of the defending men, Calum and I are armed with the latest flintlock muskets, which can be fired without the use of a burning match cord. We've got ourselves a position close to the bridge where the most intensive fighting will take place. If the enemy gets to this side of the river, then we'll watch out for each other, as we've done throughout life. For the moment we're resting, waiting for the return of the Covenanter delegation.

'If I've never actually said it before, I'm proud to have you as my little brother. When we get home ...' I stop because I can't actually think of what to say.

'Do you think we'll get home, Sam?'

I don't answer straight away. Such a question deserves thought, and honesty. 'I fear not all of us. The danger is too great for everyone to escape unhurt. But which ones of us may be injured, killed or captured ... God only knows such things.'

'Do you regret what we've done over the years?'

'No. You?'

'No. It's what we've had to do.'

'I wish Violet had stayed in Ayrshire, like your Sarah.'

'Well, with wee Calum to take care of ...'

'Yes, a son makes a difference. I guess that's my biggest regret, that for some reason we don't understand God did not bless us with children.'

'Welsh is coming over,' says a man nearby, joining our conversation.

'His expression isn't encouraging,' notes Calum.

'Brother, he always looks like that.'

Like many men before a battle, I make an attempt at humour and those close by respond by laughing loudly. It's all forced but nonetheless a ritual, like praying, touching a cross or lucky charm ... anything that might help a man stay alive and unhurt. We assist the returning figures over the barrier. Someone calls out a question and people fall silent in order to catch the answer.

'Reverend Welsh, what was the duke's response?'

'That we have to lay down our weapons before he'll even entertain discussing anything.'

'We might as well hang ourselves where we stand,' says another voice.

'I suspect that's what Sir Robert will say,' replies the minister, before setting off up the hill to confer with the waiting officers.

* * *

John Welsh's guess was right and shortly afterwards the fighting begins when the enemy discharges muskets and its four cannon moments before a troop of the King's Life Guards gallops across the bridge. Our officers Hackston and Turnbull are inspiring leaders, giving clear orders that we willingly follow.

'Wait! Wait,' calls Hackston from his grey courser, ignoring the shots that whip through the air around him.

I'm staring at a potential target as our cannon fires and I never in my life want to see such a scene again. People and animals explode in a mist of red as the cannonball tears through arms, legs, bodies, heads ... they all just become one mass of gore lining the parapets.

'Dear God above,' says Calum, his voice cracking with shock. 'Did you see, Sam?'

'I saw, and I fear we'll never unsee it. Steady your nerve, Calum. This will get worse. Every scene like that will beget another in revenge.'

The closest forty men either side of our cannon have been ordered to concentrate only on the bridge. I had been aiming at one of the leading horsemen, but he's disappeared before my eyes and I'm just trying to pick a new target when Hackston shouts at us.

'Aim at the far end of the bridge. The far end of the bridge.'

Hundreds of Royalist foot soldiers are jammed together in a huge mass with nowhere to go now that the charge on horseback has been stopped so completely. I merely aim at the group. Even at this distance, it's almost impossible not to hit someone.

'Fire!'

We discharge our muskets and I immediately use a finger to quickly rid the pan of any embers before priming it with loose black powder from my flask. We've been drilled in the procedure and around me men cast about their muskets, putting the stock on the ground so that the barrel points to the sky and can be loaded with a charge, ball and wadding. I ram the components down the barrel with a scouring stick, my heart pounding in my chest; the longer this takes, the longer I am vulnerable to the enemy's fire. The barricade is nowhere near high enough to protect us.

Earlier that morning, men joked that the man operating our cannon had been born holding one. He's so skilled that people call him 'Gunner', his true name unknown to anyone except his mother. I'm astonished when I hear the cannon fire again so soon. I can't help looking up from my task and see that the ball has torn into the foot soldiers. In their terror, a couple of figures jump into the water and are instantly swept away, their cries for help joining the cries of the wounded.

'Sam, this is slaughter,' says Calum, who has also stopped to watch.

'It will turn if they get across. Then it will be us who are slaughtered. Remember your training and just concentrate on the job in hand.'

'Job, Sam! Is killing Scotsmen now a job, like ploughing the land?'

I'm as scared as my brother but am saved from having to reply by Hackston, who is close by and shouts out.

'Reload! Reload! The enemy will come to you soon enough. Reload fast and fire slow. Pick your target. Allow for the wind.'

We reload, fire and kill, then reload, fire and kill until the air is thick with the stench of blue-grey smoke and the bridge is soaked in the blood of men from Perth and Aberdeen, Inverness and Edinburgh ... strangers we could have met in some remote tavern and enjoyed an ale with. All around me men wipe their eyes and blame the smoke, but that's not the cause of our tears.

'I'm running out of powder and shot,' says Calum.

The three hundred of us started this fight with extra bandoliers of powder charges, plus plenty of spare shot and waterskins, which we filled in the Clyde under the cover of darkness. Once a musket has been discharged about a dozen times, it's unusable until the barrel has been washed out.

Empty waterskins litter the ground at our feet. After two hours of fighting there's not even a mouthful of water remaining and men can barely speak for thirst. A bone-deep weariness overtakes me and I slump down behind the shelter for a brief rest next to Calum.

I check the leather bag holding my shot and a few moments later hold up the one remaining ball between my fingers, so blackened with powder that it's difficult to tell metal from flesh.

'That's all you've got?'

'One ball and just enough powder to fire it,' I reply.

'What then?'

I look at my brother, his handsome face so altered by dirt, horror and fear that even the angels would struggle to recognise him. I replace the ball then gently pull Calum towards me and kiss his head. I hold him tight, like I used to when we were children in our box-bed.

'The end, Sam?'

'We are more in God's hands than ever, for there is little left for us to do in this fight.'

'I am so weary of it.'

'I know.'

'I wish I could have seen Sarah and wee Calum again, even just once more.'

'I know.'

I stroke his long blond hair and we lie without speaking because there are no more words to be said. The battle seems far away. But it has not forgotten us and soon Hackston rides towards our position. I watch him in awe – up on that horse, he must be a target for half the soldiers in the king's army, yet he seems fearless. We sit up when he gets close.

'Sir,' I say in a rasping voice, 'we're out of powder and shot.'

'I've already sent word up the hill.'

I look 'up the hill' to a sight that's beyond all understanding. Thousands of Covenanters stand idly watching the carnage taking place in front of them, yet despite our obvious desperate situation we've not been relieved by a single man. They've been turned to stone by dispute and distrust. Captain Turnbull rides up, his face red with fury.

'No one will give us shot or powder! I've ridden around begging fellow officers, yet they all say there's none to spare.'

It's a testament to Hackston's character that he retains his composure. 'Calum and Samuel, run up and down the lines. Tell men to share out their powder and shot. Let them know that there is no more coming and we will soon be finished here.'

With a nod to Calum I rush off, keeping low and stopping at every fifth man to pass on the message. Men swear and curse but readily follow the command. By the time I've reached the end of the line our cannon has fallen silent and figures are beginning to run back.

On the bridge, a fierce fight has broken out between our dragoons, led by Hackston, and the King's Life Guard. I see that some of the barricade has been pulled away to allow our horsemen to attack the approaching enemy, no doubt with the intention of holding them back while the exhausted men on foot get away.

I load my musket then set off towards the relative safety of our own line. Firing one ball will make no difference now in defending the bridge, yet to have this for the hand-to-hand fighting that is to come may be much more useful. I'm still some distance from the main Covenanter army when shouts of alarm make me turn.

Enemy horsemen pour on to the south side of the Clyde and stragglers on foot are their obvious target. Some Covenanters throw away their unloaded muskets to run faster but it's a futile gesture for most of them. I drop to one knee and aim at the rider heading in my direction, his sword held out and urging on his mount with kicks and shouts as if he simply can't wait another second to kill me.

* * *

Violet

There's a slight rise in the ground off to one side that provides a view of the bridge and of the two armies. Huddled together with a dozen other women, I watch in horror as the few hundred men who so bravely defended the crossing run to join the main Covenanter force. Too soon the enemy's horsemen cross the bridge and gallop after them.

'Our men are going to be caught and they're the only ones who've fought,' says a terrified voice nearby.

When it seems that a slaughter is about to occur, hundreds of Covenanters on horseback charge down the hill and quickly drive the outnumbered Life Guards away.

'The bridge!' cries another woman.

Large numbers of foot soldiers rush over to the south side of the Clyde, where their lines grow longer with every minute.

'We've lost,' I say, turning to the others. 'You should go now. Head back over those fields towards the woods.'

'What about you?' someone asks.

'Almost everyone I love is on that hill. I'm staying.'

'So am I,' says another.

'Me too,' agrees a third. 'I wish I had a weapon.'

After standing doing nothing for the last couple of hours, some men hurry down to meet the advancing government soldiers but there seems little co-ordination. Plenty of Covenanters hesitate and all the time more Royalist soldiers join in the fight.

'Officers are leaving!' cries a shocked voice behind me.

I look over to see several Covenanters on horseback gallop away, a few forcing apart the formations in their desire to escape and creating even more confusion amongst those on foot. Soon others begin to flee in the same direction.

'Come on!' I urge. 'We can't stay here, or we'll become trapped.'

With this we run from our vantage point and are soon surrounded by groups and individuals fighting. The air is filled with sounds; cries of pain and fear, curses and shouts, those begging for mercy, those calling for their mother. There are bodies and the injured everywhere. I quickly lose contact with the other women.

Surprisingly, no one bothers me but then I'm unarmed and men are in such fierce conflict that they only have time to notice the immediate danger in front of them. I'm trying to reach the area that I believe my father is in. As I step over a body, the man's eyes open and he grabs my ankle, giving me such a shock that I cry out.

'Help me!' he says.

Blood flows freely from a wound to his side. I kneel next to him, but there is nothing I can do.

'Don't let me be taken.'

I try to prise his hands off my ankle. 'I can't help you, I've got to find my own family.'

'It's your duty. Get me away from here.'

His grip is so fierce I have to use both hands to try and force open his fingers.

'I'm sorry, I can't stay.'

'You must.'

People are fighting and dying around us while this stranger and I are locked in an oddly intimate trial of strength. With a desperate cry, I yank my leg away and he looks up at me, pleading now.

'Please.'

'I'm sorry.'

I run from him with a terrible feeling of panic growing in my chest. I should not have delayed. The movement of troops has flowed one way and then another and when I reach the spot where I thought my father should be there is no sign of him or anyone I know. I'm suddenly alone in the centre of a desperate struggle for survival when I hear a voice – one that used to sing to me as a child, one that taught me about medicine, plants and diseases. Frantically, I try to find the source.

He is there, clearly wounded, fending off a soldier who is attacking viciously with a sword. I run with no thought of what to do when I reach them. Scattered on the ground are various weapons and I stop just long enough to snatch up a knife. As I get nearer, the soldier catches my father in the chest. His sword drops and as he falls to the ground, the private pulls back his arm for a killing blow. I can't do anything other than strike at the man's back. He cries out in shock and turns quickly, sweeping his sword in a large arc, expecting his attacker to be standing further away. Before he can react again, I thrust the knife upwards just beyond his chin. He looks utterly surprised as I push the blade higher and for a brief moment we're locked together in this embrace of death.

Slowly he sinks to his knees, gurgling horribly. I step away and am about to go to my father when someone charges into me with such force that I'm lifted off my feet before sprawling upon the ground, so stunned that I'm helpless.

'Violet,' croaks Father, reaching out his arm.

A huge soldier stands above me with an expression of fury.

I can't do anything to protect myself and stretch out so that my fingers entwine with those of Father's. He smiles. It was his wish to name me Violet, after his favourite flower. He told me that day when I was six, after I brought home the flowers that Samuel had given me. Strange that I should think of that now.

The soldier raises his sword, holding it with both hands to drive the point into my chest.

We'll die together then in the cause we both believe in. It's not such a bad way to end. I gaze into Father's face, happy that this is the last thing I'll see on earth. In this moment all the violence and death and hate in the world mean nothing to us as we lie upon that ground. We'll soon meet again in Heaven.

But nothing happens. Nothing ...

I glance up again, this time to see the soldier above me staring in disbelief at the pike that's been driven deep into his body. With another push my saviour sends him stumbling away beyond my feet, where he lies motionless.

'Violet!'

'Hamish! Father's badly hurt.'

My brother helps me up, retrieves his pike and stands guard while I try to assess Father's injuries.

'Violet,' Father splutters, blood pooling at the corners of his lips, 'you can't do anything. Get away while you can.'

'No, we'll stem the bleeding and carry you to safety.'

'Child ... I'm dying. You've done what's been possible, you and Hamish, Samuel and Calum. Find them and go home. Let others take up the struggle.'

'I can't leave you.'

'Drop it! Do it now or I'll order my men to fire!'

Four soldiers have surrounded us, pointing muskets at Hamish. They're just out of reach of his pike. An officer steps up between them, his sword drawn.

'The Duke of Monmouth has ordered quarter to be given,' says the officer, 'but you must drop your weapon or I'll have no option than to have you shot.'

Hamish looks at me. There's no way he can win. If we're out of the fight we can tend to Father. I give him a nod, and my brother throws down the pike.

A couple of soldiers step forward and bind his hands. Around us the fighting seems less intense, as if it's thinned out and perhaps moved beyond the hill.

'Father, we can see to your wounds. You'll survive. I'll save you.'

But I can't. He stares at me, but doesn't see me any more. He doesn't see anything.

14

Samuel
22 June 1679, Bothwell Bridge, Lanarkshire

THE STENCH OF DEATH AND despair hangs in the air like smoke from a fire that fills a room to such an extent it's impossible to breathe, only we can't escape by simply stepping outside. More than a thousand of us have been taken prisoner. Many Covenanters fled the field, some early on and others when it became obvious that the battle was lost. The number killed runs into hundreds.

To his credit, Monmouth ordered that quarter should be given and those taken were not to be treated harshly. However, he left the area soon afterwards and we're in the hands of men who hate us beyond any sense of reason or humanity, held in isolated groups. We can offer little comfort to the wounded and there are plenty who won't live to see the sun rise.

Everyone is beyond exhausted, for we are weary not just in body but in spirit also. Calum and I sit on the ground, leaning back to back, a habit we've had since boyhood. Violet is curled up with her head on my lap, overcome by the loss of her father. A short distance away, Hamish sits by himself, as numb as Violet seems to be devastated.

The cries of those in pain and the groans of those dying are unbearable to hear. There are men who have been slashed and have huge chunks of flesh hanging from their bodies by little more than a strip of skin and they hug the hideous mass tightly as if this will somehow save them; others have been stabbed and the damage is obvious only by the flow of blood that they desperately try to stem with their bare hands.

A little way outside of our guarded group, soldiers search amongst the dead, taking anything of the slightest value. Some bodies are almost naked because they've been stripped of clothes that could later be sold. There is not a shred of respect or mercy for the living or the dead.

'How's your head, Sam?' asks Calum from behind me.

'I'll live, although God only knows how many will have left this world by the morning.' In truth I feel that I've got an axe embedded in the side of my skull and the fact that Violet has made no attempt to examine the wound shows how affected she is. I will not intrude on her grief. I cannot remember anything after firing my musket at the rider, not even if I hit him. Someone certainly hit me.

'What do you think will happen to us?' asks Calum.

'At the moment it's difficult to think, but I guess we'll be taken somewhere and held prisoner,' I reply.

A figure I hadn't seen approach kneels by my side and gently takes hold of my head.

'Father, are you unhurt?' I ask.

'Shh, keep still,' he replies, checking the injury. 'I'm fine, in body at least. You're lucky that blow wasn't any harder.' He lays a hand on Violet's shoulder. 'I'm sorry, daughter. Your father was a good man. He'll be greatly missed.' He turns to my brother. 'Calum?'

'I'm unharmed, Father. Hamish also escaped serious injury.'

'Well, that's a blessing to be sure. But I must leave you. There are people dying almost by the minute and I have to give what spiritual comfort I can.'

Violet surprises us by speaking. She doesn't move or even open her eyes. 'Don't try to leave this group to help those in another, for the soldiers will be keen to have the chance to kill a minister.'

'You're right,' he says, 'and sadly there's enough for me to do here without seeking others in need. I'll return when I can.'

'I don't believe we'll have gone anywhere,' says Calum bitterly.

* * *

We've been kept overnight without food, water or shelter from the rain. At first light we're ordered to bury those who've died. It's a wretched task and we can do no more than dig a long trench to lay out bodies side by side ... sons, brothers, fathers, cousins, friends, neighbours, strangers who believed in the same cause ... they're all put into that shallow trench.

There are also women caught up in the butchery and we lay them out as respectfully as possible, but there is no option other than to include them in the same ditch. Then we come to the body of Doctor Milligan. Violet is sitting by his side, holding one of his hands. I kneel beside her.

'Violet, we must lay your father to rest. His soul is with God and we have to put his body in the earth.'

'He wasn't a violent man,' she says in a broken voice.

'No, he wasn't.' I do not want to upset her further, but we are not out of danger. 'It's safer if we don't draw attention to ourselves.'

She nods, releasing his hand and standing up. 'I want to help.'

'All right, you and Hamish take his legs. Calum and I will take his arms.'

We try to make the process dignified but we slip in the mud, a nearby guard shouts at us to hurry and the trench is already half-full with water. In the end, Violet's father splashes into his final resting place and we're not permitted to do anything other than fetch the next body. Some are so mutilated that their own mothers wouldn't recognise them.

'These men haven't just been killed, they've been utterly destroyed,' whispers Hamish, the first words I've heard him speak this morning.

I nod sadly. 'They're victims of vengeance, hate and fear.'

'Fear?'

'No one goes into battle not being scared and they faced an enemy that has beaten Royalist soldiers in the recent past. We know how many lies have been spread about us being traitors and seeking to bring down the monarch. Every person in the Royalist army, from the common soldier to the most senior officer, will want to show that they have carried out their duty to the utmost.'

Hamish returns to his silence and we continue digging the ground and burying bodies for another couple of hours. We're totally spent by the time we've finished. Most of us haven't eaten since before the battle the previous day and trying to slacken our thirst by catching rainwater in our hands is almost futile.

The others around us have mainly been trying to help the wounded and we're dismayed when soldiers order us to prepare to move on within minutes of covering the last body. I see my father walk over to a soldier and instinctively know that there's going to be trouble. Calum and I move nearer.

'I'm Reverend Colvil. We need food and water and our wounded require proper treatment before anyone can move on.'

'You were a minister of the Kirk?'

'I *am* a minister of the Kirk, and I need to speak to an officer.'

'This man needs to speak to an officer, lads!' crows the man. 'Are we not good enough for you?'

'You don't have the authority for what's needed.'

'Oh, I have the authority all right.'

The soldier swings around his musket with surprising speed and hits Father in the stomach with the stock. He raises the weapon to hit him on the head when a figure rushes forward between them.

'Stop! You've proved you're in charge. Beating him will only create yet another person who has to be carried and we'll be slow enough as it is.'

I hadn't even realised that Violet was so close by. The soldier hesitates, which I guess was her intention, although I wish she hadn't put herself in such danger. To assume she won't be hurt because she's a woman is a shield made of paper. If we move closer we're likely to tip the standoff into violence so Calum, Hamish and I remain motionless, while Father is bent over, trying to get his breath.

'We'll start to get everyone ready to move,' says Violet, who then turns her back on the soldier to indicate that the conversation is over. She takes my father's arm. 'Come along, Reverend Colvil, let us sort out how those who are badly injured can be moved. We'll need relays of able-bodied men to help.'

As she speaks, Violet steers my father, still doubled over, away from the immediate potential danger. The soldier appears uncertain what to do, but seeing that the Covenanters are no threat, he returns to his comrades.

'Violet—' I start.

'Yes, I know, Samuel, but it worked. Now we need to decide how we're going to transport so many who are unable to walk.'

I watch my wife in awed silence, marvelling at the strength she displays, even as my heart breaks – because I'm certain there will soon be another death within our families.

15

Violet
24 June 1679, Edinburgh

OUR JOURNEY TO EDINBURGH HAS been marked along its route by hurriedly made graves which were sometimes no more than piles of stones. To our shame, there were occasions when a body was simply laid by the side of the track and left because we weren't allowed to stop, although the militia escorting us always found time to strip it of anything valuable. Perhaps some kindly souls may come across the remains and put them in the earth.

A handful of Covenanters have been killed trying to escape but several were successful, normally in ones or twos. We would only attempt such a thing if the five of us could get away – a plan so dangerous that it's never been discussed in earnest.

The residents of the city are silent as we stumble and stagger through the first few streets. Even the tall, dark buildings seem to look down upon us with disdain. We are such a miserable, wretched group of filthy, stinking people that folk in the street recoil from us.

When a figure rushes out from the watching crowd towards me, I instinctively flinch in expectation of being hit, but the woman thrusts a hunk of bread into my hand. I'm too surprised to speak, though tears make their way slowly through the dirt on my face. Others try to follow the example but the guards force them to keep away. It's as we slowly make our way further into the city that the attitude of those looking on changes.

'Where's your God?' jeers a man, as if we somehow worship a different one.

Nobody replies and the question is soon taken up by others, who call out repeatedly:

'Where's your God? Where's your God?'

It becomes a chant, yard after yard it's thrown at us like a weapon on the battlefield until the streets echo with the words. The hostility is relentless, burrowing into my heart until it too takes up the chant.

Where is our God?

Eventually we leave the calls behind as we trudge through imposing wrought-iron gates into a large grassy area surrounded by high stone walls.

'What's this place?' asks Hamish.

'Just the other side of that wall is Greyfriars Kirk, where the National Covenant was signed in thirty-eight,' says the Reverend Colvil. 'So many men of influence, power and wealth added their signature that day and those that followed. I doubt there's ever been a document like it before or since in the history of the world. My father was there, and he often spoke about the great hope there had been for the future.'

'And look what it's come to,' says Hamish. 'The authorities can't possibly mean for us to be held in this space. There's no shelter here ... nothing.'

There's been a deep change in my brother since our father was killed. He rarely speaks and, when he does, he seems lost. I suspect he's not alone amongst the prisoners in this.

'The Edinburgh gaols are probably full,' says Calum.

'If they hold us here long enough then disease, hunger and despair will rid them of the problem of what to do with so many captured Covenanters,' says Samuel.

We watch as hundreds of figures enter the enclosure. Those brought on carts or carried are being laid out in one particular area and after a while the captain of the dragoons that escorted us along with the militia starts walking up and down, studying the wounded.

'I shall find out what's happening to them,' says Samuel's father.

'Reverend Colvil, the question may appear less confrontational if it comes from a woman,' I point out.

He studies me for a moment, then sighs in resignation. 'Yes, daughter, you're right ... as ever. The place is filling up. Let's claim a spot over there. Violet, that's where we'll be.'

'I'll wait for you,' says Samuel.

'Go with the others, my love. I promise, nothing is going to happen to me.'

I approach the officer while he's still walking along the line of injured men. 'Captain, may I ask what plans there are to care for the seriously wounded?'

The captain studies me in silence for several moments and I know that I was right to be the one to put the question. Samuel's father would be in an argument with the man by now and we don't need more animosity.

'The only possible place to put them is Heriot's Hospital. It's just the other side of that wall.'

The upper part of the large building is visible and I take a few steps in its direction before stopping. He hesitates a moment then follows me and with that gesture I'm reassured he is a man of some compassion. To speak of death in front of dying men would be cruel beyond measure.

'Thank you, captain,' I say with a lowered voice. 'I fear many of these men will not survive a night in the open.'

'That's what I was thinking. I'll order them to be moved as soon as the remainder of the prisoners are inside.'

It always amazes me how men so young can have such responsibilities that they are forced to make quick decisions over life and death.

'What on earth were women doing at Bothwell?' he says.

'What were any of us doing? All we ever wanted was to be free to worship as we had been.'

'Well, that's not a question for me to answer. I'm a simple soldier.'

'Captain, I believe you are much more than that.'

For a few moments we stand and watch as exhausted figures stare in disbelief that this is where we're being held. It's a strange feeling, for a couple of days ago the officer and I could have faced each other on the battlefield. I thank him again then rejoin the others and tell them of my conversation.

'A soldier with honour,' says Calum.

I'm so thirsty it's difficult to speak. 'The troughs?' I say, indicating several stone troughs in a line near the gate.

'Dry,' says Samuel. 'I've checked them. I doubt we'll get any water tonight. This land may belong to the Kirk, but for us it's going to be Hell, one that will soon start filling up with the dead.'

* * *

The morning brings a sight of such misery that I fancy it can be tasted upon the air, which is already tainted enough with a mixture of putrid smells from the capital. Now we're adding to it; a dyke runs the length of one side of the enclosure and this has become our latrine, the water already filthy before coming in under a wall. At least the captain proved to be honest in what he said and about thirty Covenanters were carried away last night to be held where they can be better cared for.

Samuel and I walk around in an attempt to understand our new prison and gain a better idea of the state of others. I've spoken to several people and inspected a few wounds, but there's little that can be done for anyone here.

'Violet, there are only a handful of women.'

'I've counted five and I hear there are two more, although I haven't seen them yet.'

'So, fewer than ten out of more than a thousand men.'

'Do you worry for my virtue, Samuel?'

'I worry that you're going to be punished as if you had actually fought at Bothwell.'

'I *did* fight at Bothwell.'

We fall silent, walking past figures lying on the ground, groups gathered around preachers and others walking as we are, trying to make some sense of what's happening. Samuel fears that I'll be haunted by the memory of the soldier I killed, but the truth is I haven't thought about him. The man was about to murder my father lying helpless at his feet and I won't waste time remembering him.

My father's death, however, is like an open wound that someone is constantly rubbing salt into. I'm surprised there's any moisture in my body to produce tears, but they fall freely down my cheeks. Samuel takes me in his arms.

'You are my life, Violet. I wish there was something I could do. If women are given the offer to be set free, then you must go with them.'

'I said it at Bothwell ... All the men I love are together and I'm not about to leave them, regardless of the danger.'

* * *

Samuel
1 July 1679, Greyfriars Kirkyard, Edinburgh

Hope seeps away from us like the stinking sludge that flows under the far wall. Every day I see friends who faced battle without flinching lose their strength and will to go on. They shun all company and refuse their food rations, choosing an isolated spot to simply wait for this misery to end. Who knows, perhaps they are wiser than the rest of us.

Each of us is given a penny loaf per day, handed out at the gate along with some biscuits, both of the poorest quality. People are so hungry that they've already eaten the grass in the enclosure. The troughs are filled with water each morning but by noon they're empty and our thirst is fierce.

Local men are not allowed to approach the gates but women can, and many who are sympathetic to the cause bring us food, clothing, blankets and small items to make our lives a little easier. The militia check their baskets and can be distastefully abusive but don't actually prevent them, although a few demand bribes.

Deaths are common and this morning is no different. I help carry one of two Covenanters who have died during the night to the gates. It already feels like months since we walked through them that first time. The guards take no chances and when the gates are unlocked, they stand with muskets aimed almost as if wishing someone would try to escape.

The idea is ludicrous. Most of us are so weak that it takes four of us to carry one person. We shuffle through and gently lay the body on a hand-drawn cart belonging to the gravediggers. We haven't found out where Covenanters are buried and suspect it's somewhere unwholesome. There's a corner in Greyfriars cemetery for 'thieves' but even Calum, with all his charm and skill at gaining information, hasn't discovered this answer. A guard shouts at us to return to our prison, so we walk back inside to allow the second body to be carried out.

'You know,' says Calum when no one is near enough to hear, 'the soldiers never check the bodies.'

'What do you mean?'

'They watch us through those bars every single moment of the day and night, but someone being laid on the cart is never even glanced at.'

I take care to keep my face expressionless as I whisper back. 'Escape?'

He gives the barest of nods. 'It's a possibility.'

'What about the gravediggers?'

'They're just gravediggers and there's still quite a lot of coin amongst us.'

For all the thieving by soldiers, most Covenanters have been able to hide some of their money. Even amongst the five of us we could put together a decent bribe.

'Die here, or die trying to escape,' I say. 'I suppose it's something to consider, brother.'

* * *

Violet and I walk slowly around the enclosed area along with many others ... round and round. She listens in silence as I recount Calum's idea.

'Assuming they weren't discovered at the gate and killed, how would we ever know that it's succeeded?'

'What do you mean? People would have got away.'

'We would see people taken on the cart but could never be sure the gravediggers hadn't later killed them and taken the money, ready to do the same deed again. They could be paid without the risk of an escaped Covenanter being recaptured and tortured into revealing the truth.'

I've never known someone so astute as Violet, but her ability to instantly spot the problem in something can be bloody infuriating. Nothing gets past my Violet.

'Why are you smiling, Samuel Colvil? I've not seen you do that in a very long while.'

'I'm smiling because I love you so much and whatever happens, I've been blessed to have shared my life with you.'

'We've been through a great deal together. While we remain on this earth I struggle to see any joy ahead, yet I wouldn't alter anything we've done. I love you, Samuel. I've loved you since we were six years old.'

'Were we ever that age? Where did that innocence go?'

'Just life, I guess. You can't grow older and keep the innocence of childhood.'

'It's sad that we've never been blessed with children.'

'I think the Lord has other plans for us,' I say.

'What plans, I wonder, does He have for us now?'

Our conversation is stopped abruptly by the sound of shouting and we turn around to see about two dozen men near the gates, angrily calling to the soldiers, who start running from other areas to join those already with muskets levelled.

'What's brought this about?' I say, half expecting Violet to have the answer.

We're near the latrine end of the compound and everyone's attention is on the loud exchange taking place at the other end, where more people are joining in, either side of the bars.

'It's a deception,' says Violet.

'What?'

'Don't make it obvious ... glance over your shoulder.'

I see what she has already spotted: three men are climbing the wall just beyond the dyke.

'Well, that's taken some organisation,' I say, annoyed that we haven't heard of the plan, yet also impressed at the scale and, so far, apparent success. I don't want to attract attention to them so return my gaze to the argument.

'It's a dangerous thing to do,' she says. 'It would take very little for those soldiers to fire a volley.'

As if her words have power, the crowd suddenly begins to disperse, a few men shouting back over their shoulders but otherwise moving away. The guards lower their muskets, puzzled.

'Come on,' says Violet, 'let's start walking again and make everything appear normal ... as if there's anything at all normal about our lives.'

When we turn, I glance once more at the wall, but there's no sign of the three Covenanters.

'God's speed,' I whisper.

And I wonder if we will also escape before this prison kills us.

16

Violet
3 July 1679, Greyfriars Kirkyard, Edinburgh

THE FIVE OF US HAVE discussed Calum's idea that Covenanters could escape by pretending to be dead, but none of us will leave without the others. However, Samuel has suggested it to a couple of men he believes will be keen and can be trusted, so this morning a man called Walter is going to attempt it.

'This waiting is awful,' I say to the Reverend Colvil, who stands with me and Calum, trying to appear as if nothing unusual is expected.

'Patience, daughter,' he says. 'We're in God's hands and there can be no safer ones to hold us.'

One person has died during the night and Walter lies on the ground next to him. Hamish walks over from where he's been keeping watch by the gates.

'The gravediggers are coming,' he says.

Hamish, Samuel, Calum and the Reverend Colvil walk slowly towards the bodies. I move a little nearer, but don't want to appear as if I'm part of anything. My heart is pounding. How can Walter pretend he's dead realistically enough? Surely something will give him away? My fear is not for him. If he's discovered, then the four men I love will be in great danger.

As usual, soldiers position themselves beyond the gates and when the handcart stops, they raise their muskets. The gates are unlocked. I can barely draw breath and when some men move to lift Walter, I think my heart stops.

'We'll lift him,' says Reverend Colvil authoritatively. 'He was a friend.'

With a shrug, the men take the other body and we all watch as it's carried out. When the body is laid down it makes a loud moaning noise. I've heard of this happening from Father, how air escaping from a body can make a sound that terrifies even the toughest. A couple of the Covenanters step back quickly while one of the soldiers moves forward. He pulls out a dirk.

'Shut up, you filthy traitor!' Without any hesitation he stabs the body hard in the side, but there is no reaction or further sound. 'You moan in life and don't even shut up when you're dead!' Several soldiers laugh. 'Get that other scum out and be bloody quick about it!'

Samuel glances at me and his expression makes me wonder if he thinks they may all be killed in the next few minutes. They have to wait until the first Covenanters are back within the enclosure before they lift Walter and slowly carry him towards the cart. I'm sure I can see his chest moving, a finger twitching, his eyelids flutter; I cannot breathe, terrified the soldier will stab him just like the other body. The four men turn around and head inside. Samuel comes to me, but the others walk away as if they intend to go around the enclosure.

'This is terrible,' I whisper.

'Shh. We'll know soon enough if Walter's discovered.'

We move to a place where we can watch without it being obvious. The gates are locked. Soldiers begin to disperse. The gravediggers move to the cart. An arm hangs over the edge.

One of the gravediggers takes hold of it and tucks it back. Some comments are made but I can't make out the words.

Then the cart is pushed away, the uneven ground making the figures on board jostle and move around. The arm hangs over the edge again. Never have minutes gone by so slowly. Every second feels like a lifetime. Eventually, when I have died more times than I can count, the cart moves out of sight and I almost collapse into Samuel's arms.

* * *

'It's too much of a risk,' says Hamish bitterly. 'If we four always carry out the person trying to escape, then at some point we're going to be found out and likely killed for it. I'm not prepared to do it any more.'

The five of us have been discussing the next potential escape and we're split about how to continue.

'What else are we doing to help the cause?' says Calum. 'If we do nothing, then we're simply waiting to die in this hellish place.'

'You can't keep getting away with it,' I say. 'There should be an agreement with those who carry out a person that one of them can be next if they wish. In this way those who risk their lives know they have a chance to get away on another occasion.'

'Well, I'm out of it,' says Hamish. 'I won't be involved again.'

'We *have* to continue,' says Calum.

'In that case I'll take Hamish's place,' I say.

Samuel immediately rounds on me. 'You'll do no such thing!'

'I'll do what I like. You need four people to carry someone, so I'll do it and if we're caught, at least I'll be killed alongside those I love.'

I know they won't let me help carry a body, which means that an outsider would have to be brought into the secret and I'm relying on this fact to make them stop altogether. I actually agree with Hamish that the risk is too great.

Any further conversation on the matter is ended by the sound of shouting. We turn towards the source and see a man violently smashing his head against a wall. Together, we rush forward yet don't reach him until he's hit his forehead twice more. Samuel and Calum take hold of him as gently as they can, but his despair makes him strong and Hamish also has to help.

'Be careful with him,' says Reverend Colvil. 'Be still, my son. God is with you.'

The man looks quite mad. I've seen this expression on a few others, including one Covenanter who later managed to take his own life. I can hear soldiers laughing by the gate and, as we lie the person down, they shout vile abuse. The poor wretch before us is too far gone to understand and even Samuel's father is powerless to calm him.

I can think of nothing else to do, so I force my way between Calum and the man, lie down beside him and take him in my arms. Whimpering, he curls into my body the way that Samuel used to when he was young and I hold him tightly, speaking quiet words of comfort. He settles against me, his head upon my breast as he cries.

How have we come to this?

The others form a semicircle facing outwards to provide a little privacy, while I lie on the hard ground with this stranger and try to reassure him that everything will be all right and he must not give up hope. But the words, I know, are really for myself, because I cannot see how we can survive without betraying our beliefs.

17

Violet
10 July 1679, Greyfriars Kirkyard, Edinburgh

It's known as the 'black bond', at least by those who refuse to take it. Prisoners are being offered their freedom if they swear an oath never again to take up arms against the king and obtain a bond for their future good behaviour. News has reached us that this 'King's Peace', as it's officially called, has already been accepted by hundreds of Covenanters who fought at Bothwell Bridge and weren't captured, but whose names have subsequently been put on wanted lists held by the authorities.

'They're giving up the freedom of their souls for the freedom of their bodies,' seethes the Reverend Colvil, who is set against the offer.

'Many will take the oath, both around Scotland and here in this prison,' says Samuel.

'Then it's taken by weak men whose hearts were never truly for the cause,' says his father.

'If they fought at Bothwell then they showed courage,' says Calum.

'There were plenty at Bothwell who showed us the soles of their shoes as they ran off without firing a single shot, or swinging a weapon even once, including some officers!' his father thunders.

The Reverend Colvil is like an ancient oak tree that cannot bend. He'll accept no course of action, no argument, that goes against his beliefs. One day, when the wind is strong enough, he'll break in two. I don't want the acorn to be like the oak.

'I've spoken to the other women and they are set on taking the bond,' I say. 'Many have children and need to return to their families. They shouldn't be here.'

'You shouldn't be here,' says Hamish.

Samuel nods his agreement. 'You can't be the only woman left.'

'I won't leave ... nor will I remain as a woman.'

The reverend turns a questioning gaze on me.

'I've already spoken to one of the people who bring us food. Later today she's going to slip me some men's clothing, then I'll live disguised as a man.'

'That's madness,' exclaims Hamish. 'Tell her, Samuel. She's your wife.'

'And you think that's enough to make her listen?' He shakes his head at my brother, but I know there is no anger there for me. 'Go on, Violet.'

'I won't leave, and you can't actually make me. However, I don't want to be known as the only female here. Look at us. We're becoming so reduced by starvation that it won't be long before the good Lord Himself will struggle to tell man from woman.'

'Your hair—'

'I'll cut it, Hamish! I'll live as a man and there's not a Covenanter amongst us who would betray my secret.'

And perhaps it is testament to how beaten we all are that no one argues. Samuel takes my hand and squeezes it, hard.

* * *

Hundreds agree to take the Black Bond. Some ministers preach that it should be sworn and others preach that it should not, including Samuel's father. Prisoners line up at the gates and in small groups they're taken under guard around the corner to Greyfriars Kirk where they give their details, speak the words as set out in the King's Peace and sign their name to the document. They are then free to travel home as best they can; betraying the cause with every word spoken, with every word written, with every step taken.

'The enclosure is emptying,' says Calum, who's standing with Samuel, Hamish and me, watching as line upon line walk through the gate. 'I didn't think so many would accept.'

'The authorities can't deal with this many prisoners all in one go,' says Samuel. 'There aren't the courts, judges or jails to cope and so they've made an offer that's simply too attractive for many to refuse.'

'We're fighting for freedom to worship and they've gained freedom from being prisoners,' muses Hamish. 'They've lost one to gain the other. I don't know that I can condemn them for it.'

Calum glances over his shoulder as if to check who is listening. 'Don't say that to our father. What these people are promising is never to fight again for the Covenanter cause. He won't forgive anyone for making such a decision.'

'I need to speak to him,' says Samuel. 'His outspoken criticism is making him too obvious a target for further punishment.'

'He'll not be silenced, Samuel,' I say. 'And will accept the consequences as God's will.'

Under my arm I have a large bundle of men's clothes that my saviour handed over. I gave her what few coins I had plus all of Calum's. He was the only person I could ask who would simply give me his money without querying why I wanted it. Tomorrow I'll give her my clothes as well.

'I need to change. There's a great deal of confusion at the moment and if I do this now then people will simply assume I've signed the bond and left.'

My family shield me while I swap my clothes and my identity. I've been given a long strip of cloth and, as tightly as I can manage, I bind my breasts. They're not large. I put on the shirt and jerkin then remove my filthy petticoats before pulling up hose and breeches. I silently thank the woman, for although the items are old, they're clean.

The strangest item is the shoes, which are too big. I tear up part of a petticoat and stuff material into the ends, which helps a little. I finish by slipping into a threadbare coat. The Edinburgh woman who has aided me also included a small pair of scissors.

'Samuel, I would like you to do this.'

He hesitates. 'That I should cut off your beautiful hair …'

'We've no choice. Cut it short so that it's easier to keep free of vermin.'

We're silent as he does this. Across from us prisoners continue to line up by the gates. The whole process is slow as every person has to swear his oath in the kirk and an official record is made of who they are. All of this takes place only yards from where the famous National Covenant with God was signed all those years ago.

Ties with the Covenanter cause are being cut as surely and completely as the strands of black hair falling by my feet.

'I need a new name,' I say, pretending not to notice the tears in Samuel's eyes now that he's completed a task he could never have imagined doing. 'From now on I'm to be called Douglas, even if there's no one else nearby. Calum, will you explain this to your father?'

'Of course. Where is he?'

'Over there,' says Hamish, nodding to the queue by the gates, 'trying to persuade people not to sign the bond.'

'That must be dangerous,' says Calum.

'Too dangerous,' agrees Samuel. 'He may not be signing the Black Bond, but I fear he's signing his own death warrant.'

Gently, I take the scissors from Samuel's hand. 'My love, I think he knows.'

18

Samuel
10 August 1679, Greyfriars Kirkyard, Edinburgh

Four men have escaped by pretending to be dead and being taken away by the gravediggers. We no longer have any involvement in this and generally watch on from a distance that allows us to hear and see what's happening but doesn't implicate us in any way should the ploy be discovered. For a while we weren't certain if these prisoners were subsequently killed by the gravediggers, but then we received a message via one of the women who regularly brings food which confirmed that men are getting away alive.

Violet shivers, despite the fierce heat that's beaten down upon us without mercy these last few weeks. I put a hand on her brow.

'You're hot.'

'I feel cold.'

Even the strongest amongst us can't avoid the fevers and diseases that increasingly race throughout the enclosure. The air seems trapped within our high prison walls and it's so fetid there's almost a sense of evil about it, as if breathing will allow something unwholesome to enter one's lungs. Everyone is so desperately thin, our bodies covered in sores from lying on hard, dusty ground, and our voices are cracked like our lips.

'Another attempt,' says Calum, joining us to observe from our safe spot.

The gravediggers have arrived, and the gates are opened. This morning there is only one dead body. Loading more than two on the handcart would make it even more difficult for a person to pretend they're not alive.

'Do you know them?' says Violet.

'The one with the brown hair is Giles,' Calum replies. 'He refused to sign the Black Bond.'

'The authorities are still offering it,' says Samuel. 'There are those who may yet accept.'

We watch as Giles is lifted by his friends, taken through the gates and laid gently on the cart. The same men come back and carry out the dead body, which they lay alongside. As they turn away there is a loud moan that freezes everyone to the spot in shock.

'You miserable moaning traitor!' shouts the corporal.

We look on in horror as he pulls out his sword and sticks it into the side of the second figure. The soldiers laugh and call out encouragement to stab the other one as well.

'Dear God, no,' whispers Violet.

The corporal pulls out the blade, hesitates as if he's an actor entertaining an audience, then plunges the blade into Giles, who cries out in agony, pushing himself away and falling to the ground.

'He's alive! Kill the bastard! And those who carried him.'

Suddenly there's mayhem as people scatter, rushing away from the gates while the wounded Covenanter crawls along the ground. Shots are fired. One man falls. Another is hit but staggers on. We run, although not before I catch a glimpse of a private thrusting his sword into the back of Giles crawling in the dirt in a bid for a freedom he could have had for uttering a few words and signing his name.

* * *

Four days after the failed escape attempt by Giles, Violet and I walk around the enclosure, discussing the strange tension in the air this morning. Since taking on her disguise we haven't been able to show each other any affection and we hadn't appreciated how difficult or unnatural this would be.

'It's odd that the soldiers seem so nervous,' she says. 'And look how many more there are than usual.'

We're close to the gates and I see clearly what she means. 'They're about to enter.'

As we move away there's the sound of the gates being opened behind us and large numbers of soldiers entering. We don't stop until we're at the far wall, from where we watch a captain move slowly amongst the Covenanters, obviously asking questions before moving on. He stops to speak to my father, who then comes over to us, his face almost lit with joy.

'Father, what's happening?' I ask.

'Samuel ... Violet ... God calls me along with four others, including the Reverend Kidd and Reverend King. It will be a privilege to be amongst such men in my journey to Heaven. I know you'll take care of each other, as well as Hamish and Calum. You'll need to find a greater inner strength than you've ever known, but never doubt that our cause is right. The soldiers have orders that five named individuals are to be taken to the Grassmarket.'

'Oh God!' I almost collapse into my father's embrace. 'No ... no.'

Calum runs over to us, tears pouring freely down his face. The four of us hug each other, a tiny group of utter despair.

'How has it come to this?' sobs Calum.

We pull away from each other to speak, and Father turns first to Violet.

'Violet, you've always been like a daughter to me.'

'And you a father.'

'Calum ... my dear son. We'll meet again when there is no hunger, no fear or pain.'

Calum is so distraught he can't reply. Violet takes him in her arms to comfort him, just as Father and I stare at each other.

'I don't want you to face this alone,' I tell him, sounding hoarse and hopeless. 'If there's any chance that I can at least be with you, then I will come.'

'You've proved your courage many times, Samuel, but this is not a sight for you to see. And I won't be alone, not for one second.'

'Samuel,' says Violet, 'they're coming.'

Father embraces me then walks away, calling out with his clear, authoritative voice as though he's stepped into a pulpit and is about to give a sermon. 'I am the Reverend Colvil and the threat of death holds no fear for me.'

Soldiers bind his hands. It's a scene being repeated around us. Some people cry and shout out, but most are quiet, as if this fate is both expected and accepted. The five condemned men appear serene, a couple of them making comments between themselves. The captain in charge has been in here before and, without giving Violet the chance to stop me, I stride over to him. A nearby soldier levels his musket, which I ignore.

'Captain, if you are to hang my father this day, I ask that I can accompany him so that I may stand by the gallows and offer some comfort by my presence.'

'Those are not my orders.'

I consider I've nothing to lose by making a guess. 'But you don't actually have orders saying you can't allow it, and to have witnesses who can report back to those left here may be useful to you.'

'What's your name?'

'Samuel Colvil. My father is the Reverend Colvil.'

The captain nods at the familiar name. 'Private, help those men.'

'Yes, sir.' The private marches away, leaving the two of us alone.

'I'll allow five men to be witnesses. Your hands will be bound.'

'I understand. I have one more request.'

'You expect a lot for a rebel.'

'My younger brother, Calum – the blond man over there – he will want to come. I ask you as a man who no doubt has some family yourself ... please don't let him. He wouldn't recover from it. Don't doubt his braveness, but there are some things—'

'You may think us evil, Samuel Colvil, but we follow our orders as soldiers in the king's army. I know there are some who carry out those orders too ... eagerly. But we are not all like that, and I dare say there are men amongst those you follow who are too eager, like those who murdered Archbishop Sharp.'

I don't disagree with his observation, yet can't bring myself to say so. 'Many say that we Covenanters are traitors. We're not. We follow our beliefs and, certainly at the start of this war, we had no ill will towards the king.'

He nods. 'Wars are brutal. Civil wars the most brutal of all. You can't hurt kinsmen without hurting yourself. Such wounds will take a long time to heal. I doubt that we'll see it happen in our lifetime.'

Perhaps his words should add to my grief, yet there is some comfort in finding common ground. 'Thank you, Captain. You are a man of honour.'

'Be quick in informing the other four men.'

With this instruction I rush to those Covenanters I believe will have the same wish as myself and we gather in a small group. Violet and Calum chase after me.

'Samuel, what are you doing?' says Violet.

'The captain is allowing five men to accompany the condemned to the gallows. I will be by my father's side at the end.'

'I must go,' says Calum, as I expected.

Violet and I both say 'No' at the same time. I then add, 'Calum, those with connections to the others should be allowed to attend.'

He stares at me, saying nothing. My brother's no fool. He knows I'm protecting him, but it hurts just the same. I'm in awe of the bravery of the men who are about to die and despite my size I feel small in their company as we're taken out of our prison and escorted to the Grassmarket. A large crowd has gathered near to the enormous scaffold, a structure of death which is in such regular use by the authorities that it's a permanent feature within the city. Soldiers move amongst us to separate the spectators from the others.

'Father!' I call out, unable to stop myself.

He calls back to me, his voice clear and loud. 'I am not afraid, Samuel, for I go to a better place – where we are free of tyranny, of pain and hunger and grief. We will meet again there one day, son.'

It's the five of us being left behind who make a noise as we're pushed further away. In the end we're silenced by the calmness of the condemned. The first of those brave, brave men walks up the steps to the platform, his head held high. Even the guards hold back when it's so obvious they aren't needed to restrain him.

'Where's your God?' shouts a man, but no one joins his mockery.

The Covenanter simply holds the crowd in his gaze and replies stoically, 'My God waits for me and I'll be with Him soon. Where is your God that you should stand down there in such dread?'

Nobody replies and as he climbs the ladder the four other condemned men begin to sing. We five join in. The executioner looks bored as he waits on his own ladder and without any hesitation he places the noose around the Covenanter's neck as soon as he is level with it. Unlike the drunken display by Cornelius, the stocky hangman knows his business and he reaches over to take a firm hold of the condemned man's ladder, then he casts it over with one fierce heave, dislodging the Covenanter, who drops a few feet to endure that terrible dance of death that no person should ever have to learn.

And so the living become the dead and the last figure to walk up the steps to the platform is my own father. He looks fondly upon the four bodies that have been thrown to the ground below.

'I shall be with you in a moment, my dear friends, and together we will watch from Heaven upon these misguided people.'

He's stopped singing to speak and my four companions are too overcome by grief to continue. My own throat closes up and everything falls so silent it seems as if the air itself is stilled.

'Take care, my son. I love you.'

I can't watch and keep my eyes closed until finally ... finally ... a voice announces that he is dead. This war has taken so much from us, our home, our innocence, the lives of friends and neighbours, Violet's father ... now it takes my father too. Will there ever be enough deaths to bring it to an end?

The other witnesses and I weep openly, expecting to be taken back to the enclosure, but at that moment an official walks up to the scaffold's platform. He doesn't even wait for my father's body to be taken down. It swings gently behind him as he speaks.

'As is right by the laws of God and man, these traitors have met their death. Now their bodies will be used to demonstrate to others what will happen to those who show disloyalty to the king. Their heads will be removed and sent to the places from whence they came, where they will be displayed publicly for all to see. What's left of their bodies will be hung in gibbets to rot. Let no one doubt the outcome of traitors. Long live the king!'

That Father's head should be removed ... something breaks within me, and even with my hands bound I push, kick and headbutt the unsuspecting guards until several lie on the ground around me. My rage is finally brought to a sudden end when the stock of a musket slams into my head and everything goes black.

* * *

Violet
24 August 1679, Greyfriars Kirkyard, Edinburgh

'I need to speak to you about something.'

I'm bound to Hamish in a way that's impossible for anyone to understand who is not a twin. We shared a world even before entering this one and since the moment we were born, we've slept, eaten, played, laughed, fought side by side and cried as if we were not two people but one. I'm instantly worried about what he wants to say when we've never had a secret from the others, and I try not to show I'm concerned. Of course, he knows I am.

'Let's walk,' I say.

We slot in between small groups of people moving slowly around the enclosure. The number held here has grown following the mass departure of those agreeing to the Black Bond, with Covenanters captured after Bothwell plus others taken prisoner for different reasons being brought to Greyfriars.

'I'm not brave like you, Samuel and Calum. I can't go on, Violet, not like this.'

I don't understand what he's implying. The reality is that we have no choice, unless he's planning an escape, but such an act would be out of character.

'Hamish, we've all felt like that over the weeks ... over the years even, when we've been hunted and attacked, homeless and despairing. You're not alone and the feeling will pass.'

'No, it won't.'

'We have no option but to go on.'

'There is an option. The government is still offering the King's Peace.'

I stare at him and for the first time in my entire life I don't recognise the man in front of me.

'Hamish, you can't betray the cause now!'

'I'm not. I just can't go on living like this.'

'I don't believe you'll sign, that you would go home to Mother and leave us here.'

'Then come with me, Violet.'

'After everything we've been through! I held Father in my arms at Bothwell while he bled out his life upon my breast. Samuel watched his own father hanged less than two weeks ago. How many others have died over the decades that people in Scotland might one day worship freely, and you would walk away from all that? People have fought for this even before we were born.'

He's crying now, huge sobs bursting out of his emaciated body in a way that would have broken my heart until a few moments ago. I can't hold him or offer comfort, and that is so utterly unnatural to me that tears flow down my cheeks.

'Yes, I know.'

'Have you lost your faith in the cause?'

'No, I've lost the strength to fight for it ... in my body, in my mind, in my soul ... I no longer have the will to go on.'

We stand facing each other only a few feet apart, yet it represents a chasm that is so deep and wide we cannot reach across it.

'Many people have signed the bond,' he says.

'Does that make it right?'

'No. There's what's right and there's what's real, and this is the reality.'

'Then here is my reality. You are no brother of mine!'

Never have I felt or meant words more strongly than the ones I've just spoken ... and never have I regretted or hated words more than the ones I've just spoken. Those eleven words have cleaved me in half more surely than the sharpest Claymore ever could.

His voice is barely a whisper. 'Please don't say that.'

'This is all there is to say. There is nothing more, Hamish. Nothing. We are no longer blood and kin.'

'Violet?'

'My loyalty is to Samuel and Calum and our beliefs, for that is what's left for me.'

With those cruel words, I turn and walk away.

* * *

Samuel and Calum refuse to speak to Hamish, so we've had no contact with him since he confessed his intentions. Now, on the last day of August, he's one of a handful of men standing by the gates waiting to be taken to Greyfriars Kirk, where he'll sign away his soul. Everyone in the entire enclosure has gathered in silence, watching.

Hamish keeps his eyes firmly on the ground by his feet. The guards make them wait a long time and I suspect they're doing this deliberately. Eventually, someone unlocks the gates and the five figures shuffle forward, appearing more like condemned men than those who so nobly walked out to be hanged in the Grassmarket.

Hamish is the last. As he's about to step through the archway, he stops to look back at me. I meet his gaze without friendship or love, a woman of granite and a sister of mist. He has betrayed us. Those that leave this morning will never be forgiven by those left behind. With tears falling down his cheeks he walks slowly through the gates and out of our lives.

Part III

The *Crown of London*

19

Violet
15 November 1679, Greyfriars Kirkyard, Edinburgh

Samuel and I tremble uncontrollably as we hug each other, the thin blanket wrapped around us doing little to help. We've known lower temperatures but without the ability to light a fire and still with no shelter except the four walls of the enclosure there's no escape from the cold. For weeks it's been seeping into our bodies every single minute of the day and night. Hot food is a distant memory.

People are beginning to fear that the authorities will let the harsh weather kill us and solve their problem. Two Covenanters have died since the beginning of the month, the bodies stripped of clothing before being laid out for the gravediggers. These days they come in through the gates and pick up the deceased themselves.

My chest feels so constricted that speaking is difficult. 'There's one good thing about the cold,' I stutter.

'I'm struggling to think of it.'

'Nobody considers it odd that we hug each other.'

All around us men are gathered in small groups, so desperate for warmth that they embrace each other as tightly as lovers.

Calum comes towards us. Like everyone else he's swaddled in multiple items of clothing that make him appear misshapen, a parody of humour at which no one laughs. Clothes have been stripped from the dead or bought from the women who visit, using the remaining coin that hasn't been stolen. His blond hair is hidden under a large bonnet held down firmly with a woman's kerchief tied under his chin. Nobody moves quickly. When he reaches us Samuel opens the blanket and includes his brother within it, then the three of us stand, our limbs trembling and our teeth chattering.

'Something's happening,' says Calum. 'There's a large number of soldiers gathering beyond the gates. I think they're going to come in.'

'To kill us?' I say.

'Why bother now?' says Samuel. 'Unless the authorities have finally lost all patience.'

'We're about to find out,' says Calum.

The gates are being unlocked and moments later dozens of soldiers rush in, bayonets fitted to muskets in a show of force that is so unnecessary it's almost laughable. The majority of us can just about walk.

'Fall into lines! Fall into lines!' shouts a sergeant.

Everyone is taken aback and many stand around without moving until soldiers start pushing prisoners forward and getting them into lines three abreast.

'Violet, keep between us,' whispers Samuel.

We join the others. There is some muttering and a few cries of pain when someone is hit or shoved too hard, but otherwise people line up without protest. There are over two hundred and most of us have lived within this open prison for almost five months. It seems unreal that we're actually about to leave. But we do.

We stumble through the stone archway and into the first street, where crowds wait in silence. I assume that news of our departure has been deliberately spread throughout Edinburgh and residents are probably expected to come out and see what happens to those who defy the king's authority. A couple of men call out insults, but most don't comment. Whether they feel shock, disdain or pity, I've no idea and am too weary to care.

'Why do they need so many soldiers?' I ask. 'We're far too weak to fight.'

'I don't think they're for us,' says Samuel. 'They must be worried that there could be an attempted rescue.'

We certainly see no sign of such a thing as we're taken down street after street. Covenanters fall and are helped back up only to fall again as we trudge along on our journey of punishment. Finally, when there are more of us falling than walking, we arrive in Leith and are taken to the harbour, where we're brought to a halt near a two-masted ship called the *Crown of London*.

'It's small,' I say.

'Too small,' replies Samuel. 'This isn't big enough for so many.'

'Look!' says Calum. 'Dear God above. Are those who I think they are?'

Arriving only minutes after us dozens of militia approach along a different street. They're got cloths and scarves wrapped around their faces and some are carrying stretchers that, at first sight, seem to have dead people on them.

'Samuel,' I utter in horror. 'These are the wounded Covenanters who were taken to Heriot's Hospital when we arrived.'

'I see them,' he says, 'though I don't believe what I'm seeing.'

There are around twenty and the stench of their bodies overpowers every other smell around the harbour regardless of how unpleasant or powerful. It's clear that most have lost control of their bodily functions and the poor souls haven't been cleaned, or certainly not properly. I can hardly believe they're still living. Everyone from the enclosure stares in shock at the sight and murmured comments are increasingly interspersed by angry shouts as more people realise what we're facing.

Any further conversation about their arrival is prevented by the appearance on deck of someone I take to be the captain. He looks down upon us with such loathing that my skin suddenly feels even dirtier than it did moments ago.

'I'm Captain Teddico,' he says, 'and you are the worst treacherous scum that ever walked this land. For your heinous crimes, you'll be transported on board my ship to your final destination. I will brook no ill behaviour and any man who angers me will feel the lash of the whip. You're going to stink my ship like rotting fish.' He wrinkles his nose with a sneer before barking orders. 'Get them aboard!'

We're pulled and shoved into a line so that we can walk across the gangplank. I follow Samuel on to the rocking vessel, where sailors order us down a ladder and into the hold. It's a slow process, as many need help. The captain's anger grows by the second and he's soon shouting obscene abuse at us while ordering sailors to push those who are considered not quick enough. Desperate cries of pain and warning reach us from Covenanters who have fallen off the ladder and landed on the hard floor below.

'Calum, you go ahead of Douglas and I'll go after him,' says Samuel, trying to work out how best to protect me, although in fairness I'm more able than many others.

I descend into a world so unlike the one we've been held in since June that the breath is snatched from my lungs. Instead of an open space with no shelter we're encased by walls of wood, pressing on us closer and closer.

'It's like a huge coffin,' Calum whispers fearfully.

'Let's find a space,' says Samuel, indicating a place not far from the ladder. 'It's going to get unbelievably hot and we need to get as much air as possible. And we want to be away from those.'

Samuel indicates a row of buckets against one wall and my heart sinks at the realisation that this is all there is for our natural needs. We spread out the thin blanket and collapse upon it, then watch as more figures come into the hold. Most people are shocked into silence. A few moan as though fighting some inner terror.

It doesn't take long to study our new home. Half a dozen lanterns swing gently upon hooks in the ceiling and cast a flickering, yellow light upon the surroundings. Every surface is wood, without a single item to provide comfort.

'We may be out of the wind and rain but even a cow in the meanest of barns would have some straw,' says Calum.

'I fear, brother, that we've swapped our hell for one even worse.'

Starvation has reduced our bodies till we are little more than walking skeletons. While Covenanters are still shuffling into the hold, I feel pain streaking up my legs and back in whatever position I sit.

'Douglas?'

'I'm all right, Samuel. I just need to settle down.'

'Here they come,' warns Calum.

Whatever discomfort, pain or fear we're experiencing is forgotten at the sight of the wounded Covenanters. Men on deck lower them by their arms while others at the bottom of the ladder reach up and take the emaciated bodies, carrying them to various corners of the hold, where they're gently laid.

'There's not going to be enough room for everyone to lie down at the same time,' says Calum.

The wounded continue to be lowered, some unconscious, others moaning and a few piteously begging to be taken back up or to be killed. Their pleading is heart-breaking.

'Are we really in Scotland?' says Samuel, shaking his head in utter disbelief.

In the confined space the smell is like nothing I've ever known. A couple of men nearby retch, but they've nothing in their stomachs to bring up. Eventually all of the wounded are here and the remaining Covenanters start coming down the ladder. Upon reaching the bottom, one man suddenly screams. Two friends take hold of him and try to move him away, but he holds on to a step with such fierce determination that he can't be shifted, no matter how much they try. Others have to squeeze around him to pass.

Someone calls out, 'Get him away before a sailor comes down!'

The warning is too late, for moments later we hear angry shouts from the hatch followed by a stocky figure quickly descending the ladder. The sailor assesses the situation in an instant and the next moment he removes a wooden cudgel from his waistband and hits the hysterical Covenanter until he's nearly unconscious. His friends pull him away from the danger as soon as they can. Everyone has fallen silent, shocked at the brutality but also at the way this foretells how we will be treated. The sailor stares around, completely unafraid at being surrounded by so many prisoners.

'His certainty that he's safe is worrying,' says Calum.

'The sailors must have clear orders from the captain for this one to be confident that he can treat us so harshly,' says Samuel.

Taking his time, the sailor climbs back up the ladder and the flow of people coming into the hold continues once more.

* * *

As ever, Calum is quick to get involved in any activity that might be useful and later that day he's one of the men who carries up buckets to empty over the side.

'We're being treated like animals,' he says upon his return. 'Some bastard Edinburgh merchant called Paterson has got the king's approval to do a deal with the Provost of Edinburgh for us to be transported to America or the West Indies to work on the plantations.'

'But we can't be sold like slaves,' says Samuel. 'We're Scotsmen.'

'No, not slaves. It's our labour that will be sold, and it'll simply be bought by the highest bidder. We'll have no say in any of it, so we could even be split up.'

This unconsidered possibility fills me with such dread that I can't stop the tears rolling down my cheeks. That we should have endured so much to then be separated . . . Is it not enough that I had to be parted from my mother, my father, my own twin, and now I may lose Samuel and Calum too?

'But how long can we be forced to work?' I ask.

'Nobody knows,' says Calum. 'I've heard that prisoners of war can be held for as long as ten years and Parliament says we're rebels, which they consider to be an even greater crime. And the king proudly declares that he's showing mercy by not having us executed.'

'I can't do this,' I say, openly crying.

'Enough for now, Calum.'

'No, it's not, Sam. You need to hear the rest. We should have been split between two ships, but the other one hasn't arrived, which is why we're so overcrowded on this one. Until that vessel gets here from London we're going to remain in the harbour. However, the Edinburgh authorities are scared there might be a rescue attempt, so they're pressing for the *Crown of London* to sail.'

'If we're meant to be distributed between two vessels, then this one alone can't carry sufficient supplies for everyone,' I say. 'We wouldn't survive a long journey.'

No one replies, for there is no denying the truth. We may yet die long before ever reaching a plantation.

* * *

It didn't seem possible to us when we were held in Greyfriars Kirkyard that our conditions could possibly be worse, but being kept in the hold is beyond any horror we could have imagined. Calum was correct when he said it was like entering a huge coffin. Without enough room for everyone to lie down at the same time, there's certainly no opportunity to walk or stretch.

A trip to the stinking buckets requires others to twist and lean their bodies over so that you can get through the mass. No one has spoken openly about me being a woman, if anyone's actually noticed, or even cares. My new identity has been aided by the fact that I've not had a monthly bleed since Bothwell. I know from other women that enormous grief or shock can cause such a sudden change, and I assume losing Father has done this to me.

Everyone suffers with terrible crushing headaches, while there's no chance to get relief from the sores that cover our backs and legs. Two poor souls have completely lost their wits and have had to be tightly bound to prevent them causing injury to those nearby. Their constant whimpering and that of the wounded Covenanters is pitiful.

Without supporters to provide extra food as they did in Greyfriars our diet is so poor that we can't possibly survive for long. One man has died during the twelve days we've been here and there appears to be no sign of this second ship which is meant to take half of us on our journey across the Atlantic.

Despair eats away at our resolve and hope as sharply as the teeth of the rats that run about, biting unsuspecting victims when they can. We're also tormented by lice. During those last few weeks in Greyfriars Kirkyard they had been dying due to the cold, even upon the most intimate parts of our bodies, but in the heat of the cramped ship's hold they've multiplied out of control.

On occasions news reaches us and we heard that five Covenanters were recently taken from an Edinburgh gaol to Magus Muir in Fife and executed at the site where Archbishop Sharp was murdered.

'Never doubt that God is on our side!'

There are those who still preach that all of this misery is merely God testing our faith. I don't know where they find the strength to give sermons. Most of us struggle just to stand up.

'There will be greater glory in Heaven because of the suffering our earthly bodies endure in His name …'

I've got my head on Calum's shoulder and I'm only half listening to what's being said. I shift slightly and, though I try not to, I moan at the pain in my right leg.

'It's bad?' asks Calum.

I lay my head back down and he puts an arm around me. 'Not so bad.'

'Liar.'

'All right, it hurts a bit. How's that sore on your thigh?'

'Almost healed.'

'Liar.'

'I try not to think about it.'

Samuel sits on my other side. The cramped conditions are particularly restricting for someone so tall. 'It's difficult,' he says, 'not to think about things.'

We fall silent. The preacher is still speaking. For some reason Hamish comes into my mind ... our parting words, the terrible hurt and feelings of betrayal. Yet now ... now I wonder if he wasn't right in signing the Black Bond and gaining his freedom. Such doubts are not to be said aloud. I'm glad that Hamish, at least, is not having to endure this ordeal.

'What are you thinking?' asks Calum, well aware of Samuel's morose mood.

'Too many things from the past, brother ... Rullion Green, Bothwell Bridge, the execution of George, Alexander and the others in Ayr. Father's murder ...'

I know from the cries he utters during his sleep that terrible images haunt Samuel's dreams.

'Father didn't deserve to die as he did,' says Samuel. 'And I worry what's happening to our mothers.'

'Hamish should be with your mother, Violet. At least she's not alone and between them they'll make sure that our mother is as well as can be.'

An angry shout from somewhere on the other side of the hold grabs our attention. The light from the hanging lanterns is gloomy but we see a rat flying through the air. It hits someone on the head before dropping into his lap and scuttling over legs, resulting in more angry calls of alarm.

This is immediately overshadowed by footsteps running on the deck. Everyone falls silent, including the preacher, who is forgotten along with the rat. A murmur of shock runs through the hold as the creaking of the ship and the slapping of a sail are accompanied by a gentle movement.

'Teddico can't be serious!' cries Calum. 'He's not waiting for the other ship!'

'God help us now,' says Samuel.

But God has not helped us much so far in our fight, and as the ship finally leaves the harbour for the unknown of the seas, I wonder if He ever will.

20

Violet
10 December 1679, *the* Crown of London,
sea off Deerness, Orkney

THE STENCH IS BEYOND BELIEF. Each breath feels as if it's not air I'm taking in but something physical that is hot and sharp, slicing my lungs painfully. Many prisoners have been terribly sea-sick and people vomit over themselves and their neighbours as there's no time to reach the buckets which are overflowing anyway, their disgusting contents slopping along the floor as the ship rolls and pitches. Figures sit squashed side by side, soaked in filth yet too ill to care.

Our initial fears have turned out to be true and the rations of water and food are so poor that we're certain the ship isn't provisioned for a long journey with this many people. If the authorities mean to kill us, I wish they would get it over with.

We've been heading north, a strange route in winter. Nothing about this voyage makes sense to those amongst us who understand the sea. The weather has been rough since departing Leith and now we're anchored off Orkney. The hatch has been opened so that the buckets can be emptied and water brought down. At least we're not made to use the same containers for both functions. I'm as fit as many in the hold and so the three of us are quick to volunteer.

Putting my head outside is extraordinary after so long below. Like everyone else I've discarded most of my layers of clothing and the intense cold is quickly numbing my body. I can only get on to the deck on my hands and knees, then find that the wild pitching of the vessel means I can't get up. If Teddico appears now, he's going to order me back down. Without any warning a hand grabs my arm and a sailor lifts me to my feet as if I weigh hardly anything at all. With a rough kindness he holds me upright until I'm finally able to stand by myself.

'Empty them over that side,' he says, pointing. 'Don't mess the deck!'

I nod my thanks and he leaves. There's a lot of activity going on about me and sailors seem too busy to bother with what I'm doing. Samuel's head appears out of the hatch.

'Are you all right?'

'Yes, it's just difficult to balance,' I say, though I'm also scared I won't have the ability to carry a bucket without spilling the contents.

He goes back down. Calum is at the bottom. Despite the apparent enormity of my task I'm grateful that they're letting me have this experience. There have been times when I felt I could have killed someone just to have five minutes in the open air. I take the opportunity to look around. The nearby land appears black, while the grey of the clouds and the angry sea merge together as if one is lifted up and the other dragged down in a kiss that foretells of death.

'Violet!'

Samuel has placed a stinking bucket on the deck. The handle is covered in human waste but I have no other way to carry it, so lift it up and weave towards the side. It's only at this point I become aware that there's a group of officers a little further along. Teddico is shouting down to someone and I position myself as far away as possible, yet still able to hear what's being said. Below is a small boat that's obviously been rowed out from the shore and is taking shelter on that side of the ship. One man calls up in the strange accent these islanders have.

'I tell you, Captain, the storm is going to be severe and you would be safer anchoring farther into the sound, particularly if it comes from the north. I can put a man aboard to guide you, if that helps.'

'As I've already told you, my decision is made. We'll ride it out here at anchor,' shouts Teddico, who then walks away, leaving his officers and the four men in the boat staring at each other in apparent disbelief.

As soon as it moves away, the small boat is thrown around dangerously and it's clear the Orcadians have put their lives at great risk to deliver this warning. Then, shaking their heads, the officers disperse. I tip the bucket into the sea and wonder if, before long, we'll all be following the slop.

* * *

The storm worsens and our misery is replaced by fear, which is then nudged aside by terror as the ship lurches and twists, rises and falls. We're all intensely focused on a Covenanter called Fergus, an experienced sailor who understands sounds that to us are merely creaking and banging, flapping and clanking.

'The anchor's being dragged,' he announces.

'What does that mean?' asks a voice.

'If it continues then the ship will likely be forced on to the rocks. Quiet!'

He climbs up the steps and bends his head so that his ear is pressed against the hatch. His expression of concentration is fierce. He's like this for an age before suddenly shouting out.

'Bastards! They're lowering the boats. We're being abandoned. Hey! Hey! Open the hatch! Don't leave us down here!'

His comments send panic racing throughout us. Calum joins Fergus to push against the hatch. People cry out to be freed and pray for God's intervention, while outside the wind howls its rage and the ship is pushed further and faster until finally there is a huge explosion of noise as the hull is lifted up then smashed down on to rocks.

Men cry out in pain and shock as we're thrown around violently, heads and limbs bashing against each other or the walls of the hold. Fergus falls off the ladder into a pile of bodies, those at the bottom screaming to be released. Several lanterns smash, and as the gloom increases, so does the madness. I can just make out Calum still heaving against the hatch.

Samuel holds me tightly in his arms, trying to protect me as best he can. Above it all, I hear him say he's sorry. I pull back to look up at him.

'Samuel, I would rather die than continue alone. I have no regrets. Better that we end this very night than be banished to a strange land. We've kept true to what is right, and for all his wealth and power the king is merely a man who'll eventually die and be replaced by another. Never doubt that others will continue our fight. We might not see it, but the time will come when Scotsmen don't have such hate in their hearts that they murder countrymen on sight for carrying a Bible.'

'Violet, if you get the chance, you must swim for the shore.'

'Not without you.'

'Please! I'll try to keep us together—'

The ship shifts violently and, with one last scream of breaking timbers, icy water pours through the broken hull.

21

Samuel
10 December 1679, sea off Deerness, Orkney

THE INSTANT I'M THROUGH THE shattered hull of the *Crown of London*, the sea embraces me with such ferocity that my body tumbles, turns and twists helplessly in the currents. My chest feels squeezed in straps of iron as I fight the panic that threatens to overwhelm me, and when my head crashes into something, I almost lose my wits completely. With no compassion for the poor soul so recently departed, I harshly push the lifeless body away. It's instinct that takes me to the surface.

For a long while I'm aware of nothing other than the urgent need to fill my lungs with air and not swallow more water. The fight is a close one. Finally, some sense of sanity comes back to me. The clouds are breaking up and as the full moon illuminates more of the surroundings, I realise that Hell is not flames and heat but dying men thrashing frantically, calling for help amongst the wreckage of the ship and those who will never call again.

The shore is close but there is no way through the mayhem and what strength I have is failing so fast I doubt that I can swim around it all. Without any warning a hand grabs my leg and drags me under. The man could be a friend or a stranger yet there is no thought in either of us to aid the other, just a primitive urge to survive as we wrestle under the waves.

In his terror he won't let go, unaware that his actions will doom us both, while I alternate between punching him and trying to prize open his fingers. Soon we're so exhausted that neither of us can do anything other than simply drift apart. I see moonlight above but have nothing left within me to try and reach the surface.

Violet ... I love you ...

Just as my eyes close my hair is yanked painfully and my body pulled to the surface.

'Take the rope.'

I'm too confused to follow what is said, so my saviour forces my arm underneath a rope that is fixed to a large piece of floating timber. Now I'm bound firmly and lay my head upon a wooden beam while once again I cough and splutter water from my lungs. When I can eventually take in what's happening nearby, I'm surprised at how far we've drifted.

The cries of drowning men are faint, either because of the distance or because there are few left alive. There doesn't appear to be anyone close. The broken outline of the remains of the *Crown of London* is visible on the rocks. For the first time I look at the man who's saved my life. I recognise his face, though I don't know his name.

'Thank you.' It's a poor acknowledgement of what he's just done.

'If we get the chance, we should move inland, as far from the shore as possible because the crew, damn their souls, will search for survivors to rearrest.'

'Do you think there'll be many?'

'Survivors? We're alive. Most bodies will likely end up near the wreck ... the dead and the living.'

'There's someone I have to search for.'

'Your wife, Samuel.'

'You know!'

'Do you really think you could keep such a thing secret? Many men knew but we would never betray a fellow Covenanter. Your reputation, and your hair, make you a well-known figure. I hope you find her. She's a brave— Look out!'

I twist around to see a huge piece of wreckage heading straight towards us. It's travelling at a much greater speed than we are and I'm still frantically trying to free my arm when it hits. Something sharp pierces my left thigh as we're dragged aside, then once more I'm under the water. This time I'm trapped and my arm feels as though it's being stretched out of its socket.

I fear the sea is so hungry for my soul that it won't let me go a third time, yet the wreckage continues its journey and I surface, so near unconscious with pain, exhaustion and the need for air that it's several minutes before I realise there is no one else. The man who saved me, whose name I didn't even get, has gone.

'Hey! Hey! Where are you?'

I call out to the empty water until I'm hoarse, but there is no reply or sign of him. I'm as alone as it's possible to be. This final tragedy breaks me and I weep and cry and wail until I am no more than flotsam floating wherever the currents take me.

* * *

The first thing I'm aware of is vomiting water and coughing as I try to suck air into lungs that are soaked, like wet breeches hanging limply on a dreich day. The second thing is cold so intense that my very bones feel as though they're made of ice; each beat of my heart seems like it must surely be the last.

Through heaving gasps, I force myself to think. Sand ... I'm lying on sand. My arm is still bound to the wreckage that has given me another chance of life. Slowly, I sit up. The pain from my thigh makes me shudder and I have to remain still until the nausea passes sufficiently to move again.

The storm is reduced to gusts that blow spray over me from the receding tide, though the sea remains angry, as though the numerous souls it's devoured this night isn't enough. With fingers that barely move it takes ages to release my arm, which is so numb, it could be broken without me knowing. There's nobody else in sight.

Inch by painful inch, I turn myself on to my knees then pause, not sure if I can stand. But I have to walk if there is any hope of finding Violet. Initially, the dizziness just about puts me flat on my face. I carefully take a few steps. My leg is obviously not broken, though it's doubtful I'll get far.

The beach is long and narrow, bordering low cliffs. Finding a path doesn't take long but it's treacherous to climb. I slip, stumble and fall so often that my resolve begins to fade. When I reach the top I'm forced to sit on a rock before deciding which direction to take. There's not a dwelling in sight and I begin to wonder whether this part of Orkney is inhabited, yet there is a track heading into the distance and the only option is to follow it, hoping that it's made by humans and not animals.

I stagger, weave, beg for God's help and mutter fragments of prayer that He will take care of Violet. There is no reply, just the sound of the wind combined with my cries of pain and grief. It seems impossible that I can walk far enough to reach any sort of habitation, yet I continue, a journey of horror that has no end, no pity. Then I fall and can't get up ... can't go on.

The urge to sleep is unbelievable. Violet is likely dead. Perhaps if I simply lie down and rest I'll meet her soon in Heaven. Maybe she's watching, waiting patiently for me to realise that all I have to do for us to be together is rest my head on that nearby rock ... It's soft ... not a rock but a pillow, filled with hens' feathers like the ones my mother used to have. When Calum and I were young she always tucked us up in the box-bed, kissing our foreheads before leaving.

'Mother ...'

My head is almost on the pillow, eager for my mother's kiss, when I hear a man shouting. It's not real. He calls again ... a name? I look up and in the distance see a light, then a dog barks and the man's voice is gentler, almost lost in the wind, before the light disappears.

A door closing? A man and a dog? I glance down at my hand resting on the rock, which is hard and cold and slimy.

The Devil's work!

In the end, it's anger that gives me the strength to go on ... anger at the injustice, the brutality, the killings of innocent people. When I try to walk my legs will barely move and I only manage a few yards before stumbling badly. I'm so weak, I suspect my thigh is bleeding heavily.

The world spins but I'm not giving up, desperate step after desperate step, my body shaking so violently that it seems my limbs must surely shatter like glass. Despite my determination, I sink slowly to the ground. God knows I've tried, but I've failed. In everything, I've failed.

Violet ... my love. I'm sorry.

I manage to roll on to my back so that my last sights on earth may be of the stars and sky. Far away there is a strange noise. A light appears just above my body. Has God sent an angel? Suddenly the hideous face of a black beast fills my vision, its fierce, evil eyes so close to mine that I am gripped by an all-consuming terror.

The Devil has come for me.

22

Violet
10 December 1679, sea off Deerness, Orkney

I THROW MY ARMS AROUND SAMUEL but the unstoppable rush of seawater tears us apart in an instant. I'm stunned by the force of it, powerless to fight back, and instinctively let the current take me, holding my breath, though my chest feels as though it's being crushed under the weight of a mountain.

When I finally surface, my lungs are on fire and I can do nothing except try to keep above the water and gulp air as frantically as possible. I'm not too far from shore. Many men are ahead of me, struggling against the waves or wading wearily over the last few yards. The ship's crew is spread out thinly along the shoreline, some holding oars to help pull people to safety.

Then a sailor raises an oar, hesitates a moment, and brings it down heavily upon the head of the nearest Covenanter. The man falls to his knees and is beaten repeatedly until his body disappears under the waves. I watch in utter disbelief as sailors push defenceless men back into the sea or beat them down where they stand.

Heart-breaking calls for mercy carry across the water even above the roar of the storm. I'm frozen as much from shock as the cold. Only death awaits me here. Away left, in the opposite direction to the ship, there is a large projection of rock into the sea. If I can get beyond that point, then I should be out of sight of the sailors. There is no choice.

I begin swimming and notice that others have the same idea. It's a desperate battle. The chill in my limbs is frightening, sucking my strength even as I try to swim faster, harder. Someone nearby flounders.

'Keep going,' I shout.

'God help me!' he cries, and is gone.

By the time I've got around the rocks, there are hardly any swimmers remaining, and when I finally crawl up on to the shore I'm too exhausted to do anything but lie there, gasping and crying. If a sailor came along now he could murder me at his ease. Shivering violently, I look about. Three – there are just three others.

Where is Samuel? Why isn't he with me?

One man struggles to sit up. I've heard his name before but can't recall it.

'We can't stay here,' he says.

'I can't move,' says another. It's clear that he will not even try to get up and we are too weak to help.

'We need to head away from the ship,' I say, once I've stood and my two companions are on their feet alongside me. We look down at the fourth Covenanter. There is nothing we can do. 'God bless you.'

We leave, making our way along the beach in search of a track that will take us inland. Soon we're shaking so much that it's difficult even to speak and when we find a likely path we simply nod at each other and carry on. As we trudge along the intensity of the cold makes us groan as though we're being tortured. Increasingly one of us stumbles and gets up only for someone else to fall moments later.

Alan – that's the man's name. I've heard him call the other Iain. It's while waiting for Iain to stand that I see the outline of a building in the distance. I point and Alan follows the direction of my arm, nodding vigorously. We all head straight for it, which is a mistake because we end up going across rougher ground. At one point we fall into a ditch and lie there like drunks so in their cups that they can't speak or move with any sense.

I'm filled with dread that the building may be a ruin, because we can't possibly search any further. As we get close, there is smoke in the air and a dim light behind the curtain at the small window. Alan kicks the door several times, too exhausted to do anything else. He's feebly kicking it again when it opens so suddenly that he almost loses his balance.

'Dear God above.' The man takes in our situation in an instant. 'Get inside.'

He ushers us in before closing the door. Like all such places, it's basically one room where people sleep, eat and live out their lives. Two figures stare at us, a wife and daughter of about sixteen. It's the wife who is suddenly alive with orders.

'You can't keep those clothes on. Strip everything off. Just do it where you are. Meg, stoke up the fire and reheat the broth. David, fetch blankets and cloths to dry them. Light some more candles. They may be injured and I need to see what I'm doing.'

Neither of my companions has the strength to move, not even to remove their garments. David realises he has to do it for them and they stand like children while a parent undresses them. In my need to survive I hadn't considered such a scene. My secret is about to be revealed.

The wife studies me for a moment then pulls a blanket out of a nearby box-bed. 'Come with me, lad.'

She gently takes my arm and leads me a few feet away from the men before unfolding the blanket so that I'm shielded from view. I look at her face and she gives a tiny nod of reassurance, because men see what they expect to while women see what's there.

'Meg, come around here and help the lad undress.'

'Mother?' The girl sounds shocked by the suggestion.

'Do it quickly.'

Meg joins me behind the blanket and reluctantly begins to remove my sodden garments. A few moments later she looks up in surprise at her mother, who replies with a tiny shake of her head. Women keep each other's secrets and for now mine is safe. Meg quickly finishes her task and rubs me vigorously with a large cloth before I'm wrapped in the blanket and sat in an armchair by the fire. A thick woollen kerchief is draped over me and then another blanket.

Alan is in the armchair opposite, while a wooden chair is brought over for Iain. In the safety and warmth of this house, away from the terror of the storm and the death-pull of the sea, we all begin to cry.

'Here, get a tot of this into you,' says David, who has produced a cup containing whisky by the smell of it. He holds it to Alan's lips.

'Not too much,' instructs the wife. 'They need something hot inside them.'

One by one we take a sip and bend over coughing, uncertain as to whether we are better or worse for taking the liquid, then David stands behind the armchair opposite and starts to massage Alan's shoulders. He does it firmly yet with obvious kindness; perhaps this is not the first time that people have arrived at their front door frozen near to death. My head drops suddenly.

'I know you're exhausted,' says the wife, 'but you mustn't sleep until you've warmed up, otherwise you might not wake. My name's Grizel. You don't have to tell us anything about yourselves.'

Grizel starts to rub my shoulders while Meg ladles steaming broth into a bowl and spoonfeeds Iain. We're shaking too violently to do this ourselves. Soon we are all being fed, slurping noises, groans and words of encouragement competing with each other for a while, until we can eat no more.

Grizel swings the large black kettle over the fire. I can't keep awake. The last thing I'm aware of is Grizel pouring hot water into a bowl, kneeling by my armchair and gently washing my feet.

* * *

The morning's bright sunshine offers no clue to the horror of the previous night. It doesn't seem believable that gulls should cry and sheep should bleat and the world continue around us as if this great tragedy hasn't occurred. I sit at the table with Alan and Iain, the three of us still wrapped in blankets. Our clothes have been washed during the night and hang on a rope outside, flapping wildly in the Orkney wind. No one has spoken. Iain can barely eat the brose in front of him while Alan is already on to his second helping. I force mine down, knowing that I have to build up my strength if I am to find Samuel.

Samuel . . . my love. Where are you?

He is not drowned. I refuse to believe it.

The door opens and David enters. Everyone stops to look at him.

'There's the wreckage of a ship on the rocks at Scarva Taing. The rumour is that it was carrying dangerous convicts to America...' He stares at us. '... but I see no dangerous convicts here.'

'Have many escaped?' I ask.

'Bodies have washed up along the shore and they'll probably continue to do so for days to come. Some will never be given up by the sea and there are probably many still inside the wreck. Apparently about two dozen people have been recaptured. The authorities are searching for others.

'You may not be safe here and I won't throw you out. However, I won't put my family at risk either. If they come, I'll say that you told us you were fishermen and we had no reason to believe otherwise. To us, you were near-drowned men needing help and as good Christians we couldn't turn you away.'

His comment is as much question as statement and requires an answer. We nod to show we'll stick to the same tale.

'That's agreed then.'

* * *

It's late morning. Behind the house there's a dyke with a small stream that runs out to sea and a secluded spot where people relieve themselves. I'm dressed in my rags, but Grizel has given me a thick woollen jumper. It's old and patched but a very welcome addition. I can't believe I will ever feel warm again. I'm pulling up my breeches when Grizel comes into sight, crouching and moving as fast as she can.

'Sailors! Four of them and as mean-looking as I've ever seen. David is arguing that they have no right to enter his home, but he's not going to be able to keep them out. Your friends are stuck inside and will be found straight away. Here, get this on.'

Grizel has brought a coat, so worn that the Orcadian wind will likely pass through it without noticing, but it's better than nothing.

'I can't leave them,' I say.

'You can't help them. Look, follow the dyke to those rocks and then go up the hill. When you get to those bushes, you can easily keep yourself hidden while watching what happens around the house.'

I hug her, realising how much I've missed being able to hug someone. 'Thank you.'

'Head south-west. You're probably safest in the town of Kirkwall, where strangers are not uncommon. I must get back. God's speed.'

We go our separate ways and soon I'm climbing the small hill, quickly out of breath with the exertion. When I reach the bushes, I lie down. There's no sign of anyone; the sailors must have gone inside and I pray our saviours will be spared any violence. It's not long before Alan and Iain are brought out, their hands bound behind their backs. One sailor starts pushing them away as the other three begin searching near the house.

For a moment I'm frozen with indecision, then I pull myself around on my elbows and crawl as quickly as possible further up the hill. Every single second, I expect to hear shouts behind me as I'm completely exposed, yet I reach the top undiscovered and roll down the other side until it's safe enough to stand.

Frantically, I scan the area for potential hiding places. There are no woods, in fact no trees anywhere. The landscape is open and the only place is a tumbled-down building a few hundred yards away. I stumble towards it, realising that it's too obvious and they'll surely search it. I'm shaking by the time I reach the remnants of walls and piles of stone.

They'll find me easily.

A short distance away is a ditch. It's shallow but I'm thin and instinctively head for it. There is one spot that's deep enough for me to lie in and be out of sight from someone merely glancing over from the ruin. There's no other option, so I lie face down, hugging the earth. It's only minutes later when I hear voices.

'And I'm telling you there's more nearby. I can smell them, filthy Covenanters!'

'You and your nose!'

I hear them moving about the ruin, muttering curses and threats of what they'll do to anyone they find. After several minutes it goes quiet. I barely breathe lest they hear the air moving into my lungs. They must surely hear my heart, for it's almost bursting out of my chest. Yet there's nothing from them. I lie, waiting for a sound or a voice to indicate where they are. Nothing. They must have moved on quietly. I remain motionless for so long without hearing anything that eventually I risk carefully raising my head.

Feet! There are feet by my head!

I'm suddenly lifted bodily out of the ditch.

'Here we are!' says one. All three sailors are laughing. 'We had bets on how long it would take you to look up.'

Everything happens so quickly. Two of them roughly hold my arms while the third one punches me in the stomach so hard that I almost pass out from the pain and shock.

'I knew I could smell one,' he says.

I'm only vaguely aware of being hauled upright. Then the man who says he has a nose for Covenanters pulls back his arm. This time his fist heads straight for my face.

23

Violet
11 December 1679, Stromness, Orkney

A VOICE CALLS TO ME. IT'S so far away, as if the words have been carried across the moors on the wind and now can't even claim to be a whisper.

'Samuel?'

'Shhh. It's Calum. You're safe, at least for now, but your face has been badly messed up.'

Slowly, I open my eyes. They feel sticky. My nose is blocked and I can taste blood. It takes a while to focus on Calum, who's cradling me in his arms. I raise a hand to my mouth, but he gently takes hold of it.

'Best to leave it for the moment.' He speaks quietly so as not to be overheard.

'Samuel?'

'No sign or word of him. I've asked everyone here.'

'Where ...'

'Almost fifty of us are being held in a storeroom in Stromness. The authorities intend to keep us here until they can find another ship.'

'A lot dead?'

He doesn't answer straight away. 'Yes. I doubt there'll be many yet to find alive. Samuel is well known and easy to recognise. The fact that no one has seen his body has got to be a good thing.'

A sob bubbles to my lips and I close my swollen eyes again, tears escaping from the corners. I cling with all my might to the hope that if Samuel has not been found, he's out there, somewhere, still alive.

* * *

One morning about two weeks later, we're told to go outside. It's raining and Stromness is grey and bleak, yet I long to stay with all my heart, for if we leave I will never see these shores again. It's obviously been decided that nobody will try to escape as the only guards are sailors, who I assume are from the ship we'll be taken to.

A couple of dozen local people watch. They're wrapped in thick woollen clothing against the biting wind, while our clothes are little more than rags. We're soon shivering uncontrollably as we wait for an order to move on. An elderly woman walks slowly towards our group. No one tries to stop her.

'Something for your journey, son,' she says, handing over a small bundle. 'It's not much. Share it out as best you can.'

'Thank you, I will,' replies the Covenanter.

Many more figures step forward, handing over food and speaking quietly to the men. A woman comes up to us. She glances at me and speaks to Calum.

'A few oatcakes.'

'Your kindness means more than I can express.'

Calum's voice cracks with emotion. She gently lays a hand on his arm, nods at me, then walks away. The two of us are silent for several minutes.

'Do you think he's still here, Violet, somewhere in Orkney?'

I don't answer straight away. Am I simply fooling myself, hoping that Samuel is alive? Should I accept what must surely be the truth, that his body has floated out to sea?

'I was so certain that if he was dead I would know it, but now ... I miss him so much. He was my life, Calum. Without him I can't understand how I've continued to live, why I would want to continue to live.'

The conversation is brought to a halt by someone shouting that we should move. We shuffle along, silent and sullen, each of us with our own private grief. As we near the quayside, my heart starts pounding and soon my entire body is trembling. I hear moans from a few of the others and realise they also feel this sudden unexpected terror.

'Calum.'

'It's all right. You're not alone and this is not the *Crown of London*.'

Despite his words of encouragement I continue to panic at the idea of boarding a ship. 'I want Samuel. I can't go on. I have to find Samuel. He may be hurt.'

Calum puts his hands on my shoulders. 'Violet, I miss my wife and son more than I could possibly have imagined, but I have to believe that we'll be reunited again. For now we've no choice, but I won't leave your side. God hasn't brought us this far only to let us die on this ship. He must have a purpose for us.' He puts an arm around my waist. 'Just put one foot in front of the other. That's it. We'll walk on side by side. One day we'll find Samuel together and until then I'll protect you. I promise.'

Slowly and hesitantly we board the *Sophia*. There's not the threat of violence that we experienced from Teddico and his crew and, unmolested, we climb down into the hold, a world uninhabited by those who live in the light. It isn't big but we're fewer than a fifth of the number who left Leith in November and we have much more space than on the *Crown of London*.

Eventually, the hatch is closed and locked. We hear orders being called out, the bumping of the gangplank being withdrawn, footsteps running, more instructions, the flapping of a sail. Strangely we all remain standing. It's at least twenty minutes after the vessel has moved away from the harbour that people begin looking for a place to sit.

Somewhere off to my left a man starts to cry.

24

Samuel
13 December 1679, Deerness, Orkney

My body is squeezed into such a small space I can barely move and certainly can't stretch out. I open my eyes. It's daylight and I'm in a box-bed. Slowly, I turn my head to see more of my surroundings. The effort is unbelievable. A curtain is across much of the opening. Without warning, the face of the black beast is once again close to mine, but before I can even draw breath to scream, it starts licking my cheek with a warm, rough tongue.

'Move out of the way, Gunnar.' The curtain is pulled back and the beast pushed away as a man gets down on one knee so that his head is nearer to mine. 'Well, lad, we've never known someone so near to death yet so determined to live. Many times we thought you were lost. We've prayed for hours by your side and the good Lord has answered.'

'Where ...?'

'Don't try to talk. The important thing to understand is that you're safe. Mary and I believe in the Covenanters' cause and we'll take care of you as long as it's needed.'

'How ...'

'How did we know you're a Covenanter? You've been ranting and raving almost non-stop for days. It seems you've been harshly treated, lad, harshly treated indeed. There's no news about your dear Violet, no news at all about a woman being on board the ship. The morning after we found you, I took my axe to the beach where you washed up. If anyone comes searching this far, they'll find no sign of wreckage to indicate that someone might have landed nearby.'

'Must search ...' I try to lift myself up but my body feels as broken as the ship.

'You're not going anywhere. Now, my Mary might be a peedie woman but she'll give me some grief if I keep you awake. Sleep, lad. And don't be frightened of Gunnar. He's an ugly brute but I promise you, he's not the Devil.'

* * *

It's daylight when I wake again, although I sense it's not the same day. When I try to shift my position, the pain in my leg is so fierce that I cry out and moments later the curtain is pulled back. I guess the woman might be around forty-five. She sits on the edge of the bed and lays her hand on my brow. I've felt this hand before, though not known its owner.

'Well, your fever has broken but your leg is a long way from being mended. We need to get food into you. Can you manage some broth if I help?'

I nod and she reaches forward, sliding her hands under my back. 'We need to sit you up a bit. Bliss me! You're so skinny.'

Her arms are surprisingly strong and she clutches me tightly to her as she manoeuvres me in the bed. Without warning, I'm crying so hard it doesn't seem possible that my tears will ever stop. Everyone I love or have loved is dead or lost. I've seen friends tortured and killed before my eyes and I, in turn, have killed. The worst feeling is that I simply don't know where Violet is, and the thought of living without her is unbearable.

'It's all right,' she says. 'I won't let you go. I won't let you go.'

This tiny woman who has helped save my life rocks me back and forth as though I'm a child. I'm utterly helpless in her arms. I cry as I've never done before. My leg might mend but my heart never will.

Finally, I'm so exhausted that blessed sleep releases me from my anguish.

* * *

Days and nights pass in a vague haze, like a delicate morning mist that could easily go unnoticed. I recall eating and drinking, the pain of the dressing on my leg being replaced, being cleaned . . . being held and soothed. When I wake again, properly this time, I feel different. The curtain is open and for a while I watch Mary skilfully gutting fish, which I guess is a common food on an island. She looks up from the table and smiles, which transforms her face in a way I almost can't believe.

'You're back with us and this time I think it's for good.' She pours water into a cup and brings it over. Having helped me to sit, she holds the cup to my lips, preventing me from gulping too quickly.

'Wait a moment and I'll call Hugh.'

While I'm alone the dog comes over, sits by my feet and places his head on my thigh, fortunately the thigh of my uninjured leg. 'Devil,' I say, stroking him behind an ear. When the couple return, they pull up stools and sit.

'You'll be full of questions, but save your strength and I'll tell you what we know,' says Hugh. 'You've been here over a week and in that time more than forty Covenanters have been captured. They're being held in Stromness, no doubt until there's a ship that can take them to their destination.

'Bodies have been washing up along the shore but no one is searching for survivors any more and the sailors and captain from the *Crown of London* have left Orkney. But even here you're not out of danger. Only those we trust can know who you are.'

'Violet?'

He shakes his head sadly. 'Nothing about a woman being amongst the men and if she's in disguise ... well, I don't know how we could find out.'

'There's been no news of a woman's body being found,' says Mary. 'That has to be good.'

'I'll go to Stromness.'

'No you won't,' she says sternly. 'I think your fever has gone for good, but Stromness is the other side of the island and I doubt you could get yourself outside without help.'

If Violet lives, she may well be amongst the captives. I can't let her be taken from me again. Despite the protests of Hugh and Mary, I move my legs around and place my feet on the floor.

'Don't try it, son!' he cries.

But I stand, harshly pushing away their restraining hands and take a step. It's all I manage, one bloody step, before the cold, hard slabs are rushing up to hit me as if they can't wait another second to bash some sense into my stupid, stubborn head.

Part IV

Servants and Slaves

25

Violet
12 March 1680, Bridgetown, Barbados

THE HATCH IS THROWN OPEN and when I emerge into the painfully bright light a sailor binds my hands with rope. The sights that confront me are so extraordinary that I then stand on the deck in stunned silence. The bay is huge and alive with boats being rowed to or from the numerous ships at anchor, all of them of such varying sizes and styles it's hard to believe they have a similar purpose.

Like the *Sophia*, many vessels are tied to moorings and the activity around the quayside is frantic. Workers stagger, almost disappearing under huge sacks that look as though they contain seed or flour; they struggle with heavy boxes and crates or fight to control the direction of barrels rolling along the ground. Men sing, shout, argue and give orders.

Mules bray and horses snort, while rats scurry between everything and everyone. Even in the most rundown ports in Scotland, I've never seen rats so bold or in such numbers. A sailor kicks out, sending one into the water, which results in a cheer from those nearby. A bell rings, though what it signifies I don't know, for people continue without apparently taking any notice.

Further away, children in rags run around between people arriving and leaving, calls of greeting or farewell mingling with those of hawkers trying to sell their wares. Not one square yard of the quayside is silent or still. The shifting breeze brings so many different smells it's difficult to identify something before it's nudged aside by another, but I recognise spices before they're overpowered by hot pitch, which is then replaced by the stench of rotting waste. After so long in the hold, my senses feel as if they'll explode.

'Is this America?' says Alan, who has come to stand beside me, and looks around us in bewilderment.

'I don't know,' I reply, squinting. The sun appears much bigger than in Scotland, although I know this can't be correct.

'It's Barbados,' says Calum, joining us.

'Is that in America?' asks Alan.

'The West Indies.' I recall how Father and I used to study maps that he had brought back from his journeys. What would he make of this place?

'Heaven save us!' says Alan. 'What's that monster over there?' He points, having to raise both hands to do so.

'I never thought to see such a beast,' says Calum.

'It's a camel,' I answer, as astonished as anyone.

Before we're able to discuss this further, sailors start ordering us to form two rows. Calum whispers to keep close, which I would have done anyway, and I notice that Alan makes sure he's on the other side of me. Like cattle at the market, we're about to be sold as forced labour to work on the plantations. Even after all that's happened, the idea seems unreal.

Five men approach the ship and walk up the gangplank, so upright and confident I fancy I can smell their reek of power and cruelty from where we stand. Once on board, they speak to the captain and I'm close enough to hear what's said.

Four of them are buying while the fifth is the local agent representing William Paterson, the Edinburgh merchant responsible for our transportation. The captain brings out a sheet containing a list of our names, which we had been made to give while in Stromness. I wasn't the only person to provide false details, as men attempted to protect their families from future persecution. There is some discussion about the two prisoners who died during the journey, before we're counted to confirm numbers.

It begins then. One man who goes by the name of McKinnon, the overseer of the Drummond plantation, is the first along the line in the front. He feels men's arms, shakes a few, looks in mouths. He's getting closer.

'They're in a bloody terrible condition,' McKinnon complains to the captain.

'Covenanters,' he says, as if this means we're not people like anyone else.

McKinnon reaches me. He grabs my arms and shakes so violently that my head snaps backwards and forwards.

'Skin and bone.'

'They'll build up once they're on land and fed properly,' says the captain.

'Open your mouth!'

Of all the punishments, starvations and ill-treatments I've suffered, the fighting, killings and tortures I've seen, this command to inspect my teeth fills me with such rage that I don't obey. McKinnon grabs my jaw and I clench it tightly. I stare back and after a few moments, to my utter surprise, he laughs.

'A small man with spirit will better survive the hardships than a bigger man who's broken,' he says to the other buyers, as if imparting wisdom like a teacher with pupils. 'Open your mouth.'

I open my mouth.

We stand for nearly an hour while the four overseers haggle. Moaning about the stink we give off, they move further away and I can no longer hear everything said. A sailor brings out a tray of drinks. It's obvious they know each other well and this sort of purchase is a common transaction that creates no animosity between them as they laugh, slap backs and shake hands like old friends.

In the end McKinnon decides on me, Calum, Alan and three others for twenty-seven pounds each. This forced servitude should be for a set period but if any particular number of years has been discussed, there's no indication to us as to how long we'll be held. I'm too cowed to ask, and no one else does either.

Our group is the first to leave and, as we walk unsteadily along the deck, I glance at each of the faces we pass. These are men I've endured so much with. Some nod. A few silently weep. Others stare at their feet, the broken men that McKinnon doesn't want. I pause at one figure – he won't look at me.

'God be with you, Iain,' I say quietly, moving on without any response. We won't meet again, of that I'm certain.

An intense loathing for McKinnon curdles in the pit of my stomach. And yet he's right to choose those who are more likely to survive. Walking down the gangplank, I wonder why I'm not broken. I've lost everything and everyone except Calum. He's all I have left. I must survive this for him – and for Samuel.

The day I stop believing he is out there, somewhere, is the day I finally break.

* * *

Nobody pays us any attention as we shuffle through the throng of people on the quayside, yet we're wide-eyed at the scenes around us. McKinnon has a brutish-looking man with him whom I've heard called Hunter and they push us along, making sure we stay together. We pass a large, noisy crowd gathered around a raised platform where about three dozen black men and women stand, their legs and wrists heavily chained. They're totally naked.

'No slaves today, Mister McKinnon?'

'Not this time, Mister Hunter.'

Hunter stares at the women. Moments later, we come upon a small, penned area where mules are being inspected by potential buyers with more gentleness than the people on the platform – or us, for that matter.

'Dear God above, Violet, what hell is this?' whispers Calum.

I have no words that could come close to giving a suitable reply. Just beyond the mules is a pen containing horses and further on again is a much larger pen with oxen. The sheer bustle and strangeness is overwhelming. Around the harbour, small groups of soldiers and armed militia stand watching the various activities.

Something kicks my leg and I look with surprise to see a boy of about seven close by. He's with two friends. They're laughing and take turns to rush in and try to kick us before running away. We're too slow to react but eventually one gets near to Hunter, who punches him so hard that the diminutive figure lands several yards away to lie still in the dirt. The others leave us alone.

We turn up a street teeming with hawkers and people with stalls selling such an array of products that I feel dizzy. There are tables piled high with fruits, of which I recognise only lemons. Food stalls are mixed between others selling clay pots, clothing, tobacco, knives and swords, hats, shoes, tools of every description ... I can't take it all in.

The shouting from people promoting their wares is constant. A man and a boy play music on a lute and recorder. Drunks outside a tavern call encouragement to two men fighting. Prostitutes stand at the end of alleyways, trying to entice men to follow them. I don't catch the words but a woman says something to Calum. I'm taken aback at his expression of hate. She laughs at him, at his helplessness. We carry on, led by McKinnon and pushed by Hunter.

Further on we catch glimpses of long, straight streets with houses that are absolutely stunning in their grandeur. Outside some stand ornate carriages fitted with beautiful horses attended by slaves dressed in gold-braided uniforms, the likes of which I've never seen.

My legs are shaking by the time we reach a sturdy wagon fitted with two oxen. A horse is tied up close by. McKinnon flips a coin to the youth standing guard, who walks away as we're ordered into the back. McKinnon unties the horse and mounts it while Hunter climbs on the wagon and takes the reins for the oxen.

'That,' says McKinnon as if he's back in his imaginary classroom, 'is Bridgetown, and you're unlikely to find its equal in badness or goodness anywhere in the world. Isn't that right, Mister Hunter?'

'That's right, Mister McKinnon.'

'And none of you will see it again for many years to come ... perhaps never.'

With these words, he laughs loudly. Hunter flicks the reins and we set off, bouncing along with dread in our hearts at what the future holds. McKinnon follows closely behind to ensure no one escapes.

But where could we possibly escape to on this hellish island?

26

Violet
12 March 1680, Drummond Plantation, Barbados

THE HOUSE IS THE LARGEST I've ever seen and is bedecked with so many extraordinary carvings and expensive decorative features that it can only have been built by someone with such immense wealth that they did not know what to do with their money. It is a blatant, vulgar statement of prestige and power – and a hint of something even more unwholesome.

The house is framed like a painting by a semicircle of large trees that have obviously been planted to provide shade. I'm still marvelling at the construction when the front door opens and after a pause a well-dressed man emerges on to the veranda. By the way he so confidently stands studying us in no apparent hurry there is no mistaking him for anyone but the owner.

He's certainly tall and powerfully built, although as he comes down the wide wooden steps and nearer it becomes clear that what might have once been a handsome face is blotched with too much alcohol and lined with too much cruelty. Deliberately slowly, he climbs into a tall wooden platform, as ornately carved as his house but appearing a great deal older. I'm so intent on him that it's with a start I realise he is standing in a pulpit.

The man has actually had a pulpit from a Scottish kirk shipped all the way to Barbados.

We six from the *Sophia* still have our hands tied, and we're lined up so that he can look directly down upon us. A short distance away to our right are several dozen men, most of whom seem utterly wretched and defeated, staring at the ground in front of them. They're dressed identically, in coarse linen drawers and shirts and canvas shoes.

On the other side of us is a group of women and a few children, fewer than twenty in total. The women wear petticoats and shoes but nothing upon the upper half of their bodies. Although my true identity has never been discovered, my unease increases hugely when I don't see any white women.

'My name is William Drummond. You will call me "master", for I own this plantation and, for the time you're on this land, I own *you*. I own the shoes on your feet and the earth beneath their soles. Everything around us is mine – everybody here is mine.'

I cannot take in what I am hearing, that this stranger actually believes he owns all of these people, including us, as if we are beasts in the field. It's clear that in Drummond's mind we're not human, and I fear this may free his conscience to treat people in ways that I cannot even begin to imagine.

'He's mad,' whispers Calum.

I do not respond, as Drummond continues.

'Now you recently arrived men will see there are other white men present . . . and there are black men . . . and there are black women. I make no distinction between heathens and Christians, only that males and females may not fraternise. That means you will not form relationships. You work together but nothing else. Anyone who ignores this rule will be punished.

'If you do not instantly obey my commands, or those given by the overseer, Mister McKinnon, or Mister Hunter and Mister Findlay ...' He indicates three men who each carry a whip and have a wooden cudgel hanging from their belt ... 'all of whom you will also call "master" because they represent me, then you will be punished. That's only right and proper.

'If you do not carry out your duties as instructed, if you are in any way disrespectful to your masters, if you steal, damage items, cause disruption or try to run away, then you will be punished. The sooner you understand this and forget the people you used to be, the sooner your lives will improve and you can settle into your new home. This is your home and I'm a fair man. Isn't that so, Mister McKinnon?'

'A very fair man, Mister Drummond.'

Drummond pauses to stare at each of us in turn. I don't think I've ever disbelieved a comment more than what he's just said. All the people who were already here are looking at the ground by their feet; it's only us newcomers who return his gaze. Suddenly, I realise how dangerous this is.

'Calum,' I whisper, 'don't look at him.'

'What?' he whispers back.

'Look down. Don't meet his eye.'

'I do not want to damage my own property,' continues Drummond. 'What sane man would? But sometimes it is necessary. The punishment of an individual is good for everyone because they and others around them can learn from that one person's mistake. See here,' he says, indicating a stout piece of timber rising about seven feet out of the ground with a cross beam that makes the structure appear like the cross of Christ. 'This is the punishment post. Anyone deserving of punishment is brought here.

'And over there ...' He points at a huge tree standing by itself, which is different to those shading the house. One sturdy branch has its end supported by a thick plank. A short distance away, two wooden stakes protrude from the ground. 'That is the hanging tree.'

I feel terribly sick. My left leg starts trembling and I can't stop it. Someone, Alan I think, groans.

'Your arrival is timely because one misguided slave has refused to obey the rules, even though I have made them as easy to understand as possible. You can see the fate that awaits anyone who does not follow instructions. Mister McKinnon, please arrange the necessary.'

I hadn't noticed that Hunter and Findlay have left and they reappear, dragging a young black man whose ankles are heavily chained. He's crying out in terror, begging for forgiveness. When they tie his arms to the cross beam, the horrifying realisation dawns on me that we've been positioned to get the clearest view – to learn from one person's mistake.

Drummond shakes his head, as if this display greatly pains him. 'Oh, Joseph, why do you make me do this?'

'Master! Master! I'm sorry. Please tell me what I've done wrong and I promise I'll never do it again. I swear.'

This brief exchange makes me wonder whether the slave called Joseph has actually disobeyed any rules – or is this barbaric display really because of us? The thought fills me with emotions I don't know how to put into words.

'It's just not that simple, Joseph. If only life was simple. Wouldn't that be good, Mister McKinnon?'

'It would be very good, Mister Drummond.'

'Well, do your duty, Mister McKinnon. Do your Christian duty.'

Terrible raised scars criss-cross the young man's back, marks of previous whippings. He's sobbing uncontrollably as the overseer moves into position, flicking the whip out to its full length behind him. Knots have been tied into it every six inches or so to cause greater injury.

The first crack of leather on skin makes several people call out, as if it's them being hit, and the swishing of the rope is accompanied by crying and wailing. Drummond watches, a tiny smile on his face. The brutality is staggering. Blood is soon flowing freely down the man's back and when bits of flesh start to come away, the whip makes a wet, slapping noise as it hits. Alan bends over, retching.

Despite all the horrors I've seen, the fighting at Bothwell, the cruelty in Greyfriars, the hangings in Ayr, this is so much worse. It feels ... intimate, as if we're all taking part, that we're the ones holding this poor man's arms against those posts. Yet I can't tear away my gaze, can't even blink. It is a sight of such inhumanity that I can only believe it's happening by bearing witness.

It's not long before Joseph makes no sound and hangs limply from the post.

'Thank you, Mister McKinnon,' says Drummond, clearly pleased by the demonstration and reaction to it. 'He can be untied and the ropes removed from the new arrivals' wrists.'

Hunter walks along our line and frees our hands. No one moves. No one speaks. There's no doubting that Drummond's barbarous demonstration has achieved its aim – we are completely and utterly terrified.

* * *

As Joseph is carried back to one of the huts, we're taken away by Hunter and Findlay with almost everyone else. I notice that it's the children and the most elderly who remain behind and I assume this is because whatever work awaits us is too strenuous for them. Goodness knows how we'll manage. We've had no food or water since yesterday and I'm struggling just to walk. About fifteen minutes later Hunter shouts out an order.

'Irish, tell them what to do and be quick about it.'

Hunter and Findlay carry on walking with the male slaves and servants while the women amongst us go into the nearest field. A large man with curly brown hair remains with us. I can't fathom his expression and he doesn't speak until the others are too far away to hear.

'My name's Rory. If you think you've arrived in Hell, you're right. If you think that Drummond is a mad bastard, you're right. If you think your lives can't possibly get any worse, you're wrong. Never, *ever* upset Drummond or his three henchmen. There is no law on this plantation other than Drummond's law. Understand that and do it quickly because he meant everything he said earlier about punishment, and also about calling them "master". The word will stick in your gullet like a copy of Laud's liturgy, but just do it.

'For what's left of today, you'll help the women weed this field so that we can plant sugar canes in it. We've lost some servants and slaves and have got behind with the work that needs to be done.'

'What do you mean, you lost them?' asks Calum.

'Oh, we know where they are,' replies Rory, deadpan. 'You'll find them in the cemetery. You'll work and eat by the bell. When it rings at six in the morning, make sure you're ready to leave. When it rings at eleven, everyone, slaves and servants, goes back for a midday meal. We go out again at the one o'clock bell and work until six. We don't work on Sundays, but if the mood takes him and he's not too drunk, we have to listen to Drummond telling us how lucky we are and about how this is all part of God's great plan.'

'We haven't eaten since yesterday,' says Calum.

'That can't be helped now. You'll have to wait until the evening meal.'

'What about water?' asks Alan.

'In that bucket over there. If it's empty, ask one of the women to refill it. Hunter and Findlay will be looking for an excuse to give you a beating so don't wander off by yourself unless you need a shit, in which case there's a ditch by that far edge. You'll find it by the smell. This is the only valid reason for you not to be working ... that or the fact you've dropped down dead, and even then you might still get a beating.'

* * *

My hands are sliced fiercely by an extremely tough vine which is like no plant I've ever encountered. We're told that these withes can rapidly invade a planted field, wrapping themselves around the sugar canes and pulling them down to the ground, destroying the crop. Apparently withes and rats are constant enemies.

The female slaves show us how to dig out the roots using a small, specially shaped spade. None of us can match them in effort or output, and by the time we hear the bell I can barely move my arms. We follow the women like ancient, bent figures almost in their grave. Behind us, male slaves and servants head in from fields further away. Calum comes up beside me. We haven't spoken since starting the work.

'You're trembling,' he says. 'Will you make it back without help?'

'Yes. I mustn't draw attention to myself. It's not far, then we can rest. We should speak to Rory, to understand more about this place. I think we can trust what he says.'

I try to smile, but my face won't respond. I want to take Calum in my arms, but we can't show any physical affection towards each other. I must always remember my new identity, though I wonder at the sanity of it and whether it's me or the world that has gone mad. How did a girl from the quiet Ayrshire village of Coylton end up on a plantation in Barbados disguised as a man?

The compound where the slaves and servants live is far enough from the big house to be out of sight of it. When we arrive, the six of us lie on the ground and I instantly fall into unconsciousness. It seems like minutes later when I feel someone kicking the sole of one of my feet.

'Wake up if you want food,' says Rory, walking along our line and waking each of us with a kick. 'You can sleep later. Come on! If you miss this meal, you'll be hungry until tomorrow.'

My entire body feels as though it's in spasm and it requires a huge effort to roll on to my front in order to get to my knees and then stand.

'You can eat with any of the men but stay clear of the women. You might work alongside them during the day, but once that bell goes, you don't speak to them unless there's a really good reason, and that needs to be a really good reason to Drummond, and even the Lord Almighty doesn't know what goes on in his head.'

Rory is surprisingly honest about the owner but, as with earlier, we are the only people who can hear him. He's looking at me and I feel as if he's almost reading my thoughts. There's a keen mind behind his gruff exterior.

'Never openly criticise Drummond or the others. What I've said to you today is for your ears only. You keep your mouths shut. Understood?'

We murmur or nod our replies and follow him in silence to an area where three of the older, less able male slaves are serving food from a couple of long planks set upon the stumps of two trees. As we shuffle forward in the queue, I can see the food more clearly. I don't know what the first item is. Calum has obviously had the same thought as he asks Rory, who's just in front of us.

'What's the yellow stuff?'

'Loblolly,' says Rory. 'It's maize, pounded with a mortar and boiled in water until you get a thick substance that can be cut up into slices. You won't be here long before you have nightmares about having to eat more loblolly. Isn't that right, Abraham?'

'I dream every night it's chasing me through the fields,' says a black man ahead.

'Do you ever get caught?'

'Not yet, Rory, but I'm slowing down.'

'Keep running, my friend,' says Rory. 'In your dreams you can run.'

We each pick up a wooden plate and spoon then we're served a slice along with a ladle of green beans which I don't recognise. We help ourselves to something called a potato, which is hot, and a hunk of strange-looking bread. Trying to work out what this is made of defeats me. It's not from any type of flour that I know.

As if an unspoken decision has been made, the three of us find somewhere together. Around us, small groups gather and sit quietly talking and eating. The women and children are further away. As usual I let Calum speak for both of us.

'I'm Calum and this is Douglas. How did you end up here?'

'Because I was stupid enough to believe the lies that the English bastards told us in Ireland. The whole country was starving. People were dying in their beds and dropping in the street. So the English, ever keen to rid themselves of the troublesome Catholic population, promised us a new beginning in America ... plenty of good jobs and food plus fertile land just waiting to be ploughed.' He shakes his head ruefully.

'Of course, no one had money for the journey, so the offer was that if we agreed to be indentured servants for five years, that would cover our transportation and after that we would be freed and given an agreed amount of money.'

'There were others with you?'

'Three of us from Kilmurry in County Clare. On the day we arrived, it became clear immediately that we weren't servants in any sense that we would have understood, and if we broke any Barbados laws, we would be punished by having our period of servitude extended. I've had mine increased by four years.'

'That's a huge amount! Why?'

'Because one day I ran away. I hardly got beyond the next plantation before the slave hunters and their damn bloodhounds caught up and brought me back in chains.'

'And the other two from Ireland?'

'Dead from being overworked, poorly fed, disease. There's always sickness somewhere but every few years something serious sweeps throughout the island, killing large numbers. The only things you can guarantee will grow are cemeteries and sugar cane.'

We're silent for a while, trying to digest the strange food as well as the information we're being given.

'Don't try to understand Barbados by comparing it to anything you've ever known in Scotland,' says Rory. 'The rules are made by a handful of powerful men who are themselves ruled by making money. In years gone by there were ex-Cavaliers and Roundheads who would have been the fiercest of enemies in Britain, while here they were great friends because their success as landowners depended upon them sticking together. Now we're into the next generations of those people.

'Amongst the forced indentured servants like you, there used to be captured Royalist soldiers defeated by Cromwell working alongside captured Covenanters sent here by the king. Poor Irish and rich Scottish lairds worked alongside convicts and killers, as well as a few ordinary folk spirited from the streets.'

'Spirited?' asks Calum.

'Kidnapped. It's a very lucrative business. Gangs operate around ports like Liverpool, Bristol and London. But those unfortunate souls tend to be shipped to Virgina or Maryland, in America. There are even a couple of free men here on the Drummond plantation.'

'What, completely free?'

'Yes. If people have the money to pay for their passage, then they emigrate, arriving at their destination without any obligations. They can then sell their craft. The blacksmith and carpenter make a good living from their labours. Despite being English, they're good men – just don't cross them. The most important man here is a slave called Thaddeus. He runs the boiling-house and has the greatest understanding of the entire sugar-making process of anyone. That's him over there, talking to Shoshana.' He dips his head in their direction.

'I thought men couldn't talk to women.'

'Even McKinnon would hesitate to hurt Thaddeus.'

Calum and I are silent. The enormity of what we are being told is almost beyond our comprehension.

'Whatever you may be feeling, be grateful you're servants and not slaves,' says Rory. 'These days, they provide the main labour on the plantations. You'll find every type of owner, even religious groups like Quakers and Anglicans who conveniently convince themselves that it says in the Bible they can own heathens. They're brought from all over Africa and often deliberately mixed up so their different languages make it much more difficult to organise a revolt.'

'Revolt?'

'It happens. In the past the blacks and the Irish have sometimes risen up together.'

'They've never succeeded?' asks Calum.

'No, and the retributions have been terrible. Oh, the owners might despise the blacks, but by God they hate the Irish.'

A man who barely looks eighteen walks past and Rory calls him over. 'Thomas, this is Douglas and Calum. They're Covenanters.'

We say hello and the man nods in reply before walking on without speaking or even looking at our faces. Once he's moved away, Rory speaks again.

'Thomas is a Covenanter.'

'A Covenanter! I must speak with him.'

Calum rises to his feet as if to go after the man that very moment. He's so impulsive at times, like Samuel.

'No, leave him be,' says Rory firmly. 'Let him come to you if he wants. Thomas has only been here a few months and he's a very troubled young man. I watch out for him where I can.'

'How did he end up here?'

'That's a story for him to tell. Everyone here has their own story.' He studies me closely. 'You're quiet, Douglas.'

'I listen.'

'Well, listen to this. Be careful not to draw attention to yourself in any way. Calum, watch out for Findlay.'

I peer at him, puzzled. 'Why Findlay? What would he want with Calum?'

'Just watch out. While you're here, you'll encounter cruelty, desires and activities such as you wouldn't believe possible from another human being. Hunter and Findlay are amongst the worst. They were forced indentured servants once, before my time.'

'Servants!'

'Convicts, sold like thousands of others. Every so often the British government decides that emptying the jails in England by transporting the inmates is a good way of solving a problem and making money. Those two proved themselves to be so sadistic that Drummond released them to work for him. They're fanatically loyal. Even without orders, they'll hurt people because it's what they enjoy.'

'Lord save us,' whispers Calum.

'Yes, well there's a question. Drummond will preach at us on a Sunday about forgiveness from that bloody pulpit of his, then have a man whipped an hour later because the fancy takes him. Yet there are owners who would leave a worse taste than him.'

'Are there no good plantation owners?'

'There are some you might consider decent, even caring in their own way for those who work the land. It's mainly chance where anyone ends up. The degree of misery of slaves and servants is largely determined by the character of the owner. I don't understand what we've done in our lives to be punished so severely, yet here we are under Drummond. He's as mad as a March hare, and it likely won't take long before you're hopping around in the same field.'

* * *

There are four men's huts. Alan and the other three have been allocated the second hut, while Calum and I get the first. Inside we find half a dozen beds that have been built with rough bits of timber. There are a similar number of hammocks, all occupied. The rest of the space is taken up with thin straw mattresses. We can smell them from the doorway but after so long in the hold of the ship, all I care about is not sleeping on a hard surface. We find two together with no one in them.

'It'll be better when we understand the routine of the plantation,' whispers Calum.

I've been feeling increasingly ill all evening and am trying hard not to cry. 'I guess so.'

'And tomorrow's Saturday, so we just have to get through that and on Sunday we can rest and get ourselves sorted, maybe get cleaned up and be given new clothes.'

I try to speak but it comes out as a huge sob. Calum reaches across and takes my hand. It's gloomy enough for nobody to see, and who's bothered anyway?

'It will get better. We haven't suffered everything for our lives to end here. God hasn't forgotten us.'

Perhaps, but right now, in this dirty hut at the end of the world, it does feel as though we've been misplaced. I sniff. 'Let's get to sleep.'

He squeezes my hand then lets go, and I try to find a position that offers some comfort. Men are still coming into the hut and a figure lies on the mattress on the other side of me. There are some murmured conversations but mostly people are too weary for anything other than rest.

I want it so much, but as the minutes pass, I find sleep evades me. My mind is like an overflowing river, too full for even the tiniest part to be still. Images of the day push each other out of the way, demanding my attention – the extraordinary scenes at the harbour, the unfettered violence on the plantation, the insanity of Drummond. I sense such a terrible danger from this man, and in the darkness I can't shake off the notion that our lives will be bound together in some unnatural way.

And I wonder about Samuel, whether he's alive. And if he is, how will I ever get back to him now?

There are a great many noises outside, with chirping, screeching and howling so strange to me that I can't identify if they're made by birds, beasts or demons. Something bites my leg and I kick out. I hear a rat scuttle away. That sound at least is familiar.

Next to me Calum snores quietly, something else I know well. Somewhere a man weeps. This must be a person who has been here for a while as we're the only new people in this hut. There's more than Thomas in this place who's troubled beyond endurance. I shift, trying to get more comfortable. The mattress is alive with vermin. Eventually, I fall into a troubled sleep and dream of being eaten by cockroaches.

27

Violet
13 March 1680, Drummond Plantation, Barbados

Someone is gently shaking my shoulder and I finally open my eyes to see the outline of the slave who had been next to me.

'Eat,' he says, before heading to the door.

Other figures are already moving about in the gloom. I realise that my dream reflects something of reality. The sweat and heat from my body has attracted the occupants of the mattress and my back is on fire with insect bites.

'Calum. Calum, wake up.'

I have to shake him several times before he shows any sign of coming around. He was like that as a small boy, when he would stay overnight with us instead of going home with Samuel and his parents.

'We have to get up.'

'We've only just gone to sleep.'

'Tomorrow we sleep. Now we eat.'

We follow the stooped figures heading silently towards a nearby ditch that's used by everyone as a latrine. People find as private a spot as they can and no one takes any notice of me. Drummond's strictness about men and women not fraternising wouldn't be out of place being mentioned in a staunch

Presbyterian sermon, yet at the same time we're thrown together in the most intimate of situations that makes the idea of not speaking seem ridiculous.

As we trudge out to the fields, I can't believe that I'll get through the day. My entire body hurts more than I've ever known and I dread having to dig out more withes.

'You don't look well,' says Calum quietly.

'I'll be all right. I'm not sure if the food helped or not.'

'More loblolly to start the day.'

To our surprise, we leave the women to continue clearing the area they were working on yesterday and are taken with the other male slaves and servants to fields further away. The six of us stay together and also keep close to Rory, whom we look to for advice almost as if we're frightened children seeking reassurance from an adult. He's aware of this and in his gruff way is kind.

'We plant sugar canes throughout most of the year,' he explains, 'so that we have a constant supply for the Ingenio.'

'What's that?' asks Calum.

'A monster. It's part of the processing plant and you'll not see its equal anywhere in Europe. The cane is usually ready to harvest at fifteen months but once cut it has to be processed within a couple of days otherwise the damn stuff starts to ferment and then it's useless.'

'So what are we doing?' asks Alan.

'You're going to cut canes, and if you thought yesterday was tough, I can promise that you'll wish you were back weeding within ten minutes.'

We pass field after field of sugar canes, gently moving seas of different colours and hues depending upon the maturity of the plants, some of which are less than a foot high. Others are taller than me and I can't see beyond the nearest rows. Finally, we reach an area that is currently being harvested.

A few slaves have been carrying boxes and when they lay these down many men go to them and take out a small billhook, the curved blades of which appear to have been recently sharpened. They immediately set about cutting down canes and we watch with a mixture of fascination and dread.

Off to our right is a field that has been completely cleared of any remnants of vegetation. Here, other slaves and servants work side by side digging narrow trenches about six inches across and the same in depth. I assume this is for planting, but I don't give this any further thought because my attention is suddenly taken by an animal noise close behind me. I turn to see five mules standing in a line.

'Irish! Get them bloody working!' shouts Hunter.

'Pick up a billhook and follow me,' says Rory, who has stayed silent as we've gazed in wonder.

We gather a little way from those already frantically busy. He puts a hand around the stem of a sugar cane as though he would like to strangle it.

'You will learn to hate this plant. You will hate it waking up in the morning and going to bed at night. You will hate it while forcing down yet more loblolly and when you're squatting over the stinking latrine. Every second of your life here you will have a hatred in your hearts that you wouldn't have believed possible for something growing in the soil. It's because of this plant that we're here. Growing and harvesting these bastards kills people more quickly than any other crop in the colonies.

'Listen carefully. Hold the cane like this and cut it about six inches from the ground, with one swipe of the billhook. Don't damage the buds near the bottom or you'll be punished. This is where next year's shoots grow from.'

Rory demonstrates and seconds later the cane is free. 'Looks easy, doesn't it? Take off the top with one stroke then trim off all the blades growing out the sides.' The billhook is almost a blur as the metal edge slices off each leaf precisely where it comes off the stem, while not once even nicking the latter. Moments later he's holding a perfectly trimmed cane, about six foot in length and one inch thick.

My panic grows with every heartbeat. I'm so awkward with tools that require judging distances and I fear I'm about to lose some fingers.

'You work without stopping until the bell at eleven.'

'That's five hours!' says Alan.

'You won't last,' says Rory. 'I'll tell you that now.'

'Then what do we do?' asks Calum.

'Pray, if you still believe there's a God.'

Slaves walk by carrying bundles of canes that they've cut and tied in the time we've been trying to understand what we're meant to do. We watch as they lay them across wooden crooks that have been fitted to the packsaddles on the mules. I'm surprised at how calmly the animals stand. When the first mule has three faggots loaded on the crook, a man pats its rump and the beast moves off, heading back towards the compound by itself.

'Hunter isn't going to give us any more time,' says Rory. 'And he's put me in the other field so I'm not going to be with you. Good luck.'

With this Rory returns his billhook to the box and walks away. We stand looking at each other in disbelief.

'Let's get started,' says Alan.

We spread out, finding spaces amongst the slaves and servants. No one can help anyone else in this and as I take hold of my first sugar cane it's not hate I feel but fear. This innate plant will sweeten the drink and food of people with no knowledge of the pain involved in bringing it to their table.

Remember Bothwell . . . Remember the cause . . . This is a plant.

I put a hand between the leaves and take firm hold of the stem, then I position my feet and body as I saw Rory do.

It's just a plant.

I aim for a spot about six inches above the ground, making sure my other hand is clear in case I misjudge. I've never used a tool like this before, and the balance is odd. I move my hand further up the stem but this makes my stance awkward. Finally, I swing the billhook as hard as I can. It bites into the cane without cutting it.

'Damn!'

I glance around, worried that Hunter will have noticed my failure. There's no sign of him, so I wiggle the blade free and hack again. As soon as the stem is cut, the weight of the plant simply pulls it out of my left hand and it falls to the ground. As quickly as possible I remove the top, which contains a lot of foliage, and work my way along, cutting off the leaves. It must be more than five minutes later when I'm left with a cane that's shorter than it should be and which has bits of leaf still poking from a stem that's been damaged in several places.

I don't know whether to try and make this one neater or start another one because I'll be punished for not working fast enough. I can't help it and start to cry. I feel so terribly alone. The tears won't stop. I'm going to be beaten. I stand holding this stupid, overgrown stalk and can't stop crying because I'm so frightened.

A slave walks nearby, carrying canes. He stops, glances around then quickly lays down his bundle and comes over. Without speaking he takes the stem from me and within seconds removes the remaining leaves. With astonishing speed he cuts and trims three canes and puts them by my feet, then he takes my damaged one and feeds it into the middle of his bundle. He picks up his load and continues to the waiting mules. It's only as he walks away that I notice the fresh lines of blood coming through the back of his shirt.

* * *

There's a shadow across my face.

'You Covenanters should be drowned,' spits Hunter.

He's already kicked me once, but I don't attempt to get up. I fainted, and when I woke I lay where I fell, unable to continue. My billhook is nowhere in sight. This work is so far beyond my ability that no threat will make me carry on. I think Hunter knows it and there's less pleasure for him in beating someone who's beyond the point of responding.

'Get up!'

He kicks me again and I gasp at the pain in my ribs but don't move. He's frustrated yet seems to accept that all he can actually do is stand there kicking me, without obtaining the result he wants.

'Drink some water then start carrying the bundles to the mules.'

With this order he storms off, muttering curses about Covenanters. In a strange way I feel that I've won a small victory.

Rory was right. Long before the bell rings at eleven, we six from the *Sophia* have had to stop cutting canes. We've been helped in this by the arrival of McKinnon, who rode by during his regular inspection of the plantation. The overseer is evil, but he's driven by profit, and it was instantly apparent to him that it wasn't productive to have the newly arrived servants cutting canes.

The sound of the handbell carries clearly across the fields and the two mules waiting to be loaded turn around and plod back to the compound. We follow and our small group is soon joined by Rory.

'You didn't last,' he says.

'No,' says Calum.

'Well, Hunter won't be able to make you attempt that work again, not until McKinnon is certain you can handle it.'

'Is that meant to make me feel better?' asks Calum.

'While you're on the plantation you have to make the most of even the smallest improvement to your life. Such things can make a big difference.'

I sense that Calum realises he's being ungracious to someone who is not only trying to help but probably represents our greatest hope of surviving.

'Thanks,' he says.

'Save your thanks,' says Rory. 'There are terrors and torments on this plantation that are beyond anything you could imagine in your worst nightmare. You're only just getting started.'

28

Violet
14 March 1680, Drummond Plantation, Barbados

It's Sunday morning, there's been no bell and the pleasure of sleeping is unbelievable. I eat another meal of loblolly while sitting outside amongst servants and slaves. People are mainly quiet and reflective, although there is definitely a change compared to the last two days.

Hunter comes over. 'Irish, collect clothes for them before going to the beach.'

'The beach?' asks Alan, once Hunter has left.

'This plantation reaches the shore,' says Rory. 'Every Sunday morning we all go there to scrub ourselves and our clothes. You can stink like a corpse during the week, but Drummond expects everyone to be clean on a Sunday.'

Rory goes off and returns with a new pair of coarse linen drawers and a shirt plus shoes for the six of us. Shortly after this we set off with everyone else, some slaves carrying large wicker baskets fitted with lids. I can just make out near the front that children and adults with long sticks are herding dozens upon dozens of noisy turkeys, which set the speed for those walking behind.

We head in a different direction to the one we've previously taken, through parts of the compound we've not been in. The number of buildings, huts and structures is greater than you would find in many Ayrshire villages. The purpose of some is obvious, like the blacksmith's forge, but the reason for many is a mystery; presumably they're needed for processing the sugar cane. We pass enclosures containing mules and hogs, as well as pens for hens and a species of black duck I've never seen before.

Until now I've only been aware of sugar canes disappearing into the distance as far as I can see, but this morning we pass large areas set aside as pasture for horses and oxen, which munch away with no interest in people passing by. Thomas is close to us. We've yet to speak to him following our brief introduction by Rory, but Calum sees his chance now.

'Thomas, why are there turkeys ahead?'

The young man studies us as we walk, until finally, he replies. 'They're being taken to the potatoes.'

'To eat them?'

'To eat caterpillars. The crop is infested and the most effective way to get rid of them is to let the turkeys roam free. They won't stray and will easily be gathered up and driven back later today.' Thomas looks at the ground to indicate that the conversation is over.

We continue in silence for a short while before I speak quietly to Calum. 'Samuel once said that my eyebrows were like caterpillars.'

'Did he?'

'We were so young and innocent and in love back then.'

'I miss him every minute,' says Calum. 'He was always there watching out for me.'

'How did our youth and innocence leave us so totally, almost without us realising?' I ask.

'But there's still love,' he says. 'And that has to be the most important.'

It's not long before we reach long rows of mounded earth and watch as the turkeys head eagerly into the foliage to gorge themselves on the tiny enemy. They've clearly done this before and are left to it while everyone moves on at a faster pace.

We pass fields growing cotton, corn and the green beans we've so far had with every meal and which I've heard called bonavist. A little further on we walk by several acres used for fruits and there are extraordinary, lush displays that leave us wide-eyed.

'Is this real?' says Calum.

I'm too astonished at the scenery to ask which bit of the surrounding land he's referring to. For a while everything is hidden when we enter an area enclosed by thick vegetation that's growing wild, then the path suddenly opens up to reveal the beach. I'm so awed by the view that I don't immediately realise the hot, white sand is teeming with crabs crawling in every direction.

'I've never even imagined there could be somewhere like this,' says Calum.

People come past us on either side and those already ahead make for the water, stripping off their clothes as they get nearer ... slaves and servants, men, women and children.

'Calum.'

'I see.'

'What am I going to do?'

Without me realising, Alan has caught up and overheard our exchange.

'Douglas,' he says, almost hesitating, 'we know there is an important secret to be kept. Why don't the six of us go to the furthest point allowed and keep close together?'

I can't think of anything else to suggest so we survivors of the *Crown of London* walk along the beach to a tall wooden post that marks the boundary of where we're permitted.

'What happens if we carry on?' I ask.

'We get shot, or at least shot at,' says Calum, tilting his head towards the rocks. 'Look up there. Apparently McKinnon always sits on that rock with his musket. Findlay is somewhere close by with his. Even if you could avoid them by swimming out of range along the shoreline there's nowhere to escape to around this part of the island.'

I wonder how much thought Calum has already given to escaping. Just like in Greyfriars, he's not one to give up.

'Well, let's try to get ourselves clean,' I say.

The men position themselves so that anyone looking in our direction while we undress would be unlikely to see anything amiss and we walk into the sea in our little group. I've unwound the long strip of material that I use to bind my breasts and carry this with me so that I can wash it.

My skin has been cut, bitten by insects and rats and is still covered in the sores that developed during our long imprisonment. We're all in the same sorry state and enter the sea with small, hesitant steps because every inch that the water creeps up our bodies results in severe stinging, making us gasp and cry out.

However, once I've reached a certain depth, I let myself fall forward to be immersed and get the last of the stabbing pains over with in one go. Sound and vision are instantly muted and I expect it to feel good, but within seconds my lungs squeeze tight with panic. The sea pulls me violently through the broken hull of the ship. There's no air, only water. Samuel's gone. I'm drowning, drowning. Frantically I thrash about as if I've never swum in my life. My head eventually breaks the surface.

'Help me! Help me!'

Calum has hold of one of my arms, although at first I don't realise. 'You're safe. Put your feet down.'

'What!'

'Put your feet down.'

I stand and discover that the water only comes up to my shoulders.

'I thought ...'

'Yes, I know. I've already had to stand Alan upright. We've all got that memory. Just swim about here for a while and don't go out of your depth. You'll soon be fine.'

I stick close to the shore. Further along the beach people wash themselves then retrieve their clothes and clean them. I do my best to wash the strip of binding material and Calum takes it back to lay out on the sand. When I try to remove the dirt from my body, it's so engrained into the skin that I'm having little success. Calum comes over to me holding a clump of seaweed in his hand.

'Your back looks awful. Let me try this.'

Gently he begins to wipe my neck and shoulders. The seaweed is much more effective than using fingers and soon we've each of us got a handful of the plant and are rubbing our arms and legs, with people helping others when they can't reach an area. Inch by inch, the layers of dirt wash off. I could weep with relief to feel a little more human again.

When our group walks back on to the beach the men shield me, acting so like older brothers that I'm reminded of the time Calum, Hamish and Samuel shielded me while I changed into men's clothing in Greyfriars Kirkyard, in a life so long ago it's difficult to believe it was mine. I quickly rebind my breasts then we dress in our new clothes. With no orders to do anything else, we find a spot clear of crabs and lie down to watch the activities taking place.

I hadn't realised that nets had been brought with us and a large number of the male slaves and servants are spread out in the water in a huge semicircle. It's obvious they've done this before as they're working efficiently together to force fish into the shallows, where women and children skilfully scoop them up using shallow trugs made of something that looks like willow. Others pick up crabs and put them into the large wicker baskets, the lids held down with a heavy stone or a small child to prevent escape.

'This is an extraordinary place,' says Alan. 'It could be paradise.'

'Perhaps it is for a few,' says Calum. 'As for everyone else ...'

'It's Hell,' I say, 'worse than the strictest of ministers has ever described during the fiercest of sermons.'

Everyone agrees.

* * *

People rarely know if Drummond is going to speak from his pulpit on a Sunday until he actually does. Today he's ridden off to another plantation with Isaac, his personal body slave, so we know this is not happening. It seems there's always an unease about the place whether he's here or not. McKinnon beats people to make them work faster but he tends not to bother much when they're not in the fields. However, since Hunter and Findlay enjoy inflicting pain, Sundays can be even more dangerous if they can get away with their brutality unchecked.

Everyone heads back together, the baskets so heavy with the catch that they're carried between two men. When we reach the fields growing fruit, people stop at the plantains and I discover adults are allowed one bunch each per week. An older male slave takes charge, ensuring that a similar amount is handed out to each person. We wait our turn then continue our journey carrying a bunch of plantains. It's far heavier than I expected.

Talitha, the cook from the big house, chooses a selection of fish plus several crabs, which have had their claws tied together with short strips of withes. A couple of slaves carry them in baskets to the big house and I assume these will feed Drummond over the coming days.

People disperse around the compound, a few of the adults help the children tend to the larger animals, while the smaller children feed the hens and other fowl. Over to one side two older men run whetstones along the edges of the billhooks used to cut the sugar canes. Others are preparing fires. Some of the women are mending clothes or doing something with withes and at first I can't understand what until I realise they're making ropes. Everyone seems to have a purpose except us.

'What do we do now?' asks Calum, the two of us somehow ending up standing alone.

'I don't know. Perhaps we can just look around?'

For a while we watch the various tasks being carried out but then we wander away with no particular aim. There's no sign of Hunter or Findlay. At the stables the horses are being fed and groomed and it's obvious that they're well cared for. Our astonishment at the complexity of the place increases every few minutes and we soon come upon men, women and children tending to areas that have been set aside for people to grow their own food. Calum and I watch for a while.

'What can you identify?' I say.

'How did I know you were going to ask me that? Mmm ... cucumber ... peas ... pumpkins. That's it. I don't know what the other things are.'

'There's a pile of yams over there,' I say, 'and those dirty roots are casava, which is what the bread is made of. I overheard one of the woman explaining to a girl how poisonous casava is if it isn't used properly.'

'No wonder it tastes odd. I bet that's not what Drummond eats. Did you notice that men and women talk to each other without any hesitation?'

It's only as he says these words that I realise this is what's been going around in my head as the thing that shouldn't be happening. 'It seems there's no problem fraternising on a Sunday,' I reply.

We're curious about the sugar-making process but wary of walking somewhere that's forbidden, so we look upon the group of stone-built structures from a short distance away. The door of the nearest building is open and we finally gain enough courage to go up the stairs. The man we know as Thaddeus is inspecting the insides of five huge copper vessels. When he realises we're present there's a moment of indecision with none of us knowing how to respond.

'What's this place?' asks Calum.

'The boiling-house,' says Thaddeus, beckoning us inside.

'Can you explain what happens?'

'Juice from the nearby millhouse flows into this cistern,' he says, pointing to a large iron container set against a wall, 'and from here it goes into the first clarifying copper then on to the next copper and the next. We keep the liquid boiling with fires in the room below. Each copper has its own man skimming the debris that floats to the top so that when the juice reaches the fifth copper it's clear.'

We study the structure in front of us and I see that the bottom of the vessels sits lower than the floor we stand on.

Off to one side steps leading downstairs are visible and when the furnaces are lit it must be like walking into Hades. Several shallow wooden ladles lean against a nearby wall, which I guess are used for stirring and scooping out bits of leaf and plant that have reached this far. Father would have been fascinated by this, although not in these dire circumstances.

'But the juice is still a liquid?' asks Calum.

Thaddeus nods, appearing to appreciate that Calum has grasped this point. The man is clearly proud of his knowledge.

'It would never turn into sugar if I didn't add temper, made from wood ash. If the moment isn't chosen correctly then that entire batch will be ruined. Every stage in the boiling-house requires skill, even running the furnaces because the coppers are heated to different temperatures.'

'So what's happening now?'

'I'm checking that the coppers have been cleaned properly. At midnight we'll light the furnaces and begin processing the sugar canes. This work won't stop until next Saturday evening when we'll let the fires go out.'

'Day and night?' asks Calum in shock. 'That means there have to be men working here around the clock!'

'The canes cut yesterday have to be processed during Sunday night as they can't be left any longer. As long as canes are brought in from the fields, we have to be running everything here, and we can't have fires with no liquid in the coppers or they'll be damaged. There's no halt to any of it.'

'What's going on here!'

We turn to find Findlay standing in the doorway. He's clearly been drinking heavily and intent on inflicting violence on someone if he can find the right person.

'I'm explaining how the process works to the new servants, master.'

'They don't need to know!'

'They asked me to explain, master.'

There's a tense standoff. Findlay has a hand on his cudgel and is struggling to control his anger. I suspect that faced with any other slave on the plantation he would be brutally bludgeoning them by now, but he can't touch Thaddeus, whose judgement can mean the difference between profit or loss. Findlay stares at Calum for a long while then glances at me. It's enough to make my flesh crawl.

'I'll be dealing with you two another time,' he says, before turning around, almost falling down the stairs and staggering off.

* * *

In the evening we sit around the compound in large groups, eating boiled crab and fish baked over open fires with potatoes and sweetcorn. Every moment on Barbados is so extreme it's impossible to know what the next few minutes hold for any of us. Danger and fear are interspersed with kindness and friendship like two sides of a coin that's spinning in the air – and you don't know what side will land facing you.

Thaddeus has been explaining to Calum and Alan how he ended up in charge of processing the sugar canes and that he's training other slaves because men working in the boiling-house often die young.

'Why?'

I shouldn't have blurted out the question, but for once my curiosity has overcome my caution.

Thaddeus shrugs. 'I don't know. They just normally do, despite our better conditions.'

'Better conditions?' says Alan.

'We all have hammocks in our hut.'

It doesn't seem much of a benefit if the work means people don't live long, although the prospect of keeping off the floor at night is very appealing. I've heard that scorpions are one of many constant dangers.

We watch how others bake plantains on the edge of the fires, wrapping them first in large leaves. Calum removes several plantains from one of our bunches and follows the example. He sits down as Rory joins us, carrying a jug and wooden beakers.

'Here,' he says, handing out the beakers to Calum, Alan, Thaddeus and me. 'It's slightly better than water.' He pours out a dirty-grey liquid.

'What is it?' asks Calum, sniffing suspiciously.

'Mobbie. It's made from potatoes. Don't let your plantains get overdone.'

Alan retrieves them and hands a couple to each of us. We sit in silence for a while then Thaddeus gets up, thanks us for the food and drink, and walks away.

'Where's he going in such a hurry?' says Alan.

'You'll soon find out,' says Rory. 'What's wrong with your foot, Calum?'

'An insect bite, I think.'

I've been aware of him scratching an area of his heel but we're all so covered in bites I hadn't thought to query it.

'In the morning ask Naomi to check it. The old woman over there. Most of the things in Barbados that want to hurt you are visible, from rodent rats to human rats, but some of the insects are so small that you don't know they're on your body until much later. You have to be careful of small bastards called chegoes, because they love to burrow under your skin and need to be removed. One in a foot can make someone go lame.'

At these words every inch of my skin is crawling with invisible chegoes; Scottish midges don't seem so unpleasant any more. But images of burying insects are suddenly swept away by a sound so loud and unexpected that I almost cry out in alarm.

Thaddeus appears around a hut, leading several male slaves beating upon drums with hands and sticks and altering the atmosphere around the compound so dramatically that the change is difficult to comprehend. Many women jump up and begin dancing, hands and feet moving to the furious rhythms so fast that their limbs are almost a blur. Voices sing loudly to the night sky. Then the young men not playing also jump up and begin to dance, though they remain separate to the women.

We sit wide-eyed and open-mouthed at something that could not be more different to the unaccompanied psalms permitted by the Kirk. The power and force created in the small area in which we are gathered is unbelievable.

I've never seen, heard or felt anything like it. And I can *feel* it, in my chest and in my head. As the evening goes on everything is driven out of me ... thoughts, memories, fears ... until I don't know where I am or who I am, except that while those drums continue to vibrate throughout my body, I know I'm not a prisoner.

We are all of us set free.

29

Violet
25 April 1680, Drummond Plantation, Barbados

We've all been gathered near the punishment post. Drummond (I may call him 'master' when speaking but never in my head) is standing in his pulpit. He stares at us in silence and I've come to realise this is part of his method of instilling fear amongst us. It works. The longer he remains silent the more I hear people around me moan and break into sobs. Near to me, Joseph stands, hunched over like an old man and trembling uncontrollably.

'It pains me to damage my own property. What sane man would want to do such a thing?'

He says the same words every time someone is to be punished. It's sickening, as if implying he's the one suffering. I'm not the only one to have been shocked beyond belief at the brutality inflicted upon the slaves, and this is often in situations where they can't possibly work any harder or faster. I've come to understand that sometimes this is not the aim, it's to create a constant state of terror.

'You know what I'm talking about. One of you is guilty of stealing. Come forward now and own up to your theft.'

Nobody moves.

'If no one admits to their heinous crime then one of you will be chosen at random.'

A couple of the women begin wailing and I sense that some of the men are not too far behind. Drummond's control over people is astonishing. We all look at the ground as if this will make us invisible. Without any warning Findlay grabs my arm and pulls me out of the line.

'So be it,' says Drummond. 'Let this man take the blame.'

'Master!' cries Calum, stepping forward. 'It was me! I stole. You should punish me and let this innocent man go.'

Drummond studies both of us. 'Well, what do we have here, Mister McKinnon? A man offering to take a flogging for another.'

'It doesn't seem right to me, Mister Drummond.'

'Nor me, Mister McKinnon. Nor me. The strange thing is I don't believe him, so why would a man make such an unnatural gesture? Tie him to the post.'

Calum takes a step, but Hunter pushes him back and I'm pulled roughly towards the whipping post. My legs collapse beneath me and I plead for mercy as I'm dragged along the ground. I try to hold on to my garments, but Findlay and Hunter take an arm each and rip the shirt from my body.

In front of me McKinnon looks on in surprise. 'What's this?'

He finds a loose end of the material around my breasts and starts to unwind it. Layer by layer, the overseer peels away the binding and my secret. My back is to Drummond and he doesn't understand why McKinnon stands staring at me once the material lies on the ground.

'What's the problem, Mister McKinnon?'

'Tits, Mister Drummond.'

'What!'

'This person has tits.'

Findlay and Hunter laugh. Moments later Drummond stands in front of me and without warning he grabs my breeches and yanks them down to my ankles. Now I'm naked, my arms held outstretched and no way to shield any part of my body.

'Not just tits, Mister McKinnon.'

I'm crying. I can't help it.

'Well, in all my years,' says Drummond. 'A woman disguised as a man. Why would anyone do such a thing, I wonder?'

'Shall I continue?'

'No, Mister McKinnon. Indeed, no. You don't spoil a rare gift such as this.' Drummond lays a huge hairy hand on one of my breasts and leaves it there while he considers. 'Let her go. Whip the blond. Extra lashes, Mister McKinnon, for he's tried to make us look foolish by keeping such a secret.'

* * *

Four men carry Calum into the hut and gently place him face down on a bed. His back is hardly recognisable as flesh and it's all I can do not to be sick. My father had to treat men on board ship who had been flogged and even he used to say there was little that could be done. Calum is barely conscious, moaning occasionally but not moving.

A slave brings over a jug. 'It's Kill-Devil. If you can get him to drink, it will help ease his pain.'

'What else can I do?'

The man shakes his head. 'Keep the rats off him. They'll be attracted by the smell of blood.'

However, we hear Hunter shouting from outside that we're to go back to work. Those around me start to make their way outside and I don't know what to do. I can't leave Calum alone.

Just at that moment a figure slips into the hut. It's Naomi, who is considered the wisest of the women. She's certainly the oldest.

'I will sit with him,' she says. 'You must go. I will stay until you return.'

'Thank you.'

I take one last look at my beautiful Calum, who I held in my arms as a baby, and leave him to the care of this stranger.

* * *

I sit by Calum's bed that night, thinking how people are bound to the plantation by chains of fear that hold them more securely than those used with the largest of ship's anchors. That's why the door to the hut isn't locked and there are no fences. The boundaries are as much in our minds.

And now my secret is out. I'm a woman in a hut full of men, yet everyone carries on as if there's no difference and I feel completely safe, for there is more honour and decency in this stinking, festering hut than in the grand court of the King of Scotland. Calum moans and I take his hand in mine.

'Shhh, I'm here, my love. You're safe now.'

Around me are the sounds of the night. The noises of animals and birds outside join snoring, weeping and the occasional cry of someone reliving in their dreams the nightmare that is their life. I'm so exhausted I feel my head dropping and have to force myself to keep awake. A figure walks quietly towards me in the gloom and for a moment I'm not sure if I'm imagining it.

'You can't sit awake all night,' he says.

'I must.'

'I promise I will keep him safe for the next few hours and then hand over to another who will do the same. We look after each other and you cannot do this alone throughout the night.'

He's right. I can't do it. For the second time that day I rely on strangers for the care of this person I love so much.

* * *

Three days have passed since Calum was beaten and he's been cared for more by the male and female slaves than by me. They're used to having to look after someone who's been whipped. They say it's unusual for a servant to be pulled out of a line and beaten like this, but that strange things happen on this plantation. Rory is right: Drummond is a mad bastard.

I've fallen asleep on the floor when something wakes me, although I'm not sure what. In the gloom of the rushlights I see Abraham sitting by Calum's bed, gently fanning him with a large plantain leaf to try and cool him down as his temperature has been fierce. What's woken me is a strange light and when I glance towards the source I see McKinnon holding a lantern, walking silently amongst the sleeping figures. He's checking faces.

When he gets nearer, I close my eyes and pretend to be asleep. It doesn't do any good. Moments later I feel him kicking my foot. I can't simply ignore it and when I raise my head he indicates that I should follow him. I stand up. Abraham has stopped fanning and watches in silence. Cautiously I step between the men. Once outside McKinnon quietly closes the door.

'The master wants you.'

'Why?'

He laughs. It's a horrible sound. 'Don't be stupid. He *wants* you.'

The overseer grips my left arm firmly and marches me all the way to the big house. The opulence in the entrance hall is staggering but there's no time to notice details as we walk up the wide staircase and along a corridor. He knocks on a door, opens it without waiting for a reply, and pushes me inside.

The bedroom is enormous, the expensive furniture and fittings illuminated brightly by numerous tall candles. Drummond stands near a bureau drinking from a crystal glass and studying me across a deep red rug that probably cost more than the manse in Coylton.

'What's your name?'

My body is trembling so much I can hardly speak. 'Violet.'

'And why are you here, Violet, pretending to be a man?'

I hesitate yet can't think of a benefit in not telling the truth, at least enough of it to explain how I've ended up in Barbados. He watches me intently as I relate my story and, surprisingly, he appears genuinely interested. There is intelligence behind those eyes, alongside the evil.

'I've not had a white woman in a long time, so you and I are going to get to know each other really well.'

He says this as if speaking at a town meeting while I almost collapse on the floor in fright. I force myself to reply with as much confidence as possible.

'I'm a decent, Christian, Scottish woman, married before the minister to a good man. To touch me in any sort of intimate or inappropriate way would be an affront to God.'

His smile is terrifying. 'You're new, so I'll make a few allowances for your ignorance. The first thing you have to realise is that there's no God here. While you're on this plantation you belong to me, Violet, from your tiny toes to the hairs on your head and all those secret bits in between. I'm the only God you need.'

'That's blasphemy.'

He walks into the centre of the room, spreading out his arms and spilling spirit on to the rug without a care. 'Strike me down for my blasphemy!' He laughs as he turns a full circle to face me once again. 'See, no God. Now, what do you think we should do?'

'You should return me to the hut.'

'What would a decent, Christian, Scottish woman want with a hut full of men?'

I'm still near the door but trying to escape would be futile. I sense that McKinnon is outside, listening.

'Come here.'

I don't move.

'Come here.'

I take a couple of steps towards him and stop.

'Take off your clothes.'

I've been fighting the king's army for years and have even killed men in this journey of mine. There's no way I'm giving in to this heinous man because he threatens me. My fear is pushed aside by anger as I glance around for a potential weapon. There's nothing within reach.

'No.'

'Do it!'

'You only bought my labour, not me! I'll let no man defile my body, no matter who he is. You—'

His punch to my stomach is so fast I've no time to react and I'm knocked backwards several feet before landing on the floor, gasping and helpless, the world a blur through my tears. He lifts me as if I weigh almost nothing and throws me on the bed, then he takes hold of the bottom of my breeches. I raise my knees and hold on to the waistband, but he pulls them off without any effort and when I try to stop him removing my shirt, he slaps my face so hard my ears ring like a cracked church bell.

I'm sickened by how easily he's stripped me naked and watch in shock as he removes his clothes. I slide across the bed. He takes hold of one of my ankles and pulls me back.

'Let go of me! Have some mercy. I beg you. I'm a decent woman.'

With all my strength I force my knees together, but he takes hold of both ankles and simply pulls my legs apart. I thrust my hands down to hide my privacy.

'No! No!'

Drummond must be twice my weight and when he lies on top the air is squeezed out of my lungs in a huge gush. It's difficult to breathe. I try to gouge his eyes, but he's obviously experienced in rape and anticipates the move, catching my wrists and pinning down my arms. With despair, I realise that he enjoys this. I attempt to twist and turn yet can barely move as he positions himself, deliberately slowly, as though this is all part of his pleasure.

I can't stop him. I can't stop him.

'You're mine!'

'No! Please no!'

But screaming and fighting back only excites him more.

Samuel, where are you ... Where are you?

'I'm the master!' he crows. 'I'm the master!'

In that moment, he is a man possessed, repeating the words again and again. Desperately, I try to take my mind to another place, when life was safe and whole and Samuel drew pictures of me because we were in love and he—

I'm the master! I'm the master!

I can't get myself away from this bed and what's happening. The brutality is too real to escape it in my mind. I'm trapped here in every sense because every sense is being assaulted, defiled, ripped away from the certainties I used to have.

Suddenly Drummond screams the words, then he goes limp, panting and sweating. I can't do anything except lie here, crying and waiting for him to move.

During all those months in Greyfriars Kirkyard when there was no water to wash with, or as we sat amongst the filth sloshing about in the hold of the *Crown of London*, I never felt dirty in the way I do now. That was dirt on my skin, but this ... this has made *me* dirty.

Eventually, he gets up and stands looking down upon me. I curl in on myself, trying to cover as much of my body as possible. He laughs.

'Decent, Christian, Scottish woman. I'm already looking forward to your next visit, Violet.'

Not even bothering to dress, he walks over to the bureau and refills his glass. I get up and, with my back to him, hurriedly dress. When I glance around, he's reading some papers as if I'm not even here and with no other instructions I escape from the room.

As soon as I set foot in the corridor, McKinnon takes me roughly by the arm and pulls me downstairs. Once we're outside he drags me away from the direction of the huts.

'Where are we going?'

'You have more than one master.'

The realisation of what he intends suddenly washes over me like a wave, and I struggle against him more fiercely than I've ever fought before.

'No! Let me go! You can't! You can't!'

The reality is he can.

He does.

* * *

I don't remember how I got here. The sky is above. I'm lying on the ground. My clothes are nearby. Fragments of the evening begin to take shape in my mind. Every part of me hurts, inside and out. My soul hurts the most. Without warning my entire body goes rigid. When the spasm passes, I'm trembling uncontrollably.

If I stay here it's likely I'll die. There is a part of me that wants this ... to let all the pain in my life fade away with death. Maybe Samuel is waiting and we could be together again if I would only give in. I can't. The effort needed to stand leaves me gasping, and without the strength to put on my clothes I merely hug the bundle to my chest.

When I open the door the murmuring stops instantly. A few rushlights reveal a hut similar to the men's, with some women and children in beds and others on the floor. I just remain there, whimpering and shaking. No one speaks for several moments, then suddenly figures move in the semi-darkness. A woman gently takes my arm, leading me into the centre. The door is closed.

They know. They know.

A few precious candles are lit. Someone removes the clothes in my arms and I stand naked in front of everyone. Naomi kneels at my feet. She has a basin of water and a cloth. With extraordinary tenderness she wipes my thighs and between my legs.

I don't have the words to describe my gratitude. There are no words.

I'm wailing now, huge sobs wrenched from deep within me are flung around the hut to splatter every inch with such misery and despair that the wood will be forever tainted … like me.

Another figure leads me over to an empty bed. I'm like a child as she puts me in it then lies beside me. This total stranger, who can surely have no reason to help, gently moves my head on to her chest and holds me tightly, while I cry my broken heart out until I'm finally overcome by exhaustion and grief.

* * *

When I wake, daylight is creeping into the hut. I'm still lying in the same position, held by the woman who cradled me last night. Has she lain with me throughout the night? Slowly I pull back to look at her face.

'You'll live, sleep and work with us,' she says.

'Thank you.' My voice is so hoarse and rough I can hardly speak. 'My name's Violet.'

'I'm called Shoshana. You will not think it possible, but you must find the strength to work. For the next few days, the masters will be watching carefully to make sure you don't run away or harm yourself. Some women try after the first time. Stay close to me. Later we can talk.'

I keep within the middle of the women throughout the morning, clearing yet another field of withes. Occasionally I'm aware of McKinnon, Hunter or Findlay watching me but they don't come near. They're mainly busy abusing the men harvesting sugar canes a couple of fields away.

A girl of about ten walks by, carrying two containers of water that must weigh almost as much as she does. The children are used to looking after the animals and I know this water is being taken to the mules waiting to bring back the cut canes. She stops and speaks briefly to Shoshana before continuing.

'Tamar says Calum is speaking this morning,' says Shoshana when she's beside me once more. 'That's a good sign he'll recover. He's asking about you.'

Panic grips me like a vice. 'He mustn't know!'

'Don't worry about that. Nobody will tell him what's happened until he's strong enough to learn of such things, and then you must be the one. You can visit him later, after the first bell.'

I think back to when I entered the hut last night, and how Shoshana held me like a mother holding her frightened child. She did not even know me.

'Why are you so kind to me?' I ask.

'Because we're not what the masters make us out to be. They have their muskets and weapons and force us into this life, quoting from their book that this is what our lives should be. It never was until they captured us.'

'You held me throughout the night. Thank you.'

'We're women,' she says by way of explanation. 'Every woman in our hut has been raped and many continue to be by Drummond and his men. Only the very young and the old escape it. I was barely fifteen when it first happened to me.'

Deep lines of despair and pain have aged her beautiful face, while the harsh work has made her hands hard and calloused. She has been forced to endure this abuse for so many years, yet her heart has not been hardened and I stand in awe of a generosity of spirit that I don't have.

'You were so young,' I whisper.

Some of her anger spills out now. 'Yes, and I had Tamar because of it! The birth was so brutal upon my body that I never had another child. And I held you because I'll never forget the terror of that first rape, just as you won't forget last night. It will always be a part of you, Violet. Always.'

* * *

Several days later I end up in Drummond's bedroom again. Since the first attack it's been impossible to think of anything other than this inevitable second assault. The women in the hut have told me it would happen again – there is no escaping it – and all I can do is try to survive as best as I can. My only chance to reduce this new horror in my life is to use his weaknesses, because like all men of his type he is vain, greedy, mean and jealous.

'Master, am I your property?'

'As long as you are on my plantation, you belong to me.'

I'm careful not to accuse him of anything bad. 'After you and I were together, your overseer raped me.'

According to Shoshana, Hunter even used to rape women in the fields while other slaves carried on working only yards away, but Drummond put a stop to this because it interfered with productivity. Now I'm relying on him considering me to be a different type of property, a different type of trophy. The words almost choke me.

'Master, I told Mister McKinnon I am your property alone, but he didn't respect that fact.'

I wait in petrified silence while he stares at me, his anger becoming increasingly clear as he thinks through the implications of what I've said, that it's he, Drummond, who is not being respected sufficiently. Suddenly he marches towards the door and into the corridor. A furious row erupts between the two men but there is only one plantation owner and when

Drummond comes back I know that the other men won't be allowed to physically hurt me, at least ... not rape.

My 'victory' is accompanied by crushing shame. The other women will be assaulted more often because the men cannot touch me. My Christianity gives me a voice they don't have. The consequences of my cowardice will have to be faced, for the others will find out what I've done and I can hardly expect them to forgive me.

And I am not free of abuse. For now I must endure what I cannot prevent and my courage is failing rapidly. I'm on the verge of throwing myself on the floor and begging him to leave me alone.

'Well,' he says, after we've stood for a while watching each other.

I must do this terrible, sickening deed and not reveal how repulsed I am by it, because I have to make Drummond think I've submitted to him in order not to be closely watched in the coming weeks. How many times I must do this I don't know, but I do know that Calum and I will escape and that secret knowledge gives me some strength.

Slowly, reluctantly, I remove my clothes.

30

Violet
6 June 1680, Drummond Plantation, Barbados

EVERY SINGLE PERSON ON THE plantation, from the blacksmith to the cook, knows that Drummond rapes me whenever he wishes. Only Calum doesn't. I've delayed telling him to let him get stronger, but I can't risk leaving this any longer because news that will break his heart has to come from me. Today is Sunday so I've suggested we walk together.

Most of his back has healed from the whipping, although he will forever bear those marks. Now I'm about to add to the scars in his mind and I still don't know how to tell him.

'Your limp isn't any better,' I say.

He nods. 'My own fault. I should have followed Rory's advice and got Naomi to look at my heel when he told me to. It's hard to believe that so small an insect can make you lame.'

'And your back?'

'Getting better. McKinnon wants me in the fields tomorrow. I can't keep doing work around the compound with the old men.'

We continue in silence. There's nobody about as everyone is at the beach.

'Calum ... there's something I've got to tell you.'

'Well, you can tell me anything.'

Not this. Not this.

My words come out slowly, as if each one is a sentence and deserves a pause. 'Shortly after it was discovered I'm a woman, Drummond started taking me to his bed.'

He stops to stare at me, not immediately understanding what I'm saying. Then he lets out such a terrible keening sound that my spine feels as though it's turned to ice. Sinking slowly to his knee, he covers his face with his hands.

'Nooo! Nooo! Nooo!'

I've never seen or heard him like this, not as a child or even when his father was hanged, never. I kneel and take him in my arms, but he's inconsolable.

'I should have protected you!'

Now words pour out of me. 'Calum, you were gravely wounded and ill. Nobody could have stopped him. Not even Samuel could have prevented this. The other young women are often raped by Drummond. It was always going to happen to me once he knew I was a woman.'

'I promised to protect you!'

'I know, my love. I know. But sometimes we can't keep our promises, no matter how much we try. Drummond is too powerful.'

'You'll never be the same again.'

'I'm still your Violet, still the sister who helped bring you up, still married to your brother.'

I try to give comfort, but his words are like daggers to my heart, for he is right ... I will never be the person I was before we came to Barbados. That Violet is gone forever.

* * *

By the time Calum and I return to the compound most of the others have come back from the shore. Many of them are gathered around the large open entrance into the barn and they stare inside, silent and still. Rory is standing with Joseph and upon seeing us, he comes over before we've reached the building.

'This time it's Josiah,' says Rory, his face grim.

Another slave has hanged themselves.

'Josiah!' I cry. 'Oh, no. He once cut three sugar canes and laid them at my feet so that I wouldn't be punished for being slow.'

'He was a decent man, a kind man,' says Rory. 'And here comes the mad bastard who killed him.'

Drummond and McKinnon stride towards the barn, obviously having just been made aware of the latest death. We move nearer to hear. Drummond glances inside, but it's no more than to confirm the identity of the person.

'How can people be so selfish?' he shouts angrily. 'I do so much for you all and this is how I get repaid. Where's your loyalty? Where's your gratitude? Now I'll have to buy another one.'

Slaves and servants stare at the ground and try to back away without drawing attention to themselves, but they can't actually leave while Drummond is speaking so we're all of us stuck. He's becoming almost speechless with rage and it's clear he's been drinking.

'Mister McKinnon!'

Drummond is shouting but the overseer is only a few feet away.

'Yes, Mister Drummond.'

'I want his head stuck on a spike at the main entrance!'

'Vicious, evil bastard,' whispers Rory.

Most slaves believe that the body has to be buried whole for the journey to the afterlife. This is the only way that Drummond can punish a dead person, while also instilling even more terror into the living.

Calum takes my hand and holds it tight.

* * *

As we move further into summer, the heat becomes fierce. Calum's fair skin is burnt without mercy, despite the large hat he now wears. I no longer bind my chest but I've continued to wear the linen shirt and drawers worn by men in order to protect my own skin and because I refuse to walk around barebreasted. No one has commented, which I suspect is due to the fact that I'm considered Drummond's personal property and nobody else's.

There's a rhythm to the plantation, and the cruel beatings, whippings and back-breaking work are a part of that rhythm as much as the bell, loblolly and rats. So we fight the withes and rodents, dig trenches to plant new canes and cut those that are ready, while the horses and oxen go round and round in the millhouse, unable to leave the madness behind them no matter how far they walk, as the cane juice is squeezed and boiled and cleared in a never-ending process of inhumanity that is beyond understanding or describing and so often beyond endurance.

I don't see as much of Calum now that I sleep and work with the women and one day early in July I hurry to catch up with him as everyone heads back from the fields. He's alone, hunched and walking with the air of a condemned man on his way to the gallows.

'Calum,' I say upon reaching him. He doesn't respond, which is so utterly unnatural that I'm momentarily lost for words.

'Calum?' He continues walking without acknowledging my presence. In the end I grab his arm and force him to stop.

'Calum! What's happened?'

Then I see his face and it's a face I don't know. If the Devil himself had visited Calum during the night I wouldn't have expected him to look more changed. 'Dear God, what's happened to you?'

He's holding back tears of despair, but his expression also shows enormous anger, fear and something else I can't place. It's as if many different conflicting emotions are fighting for dominance of his features and the result is a battlefield of confusion and ... what? Then I realise. Calum is *haunted*. He's so different to the person I know that it frightens me.

'Never ask.' There is such pain in his eyes, and his voice. 'Never ask.'

Without speaking further, he pulls his arm free and walks on, leaving me to stare at his back, overcome with shock and a terrible sense of loneliness and loss.

* * *

It's one evening a couple of weeks later when Calum hunts me out and almost drags me away from everyone else so that we can be alone. We haven't spoken without others around us since the strange conversation we had when he had changed so dramatically overnight.

'We have to leave, Violet. We have to get away soon. I can't stay here any more and neither can you.'

To escape Drummond is what I want so desperately, and although confused by this sudden urgency I readily agree.

'All right. Whatever the risk, we'll go together, Calum. I'm done with being good at waiting.'

The next evening we sit with Rory after the evening meal, far enough from anyone else not to be overheard but not so isolated that we appear as if we've deliberately sought privacy. As a woman I'm not supposed to be with the men at this time of day, yet I walk a path in this strange place that has no footprints other than my own. Everyone knows I'm a woman but I've lived as a man and with the men, so no one has ever made a comment when I've joined Calum, Alan or the others.

'You're thinking of escaping,' says Rory, after we've been sitting for a while in silence.

'How do you know?' asks Calum, eyeing the Irishman warily.

'Christ Almighty, I've been here long enough to spot the signs. You want information about the island.'

'Yes,' I say, 'but this puts you in danger.'

'I'm willing to take the risk, though I've got to warn you how little chance there is of success. If you're caught, the length of your forced indentured servitude is likely to be extended by years.'

'We don't even know how long it is now,' says Calum.

'Why did you try to get away, Rory?' I ask.

He hesitates at answering. 'Something happened. It was pure instinct and stupid beyond belief.'

'Where can someone escape to on an island?' says Calum.

'Unless you can smuggle yourself on board a ship or steal a boat, there's only one place to consider. Over the years slaves and servants have made for an area of high ground in the middle of Barbados that's so inaccessible it's impossible to grow anything other than the trees that already exist in large numbers.'

'Don't the authorities hunt people?'

'In the early days they tried, but those who had liberated themselves were so few in number they could easily hide. Now there are so many it would take a small army to capture them and the cost to the plantation owners would be too great. It's all about investment and return and as recaptured slaves are generally hanged, the whole exercise would be pointless, apart from trying to deter others.'

'Yet their freedom gives hope?'

'It's a burden that the owners are forced to endure. If you succeed in reaching this territory, then you'll gain your freedom from the plantation but you'll be trapped in those woods for the rest of your life.'

Calum and I look at each other.

'We have to do it ... or die trying,' he says eventually.

31

Samuel
17 July 1680, Deerness, Orkney

DESPITE THEIR KINDNESS AND BRAVERY, Mary and Hugh's small home began to feel like yet another prison and I increasingly chafed against the enforced captivity. The large network of people in Orkney who support the Covenanter cause means that we're always kept up to date with relevant news, so we heard soon after it had sailed that the *Sophia* left Stromness with the recaptured Covenanters. That was in December, when I could barely get out of the box bed.

My leg recovered slowly over the following months but my mind pitched like a ship in a storm, disappearing into the troughs of despair before rising to the light, only to drop back into the darkness. Much of this period of my life is lost to me. From what I do recall, that's probably for the best. My poor, dear saviours. It was one thing to look after a man so ill that he was little more than a child in most ways, quite another to try to calm a six-foot-three lunatic, ranting and storming around, smashing objects ... sometimes deliberately.

I remember occasions, when the Devil had left me, that I was so ashamed of my actions I wept upon Hugh's shoulder, begging for his forgiveness. This gentle man held me like a son, forgave me like a son. Whatever they say to reassure me, I will feel that shame until I die.

It was during this dark period that news reached us of another survivor from the *Crown of London*, someone who had also evaded the sailors that terrible night and avoided being recaptured. I became obsessed with meeting this man. From the description of him it certainly wasn't Violet or Calum, but my fevered mind was certain he had important information.

Apparently, this Covenanter hadn't been injured and had been moved quickly from the area of the wreck by sympathisers, until eventually reaching the north end of mainland Orkney. He's settled there now and, although aware of my own presence, wishes no contact with me. Hugh has stressed again and again that it would be dangerous for both of us if I were to try and track down this man. I've eventually accepted that he is right, though I can't help wondering at times.

Over the months people have brought clothes for me, often altered or made to suit my size, as well as other items so that I will be better equipped to journey where fate takes me and not look out of place. So on this day of July I say farewell to the two kindest people on earth.

'You'll always be welcome here,' says Mary, who can hardly speak for crying.

'There are no words that would be enough to express my gratitude.'

'I know, peedie boy,' she says, reaching up to wipe away some of my own tears.

Hugh and I simply hug each other for a long time, then I bend down to stroke Gunnar. It was the dog's incessant barking that night which made Hugh go outside to investigate and discover me lying more dead than alive.

'You saved my life. Sorry I thought you were the Devil.'

Gunnar wags his tail and licks my hand. I stand, pick up my satchel and go outside. The sun is shining and gulls wheel about the sky, screeching their familiar cries which sailors say are the spirits of those who have died at sea. I wonder if any are from the *Crown of London*.

There is a sharpness to the air and the keen wind carries the salty tang of seaweed, strong yet fresh and with it an unexpected sense of freedom. Freedom, even though I don't believe I will ever leave these islands, in truth partly because I've developed such a terror of the sea.

I walk a short way then stop to look back at the couple standing in their doorway. They smile and wave. I smile and wave. Inside, my heart feels broken, but my life must take a different path. I set off briskly and don't look back.

In my satchel I carry spare clothes and food. A shoemaker in Kirkwall made me a pair of sturdy boots and, like so many other items, these were moved secretly from dwelling to dwelling. People have also donated money and I've a good purse of coin tucked safely in my jerkin. A knife hangs from my belt, as much a working tool as a weapon, though it will serve well as both. I often wonder what happened to the Colvil family dirk.

My head is shaved as my ginger hair makes me too easily identifiable, too easily remembered by folk who might be against the cause. Many men shave their heads and, with the addition of a bonnet, my appearance should not be a reason for comment. All except my height, of course, which I can't do anything about.

My destination is a manse in Kirkwall owned by a Church of Scotland minister who knows of my situation and will help to set me up. In what, I'm not sure. Physically, I'm stronger than I've been in years and I'm not afraid of labouring work. As I walk away I can't help feeling the pleasure of being out in the countryside with the sun on my face, no longer injured, hungry or ill-treated, no longer a prisoner.

* * *

The Reverend Sinclair greets me warmly as he opens the front door and I follow him into the kitchen, where a fire burns brightly in the hearth. It's late afternoon on the day I left Deerness. In an odd way it feels as though my time there was months ago. He begs me to sit while he pours ale and produces cheese and bread, which I'm mightily grateful for.

He appraises me for many minutes with keen, intelligent eyes. I sit opposite him, eating in silence, having decided before arriving to let this stranger steer the conversation.

'I've heard your story, Samuel, and am sorry for your loss,' he says. 'You've lost your wife and brother and many good friends?'

I stop eating. 'Yes, Reverend.' I pause for a long while and he waits patiently, sensing I have something I must say yet not rushing me. In the end, I can't speak the words.

'Perhaps you've lost something else. Have you lost your faith?'

I nod a silent confession to my greatest shame. Tears run freely down my cheeks and I let them fall where they may. A couple land on the white cheese in my hand, where they sit like raindrops upon a hard surface, uncertain where to go ... like me. This is not something I've discussed, even with Mary and Hugh.

'I think I began to lose it at Bothwell. Forgive me ...'

'You may say what you want within these walls, Samuel. I'm not here to judge.'

'There was no sign of God's presence on that battlefield,' I blurt out, the words bitter on my tongue. 'Covenanters were slaughtered like sheep and many survivors then rounded up and taken to Hell. Good people died that day and during the weeks that followed in Edinburgh.'

He nods slowly. 'There was great sadness when the news reached us.'

'With the other desperate events that followed it felt as though God had forsaken us all.' I am silent for a while. 'I was present when they hanged my father in Edinburgh's Grassmarket.'

'Ah, that I didn't know. I'm sorry, Samuel.'

'There were plenty who had lost hope and willingly signed the Black Bond to gain their freedom, including men I counted as brothers.'

'But you didn't?'

'No, nor did my darling wife, Violet. Yet what good has it done me or her or any of us?'

I drop my head and run my hand across the bristles, recalling how Violet used to say it was so ginger that she could *feel* the colour.

'The answer may not reveal itself for quite some time. Until then ... well, try not to be too hard on yourself. I won't sit here and tell you that God hasn't forsaken you, regardless of what I believe, because you must discover this on your own for it to be of value. Be aware that you might never find your faith again. I've known that to be the case with some men.'

'What happened to them?'

'Oh, they live their lives ... good men still, but without God in their hearts.'

'What can I do?' I feel lost and that this minister has such integrity and wisdom that I would willingly follow his advice.

'Mmm. Let us firstly talk of practical matters. You may stay in the manse for now. If anyone asks, I'll say you're the son of an old friend, travelling for adventure as men are wont to do. I'll square that lie with the Good Lord in my own way. You need to change your name. There are many in Orkney who are against the Covenanter cause and will consider denouncing you to the authorities as their duty.'

'I'll not lose my name ... not Samuel.'

'All right, but a different surname.'

That I should call myself by a name that is not my father's seems disloyal, yet I can see the sense of it. 'Violet's surname was Milligan. I'll use that.'

The minister nods at this. 'A man taking his wife's name ... well, it's less likely to trip you up if it's one you're familiar with. We'll need to get you employment. What skills do you have?'

'It was always expected that I would become a minister and in sixty-nine I went to Holland to train and be ordained.'

'And were you?'

'Yes, but upon my return to Scotland I couldn't obtain a parish without swearing an oath and accepting the king as head of the Church. I never even preached, not once.'

'You look strong.'

'I'll do anything ... working on the docks?'

'No, you're educated and well-spoken. Some workers might be suspicious and wonder why a man from such a background was trying to be unnoticed. Better to hide in the open, though I would advise continuing to shave your head.'

'Violet ... Violet used to say my hair grew at the speed of a galloping horse.'

'I'm sorry, Samuel. I can tell you this from my own experience as an old widower, you will always miss your wife. Every single day you'll feel the absence of her presence. Have you prayed for Violet?'

The words are like knives thrown at my heart. Have I prayed? Yes, that night when the *Crown of London* broke up, then after ... ramblings in my delirium, angry demands of God. I don't need to reply. The Reverend Sinclair knows the answer.

'Perhaps we should say a prayer for Violet. I think that might be a good way to begin your life here.'

And so we pray as I should have done before, but never did.

32

Violet
21 July 1680, Drummond Plantation, Barbados

Rory is exaggerating when he talks about the hurricanes that sweep across the island. I think he's just trying to put us off. Calum and I have often been out on the Scottish moors on a wild night, so this holds no fear for us. Besides, the confusion created by a storm provides the best chance we'll ever have of escaping successfully.

We'll go with Joseph. It was Rory's suggestion as he suspected Joseph was also intending to escape. Rory has acted as the messenger between us so that no suspicion is created by conversations between people that might appear unusual. It's agreed that the three of us will head for the forest in the centre of the island during the next hurricane.

There is something Calum and I have not discussed. It's driven a wedge between us and whether we succeed or die in our attempt to get away it cannot be left unacknowledged any longer. This evening I've insisted that the two of us sit away from everyone else. I will have to be the one to speak of the dread that's in my heart.

'Calum, you and I have loved each other as brother and sister since childhood. We've grown up together, experienced unimaginable hurt and sorrow, yet have known love and loyalty beyond measure. We've always taken care of each other.'

If it is at all possible, my heart is breaking even more than it already has, but I take a deep breath and force the words out, because this is more important than any feelings of mine.

'You know what Drummond has done to me. I don't have the words to describe the utter horror and shame these visits instil. Nobody can imagine what it's like to be raped and to know that this will continue with no end in sight.'

My throat is dry as sand. I don't want it to be true.

'Calum ... you don't have to imagine it ... do you?'

He won't look me in the eye.

'Oh my darling boy.' I try to take him in my arms.

He pulls away with a shout. 'No, don't! DON'T! I'm too dirty to be touched by you ... by you or anyone.'

'I didn't understand that first day, when Rory warned you about Findlay. It made no sense to me why only you should have been at risk. It was only after Drummond raped me that I later saw in your eyes what I knew was in my own. Then I began to wonder. You were always so beautiful, but I could never have thought ...'

The tears come now. A flood of them.

'I'm not beautiful, Violet! I'm disgusting ... dirty, filthy ... no one, not even God wants me now.'

'You have great courage, Calum, and I know Findlay must have threatened you terribly for you to have let him do this against your nature.'

'He didn't! He didn't!'

'What do you mean?'

'He didn't threaten to hurt me ... he threatened to hurt *you*. I would have fought him, Violet. Even if he'd had Hunter and McKinnon with him, I would have fought him. The things he said would happen to you if I didn't agree ... I couldn't risk it. He's deranged. Even if I'd killed him and hanged for it, Hunter would have carried out his threats regardless of Drummond's orders.'

He drops his head in his hands, a broken man like those McKinnon didn't want to buy on the *Sophia*.

'I've let him use me in unnatural ways that go against the Scriptures and he's destroyed me because of it. Violet, I hope you and Joseph get away safely and that somehow, one day, you make it back to Scotland. I'll help you escape because I can't continue here like this. I'll never see my wife or son again. I don't want to live any more. There's nothing you can say that will change this ... nothing at all.'

And as I hear these words I know the man I held in my arms soon after he was born and helped to raise as a boy is speaking the truth. We must escape or die in the attempt.

* * *

Our chance comes sooner than we expect when, towards the end of July, the wind begins to increase steadily throughout the afternoon. Everyone is brought in from the fields early. Figures rush around, tying down objects with rope and stakes and locking up animals. Drummond orders the shutters on the big house to be closed and bolted. People grab food that can be eaten uncooked and make for the huts or their preferred hiding place if they feel safer there. Several go to the stone-built boiling-house.

Only Rory knows of our plans and I go over them again in my mind as I stand outside the door of the women's hut, watching. With every minute that passes there are fewer folk around.

'The storms are frightening but it will likely be over by the morning,' says Shoshana, who's come to stand next to me.

'Shoshana,' I say, turning to face her. 'I'm going to leave.'

'Leave?'

'I haven't said anything before because it's safer for you not to know. I'm escaping during the storm while there's a lot of confusion. Don't worry about me if I don't come back.'

She shakes her head. 'Violet, this is not a good idea. Almost nobody succeeds. You'll be punished. Stay here.'

'I can't. You know why.'

'It's much worse for us.'

I nod in agreement, but it doesn't change how I feel. 'I know.'

'You don't know!' says Shoshana, suddenly angry. 'Not even now, Violet. One day you'll have your freedom and walk away from this plantation, probably this island. I never will, nor will Tamar or her children if she has them.'

'I'm sorry. You're right, I'm weak. I can't continue like this until that day of freedom comes.' Tears roll down my cheeks. I'm so weak compared to her. 'I have to take this chance.'

'You can't go by yourself?'

'I'm not.'

Shoshana is silent for a long while, staring at me. 'You've kept your secret close. Leave then, if you think the risk worth it. I hope others don't suffer because of your decision.'

'Thank you for what you've done for me. I can't ever repay you.'

Our parting feels too brief ... too sharp. We hug. I don't want to let go and it's Shoshana who soon pulls away.

'The storm is getting worse. I'm going to fetch Tamar and go to the boiling-house. I hope we never meet again.'

When she walks away I'm shocked at the sense of loss.

The light is fading and as there's almost no one going around, I leave. In contrast to the wildness around me I move stealthily away, stopping now and again to glance nervously about. There's a strange smell of sulphur in the air. About fifteen minutes later I reach the ditch in the fields that's used as a latrine and hide a little distance away so that I can see anyone approach.

'Violet.'

I almost scream at the voice behind me.

'Joseph!'

'I stayed out when everyone went in. People were too worried about the hurricane to notice I didn't go back with them. There's Calum.'

I look the way he's pointing: Calum is moving as quickly as he can, the urgency in his step making his limp worse than usual.

'The last chance for anyone to turn back,' he says, upon reaching us.

There is no doubt in our faces as we look at each other. We set off north-west, Joseph leading as he knows the island much better. When we finally reach the edge of the Drummond plantation he halts.

'We can't keep going in the same direction and need to go around the border of the next plantation so there's less chance of being seen.'

The wind is getting stronger and it's increasingly more difficult to keep our balance, yet there is no stopping now. When Joseph sets off, I follow next as Calum wants to know I'm keeping up. For a while we're forced to head east, following the edges of field upon field of sugar canes. By the time we're able to head north again, I can hardly move against the force of the wind and have to turn my head away to take a breath.

'Rory was right,' shouts Calum, holding my arm to steady me. 'Scotland was never like this.'

Joseph comes back to us. 'We can't stop. There's a cave, it's known to slaves. We can shelter, but we have to reach it soon. This storm will get much worse.'

What he says is hard to believe ... frightening to believe. I nod. It's soon apparent that Joseph would have been better by himself, for I can't match his speed and I know he's going slower than he needs to. I'm so much lighter than the men that I'm blown over and get up only to stumble again soon after. It doesn't seem possible that air can have such a physical presence that it's like a solid object, slapping me about my head as a preacher once did with a Bible.

I fall over again and Calum comes beside me. He shouts. I can't hear him. He lifts me up and puts an arm firmly around my waist. I put my hand on his shoulder. Joseph is ahead, watching. He waits until we've caught up before setting off once more.

I've no idea where we are or what direction we're going in, yet we stagger on, foot after foot, yard after yard. The effort to breathe is unbelievable. It is as if the air is being sucked out of my body before it reaches my lungs. Beside me Calum is weakening and when I lose my balance yet again I take him down with me. We lie on the ground, gasping and so spent we can't continue.

I lay my head on his chest and he wraps his arms around me. The storm seems further away now. Once before I thought I was going to die, lying in the field at Bothwell next to my father, and, like that time, I think it's not a bad way to end your life, by the side of someone you love.

Suddenly I'm lifted to my feet. Joseph puts his arm firmly around my waist and holds out his other hand. When Calum is standing the three of us huddle together to hear better.

'The cave's close,' shouts Joseph.

I shake my head in reply. He shakes his in return and the next moment I'm being half carried as we continue our battle against the storm, against the cruelty and injustice that has gathered the three of us together on this strange island from such different parts of the world.

The air is alive with flying objects; branches, soil and small stones whip past our heads like shot. At any moment one of us could be seriously injured. The trees are bent like old men and even above the noise of the wind we clearly hear the cracking of trunks splitting apart. I move my legs to walk but it almost seems as if my feet aren't touching the earth and have no grip to push me forward. It's like swimming in a loch when you can just touch the bottom with your toes, only it's not enough to get you through the water.

I can't move without Joseph, but the strain is wearing him down and eventually we're forced to stop. Gently, he lets me slither to the ground then collapses to his knees next to me. Calum catches up.

'How far?' he shouts.

Joseph points. 'Up there.'

I look to where he's indicating but don't see any entrance to a cave. I can hardly open my eyes to see anything.

'I'll take her.'

Joseph nods and Calum helps him up before taking hold of me around the waist once more. We stagger, weave and stumble over the rocks as we go higher and higher until Joseph stops to study the immediate area around us. I suddenly worry that we're lost, but he heads off again and we follow close behind.

A few moments later everything goes dark as we step into another world, one of such calmness that it's difficult to believe this exists. Outside the hurricane howls as if it's angry we've got away, like the sea off Orkney which so wanted our souls. We collapse on to the floor. I'm so utterly exhausted I'm crying, then I realise we're all crying. Then there's nothing.

* * *

I don't understand where I am. I hear sounds, the crackle of flames, before opening my eyes to see colours dancing on the rocks above ... orange, red and yellow flicker amongst the shadows and shapes. They're so beautiful. There's something else ... voices talking quietly. I try to move, but my body won't respond. All I can manage is a groan.

'Violet, you're safe,' says Calum, laying a hand gently upon my shoulder. 'We're in the cave that Joseph spoke of, out of the storm, and no one will hunt for us until daylight at the earliest. We did it. We've escaped Drummond and the plantation. In the morning we've not far to go to reach the forest.'

I turn my head to see Joseph sitting close by on the other side of me. There's a fire somewhere, but I can't see it. I hold out a hand.

'Thank you, Joseph.'

He stares for a long while then takes my hand and squeezes it. 'We're not safe yet,' he says. 'We have to leave at first light.'

'You made a fire?'

'Only slaves know of this cave, its whereabouts passed on in secret to those who can be trusted. Over the years it's been stocked with wood and flint and other items. This is a safe place for a short while.'

I'm so weak I can't even get up by myself. 'Calum, help me sit.'

Once I'm up I see that the cave is big and a fire burns brightly beyond our feet, the smoke floating upwards to disappear through cracks in the rock. Calum goes to somewhere behind me and comes back moments later with a wooden ladle containing water.

'Here, drink this and I'll get you another one. The rain runs down and fills a hollow. We've plenty of water but no food.'

It's only as I drink that I realise how desperately thirsty I am. After consuming four ladles I feel some strength returning to my muscles. 'Well, we're used to being starved. I don't think one day without food will hurt us.'

We lie for a while listening to the storm become ever angrier. Calum throws small pieces of wood on the fire. It crackles, sending sparks floating upwards, where they disappear above us.

'Rory once said that everyone on the plantation had their own story and it was for each person to tell it,' I say. 'I would like to hear your story, Joseph, if you're willing to tell it.'

He looks at me in silence without replying, thinking perhaps about his story.

'It's not a long one or unusual,' he says at last. 'My parents were slaves on a plantation in the Saint Peter area and they were allowed to marry by the owner. Compared to Drummond he was at least sane, although a poor gambler. When I was eight he had to sell several slaves to pay a debt and I was taken away to a different plantation.'

'You never saw your parents again?' I ask.

'Not them or my two younger sisters. A few years later I was sold to Master Drummond.'

'He seems to hate you,' says Calum.

'He hates everyone,' says Joseph, 'but yes, he enjoys hurting me more than most others. That's why I can't go on. If I don't escape, I want to die trying.'

Calum and I look at one another, each knowing the other so well that our thoughts are like words on a page that can be read and understood clearly. In this wish to escape or die trying, he is the same as Joseph. Each of them has come to a point where living on the plantation is no longer an option. The choice is freedom or death. Calum reaches over and gently strokes my hair. It's long again now. He knows. I'm not strong like them and don't want to die if we don't make it … even though I feel I should.

* * *

'Calum! Violet! Wake up!'

I'm instantly awake at the sound of fear in Joseph's voice. We've slept too long.

'What's wrong?' says Calum.

'Dogs. I can hear dogs in the distance.'

Quickly we go to the entrance to a world filled with bright light, the smell of moist earth and freshness … and the sound of dogs. There's no sign of anyone. The hurricane has largely passed on during the night.

'Surely even bloodhounds can't follow someone after the storm we've had?' I ask.

'They don't have to,' says Joseph. 'They know which direction we would have taken and they've come here directly without having to go around the plantations.'

'How far to the forest?' asks Calum.

'Perhaps a mile.'

'Which direction?'

'We need to go higher and then head north.'

Calum turns to me and I know what he's going to say. I can't let him speak the words, because if he doesn't, I can pretend it's not going to happen.

'No, Calum.'

'Violet, what I said to you before we left was meant. This is my way out, and yours.'

'Please no.'

'We can't all escape. You know I have to do this.' He turns to Joseph. 'I'll head back down and then south. I'll make sure they follow me.'

'They'll capture you,' he says.

'Not alive. Take Violet to safety. Live your lives as best you can.'

Calum takes me in his arms. 'I love you, Violet. One day we'll meet in Heaven. I shall say hello to your father and we'll be waiting for you.'

'Oh, Calum.' I can't say any more, for what words are there that can be spoken in these last moments together?

'Give me a few minutes' head start.'

The two men shake hands and then my darling boy is gone. We watch from the entrance as he quickly moves down the rocks that proved so difficult last night. The dogs are closer and I can hear the voices of men shouting, although not what's being said.

'Violet, we need to leave. Stay close to me.'

We set off. For once I'm glad of withes, which provide something sturdy to hang on to, but there is a rough path so it's not a climb as such and we soon reach the top. Calum is quite some distance away and we can make out the tiny figures of five men with two dogs following him, as he intended.

'He may yet escape,' says Joseph.

Now that we're on more even terrain we soon leave behind the area with the cave. The wind has died away to gusts, which cause us little problem, and the forest grows ever larger in our eyes until it's less than half a mile ahead. Hope is finally creeping into my heart when the sound of a musket being fired reaches us. We look towards its source and see two men over on our right, the second one aiming at us and obviously about to fire.

'Run!' shouts Joseph.

He sprints away, immediately pulling ahead of me, and I follow as fast as I can, all caution gone. I hear a second shot, but this also misses. The men are too far away to catch us. With every step Joseph pulls further ahead, but we'll make it. The forest is so close I can smell it, smell our freedom. Then I see Joseph slow down and stop and I don't understand why until I've caught up with him.

Three armed figures have appeared from behind a large rock directly in front of us. Crying, Joseph slips to the ground and I sink to my knees beside him. The sudden certainty of defeat is crushing. How could we have come so close to freedom? Why does God not let us reach it?

'Violet ... Joseph. You really have caused a lot of trouble, and your master is very upset,' says McKinnon. 'I knew you would end up coming over this high ground and couldn't see any point tiring myself out running around the countryside, chasing some dog's arse. All I had to do was wait for you to come to me. And here you are.'

33

Violet
31 July 1680, Drummond Plantation, Barbados

WITH OUR HANDS AND LEGS chained, Joseph and I are dragged through the Drummond plantation by the men hired to find us. They kick us if we fall or think we're not stumbling along fast enough, or they kick us just because they can. In the distance I see a large group standing near the punishment post, but as we get nearer I realise that's not what they're gathered around. It's the hanging tree.

Two ropes have been thrown over the killing branch, one end of each tied to a stake in the ground while the nooses swing gently above two benches. It looks as though everyone has gathered. The faces of all the people I know watch on with horror as Joseph and I are thrown down harshly to the ground in front of them. There's no sign of Calum.

Drummond stands in his pulpit, which has been moved from its usual place. He waits until the men who have brought us back walk to one side, while we get on to our knees to listen.

'Thank you, gentlemen. You have carried out your duty efficiently as ever. It pains me greatly to destroy my own property. Why would any sane man wish to do such a thing? I tell you it's because they have no choice. I have no choice with runaways who are disloyal to their master.

'I take care of you ... slaves and servants ... providing food, shelter and clothing, aid when you're sick. Yet these two repay my kindness by putting me to great inconvenience and cost, while you have had to do more work because they have cast off their responsibilities. All it's done is lead them to the end of a rope. Gentlemen, I ask that you continue.'

Findlay and Hunter move quickly, lifting up Joseph and dragging him to a bench. They're powerfully built and he has no way of preventing them.

'Master, I beg you, don't hurt him,' I plead. 'We're sorry for what we've done.'

They manhandle Joseph to the bench and put the noose around his neck, then they lift him on to it while McKinnon reties the rope to the stake so there is almost no slack. Abraham once told me that the drop is short so there is little chance of it breaking someone's neck. Instead, people die slowly by strangulation. I can't watch but McKinnon comes over and roughly takes hold of my head, putting a hand under my chin and forcing me to look up.

'No you don't! You see everything that's going to happen to you in a few minutes' time, when he's stopped gurgling, pissing himself and twitching.'

He's squeezing my jaw so fiercely that I can't even speak and can only moan in despair as I'm forced to see Joseph murdered. Findlay steps away and Joseph is left standing precariously on the unstable bench, shaking but silent.

'This man could have lived,' says Drummond. 'He could have continued to share meals with you and enjoy your company. This is his doing, not mine. I don't want this. Carry on.'

Hunter puts a foot against the bench, hesitates a moment, then kicks it away. Joseph jerks to a sickening stop, then he's frantically twisting and turning in a futile attempt to suck air into his lungs. The hangman's jig, they call it; and there can't be a more horrifying sight. People around me cry and shout out his name but no one tries to help. Everyone is paralysed by fear.

Joseph's handsome face quickly becomes unrecognisable as his bulging eyes and discoloured tongue stick out from a head that looks as if it's about to explode. Gradually, his movements become less violent until they are little more than occasional twitches, then nothing. He hangs limply while we watch on. A few women sob but otherwise the silence is like a cloak that's smothered us in despair. His face is hideous.

Something in my brain has blocked the realisation that this is what's about to happen to me. It's too horrifying to comprehend. Then Drummond speaks.

'This pains me greatly, Violet, but justice must be done.'

McKinnon lifts me off the ground and I'm overwhelmed with a terror that goes beyond anything I've ever known.

'No ... no ... no ... no! Please, master. I'll do anything you ask. *Anything.*' I'm dragged to the hanging branch. 'I'm begging you. I promise I'll be good.'

'Too late, Violet,' he says. 'I'll miss you.'

The noose is placed around my neck and I'm lifted on to the bench.

'NO, MASTER! I'll do whatever you want. Just tell me what you want and I'll do it. Please. Anything. Not this! Not this!' My legs buckle.

'Stand straight,' orders McKinnon harshly.

I've soiled my breeches. Joseph's body swings around slowly in the breeze, the only remnant of the hurricane. His grotesque eyes stare at me from a few feet away, his pointing tongue an obscene object ... accusing.

I'm going to look like that.
'Noooo!'
'Do your duty, Mister McKinnon.'

Hunter steps away as McKinnon places his foot against the bench and looks up at Drummond. *I've gone to a place so beyond fear, and I'm screaming, screaming, screaming—*

'Do your Christian duty.'

He kicks it away.

34

Samuel
31 July 1680, Deerness, Orkney

K IRKWALL IS DOMINATED BY ITS cathedral, which is the most imposing building I've seen outside of Edinburgh. It's vast in size and scale, while the red bricks go so high above my head that I'm almost dizzy when I look up and try to understand how the structure has been created. I wander through the nave in awe of the beauty and the men who designed and built it.

In my leather satchel I carry paper and a piece of graphite held within a brass holder like the one I used to draw sketches of Violet with as she lay amongst the heather, in another life. The drawing materials belonged to Reverend Sinclair's late wife, who had been a keen artist of local wildlife. After our supper yesterday evening, he proudly showed me some of her watercolours of curlew and snipe, otter and vole. She was extremely gifted. The minister said that his dear Anne would have wanted to help a fellow artist. I wish I'd met her.

As usual, the greatest activity around a port takes place at the harbour and I make my way there out of curiosity. Two large ships are tied up to moorings and from one a constant line of men unload bags, laying them in neat piles on the quayside, where they are counted off by an official. The other vessel has men taking items on board and I watch as kegs of rum, barrels of water, food and other supplies, including huge coils of rope are carried across the gangplank. Sailors are busy amongst the rigging.

To paint a ship requires a specific skill and soon after arriving in Amsterdam to begin my training as a minister good fortune brought me together with Willem van de Velde, a Dutch painter famous for creating sea scenes. He taught me much before having to flee to England with his father. I'm so caught up in what's before me that almost without realising I sit on a low wall, remove a sheet of paper and begin to sketch.

Violet used to watch me for ages as I drew. She would often say afterwards that I was so intense in trying to capture the view before me that I appeared almost to have become part of the scene. I was no longer 'there' in the present, and not aware of anything else around me. Once, when we were alone and I was drawing a landscape, she stripped off her clothes and sat quietly nearby waiting for me to notice. I was so shocked when I finally did that she burst out laughing. I stop drawing, hearing her laugh so clearly in my head that for an instant I almost turn to speak to her.

'That's a fair hand you've got.'

I'm wrenched back to reality by the comment, unaware how long I've been sitting or that there is someone nearby who has been studying my drawing. The man walks around to face me. His clothes indicate wealth while his speech demonstrates education and the keenness in his eyes, I suspect, intelligence and something else ... humour.

'You've a great skill in capturing the detail of ships.'

'Thank you.'

'Can you paint them as well?'

'Yes.'

'How about this one?' He points to one of the two ships.

'It would be a big undertaking, but I could do it.'

'What's your name?'

'Samuel ... Milligan.'

'I'm Gilbert Linklater.' He holds out his hand and I stand to shake it. 'Are you staying in Kirkwall, Samuel?'

I'm wary of strangers asking questions, particularly about what I'm doing, but I sense no hostility from this man. 'For a while.'

'Long enough for a big undertaking?'

'Perhaps. How long will the ship be anchored?'

'It sails in four days.'

'I guess I could produce the sketches I would need during that time and a master drawing from those later on. The painting would take weeks.'

'Let's go and have a walk about the deck then.'

'Do you think we can just go aboard?'

This sets him laughing. 'I should bloody hope so. I own it.'

* * *

I haven't been on a ship since the *Crown of London* and when I walk along the gangplank my steps slow down as the firmness of the ground is replaced by movement that's so slight it could almost go unnoticed, yet it feels as though it shakes the foundations of my life. I stop, put my hand upon the rope railing and check to reassure myself that the vessel is securely tied to sturdy moorings. I force my legs to continue the journey, which is so short in distance, yet so long in memory.

I recall the first time I walked on to a ship with Willem in Rotterdam harbour and he laughed at how astonished I was at the complexity of everything, in particular the rigging and sails which appeared to me to be such a huge confusion of canvas and hemp. However, during the time I studied under him, we visited many different vessels together and I learnt much about the various designs, along with an understanding of common terms and items.

I place my hand upon a rope, which gives off a familiar smell of tar. 'Every single one has its own purpose,' I say, running my fingers along a strand that heads up to somewhere far above us. 'And the strength of each matches the task it is given, like people and their work.'

Gilbert nods his approval. 'If you placed them end to end there's almost two miles of rope on this ship and it all has to be replaced every few years because it rots so quickly. We may ride the sea like kings, Samuel, but we are never the master.'

We walk slowly around the deck and I'm introduced to the captain and his officers, who are told that I am to have unhindered access over the next few days. Everyone is courteous and there is no doubting who's in charge.

'The ship has just brought back a cargo of tobacco, cotton and indigo,' says Gilbert. 'Some has been unloaded here but the main bulk will go to Liverpool. What we need from Orkney are men. Let me show you below.'

He leads the way down the ladder, but I only take three steps when the smell hits me – and I'm on the *Crown of London* again, boxed in by death and decay, the sounds of men crying, the sounds of men dying, all hope ripped from our souls. A strong hand lands on my back, holding me firmly against the ladder.

'Samuel! Are you all right? On deck! On deck I say!'

I'm vaguely aware of two burly sailors hurriedly appearing and hauling me by my arms back into the open air, where I lie helpless, waves of grief and horror making me moan and unable to think clearly or speak with any sense.

'Violet ... Violet.'

See ... your long black hair falls towards the ground in a certain way ... no matter how often you lie again in that position your hair will never fall exactly the way it just has ...

'Please ... please ... please.'

'Samuel! Samuel!'

I'm being shaken and open my eyes to see the concerned face of Gilbert close to mine as he kneels by my side.

'I'm terribly sorry. The ship took slaves from Africa to Virginia and no matter how much the hold is scrubbed, it's impossible to get rid of the stench entirely. I didn't consider that you might have had such a weak stomach. I sincerely apologise for my insensitivity.'

He expresses remorse at not warning me about a smell, yet displays no shame or guilt at transporting hundreds of poor souls into a life of slavery.

'Come, let's get you to the captain's cabin where a tot of rum and perhaps some food will aid your recovery.'

* * *

I walk slowly back to the manse through the streets of Kirkwall, my thoughts, feelings and footsteps so uncertain of themselves that any one of them could trip me up. What am I to make of this ship owner who transports people as slaves yet can show me such kindness? Once the two sailors had me safely settled into a chair in the captain's cabin, Gilbert could hardly have been more attentive. I had to assure him more than once that I could reach the manse without the need of a sailor escorting me.

Physically, I've largely recovered, but inside I'm staggering at the memories that so completely overcame me when I experienced just a hint of that smell ... sweat, blood, bodily waste, death ... but that's not what's ingrained into those planks of wood in the hold; it's terror and despair and suicide and hate. Part of me wants to rush back and grab hold of Gilbert, to shout that no amount of scrubbing will rid the ship of the stain of evil that is now part of it. He may clean it, change its name and carry a different cargo but what has been done will always taint the ship.

I stop. I'm crying. A couple of people look at me as they pass in the street. They don't speak. I wipe my eyes and take a deep breath. The tears still come. I can't stop them. The Reverend Sinclair is sitting at his table when I enter his house and upon seeing me he immediately suggests using some of his precious tea. We sit in the armchairs either side of the hearth and once I've recounted my experience he is silent for quite some while.

'Over the years I've met many good people and bad people,' he says, 'but I've rarely encountered someone I thought was all one or the other ... We are, each of us, generally somewhere in between. Those whose actions we consider evil may believe the right of what they do as strongly as others believe it is wrong. Goodness, just look at the king!

'And now, Samuel, you don't know what to do about Gilbert Linklater. He's an example of what I'm saying ... a regular donator to the Kirk and good causes, a generous and pleasant host, not someone who has ever displayed violence or unpleasant behaviour. Gilbert is devoted to his family and treats his wife with unusual respect. I know him well and would say that these aspects of his character are genuine. We wouldn't be enjoying this tea if it wasn't a gift from him.'

'But transporting innocent people to be sold as slaves!' My eyes well up again. 'Making a fortune from their misery. How can a man's soul ever be cleansed of such evil deeds by simply doing good deeds?'

'Is a man evil when he considers his actions normal, or is he evil when he knows they're wrong but continues anyway? I'm sure your theology tutors in Holland must have debated such points during your training to be a minister.'

'How can I possibly paint his ship?'

'Show me what you've drawn today.'

I'm taken aback at the unexpected request. Yet I collect my satchel and hand over the sketches I drew earlier. He studies them with an intense interest.

'You did these sitting on a wall at the harbour?'

'Yes.'

'Come with me.'

He hands back the sheets as he stands and suddenly strides towards the door that leads upstairs. I'm confused but lay down my work and follow. Moments later he unlocks a door I've not been through.

'You need to go in alone, Samuel.'

I hesitate at the strange instruction then step inside. I'm instantly enveloped by a sense of such peace that I'm reminded of the times I used to sit in Father's kirk when there was no one around, at least no other person. I loved the calmness and stillness. That's what this room gives me. It's clearly his late wife's workshop. The simple fact that such a large space in the house has been left untouched reveals how much he loved her.

With something close to reverence, I walk into the centre, where I detect the faintest of smells ... linseed oil ... one of the scents of a painter. That's why he keeps the door closed. He's preserving his memories of her in as many ways possible. The first items on the bench are an array of brushes, the bristles made from a variety of animal hairs. Some are obvious, like the coarse strands of a hog. I pick up another and gently run my finger through the fine hairs of what I guess might have come from a badger. I replace it carefully.

The rows of glass jars leave me astonished. Reverend Sinclair must have spent almost his entire minister's salary obtaining some of the pigments made from minerals. I can identify a blue pigment made from azurite and a green from malachite. There are reds and yellows plus an ultramarine blue that looks like it comes from lapis lazuli, but this would be such a huge cost I must be mistaken.

A little further on are more commonly found pigments made from plants and insects, such as indigo from woad and cochineal from insects. There are jars of carbon ink and iron gall ink, and in a small dish nearby are several of the familiar oak galls included in the ingredients. The Reverend Sinclair's wife obviously created her images using a wide variety of different mediums and from what I've seen of Orkney very few of these materials came from the island.

An otter watches me from the wide windowsill, its stuffed body skilfully positioned upon a couple of rocks that have no doubt come from a nearby beach. A little further along is an oystercatcher. I've lost track of time and am standing by the easel when I realise Reverend Sinclair is in the doorway, watching as silently as the otter.

'You do me a great honour, sir,' I say.

He enters. 'When my wife died, I carefully cleaned everything and the room has been left as she would have wanted it, ready for another painter. Sometimes I come in here and remove the lids on a few of the jars, then I just sit quietly, close my eyes, and remember our years together. I feel her so close to me in those moments. Do you think that's foolish of me as a man of God?'

'No, Reverend, I think it's beautiful.'

'Samuel, I don't know what God's plans are for you, but such talent can only come from Him, and whatever path you may later follow there's a reason that you and this room have been brought together. You agreed to paint Gilbert's ship?'

'Yes.'

'Well then, I know you're a man of your word and regardless of what you paint in the future you should at least fulfil this promise.'

35

Violet
10 May 1681, Drummond Plantation, Barbados

Do your duty, Mister McKinnon. Do your Christian duty. He kicks away the bench. I'm screaming as I fall.

I WAKE, SWEATING AND PANTING. I'VE been calling out, again. Someone on the floor near my bed reaches up and strokes my arm. I'm not sure who it is but I take her hand and we hold each other for a few moments before letting go. The baby kicks hard as if resentful at also waking up. I place a hand on my bulging stomach.

Once more despair washes over me at the fact that for all the years Samuel and I were together I was never with his child, yet in such a short time with Drummond and in such repulsive circumstances ... What evil grows inside me? A child from such a monster, conceived during a rape, cannot be anything but hideous. I feel as though the Devil has entered my body and I'm possessed.

Oh, Samuel, my love. What am I going to do?

They broke me the morning Joseph was murdered. That had been Drummond's intention, not to kill me at all. What everyone could see except me was that when I was standing on the bench with a noose around my neck, Findlay untied the other end and held it, simply letting go when I fell.

I don't remember hitting the ground or anything from the days that immediately followed. Apparently, I was in a state of delirium, going so wild at times in the hut that it took four women to hold me down. Eventually, they tied me to the bed for my own safety and Tamar came to care for me while the others were in the fields or working elsewhere.

When I finally came out of the darkness – no, I've never fully come out of it. There is always a shadow across my soul. I didn't recognise the person I had become. There was nothing left of the Violet who had fought so fiercely beside the man she loved so passionately. Even on the outside, I changed. My hair fell out in such quantity that in the end I shaved my head. When it grew back my hair was almost white.

Shoshana said my eyes were different. When I asked her in what way she said they belonged to a dead person. A few of the women became a little frightened of me. And there's something else ... resentment. That's not a strong enough word. No one has said anything, but the reality is that Joseph could probably have escaped successfully if he had gone by himself. I know it and so does everyone else. His death is partly my fault. I think Rory also feels guilt at involving Joseph in our attempt, although he has never spoken of it.

Of my darling Calum, I've heard nothing. I don't know if he was killed that day, captured and sent to another plantation or if he evaded his pursuers altogether. Despite enquiring of everyone I could possibly ask, there's never been any news and even Rory with all of his connections has not been able to find anything out.

Since returning to work in the fields I've gone every evening by myself to the big house and asked Drummond if he wants me. Often he doesn't, normally because he's too drunk or, ironically, because he no longer has the same desire for me ... for what I've become. If he does, I simply do whatever he says. I don't speak. I don't resist. I don't cry afterwards back in the hut.

Four months ago he told me not to come back; he found my belly too repulsive. Now I'm filled with a terrible dread at this impending birth, which can't be many weeks away. I hate this unnatural creature inside me. I loathe it. The thing kicks hard, as if knowing my thoughts. It hates me. I sigh. I need to get up and relieve myself. That's the third time tonight.

* * *

I'm screaming. The women try to reassure me that it will soon be over but I know something is terribly wrong. Nothing natural should hurt like this. I'm being punished for bringing evil into the world. Why do these things always happen at night? The bed I'm in has been pulled away from the wall so that there's easy access to both sides. The children have been taken to the far end of the hut.

Shoshana mops my brow with a cloth dipped in cold water. Naomi is down between my legs. She keeps speaking and I can't understand a word she's saying.

'You're doing fine,' says Shoshana. 'Naomi says it's normal.'

'This is not normal! I've got a monster inside me and God is angry that I'm bringing it into His world. He's not letting it come out. I'll die.'

'I don't believe that,' she says.

'I hate this thing.'

'I don't believe that either.'

It's difficult to speak and almost impossible to breathe. Someone has plunged a hot knife into my back and my body feels as though it's being ripped. When I'm not screaming, I'm crying. Naomi mutters something and I'm vaguely aware of heads nodding.

Then I'm screaming more than ever and it *burns* as the pressure bears down between my legs and all I am now is pain. How many hours has it been? How many days? And with a sudden pop, like a bubble bursting, there's something between my legs and I'm wet. The monster has escaped and it's hideous. I don't want to see.

'Put out the lights!'

There's crying. Not mine. The women are busy. I don't want to see.

'Take it away!'

'You have a son,' says Shoshana.

Naomi brings me the tiny devil, wrapped in a large cloth, and lays it in my arms. He looks up at me with such startling blue eyes, as surprised to see me as I am to see him. He moves a tiny hand towards my chin. When I stroke it he holds my finger and won't let go. There's nothing about him that resembles me or Drummond.

He's perfect.

God help me now, for I love him with all my heart. I clutch the baby to my breast and I will never let go, never give up for him. Ever.

36

Violet
31 July 1681, Drummond Plantation, Barbados

It's Sunday morning and we're lined up as usual to hear a sermon about God and goodness from the most corrupt, vile, brutal hypocrite that ever walked this earth. Duncan frets in my arms. He's been particularly unsettled over the last few days. I put him to my breast, but he doesn't appear hungry and sucks so feebly that my stomach tightens in worry.

Drummond walks towards us from the big house, followed several yards behind by McKinnon, who is almost staggering. I can't believe he's been drinking this early in the day. The murmuring amongst us dies away to complete silence as Drummond climbs into his pulpit. He gazes down upon us for a long while before speaking, but I take little notice and am much more concerned with trying to get Duncan to take some milk.

'You are like my children. And I am like your father, who protects and feeds you, ensuring that you're well and happy. For you should be happy to live in such beautiful surroundings. We are all one family here.'

There have been times when I've wondered if he is completely insane, either through the overconsumption of alcohol, the unnatural climate or some inner evil that has taken over his mind, but whenever I've subsequently analysed his words and actions, Drummond's intentions are clear. His aim is complete control of those around him, which is why he alternates between severe punishments and almost saying he loves us. I wouldn't be surprised if one day he did.

My attention is suddenly grabbed by the sound of moaning and when I seek out the source, I see a figure sink slowly to his knees.

'Bartholomew! What's the meaning of interrupting my sermon?'

'Master, I feel so ill.'

Drummond is clearly angry yet appears to want to continue the false impression that he is concerned about our welfare. 'When I have finished you may have a dose of Kill-Devil. That will sort you out. In the meantime, you must stand.'

But Bartholomew has slumped even further, propping himself up on one hand and obviously in no state to rise by himself.

'Get him up!' shouts Drummond to no one in particular.

I don't know what possesses me – some fragment of my father's teaching of medicine, a memory of the Reverend Colvil's sermons, real sermons about caring for others. I cover my breast and hand Duncan to Shoshana next to me. She stares in horror, for to move out of line on a Sunday morning is a punishable offence. My actions take everyone by such surprise that nobody speaks as I walk over and kneel by Bartholomew. He's hot and when I take hold of his head to look into his face his eyes roll upwards as if possessed.

'Master, this man is terribly sick.'

'He'll be seen to later, and so will you, Violet, if you don't get back in line!'

'Master, alcohol won't do this man any good.'

As I speak, Bartholomew slips unconscious on to the ground.
'Jesus Christ!'

I look in surprise at the unexpected outburst and am even more taken aback at who's made it.

'Mister McKinnon!' says Drummond. 'What's wrong with you?'

'My head.'

As we stare at the overseer, who has both hands on his head as if trying to squeeze out the obvious pain, he vomits violently then takes a few unsteady steps towards the house before collapsing.

Now people are whispering nervously, with many stepping away from those affected as if fearful of being too near. I can't blame them and my mind races as I try to imagine what my father would do. I walk towards Drummond, who appears stricken with indecision. He leans over the side of the pulpit and I keep my voice low so as not to give anyone the impression that I'm telling him what to do, particularly him.

'Master, we have sickness on the plantation and those affected must be kept away from the others.'

'How do we do that?'

It's the first time I've seen Drummond look scared and he's certainly never asked for my advice before.

'We should put the sick into one hut.'

'Men and women?'

'If they're that ill, they won't be bothered about who's lying next to them. Everyone else should move out of that hut. Mister McKinnon needs to be somewhere.'

'Not with the slaves or servants.'

'In his own hut then. The other two will have to find an alternative unless they also become ill.'

'Someone has to take care of the sick. You do it!'

I was expecting this. 'All right,' I reply, as if I've actually got an option, 'but I have to be . . .' I'm about to say free, but realise this would not be the word to use. '. . . able to move around unhindered.'

The decision is forced upon him when a woman cries out and has to be held by two others to prevent her from collapsing.

'Mister Findlay. You and Mister Hunter will take Mister McKinnon to his quarters. You may then wish to find other accommodation for the near future. Violet will oversee the care of the sick and she has my permission to move around unhindered.'

Drummond lowers his voice again so that only I can hear. 'I'll keep to the house with Tamar. I don't want anyone else inside. You may converse with me through a window so that I'm informed regularly as to what is happening.'

With that, Drummond gets down from his pulpit and walks back to the house, adding cowardice to his list of unenviable characteristics. Now I'm faced with dozens of people, all looking to me for instruction.

God guide me in this so that I may do the right thing.

I take a huge breath to steady my nerves. 'Listen carefully! Master has put me in charge of taking care of the sick. Does anyone feel unwell?'

No one answers. It's really what I expected because many believe that to admit to any symptoms will condemn them to actually getting the illness, if for no other reason than that they're likely to be put amongst those who do have it.

'Does anyone's head hurt?'

To my surprise, Alan holds up his hand. Following his example, two of the slaves do the same. I point at the nearest building.

'All right, everyone from this men's hut who feels well must move to another hut. I want those who are seriously ill carried inside and placed at the far end – men *and* women. Those who are feeling unwell can go to the barn and remain there tonight if they don't get any worse. Do not hide your symptoms. Pretending you don't have any will not keep you safe.'

I watch as Bartholomew is carried into the hut, while others move around in various directions, some quickly retrieving their few possessions from their usual sleeping area. The women have largely dispersed. Only Shoshana remains, standing a short distance away with Duncan. I don't know what I would do without her and go over to explain that she'll have to keep him for a while longer. I'll see first if he'll take some milk. It's only as I get near that I realise how shocked she is by this unexpected outbreak.

Duncan's face is partly covered by his shawl so I gently move a little of it to one side to enjoy a few precious moments with just the three of us. I gaze down with such love in my heart and for the first time I truly understand what my father meant at Bothwell when he said he loved Hamish and me. Duncan's no longer fretting and looks so peaceful in Shoshana's arms. Then I wonder how my world can keep ending and ending and ending.

My beautiful baby boy is dead.

* * *

I sit alone with Duncan in my arms. I tell him how much he's loved and how sorry I am that I've not been a better mother, that I haven't been able to keep him with me. Everyone has stayed away. In the end, it's Rory who approaches and kneels beside us.

'Violet, I'm so very sorry for the loss of Duncan, but we must bury him. You're needed desperately. The place is unravelling fast. Hunter has left to try and get help, although I suspect he'll simply stay away as long as he can, while Findlay has disappeared with a jug of Kill-Devil. People are lost and more are falling sick.'

I gaze at Rory. His words seem to reach me from a great distance, yet a part of me realises that there is terribly urgent work to be carried out and I must say goodbye to my baby.

'Will you help dig a grave?'

Tears roll down his cheeks. I've never seen Rory cry. 'Violet … I've already done it.'

I nod.

The two of us walk to the area that's used as a cemetery and I see in a far corner that a new grave has been created. It's tiny. Just so tiny. Gently I lay my baby in the ground and as a last gesture I cover his head with the shawl.

'You can't have a dirty face when you meet God.'

We stand in silence for several moments. Someone takes my hand and I look with surprise at Shoshana, who has walked silently up behind us.

'Violet,' she says after many minutes. 'Perhaps we should leave Rory with Duncan and go back to help those still living?'

'I promise I'll carry out this task with the greatest love, respect and care,' says Rory.

'I know you will,' I say. 'Thank you.'

Shoshana and I return to the main compound to find people standing around unsure what to do.

'They're afraid,' says Shoshana. 'And so am I.'

Firstly we go to the barn, where two people are lying amongst the straw. Three others sit nearby. I bend down to examine the most serious, one of whom is Alan. His breathing is rapid and he's hot to touch, even though I can see he's shivering.

'Explain how you feel.'

'Terrible pains in my head ... around my body ... my back in particular. I'm so weak I can hardly stand. Oh God, Violet, help me sit up.'

I get my arms around him and pull him into a sitting position, from which he immediately begins to vomit violently.

'Shoshana, I need men in here to help carry people to the hut.'

'They're too scared to come into the barn.'

'Damn their bloody fear! I've no time for it.' I storm outside, where most of the slaves stand around. 'You and you, come with me. NOW!' I'm screaming and the two men I've picked suddenly seem more frightened of me than the sickness. They follow me inside.

'Carry him to the hut and then come back for this man.' I watch as they reluctantly pick up Alan and carry him away. 'Shoshana, get the women together with the men.'

I step outside. Rory is with the men now, and they go quiet as I approach. I wait until the women have joined us. A short distance away, two slaves carry the second man from the barn to the hut. I speak loudly and with authority.

'The master has put me in charge of all matters to do with your health. Firstly, we'll have full access to the food stores so that we can all eat better meals. Shoshana, I want you to speak to every woman and child and see if any are feeling unwell. Those that are, need to go into the barn. If people are feeling sick, then they won't be made worse by going into the barn. Rory, I want you to do the same to the men.'

Dozens of faces stare at me in silence.

'Violet, the food hut is locked,' says Rory. 'No one will believe that they won't be punished if we take food without hearing Master Drummond himself give permission.'

It's as if a madness consumes me, and I crave it, beg for it, because the madness is the only thing that's keeping me sane.

I spin around and march to McKinnon's accommodation. I've never been inside before and hoped I would never have to. I push open the door with such force that it slams against the wall and the smell hits me the moment I step inside. The contents of the overseer's stomach form a trail to his bed, where he lies, groaning and shivering. He almost looks scared at seeing me burst into the room.

'The master has ordered me to take care of those who are sick and to do that properly, I need access to the storeroom. Where's the key?'

He appears puzzled, as if the question is beyond him, so I go up close and look upon him with such venom that he shrinks back against the wall. 'Where. Is. The. Key?'

He points to a peg nearby. I grab the key and walk out, leaving the door open, then head straight to the stores hut, shouting over to the slaves who don't appear to have moved. 'Rory! Bring four men and start taking whatever food is needed. Take plenty to the women. Take anything else you consider useful.'

The long narrow hut is like a small wooden fortress, sitting on stout legs coated in tar to deter ants and shaded by four tamarind trees positioned so that the building is never in sunlight. Once I've unlocked the heavy door, I enter a forbidden world of food. Everything is clearly identified and it's immediately obvious that much of it has been imported.

Sacks of bread flour from England sit below shelves with stone jars holding a variety of oils, while glass jars display an array of pickled or dried items. Huge cheeses wrapped in fine linen sway gently upon wires hanging from the ceiling and nearby there are boxes of fine biscuits and other dainties. The entire hut smells of spices and herbs and there are several bags of them, plus larger bags of salt.

I come to several intricately inlaid rosewood containers that are marked with the names of different varieties of tea. Next to them is another with the word 'coffee' on the lid. There doesn't appear to be meat of any sort and the only alcohol is a barrel of brandy and one of red wine which I assume Talitha uses in certain dishes. There are baskets of recently picked hen and duck eggs and on the floor nearby is a metal container. I lift the lid to reveal what must be this morning's milk as it smells so fresh.

When I spot a huge sack marked 'Oats from Scotland' I have to open it and hold some of this familiar food from home in my hand. I'm rubbing flakes between my fingers when I hear my name called. Rory is standing outside. I put back the oats and I go to him. He's alone.

'Nobody will come. They're too afraid and there's nothing you can say that will overcome years of terror, of being beaten and whipped upon the whim of a master.'

'I'm trying to help them.'

'I know, but sometimes help can't be accepted no matter how much a person wants to give it. Don't be angry with them, Violet. They're frightened enough as it is. Come on, let's lock up. I'll take the key back to McKinnon, then together we'll do what we can.'

* * *

I've never seen anything like it. Alan has turned yellow. I mop his brow to try and reduce his fever but he's delirious, shouting words that make no sense, then groaning as if in terrible pain. Rory comes into the hut, kneels beside me and stares down at his friend for several minutes before speaking.

'I've known this before. Every few years this disease, or whatever it is, sweeps through the island.'

'Do people die?' I ask, sensing Alan too far gone to understand what I'm saying.

'Not long after I arrived in Barbados, this sickness took away many of those I had travelled with on the ship ... including my wife.'

I'm so shocked at this revelation, at my utter ignorance in never once assuming he had been married, at my arrogance in never having asked.

'Rory, I'm so sorry. I never knew.'

'I never told you.'

'But I didn't ask, and that's unforgivable.'

He places a hand on my shoulder. 'Violet, I've seen so many die here.'

News reached us a little earlier that several plantations are affected. The apothecary that Hunter went to fetch was already dead when he got there. Theories about the sickness and what causes it are so numerous they could fill a book ... it's the position of the planets in the sky, it's brought by the wind or on a visiting ship, even the hogs have been blamed.

My father used to say that if there was a sudden outbreak of illness, the first thing to check is the water people drink. The water here is generally foul in appearance but I walked around with Rory, examining the pools and other sources, and there was nothing obvious like a dead animal. In truth, the water never seems to result in illness despite my misgivings about its quality.

I look around the hut. There are five male servants, two male slaves, a woman and a child. I feel that they're at different stages of the illness rather than that some have caught whatever it is more severely than others, but I could be completely wrong. My attention is suddenly drawn by a figure at the open door, beckoning me outside.

'Master says you must come.'

'Why, Tamar, what's wrong?'

'He's sick, Violet, and wants you to care for him.'

* * *

Drummond lies on top of his bed. I've known such despair lying exactly where he is now. He looks up at me. I stare at him for a long while with neither of us speaking.

'Well, Violet, this time it's me here and you standing there. But I'm still the master and you'll remain in the house with Tamar and take care of me.'

His breathing is laboured and his skin appears unnaturally pale. I overcome my revulsion and place a hand on his forehead. It's clammy and he almost flinches at the touch.

'Your head?'

'It's bad, and pains around my back. Get me some brandy.'

I go to the bureau where he's stood so often, drinking his expensive imported spirits from a cut-crystal glass having just finished raping me as if he's done no more than get up from the table after dinner. I have to help lift his head for him to drink. Then he lies back, gasping and watching.

'You'd like me dead.'

'I think you would be no loss to the world.'

He makes a sound that could almost be a laugh. 'Will you kill me, Violet? Kill the monster who's made your life a misery?'

'There would be no tears from me if you died, but it won't be by my hand. Whatever happens will be God's will.'

'Ha ... decent, Christian, Scottish woman.'

'Lucky for you that I am.'

I feel such loathing for this man and being forced to take care of him is vile beyond description. When he eventually speaks again, his voice is so different that the sound itself is a surprise, but what he says shocks me.

'I'm sorry ... truly ... about Duncan. I should have brought you both into the house ... kept him safer.'

I didn't expect this, didn't see this coming. Didn't even know he knew his name. When the tears come, I can't stop, no matter how hard I try and in the end my legs give way so suddenly beneath me that I flop on to the edge of the bed. I'm too close to him, but don't have the strength to move. Then I feel a hand on my arm ... clumsy, patting, a grotesque attempt at comfort. Yet, his attempt all the same.

'I would have looked after him, made sure nobody hurt him.'

Why can't I stop crying? I'm so weak. Neither of us speaks for a long while.

'I've always wanted a son. I would have brought him up to run the plantation. My wife couldn't give me children.'

It's the news that he was married, and might still be, that strangely lets me gain control of myself. 'Did she die?'

'No, she couldn't cope with Barbados ... the heat and rain, the insects and rats ... the way everything rots ... furniture, materials, paintings of Scottish ancestors and the gilt frames they're held in ... people. Everything rots here, Violet, especially people.'

He suddenly moans and I see he's about to vomit so I grab a nearby bowl and help him sit up. When he's finished I lay him back down. The effort appears to have drained him.

'My head ... my head. I need more brandy.'

'My father didn't believe in patients having large amounts of alcohol unless he was going to perform surgery. I'm going to see Tamar. Rest here. I'll return soon.'

'Don't go,' he says, almost begging.

But I do.

* * *

I find Tamar in the kitchen turning the handle on a butter churn. She's growing into an astonishingly beautiful woman and although I've not expressed my fears to Shoshana, I wonder just how long it will be before Drummond forces her to his bed. I think she's too young to be in danger yet and I don't know what good it will actually do warning her.

'How's Master Drummond?' she asks.

I sit nearby at the table. 'He's suffering the same illness as the others and there's probably very little anyone can do. It's in God's hands.'

'Why does God let good people die and bad people live?'

'I'm not sure. Perhaps God calls the good people to Heaven.'

'Why?'

'Maybe because it's their time and they've completed their task on earth.'

She seems to accept this and carries on with her task, while I wonder how to broach the subject I want to discuss.

'Tamar ... has your mother spoken to you about Master Drummond and how he has no respect for women? He takes them to his bed against their will and forces himself upon them as a man can do to a woman because he's stronger. Does this make sense?'

She's still turning the handle and I want to take hold of her to have all of her attention because she doesn't realise the seriousness of what I'm trying to explain. 'You must be careful around the master, in particular as you get older and more like a woman.'

'The master won't hurt me.'

'He will, Tamar. I fear so much that one day he will do something terrible.'

'He likes me.'

Her innocence almost makes me cry. 'Yes, I'm sure he does. You remind me of Calum when he was a boy and so beautiful and innocent and unaware of how likeable he was.'

'The master had Calum whipped, didn't he? That wasn't a good thing to do. But he won't hurt me.'

'You can't be sure of such a thing.'

Tamar finally stops turning the churn. 'Violet, don't you know?'

'What?'

'The master's my father.'

I stare at her in utter shock, unable to believe how blind I've been. The instant she utters these words I can see in her features the resemblance to a younger, handsome Drummond, before drink and power reduced him to what he is today. How could I have been so stupid?

'Do others know?'

'Everyone,' she says with a shrug. She steps closer and lowers her voice even though we're the only two here. 'I once saw the master go mad when the overseer made a bad comment about me. He slammed Mister McKinnon against the wall so hard that a plate fell off a shelf and smashed on the floor. Then master threatened he would shoot any man with his own hand if he considered they had treated me incorrectly. Mister McKinnon was really scared. Even the other plantation owners treat me courteously and they're powerful men.'

I have no words to speak and hug her tightly, but then start crying and it's a long time before I stop. Eventually, I let her go and rub my hands briskly over my face.

'Well, now that the master has banned everyone from the house except us we're going to have to work out how best to take care of him – and also ourselves. We need to be able to eat. I'll sort out with Rory that we get food delivered each day.'

'Violet, there's more food in the pantry than we two could eat if we lived to be a hundred!'

'Oh, perhaps you need to show me around so that I have a better understanding.'

And so Tamar takes me around downstairs, opening door after door upon rooms filled with the most beautiful furniture hand-made from exotic woods, intricate silver clocks, ornate rugs and the paintings of masters that must have been purchased from the leading manufacturers, craftsmen and auction houses of Europe. There is not one single item that could be considered ordinary, no matter how mundane its function. Yet apart from in the drawing room all the tables, cabinets and other items are covered in a thick layer of dust. I run my finger along several surfaces, puzzled.

'Most of the rooms don't appear to be used,' I say to Tamar when we arrive back in the kitchen.

'No. Master Drummond mainly keeps to his bedroom, the study and the drawing room. It's only when he's hosting an event that lots of us have to clean and polish beforehand.'

'Can you get a message to Rory that he's to come to the house twice a day and update me on what's happening? I want to know how the illness is progressing on the plantation and around the island. I'll do the work of taking care of Master Drummond so you don't need to go into his bedroom.'

At that moment Drummond can be heard calling. I take a large breath.

'We have a lot of work to do.'

* * *

The next morning I meet Rory outside the front door and immediately know that something bad has happened.

'Alan died during the night,' he says. 'It's what I expected when I saw he had turned so yellow. I stayed with him until the end, although he didn't know I was there.'

'He knew, Rory,' I say. 'Some part of him knew. Thank you for being there. What about the others?'

'The child is very sick, but the woman seems better. The men are pretty much as they were yesterday. Those unaffected are working in the fields or elsewhere as normal. How's Drummond?'

It's a dangerous thing to do but neither Rory nor I can bear to refer to him as master if we're alone.

'A bad night but his colour is normal. I'm trying to stop him drinking so much brandy.'

'That'll be a challenge. You look awful, Violet. Are you ill?'

'No, just tired. And ...'

'Duncan?'

'Yes. I wouldn't have slept, even without having to take care of Drummond. For all those months I thought I had a monster growing inside me.'

'All babies are innocent.'

'You've not heard some of our ministers talk about predestination. According to them we're each of us born guilty.'

'I've heard them ... ministers, priests, preachers. They tell you to believe completely different things because they don't really know and only say what suits them.'

'You've no faith?'

'Lost it long ago, along with my wife and friends, my freedom and hope.'

'What keeps you going?'

He's silent for a while then he gives me an answer that I suspect he's not given anyone. 'That of everything I've lost, one day, I can at least regain my freedom.'

* * *

Three days later, Drummond sits up in bed, slurping the broth I made earlier based upon a recipe that my mother always used if someone was sick.

'This is good. I've never gone so long without eating.'

'You should have tried being held prisoner as a Covenanter. People died from lack of food and water.'

He gives a scornful grunt. 'Why stick to a faith that causes you so much misery? I'd pick something more enjoyable.'

'Because it's the truth.'

'*Your* truth. Why aren't the Anglicans right, or the Quakers or Catholics? You could even include those in your own Church of Scotland who accept the monarch as the head. Each person is convinced that God is on their side. Maybe they all have their own and there's more than one.'

His blasphemy shouldn't surprise me, yet it does. 'You don't believe that.'

'I believe in money and power, and I have both.'

'Yet you're only a man and can fall sick and die, just like King Charles.'

'Come, sit on the bed, Violet.'

'No.'

'You and I have shared this bed many times, but I've no thought of anything like that. You'll be quite safe. Sit, please. I'm getting a sore neck looking up at you.'

I'm so dumbfounded that I sit on the edge, near the bottom of the bed.

'You're not in any way attractive, Violet. I've never thought that. However, you're intelligent and well educated, surprisingly so for a woman, and just as important, in the entire plantation you're the only person I completely trust.'

Upon hearing this I'm glad I'm sitting as I fear my legs would otherwise give way beneath me.

'Trust!'

'Yes, and that's not something I've ever said. Let's face it, you could have easily murdered me over the last few days and claimed it was the sickness.'

'I would still likely have been punished for your death.'

'Perhaps. Regardless of that, I want you to help handle the accounts for the plantation.' He makes that sound of his, almost a laugh but not really. 'You have the most expressive face I've ever encountered. You'd be no good at playing cards.'

For an instant I'm reminded of Samuel in our secret place on the hill, when he said my face was brilliantly expressive.

'I won't help run the lives of servants and slaves.'

'Hear me out, decent, Christian, Scottish woman. McKinnon is a good enough overseer who understands what stock, equipment and seeds need ordering to keep the place operating effectively, but doing the accounts falls on me and I've always hated it. You though . . . I'd wager my best horse that you'd be diligent, and despite hating me and this place you would be honest in everything you did.'

'I won't do it.'

'No?'

'There's nothing you could offer that would make me.'

'I wouldn't be quite so sure.'

'Threaten me then and have done with it!'

'You misunderstand me, Violet. If you agree, you would live in the house with Tamar – I know you're fond of her – and you would never be made to carry out hard labour. Also, I promise that no man would ever touch you again, including me. Whether you consider my word to be worth anything or not, I give it. I'll never lay a hand on you.

'Think about it, decent, Christian, Scottish woman. You would never be raped again. For as long as you're here you may keep your dignity. And let's face it, whether you handle the accounts or someone else does will not make any difference to the lives of the others. You might even be able to improve it for them. And if you haven't served your time before I die, I promise that you'll be set free upon my death.'

I'm stunned beyond words and can only sit on that hideous bed, staring at this loathsome man and his offer. Drummond is a demon in disguise, for he knows exactly what to say and do in order to break someone's will.

'Now go away. I'm tired. And take this bowl with you. I don't like the taste any more.'

* * *

When I judge that everyone has eaten their evening meal, I slip out of the house and take Shoshana away from the others so that we can talk without being overheard. Once I've explained what Drummond has said, she sits in silence for ages.

'You want me to tell you what to do, Violet. I can't. I'm a female slave on a plantation in a strange country run by powerful men and I can't say anything you haven't already thought of.'

'You're my closest friend and I need your advice. I'll never forget how you've looked after me.'

'Yes, I took care of you when you most needed it, but this choice is yours alone.'

'You're angry.'

She stands, turns away from me and then turns back. 'You want my blessing because you're too guilty to say yes by yourself. At least be honest, Violet.'

'What do you mean?' I reply, getting up slowly to face her.

'Your heart has already decided. I don't blame you. What woman wouldn't grab such a chance ... never to work in the fields again ... never to be beaten again ... never to be raped again.' Shoshana lists these scenarios as if each one is a dream of hers that she knows will always be out of reach. 'Take it! Take the offer. But you make me a promise that you'll care for Tamar as if she was your own daughter.'

'Of course.'

'Swear it!'

'I promise. I promise I'll always do everything I possibly can to protect her.'

'Then become the master's book person and look after my daughter. I won't always be around to help.' A sob bursts from her lips.

'Shoshana?'

'It's Comar!' she shouts, so unexpectedly that I almost jump backwards. 'My name is Comar. Shoshana is the master's name and I'll not have you call me that any more.'

I don't understand what's happening, what it is that I'm really being told. We're both crying. I have a sense of terrible dread and want to ask why she's telling me her real name now, but Tamar is running towards us.

'Violet! Violet! You have to come!'

'What's happened?'

'The master. He's sick.'

I don't want to leave. Comar grabs my hand.

'Go. And never forget what we've agreed.'

I'm so confused, yet run back with Tamar to the big house, determined to return to my friend as soon as possible. We rush up the stairs but at the doorway to the bedroom Tamar stops when I go in. Drummond lies on his back near the bed as if he's fallen out of it. He's been violently sick and soiled himself as well by the smell. I pick up a candle from a nearby table and kneel by him.

It's then that I see the yellow colour to his skin.

37

Samuel
5 August 1681, Stromness, Orkney

I'VE MOVED TO STROMNESS BECAUSE ships leave here often for America and the West Indies. If Violet is alive, then these places are where she would have been taken; and if she ever returns to Orkney, then it will most likely be to Stromness. It's a foolish, desperate hope that she could ever come back. Yet here I am, a fool in love with a memory that never fades.

The demand for my paintings of ships continues to grow and I've already been successful enough to purchase a small but well-built stone house not far from the harbour. When I'm not in the workshop I've created, the harbour is where I'm usually found and this morning I'm sitting on a wooden crate watching sailors unload cargo from Jamaica.

The ship has been here before and I've got to know a few of the men. There's one Orcadian in particular I like to draw, for his face represents so perfectly a life spent at sea. Then I spot him, walking along the gangplank carrying a large sack on his shoulders, a strong man even at his age which, in fairness, is impossible to tell. Maybe he's a lot younger than I assume. When he lays down his burden I call over.

'Hey, Magnus, a good journey?'

His whole face cracks into a smile when he sees me. It's quite extraordinary to watch and a delight to sketch.

'Aye, Mister Milligan, sir,' he replies, touching his cap in respect. 'We've had a good sailing.'

'Have you time to pose for me?'

Magnus glances up at the deck, checking to see if there's an officer in sight. His mates continue to unload. They all know that Magnus will end up with some easily earned money in his pocket as long as he's not found out.

'Mister Milligan, sir,' a sailor calls out, 'why don't you draw me instead?'

'Sorry, Jack, you're just not good-looking enough.'

This sets all the nearby men off laughing, including Jack, who takes my jest in good spirit. They know that Magnus will use my coins to buy rounds that evening in the Stromness tavern. He sits on a sack and takes out his clay pipe while I quickly retrieve paper and graphite from my leather satchel. We've managed about five minutes when an angry voice calls down from the ship.

'What the devil do you think you're doing down there!'

Poor Magnus jumps up as if a dozen wasps have stung him on the arse at exactly the same time. The officer hasn't spotted me and I call up in as friendly a manner as possible.

'My fault entirely, officer. I forced this poor fellow into posing and he shouldn't be blamed for my interference in his work, for which I do apologise.'

'Oh, it's you, Mister Milligan, sir.'

That I'm often a guest of the most powerful ship owners in Orkney is well-known amongst regular crews and this has saved me, and my subjects, from verbal abuse on many occasions. However, I never want to appear to undermine the authority of even the most junior officer as this would be hugely unfair.

'Perhaps, sir,' I reply politely, 'if I may have your permission to quickly finish my sketch then I could draw a likeness of yourself if you wish ... maybe as a present for your good lady wife?'

I've no idea if the officer is married but suspect that the offer of a free sketch of him in uniform will appeal.

'Very kind of you, Mister Milligan, sir. I'll be on deck whenever it suits you.' He looks back to Magnus. 'Carry on there! Don't hold up Mister Milligan longer than necessary. He's a busy gentleman.'

'Aye, aye, sir.'

When the officer walks away, Magnus sits down and his face breaks into such an array of crevices and ravines that I have to clamp a hand to my mouth in case my laughter is heard on deck.

* * *

This afternoon I'm expecting a visit from the Reverend Sinclair, who will always be welcome in my house. Not long after I moved here I received a letter from him, brought by a man also delivering several large boxes. I've taken out the letter for although I know the contents by heart I still get pleasure from reading the words:

My Dear Samuel,

You will see by this letter that I received your new address. Thank you for sending it. The manse has felt rather empty these last few weeks and the other evening I went to the workshop and removed the lids from all of the jars of pigments, inks and solutions, except the one containing turpentine as I know from experience this is not pleasant to breathe. Then I sat and closed my eyes.

I could almost hear Anne's voice. She was a very generous woman and would not have wanted her painting materials to remain as a shrine to her memory. I came to understand that evening that I had been left these items only for the time my broken heart needed them. I'm their guardian and now they must be passed on.

I mentioned my idea to Gilbert. He was, as regards painting, Anne's patron. I noticed your surprise the first time you walked around her workshop, and you were quite correct, my lowly salary would never have been able to purchase such expensive materials. It was Gilbert, with his many contacts, who obtained almost everything she needed for her art.

Anyway, Gilbert arrived the very next day with two strong men carrying packing chests and plenty of straw to help me with the task. When they had gone and the room was completely empty, I opened the window for the first time in more than two years. Anne loved children and the sound of children playing nearby suddenly filled the room. It didn't feel empty any more. I'm not ashamed to say that I shed many tears, but they were not all of sorrow.

So, dear Samuel, please accept this gift. I know you will put everything to good use.

I shall of course let you know when I next plan to visit Stromness.

Your Most Humble & Obedient Servant,
Reverend John Sinclair

My thoughts are interrupted when I hear knocking at the front door. Quickly, I put away the paper and run to answer it. My face is already smiling before I get there.

'Samuel! How are you?'

'Well, thanks to you, Reverend Sinclair.'

'Ah, not my doing ... yours and God's.'

We go through to the kitchen, where the fire is crackling in the hearth. I've spent much of yesterday and this morning preparing and the table is laden with slices of ham, turkey and honeyed chicken. There's a venison pie and herring pie from the local baker plus fresh bread, along with butter, cheeses and pickles. Next to a trifle is a large plate of mince pies, the neck of lamb, fruit and spices making them so delicious that I ate one in the shop as I was buying them. There is wine and ale plus tea, which I know he is partial to but can't afford.

'A feast!' he says in delight. 'Surely not just for us?'

'Please eat what you wish, Reverend, and then perhaps together we can take what's left around to the kirk. The minister says he'll make sure it goes to those most in need.'

'Now that's an arrangement I can live with happily.'

We sit around the table and I take great pleasure in being able to repay a tiny part of the generosity he has shown me since I arrived at his manse all those months ago. When we've eaten and drunk our fill my guest sits back in his chair, his face becoming serious.

'You have some bad news?'

'I have, Samuel, I'm sorry to say. You know that there are those who supply me with information from around Scotland. I pass it on to others who keep their beliefs secret to the outside world.'

'I hear Covenanters are still hunted like animals.'

'Hunted, tortured, killed, transported to the plantations. These are not called the Killing Times without reason.'

'The cause has resulted in so much death and misery. I don't doubt the right of it, or that one day Covenanters will win, but I've no fight left within me to play any part in the outcome.' The joy at my friend's visit is momentarily nudged aside by feelings of failure and emptiness. 'I had to face the truth of this during those long months of recovery with Mary and Hugh.'

'I know it, Samuel, I know it. You've done much and lost a great deal. Edinburgh's hangman continues to be busy. The year began with the execution of young women and last week it was the turn of the Reverend Cargill.'

'Donald Cargill, executed! That's heavy news to carry. I was one of dozens who helped to keep him safe from the Highlanders who were searching in Ayrshire for him in seventy-eight. They came close to capturing him on several occasions.'

'Sadly, the Royalist soldiers eventually succeeded.' The Reverend Sinclair takes a large breath and sighs. 'It's not right that I hold back bad news that affects you personally. I'm very sorry to have to tell you that your mother died in May. That information only reached me recently. I wanted to tell you in person.'

I didn't expect this and I'm not sure quite how to react. Via the minister's contacts I had secretly got word to my mother last year that I was alive and hiding in Orkney. Of Calum and Violet I could give no news. She understood not to mention my existence to anyone, even Hamish, who I had heard was living close by with his own mother following his release from Greyfriars Kirkyard.

'The thing we feared when my father was executed, that my mother would find out about his death by the arrival in Coylton of his head ... there was no way we could prevent it.'

'That would have been so terrible a shock it's a wonder the poor woman didn't drop down dead upon the spot.'

'My mother was a strong woman, like Violet's in so many ways. The two of us often laughed that they could have been sisters.'

'Of Violet's mother I have no news, so I assume she's alive. I hardly need to ask that you still have a great emptiness in your life.'

'Sometimes I hear Violet's voice so clearly that I turn around to speak to her, only to find there's nobody there.'

'I often speak to my dear Anne. I did wonder ...'

'What, my dear friend?'

'Have you ever thought of painting Violet's picture?'

As he says those words I'm overcome by the realisation that I can't paint anything until I've created this image, this physical representation of the woman I love.

'No, but now I'll not rest until I've completed it. Violet lying amongst the heather in the place we used to meet, but not as a girl, as she was on our wedding day. I can see this image as clearly as you sitting opposite me.'

'Then that is your most important task, Samuel, and I look forward very much to one day seeing the woman who has so captured your heart.'

* * *

My workshop is at the front of the house and although it's not large, this room gets the best light and serves my needs well. With the benefit of Gilbert's contacts I have a batch of fine linen canvas, and I fitted the best one to a wooden stretcher before coating it with animal glue, successive layers of gypsum, drying oil and a final priming layer of light green paint. Because every application has to be completely dry before the next is applied these preparations take a long time, but during this period I've been producing dozens of sketches in ink and graphite of Violet.

Although I'm driven by a need to create this image to the point of hardly being able to sleep, I don't rush into it, for the task is too important not to consider every tiny detail. I've had to prepare not just the canvas and create the drawings that I want to use as a guide, but also to make myself ready.

This morning, I know it's time to begin and that's not just because the sun is shining. I feel it inside. For days I've been hearing Violet's voice almost constantly, seeing her face and the outline of her body whether my eyes are open or shut. It's a strange sensation. Since the sinking of the *Crown of London* I've never been more certain that she is alive, somewhere out there in the world. There's no logic to it, no sense, no reason ... just a certainty in my heart.

38

Violet
5 August 1681, Drummond Plantation, Barbados

BETWEEN US, TAMAR AND I clean up Drummond and get him back into his bed, a task which proves to be almost beyond us. He doesn't wake and during the night becomes quite delirious. By the light of the next morning, I can see clearly that his skin is turning a more defined yellow and I begin to think that he will die like Alan.

What would happen to me if he did? His offer of freedom would die with him as he's had no opportunity to put this in place with his lawyer, Greig. On top of this, McKinnon would be let off his leash to punish me as he wishes and there would be nothing I could do to stop him until a new owner eventually arrives, and perhaps not even then.

The only option I have feels despicable to me, but I'll do whatever I can to save Drummond, although it's almost nothing. His body is so hot it feels on fire and I sponge him down with tepid water. I've opened all of the upstairs windows to try and get a draught, but the humid temperature has been unbearable for weeks. When it rains, which it does once a day, it's as though every angel in Heaven is crying.

He appears haunted by demons, calling out and shouting, crying in terror on occasions. I'm mopping his brow when he grabs my hand and won't let go, even though I'm sure he isn't conscious. His hold is so firm I can't break it and I'm forced to sit on the bed by his side.

'You're in the grip of a fever,' I say, not sure if the words make any sense to him, but feeling I have to say something. I don't know why. He's a monster. 'You're in your own bed in the big house, and quite safe. There are no devils after you. They're just in your confused mind.' I almost scream when his eyes open and he looks at me.

'Stay. Stay.'

'All right, I'll stay ... I promise.' That's the second promise I've made. 'I won't leave you alone.'

With that he closes his eyes and lets go. I rub my hand, which feels as though it's nearly been broken, then fetch spare blankets so that I can sleep in the armchair across from the bed over the coming nights, assuming he survives that long.

* * *

Four days and nights pass and I only leave the bedroom to relieve myself. Tamar continues to bring me food and water, leaving plates and jugs at the door, but on occasions I have had to get her to help me, for Drummond is a heavy man and I can't move him by myself. I haven't seen her this morning, which is unusual, and I'm just thinking of going downstairs to get water when Drummond's voice startles me. I hadn't realised he was conscious.

'You stayed.'

'Yes.'

'Good.'

'I said I would.'

'Decent, Christian, Scottish woman.'

I walk over to stand by the bed. He looks more ill awake than he did asleep.

'Brandy.'

'Here.' I have to help lift his head so that he can drink from the nearby glass.

'Water!'

'Yes, that's all you're getting until I say otherwise.'

He makes a dismissive sound that isn't actually a word, or maybe it is but I don't catch it. He stares at me in silence for a long while. 'Where's Tamar?'

'She's been keeping me fed and watered, although I haven't seen her this morning, which is strange. I've not even heard her going around.'

'Check that she's all right.'

I find his concern surprising, but I'm pleased to get out of the room, if only to go downstairs. I can't find Tamar in any of the obvious rooms and calling her name doesn't get a response. It's then that I spot her sitting on the steps leading down from the veranda. I go out of the front door and take several large breaths of fresh air, which smells so different to the bedroom despite the open windows.

'The master is awake. He seems to be recovering.' I sit down beside her and it's only then that I see the grief on her face. 'Tamar! What's wrong?'

'It's my mother, Violet ... she's dead.'

* * *

We bury Comar in the evening. How she knew the end was coming, I cannot know, but now I realise why she told me her real name. It was her last chance to do so and to get my promise to take care of her daughter. I keep my arm tightly around Tamar as we all stand about in silence.

The body that's disappearing slowly before our eyes under spadefuls of earth held me tightly that terrible night, never once letting go. This strange island has revealed the greatest cruelty, depravity, injustice and greed that I've ever heard of, yet I've seen the best of humanity where the most brutally used and hard-pressed of people have demonstrated the greatest kindness and generosity.

Tamar whimpers and I stroke her hair. 'Shh, you're not alone. You are much loved and I will do everything I can to keep you safe.'

I try to sound certain, but the reality is that there is little I can do to protect her. Tamar is safe only because Drummond orders it, but when he dies I fear there will be such a hateful vengeance shown against this beautiful girl. She knows it. The painful truth is that I have to do whatever I can to keep Drummond alive because if he dies, we'll be in even more danger than we already are.

* * *

When Tamar and I return to the big house, I find Drummond sitting up in his bed. He looks awful but no longer on the brink of death. Although it's difficult to be certain, particularly in the light of candles, his skin seems slightly less yellow and I can only assume that's a sign of recovery. I wish my father was here with his huge medical knowledge. Instead, he lies in a trench alongside so many other Covenanters near Bothwell.

'She's buried?' asks Drummond.

'Yes.'

'What about the others?'

'There are three people still sick in the hut but no one else shows any signs.'

'The worst is over?'

Five people have died with the same symptoms. I didn't realise Comar was ill and she might have suffered from something different.

'I believe so.'

'Sit on the bed.'

I sit.

'We spoke about you living in the house and handling the books for the estate.'

I don't answer immediately. 'Apart from what you've already offered, there's one condition.'

'You don't make conditions.'

'Keep Tamar in the house, keep her safe, and make her free as well.'

'Why do you ask this?'

'Because I gave my word to ... Shoshana ... to take care of Tamar and the truth is only you can do that.'

He studies me for a while. 'I'm not like those owners who take their slave daughters to their bed. A few of them hold some of the most lavish parties on the island and the great and good turn up to eat their food and drink their wine and not one person will openly criticise them for such unnatural behaviour.'

I wonder that this is where he draws the line, after all he's done. 'Slaves are considered to be property, not people,' I remind him, as he reminded us so often.

'Slaves are property, Violet, but sleeping with your own daughter ...' He makes that sound. 'Your face! I'll keep Tamar safe. I'm exhausted.'

I hadn't appreciated the huge effort he was making to speak. His head droops and moments later he's asleep. I remain on the bed as I've nowhere to hurry to.

We've just buried my closest friend and now I have Tamar to care for. Then there's Rory, one of the most decent and honourable men I've ever known. After Joseph, Calum and I escaped, Drummond added another year to Rory's indenture because he suspected Rory had helped us.

I knew nothing of this until long after our capture, Joseph's murder and my slow recovery from the experiences. It was Tamar who told me. Rory never said anything, never openly blamed me. Yet he's not the man he was. I think something also broke in him because of those terrible events. I must remain strong for his sake.

So, I'll continue to live in the big house, handle the books for the estate and try and keep Drummond in good health. And God help me with that task. As I watch him snoring, his huge hairy hands resting on top of the sheet ... hands that have so often defiled my body ... I know I'll never hate anyone so much in my life.

39

Violet
3 October 1681, Drummond Plantation, Barbados

I HAVE A STRANGE, RESTRICTED FREEDOM that feels uncomfortable, fragile and unnatural, not that there's anything about my life that's natural. Hunter and Findlay have no dealings with me, while McKinnon and I are forced to speak daily with a certain civility so that I can record matters relating to sugar production, make a note of what supplies we need to order and inform Drummond of any other items required.

The ability to move around as I wish, at least close to the big house, means that I often join Rory, Thomas and a few of the others for their midday meal. Rory looks ill these days. I recognise very little of the person who sat with Calum and me that first night of our captivity and advised us on our new lives as indentured servants. A terrible guilt hangs over me concerning Rory, and I cannot endure it being unacknowledged any longer. I will speak to him about it at noon, although I dread the conversation.

First, I head to the stone-built millhouse, situated on a small rise in the land so that it sits higher than all of the other outbuildings. Rory once described the Ingenio inside as a monster, and long before I get there I hear a sound like the grumbling of some fearful beast. In those early months I thought that this frightening noise was what Rory referred to, but I've since come to understand what he really meant. The entire sugar-making process is the monster.

It turns the stalks of a plant into something that delights people throughout Europe, and it gives men who have sometimes come from poor backgrounds the wealth of kings, but if it doesn't kill the men who work there in an accident, then it certainly shortens their lives. I've tried to identify the cause of the early deaths of the men who work in the boiling-house, beyond the obvious excessive labour and desperate conditions, and I think it's constantly breathing the obnoxious vapours coming off the copper pans. Even strong young men seem to weaken and be more susceptible to disease and illness.

When I get to the millhouse, I stop to watch through the large open archway where the animals enter and leave. Sometimes horses are used but at the moment there are five huge oxen fastened to the sweeps that form part of the Ingenio. I feel sorry for them. They walk around in a circle for hours at a time, driving the main central shaft which turns a series of smaller brass and steel rollers. It's unforgiving, relentless work for men and beasts regardless of the temperature.

Slaves take the sugar canes passed through a hatch from the unloading platform and feed them between the rollers, while slaves on the other side catch them and feed them back through rollers revolving the other way. The Ingenio is an extraordinary contraption of cogs and wheels, noise and power which has the sole purpose of squeezing juice from the canes.

My attention is caught by a mule as it makes its lonely way towards the platform, carrying the three bundles of cut canes that were fixed to its wooden crook back in the field that's currently being harvested. This is my favourite of these animals and when the men have unloaded the bundles it stands contentedly while I rub it behind an ear.

'You're like me, aren't you?' I say quietly. 'Desperate for some kindness ... for someone to hold you.'

It stares back with such huge, sad eyes. On the nearby platform, slaves spread out the canes to quickly examine them, while others push previously checked canes through the hatch and down to those inside. During the day they need to build up a significant pile on the platform in order to keep the process running throughout the night.

Animals are well cared for across the plantations as they are generally considered more valuable than people. The mule and I now travel a similar path in life. Nobody mistreats us and we're fed and watered well, yet I see the hopelessness in those enormous eyes ... the constant loneliness that is our daily journey. As if by some silent mutual understanding the mule and I turn away from each other.

I stop to let past one of the girls carrying away an armful of pressed canes. There are three of them doing this task and they have no more rest than the men or the beasts for the creation of crushed canes is relentless. I watch for a while as she takes them to a heap that is more than a hundred paces away. Like the leaves and tops cut off the canes during harvesting this will end up as feed for some of the animals, as the hay that can be produced on the island is too poor to provide any nourishment.

I don't go to the boiling-house. On the one occasion when I went inside while the slaves were working, I fainted and had to be carried out. Instead, I enter the quiet and cool of the curing house, the shaded stone building holding row upon row of large clay pots fitted securely within wooden frames, their precious contents silently maturing.

During the summer this is one of the few places where some respite from the fierce heat can be found and I often come in, one of only a handful of people allowed to do so apart from those bringing in newly filled pots or taking away those ready for the next stage. With nobody knowing where I am this is my moment of power, sitting on the stone floor and remembering the life I used to have.

* * *

'Rory, you don't look well,' I say, once we've eaten our meal and moved away to be by ourselves.

'I'm all right.'

'No, you're not. You've lost a lot of weight in the last few months and you often appear to be struggling. Your cough is getting worse.'

He makes a noncommittal shrug. 'I guess I'm not a young man any more. The field work is difficult. Hunter can threaten me as much as he wants but it won't make any difference.'

I have to voice aloud the guilt that is consuming me. 'You would be a free man next week if it wasn't for me.'

'Just one year and four days to go, and I willingly offered my help, Violet. What's done is done and Joseph paid a much greater price. As to Calum ...'

'I think about him every day,' I sigh.

'Drummond must know what happened.'

'Of course he does, but he refuses to tell me.'

We fall silent for a while. Eventually it's Rory who speaks.

'The day that I escaped ... my wife had died that morning and McKinnon said she hadn't been useful at anything, so it was just as well she was dead. Something in me snapped. I knocked him out with one punch and ran.' Rory has to stop speaking until he's over a fit of coughing.

'I was such a fool. It was exactly what he wanted me to do because then my servitude could legally be extended. The sentences for specific acts are clearly laid out in Barbados. I got an extra year for attacking him plus three years for running away.'

'Rory, I'm so sorry. I've always felt there was something between you and McKinnon that was personal.'

'It *is* personal.'

'I'm worried that you can't survive here for another year.'

'I've no choice. Perhaps they'll give me easier tasks now that I'm no good for working in the fields. I could sit and sharpen billhooks with the elderly men, or make ropes from withes like the women.'

There's a terrible bitterness in his voice. Unnoticed by either of us, McKinnon approaches.

'Irish! Good news. The master has freed you.'

Rory and I stare in stunned silence. 'What do you mean?' he asks.

'Just that. As he's such a compassionate man, he's decided that you don't have to work your full term. You're a free man and should be grateful.'

'What about my money?'

'What money?'

'The money that I should be given upon completion of my indentured servitude.'

'But you won't have completed it and Master Drummond feels that being freed a year early is more than equal to whatever you would have been owed. Anyway, there's no land left on

Barbados for ex-servants to buy, so you can't set yourself up here. You'll be better off taking a ship to somewhere like Jamaica and setting up there.'

'I'd have to sell my labour all over again just to make the journey!'

Rory gets up, his face red with anger, and McKinnon steps back while taking hold of his cudgel.

'Don't try it, Irish, you're not the man you were.'

'That's why you're letting me go! You've worked me until I'm broken like an old man and no use to you any more.'

I stand up and get between them. McKinnon would beat Rory senseless and enjoy it.

'Mister McKinnon, thank you for passing on the master's message. I suggest we meet as usual at the end of the working day and go through the relevant figures.'

'Yes, let's do that. Irish, you can stay until tomorrow morning, then you're out.'

When McKinnon has left, Rory sinks to his knees, tears pouring down his face. The only other time I've seen him cry was when he buried my baby.

'It's all been for nothing. I've lost my wife and friends, my health, and endured these years of utter misery just to end up a vagrant, begging on the streets of Bridgetown, where they'd sooner help a dog than an Irishman.'

For the first time since I arrived on the plantation, I take Rory in my arms. There's nothing I can say that will make any difference to his despair, for every single word he's just said is true. He can't stay on the plantation and, as I hug him tightly to me, it's impossible to see where else he can live.

* * *

Throughout the afternoon I try to work in the study but it's impossible to concentrate as I'm so beset by worry and a sense that something terrible is going to occur. When I hear the bell ring to indicate six o'clock I quickly replace the various ledgers, papers and writing implements, determined to find my friend and try to come up with some sort of a plan for his future.

The cook delays me as I go along the corridor and by the time I get outside, I can see in the distance people coming back in small groups from the fields. I walk towards them in search of Rory. Ahead of me is the barn and as people reach it they stop to stare through the large open doorway. Everyone is stopping.

Everyone.

Then I'm running ... running and screaming because I know what they're looking at. This time it's not a slave. Thomas is amongst the crowd and he hurries forward, catching me firmly in his arms.

'No, Violet, no!'

'Let me go!'

'Rory wouldn't want you to see this. He wouldn't want this to be your last image of him. Please, Violet. Please don't.'

I sink to my knees, sobbing uncontrollably. Thomas gets down on the ground and holds me tightly.

'It's my fault, my fault he had the extra year that broke him. My fault. I'm sorry, Rory ... I'm sorry ... I'm sorry.'

'Shhh. Rory never blamed you for what Drummond did to him. It was his decision to help you, Calum and Joseph to escape. He knew the risks.'

'Now he's dead.'

'And that was his decision as well. You once said that as the *Crown of London* was breaking up on those Orkney rocks you told Samuel it had been your decision to disguise yourself as a man in order to remain with him, and there were no regrets, even though it was expected everyone in the ship's hold would drown.'

It's only hours ago that I knelt on the ground and held Rory exactly as Thomas holds me.

'All the people I've ever loved are dead or lost,' I cry.

'Yes, but you're not, Violet, so you must continue.'

'Why? What's the point?'

'Because there is no option other than to swing in the barn and I don't believe that's your destiny. Neither do you, Violet, neither do you.'

40

Violet
1 August 1689, Drummond Plantation, Barbados

I'M COMPILING A LIST OF items that have to be obtained and it's already more than four pages. Everyone comes to me, from the carpenter wanting a particular timber to Tamar, who says we're currently short of linen, wool, candles and a dozen other items. I also have to hire a wheelwright and I'm supposed to find someone to fix the longcase clock, which hasn't worked for nearly a year. Drummond has only noticed recently. I looked inside and the cogs have rusted. It's as he once said, everything rusts or rots.

I add *rat poison*. The apothecary in Bridgetown supplies it and at the moment the rats around the house are winning. Sometimes they do so much damage to the sugar canes that Drummond orders the entire field to be burnt. You hear them. In those last few moments, when the flames reach the centre and the seething mass of furious brown fur, they scream so loudly.

I lean back in the leather armchair and add up a column of figures relating to the output of sugar for July, which I'll later check against last year. The fortunes created by the sugar cane plantations are so vast that Barbados has become the richest British colony in the world. To some owners, money is meaningless.

When I took over the accounts, I also took over Drummond's beautiful ebony desk. At great expense, he had an identical one shipped from England. Sometimes we sit for hours engrossed in our work, a few feet apart yet separated by a distance that can never be crossed.

I hear him enter the study, so different now to the man who gave us the first of what would be hundreds of speeches from his ridiculous pulpit. He doesn't have it any more. The local ants ate it. I've got my back to him and finish the calculation I'm working on before turning around. He waits until I'm ready.

'I want you to write a letter.'

I remain silent. These days he's slow and often takes a few moments to gather his thoughts before speaking. Twice a year he receives a letter from his wife in Edinburgh and he always writes back to her soon afterwards. I know money is sent regularly and assume she lives a very comfortable life so far from the one she knew with her husband.

'It's to my brother's son ... my nephew, Mathew. He's twenty-one and it's time he came here and learnt the sugar trade.'

'Does he want to?'

'What's that got to do with it?' he grumbles. 'I've been paying for his expensive education for years. It's time he paid me back, so he needs to come to Barbados and help run the business.'

I take a clean sheet of paper and prepare to write down his words. 'What do you want me to say?'

'Oh, you write it. You'll phrase it better. Just give it to me to sign when it's done.' He turns to leave but then stops. 'You'll join me later.'

'If you wish,' I say.

For years Drummond has insisted that I join him once a week for an evening meal. Now Tamar is a young woman she also has to eat with us on these occasions. So we sit at one end of the enormous dining-room table, like forgotten guests at a long-finished party, and he talks about the plantation and his earlier life and I wonder what on earth he thinks we are . . . a pretend family?

He goes then and I listen to his steps walking along the hallway, unsure, unsteady. What will this young man find? So much has changed around the plantation since I arrived and yet so much is the same.

The voluntary indentured servants have all gone, having completed their period of servitude and gained their freedom. Drummond honoured the original agreements and gave each of them the money he owed – not that he had much choice, by law. Forced indentured servants have continued to arrive in Barbados, including Covenanters, sent here by King James, who has no more love for us than his dead brother King Charles.

These days labour is provided almost entirely by slaves from Africa. The beatings and whippings, tortures and rapes continue without end. I stay in the big house when a slave is going to be punished. Yet there are many in power who don't hear the screams or pleas for mercy. These are such a common sound around the plantations that they merge into the other noises of everyday life, like hens clucking and mules braying, and simply go unnoticed.

Now I'm faced with the task of writing to a complete stranger to tell him that his entire life is to change and he is ordered to become a part of a world that may be the most hideous and repulsive he can imagine. Well, many of us have been on that journey. I pick up a quill and realise that I need to add *ink* to the list.

* * *

It's mid-afternoon a couple of weeks into the start of the year sixteen-ninety when Tamar and I walk around the mahogany table in the dining room, marvelling at the display of cut-crystal glasses nestling amongst the large array of solid silver cutlery. Fresh beeswax candles have been put in all the candelabras and wall sconces and as more of these are lit the items on the embroidered tablecloth glint and sparkle.

Drummond is hosting a dinner party as it's his turn amongst the local plantation owners and there is a rigid rota that only death excuses one from. When he's the host, he insists that I'm present even though I have no duties and generally try to be unnoticed. People know that I'm his bookkeeper, but no one is certain quite what else (neither am I for that matter) and so to avoid potential offence visitors usually ignore me.

This enormous social occasion has resulted in Talitha the cook being in a panic all week, working late into the evenings and overseeing five people who have been brought into the kitchen to provide extra help. I've seen the menu and I doubt that the King of Scotland would have such fare upon his table.

Slaves are rarely given meat and the amount available for a table of thirty-six guests is obscene. There will be boiled chicken and suckling pig, collops of a leg of pork, a shoulder of young goat, a loin of veal, mutton plus several birds including turkeys, hens, ducklings and doves. It's almost as if Drummond wants guests to have the option of sampling any living creature on Barbados.

'How can people need so much?' asks Tamar, whose beautiful eyes are as round as miniature porcelain dishes at the sight before us.

'They don't need it, they just want it.'

'Why?'

She often reminds me of Calum when he was younger, always asking 'why'. 'Because they hope to find happiness by eating and drinking in a way that shows they're successful. They don't know what it's like to lie amongst heather on a Scottish moor with someone who loves you so much they will never tire of capturing your image. That's happiness.'

'Who's Heather?'

I laugh at this. It's a rare sound. 'I'll explain later.'

Tamar and I share a large bedroom designed and furnished for guests who never stay. Talitha sleeps in the kitchen and Isaac either sleeps on a mattress near Drummond's bed or he returns to the slave quarters. Other than that, the house is basically empty. Most owners have significant numbers of house slaves and servants, but Drummond is unusual in this manner to the extreme.

It's not long before a display of wealth starts to appear in front of the house that is beyond staggering; one after the other ornate carriages arrive, pulled by beautiful horses decorated almost as richly as the two slave drivers who are always in attendance at such outings.

Drummond chooses the most handsome of his slaves and has them dressed in identical uniforms that make them look as though they should be serving the grandest nobility in Europe. Only Tamar is different, wearing a simple dress that Drummond had made for her in Bridgetown. Everyone knows their duties and the instant guests walk into the entrance hall they are waited upon like kings and queens.

And so they come, men with their frilly wives or mistresses, men alone, men with friends. Mister Greig, the lawyer from Bridgetown, is included. He handles the legal business of several plantations. He's the only person who speaks to me. His father emigrated from Ayr, so we often have what might be considered pleasant conversions about Ayrshire. I've never told him I was present when seven men were hanged in the town by their fellow Covenanter as I suspect this might bring our pleasant conversations to an end.

Guests are shown into the dining room and gradually they sit at the table. I stand near the door and observe. A few speeches are given and then the gorging and drinking begins. The best of imported red and white wines from France and Spain are available, along with sherry, brandy, Madeira, whisky and spirits I've never heard of before coming to Barbados. There's also the all-too-familiar Kill-Devil.

I feel sick watching the scene before me. Slaves stand around the room in their golden uniforms like marble statues, but now and again I see their eyes flicker to the table. I can almost hear their empty stomachs grumbling above the noise of those eating. The evening gets noisier, drunker and messier until Drummond stands and those around the table go quiet.

'It is my great pleasure to entertain you all, for you are not just my friends but my family.' This results in much cheering, clapping and banging on the table. 'And families should take care of each other, rejoicing in good times and helping out in the bad. My nephew, Matthew Drummond' – there are great cheers for this – 'is making plans to come here from Scotland and take over the running of my plantation so that I may enjoy your company even more.'

I haven't heard this news and assume a letter has arrived that I wasn't aware of. Drummond looks ill. Unlike his guests, he hasn't drunk much this evening, yet there's an unsteadiness to him that's the worst I've seen.

'I would like to propose a toast to my nephew. I know you will make him welcome and help to instruct him in our particular ways.'

There is much scraping of chairs and noise as people stand, some of them struggling to do so. One chair tips over and Isaac quietly moves forward and puts it upright. Red wine spills on to the table, on to food, on to clothes. Nobody bothers. Drummond holds out his hand and the others follow, resulting in wine overflowing in a slosh of liquid up and down the lines.

'To Matthew Drum—'

Drummond's glass slips from his hand and smashes against the edge of a porcelain dish. He clasps a hand to his chest. There's a moment of utter stillness as everyone stares in silence. I'm already rushing forward when he utters one word:

'Violet!'

Isaac and I lower him back into his chair. There is much confusion and cries of shock amongst the guests. One is so drunk he doesn't realise what's happening and shouts, 'To Matthew Drummond,' before draining his glass and sitting down. There's no one to take charge, no one except me.

'We need to get Master Drummond upstairs and Doctor Ross sent for,' I say to Isaac. 'Will you and Adam help the master to his bedroom. Ladies and gentlemen, please sit down and continue your meal. Master Drummond would not want his temporary ill health to stop your pleasure. Tamar, please see to drinks. Elijah, could you please clear away this broken glass and let the kitchen know that the dish of pears in cream needs replacing.'

Guests flop back into their chairs as Drummond is half-carried out of the door. I go to the study and write a note for the doctor, along with a letter of authority for someone to take it. Slaves and servants are not allowed off plantations without written authority, what's known as their 'ticket', and even with this I won't send a slave as it would be too dangerous for them at night.

When I reach Drummond's bedroom, I stop in the open doorway. For more than eight years I haven't once stepped inside, yet the room is filled from the floor to the ceiling with such painful, vivid memories it's as though I had been here only yesterday. With an enormous effort, I force away the images and enter. Drummond lies on his bed. Isaac is halfway through removing his jacket.

'Thank you, Adam. Can you please go back to the dining room and help out in any way needed.' I turn my attention to Drummond. 'Where does it hurt?'

He struggles to speak. I've seen this before in older people and I assume his unhealthy living has brought it upon him earlier than might be expected.

'Arrrm ... head.'

'Doctor Ross has been sent for. Isaac and I will get you into bed. Your guests are being taken care of.'

It's only as we start removing his clothes that I fully appreciate how thin Drummond has become. Isaac is skilled at undressing him when he's too drunk to do this himself and between us we soon get him covered up.

'Thank you, Isaac. Will you please remain with him for now? I'll go and see that everything is all right downstairs.'

'Vio ...'

'I'll be back soon. You're not alone.'

Downstairs I discover that many guests have already gone while those remaining are gathering their possessions. I speak briefly to Mister Greig before he leaves. A man is slumped in his chair at the table. I'm wondering what to do with him when one of the plantation owners comes back in with the two slaves that drive his carriage.

'I'll see he gets home,' he says.

'Thank you, sir.'

It doesn't take long for them all to leave, so I go back upstairs. Isaac seems relieved when I ask him to help in the dining room. These days I'm too weary to be concerned about being on the bed, so I sit down, and in truth Drummond has kept his word. No one has touched or threatened me in any way whatsoever since I took over handling the books.

He watches me intently. 'The ... end ...'

'The end of your life? I suspect it's close,' I tell him as if merely announcing dinner is ready. 'Then you'll find out that there is a God, although I expect you'll be going to the other place.'

I can't work out his expression. I do not care to work it out.

'The doctor should be here later on. Mister Greig will come tomorrow and see to any legal matters. I'll make sure he speaks to Mister McKinnon and gives him the authority needed to continue for now.'

Drummond gives a tiny nod. 'Stay?'

'If you want.'

With great effort he slowly slides his hand towards me. The implication is obvious, like the fear in his eyes.

* * *

I wake with my head bowed as though I've only been asleep for a few moments. But it's morning, which means that Doctor

Ross hasn't visited, probably because Thomas hasn't been able to track him down.

Drummond stares at me. I stare back. I've spent more of my adult life with this man than I have with Samuel. I've had more conversations with him, eaten more meals with him, grown *old* with him ... and I've known such despair. Surely there can only be so much raw emotion that a person can endure? I've don't think there's anything left in me to *feel* much again.

I free my hand and close his eyes. If he ever had a soul, it's no business of mine where it's gone.

I'm stiff and need to relieve myself. Getting up from the bed takes a few moments and I have to stretch and rub my numbed hand. I pull the sheet over his head then go behind a screen where Drummond has a pot.

'Well, you won't need it any more,' I say to the silent room. I just need to hear a voice.

I'm coming back around the screen when there are footsteps along the corridor, loud confident footsteps of someone in authority. I open the door as Doctor Ross reaches it.

'Ah, Violet. How is the patient?'

'Dead.'

'William's dead?'

'During the night. I sat with him but fell asleep.'

'I'm sorry I couldn't get here earlier ... a very challenging situation on ... well, that doesn't matter. I'm sure your presence was a comfort to him in his final hours.'

'I expect it was.' I don't care if it was or not. As always I've done what I've had to in order to survive. 'Shall I arrange breakfast for you, doctor?'

'Yes, thank you. Some duck eggs would be pleasant.'

'I'll join you,' I say, experiencing an unexpected sense of freedom. 'It's been a long night.'

* * *

The following day, everyone from the plantation gathers in the area that's set aside for burials. Death can be a great leveller and usually someone who dies is buried in the next available plot, so slaves, servants, overseers and owners can be together. Yet differences in life can sometimes follow the deceased.

A couple of years ago, Drummond ordered the creation of a huge marble grave marker which has lain within a secluded area surrounded by intricate wrought-iron railings that took the blacksmith weeks to make. In recent months I've seen Drummond standing silently by the site and I wonder now if he knew death was close.

All of the nearby plantation owners are present, along with a large number of businessmen, traders, suppliers and dignitaries. Once the wooden coffin is lowered into place it takes eight slaves to lift and position the grave marker, the cost of which would probably have been enough to free them all. I'll have to arrange for a stonemason to add the date of death.

The local Anglican minister says the words expected of him. We say the words expected of us. Then slaves and servants go back to work while guests are invited to the house for refreshments. There's a strange void about the place. With no wife or family there is no one actually in charge.

Many people look to me and I give instructions for tasks to be carried out as I see the need. They're always done without question, but I have no authority to order someone to do anything. Also, there's now no one to tell me what to do. When I'm satisfied that everyone is being properly looked after I make the opportunity to speak to the only person I want to converse with.

'Mister Greig.'

'Violet. Well, a new beginning ...'

'That's what I wanted to speak to you about. Master Drummond promised that I would be freed upon his death if I hadn't already completed my period of servitude. I expect the paperwork is with you, sir, and I would be grateful if this could be acted upon quickly.'

'Freed? No, Violet, William never spoke to me of such a matter and if I don't have the paperwork, you can be certain it doesn't exist.'

'But he promised.'

'I'm sorry. You probably knew William as well as anyone. He had some strange ways about him and honesty wasn't, how shall I say ... I don't want to disrespect a man who's just died ... He had his own peculiar thoughts on what was truth and what wasn't. Perhaps he meant to do it but never got around to it.'

I suddenly feel like a frightened small child and can't prevent tears rolling down my cheeks, nor the tremor in my voice. 'I've been in forced servitude for nine years. There must be an end. I'm not a slave!'

'Oh, Violet,' he says, laying a hand gently on my shoulder. 'King Charles obsessively hated those Covenanters who defied him and their sentences were indeed fiercely harsh.'

I can't believe Drummond lied ... can't believe I didn't spot the lie. Samuel always used to say I had such intuition. Where has that gone?

'I can see this is a great disappointment. I don't know how long your sentence is for and if you were never told,

I'm not sure how you find out, what with William gone. What happened to the other Covenanters who arrived here with you?'

The faces of those men who had been on the *Crown of London* and the *Sophia* are still so clear to me it's as if we had eaten a meal together only yesterday. 'There were six of us. Two died and two were transferred to other plantations, one as part payment in a lost wager and another in exchange for supplies. The fifth escaped.'

'So there's just you. I'm sorry, Violet, there's little I can do. Please excuse me. I must sort out some urgent matters.'

The lawyer moves away. Even in this moment of desperation I'm suddenly struck by a thought that makes me rudely call out. 'Wait! Sir, please one more moment of your time, I beg you. The person who escaped was called Calum Colvil. We grew up together and he was like a brother. We ran away with a slave, Joseph, who was later hanged because of it. That was in the year we arrived, sixteen-eighty. I never again heard of Calum.' I don't know what else to say, but then add, 'He was an extremely handsome man.'

'Ah yes, the good-looking blond Scotsman from Ayrshire.'

My heart is like a trapped bird, fluttering wildly against the bars of its cage. 'Sir ... was he killed?'

'No, they captured him, although I gather he put up quite a fight. Calum was transported to another plantation.'

'Which one, sir?'

'Not on Barbados, Violet,' he says, shaking his head sadly, as if knowing exactly what I'm thinking. 'William ordered him to be put on board the first available ship. I know some of this because he asked me to handle the arrangements ... having Calum held in a Bridgetown gaol until a suitable vessel could be found, handling the sale of his indenture, that sort of thing. But where he went, that I don't remember.'

Greig walks away and the next moment I'm running along the corridor, a couple of guests mumbling angrily as I pass them. Plantations keep extremely detailed accounts of the transactions that take place – there must be a record, there *must*. In the study, I riffle through the ledger for sixteen-eighty. In all of the time I've had complete access to this information I never once thought to look.

It's there, in Drummond's surprisingly neat handwriting. In the column of items and produce sold during that week, immediately below a reference to the sale of a spare mule for four pounds, is the fate of my darling Calum:

Sale of the indenture for the servant Calum Colvil for the sum of twenty-two pounds. Sailed on the Elizabeth, *bound for Jamaica, 19 September 1680.*

41

Violet
30 July 1690, Drummond Plantation, Barbados

NEWS HAS REACHED US THAT the ship bringing the new master is anchored in Carlisle Bay and there's great excitement, dread and anticipation around the plantation because nobody knows what to expect. I'm busy in the study when I see through the window the first of what should be several wagons loaded with supplies from the recently arrived vessel.

We're due a huge array of items, from flour and spices to barrels of olive oil and spirit, rolls of cloth, rope, iron, copper and musket balls. The men will unload the wagon but they won't store anything away until I've checked the contents and given permission. I don't know what's on this particular wagon so gather all my lists before leaving.

A few months before he died, Drummond had a large looking glass fitted to a wall along the corridor. It's encased in a ridiculously ornate walnut frame. With no desire to see my reflection, I've always ignored it. I don't know what makes me stop this morning. I stand for a very long time.

Dear God, Violet, what have you become?

Papers slip silently from my fingers and float gently to the floor like the dried petals of a flower. Slowly, I reach out a hand to the surface. It's not the old woman who stares back at me that's so disturbing, it's that I've become as hard and cold as the glass. How did I let this happen?

If the wives of plantation owners don't hear the screams of slaves as they're branded with a red-hot iron upon arrival, then I am worse because I hide away. I don't want to know about their screams ... not even the silent ones. Slaves don't do what I tell them because they believe I'm wise, but because of my position. They don't treat me courteously out of respect, but out of fear. Even Tamar has changed towards me as she's become a young woman, perhaps realising that she's been used. The truth is I needed someone who needed me and she was simply too convenient.

I suddenly see everything as clearly as the image before me. Compassion and concern for others have been replaced by pride, a desire for comfort and, above all, my own safety. This place has corrupted me completely. Drummond said it; everything rots here, particularly people.

I eat, sleep, work and live in the big house, my education helping to run the plantation successfully but doing nothing to help those in need. It's not a decent, Christian, Scottish woman who looks back at me. It's someone who is such a stranger that I only know it's me when I reach up to wipe away my tears ... and she does the same.

* * *

When I finally gather my lists and leave the house, I find Thomas sitting on the steps. He's crying.

'Thomas, what's happened? Are you ill?'

'King William ...'

It's all he manages to say before being so overcome that in the end I sit beside him and put an arm around his shoulder. That William of Orange and his wife Mary are now king and queen of England, Ireland and Scotland was known on Barbados. Such things generally have little meaning to people in a faraway country. Thomas makes a huge effort to speak.

'William has proclaimed that the Church of Scotland is officially Presbyterian. Ministers thrown out in sixty-two can reclaim their parish. He doesn't demand to be head of the Kirk. We have our own General Assembly that's free of control by the state or the monarch. We've won, Violet. The Covenanters have won!'

I let down my arm, too stunned to offer further comfort. It's simply unbelievable. That so many thousands of Scottish men and women have died and suffered terribly for a cause that is over with a few sentences spoken by one man arriving from Holland ... one man. I should be elated. Thomas is a mess of mixed emotions, laughing and crying at the same time, yet I'm empty inside at this momentous news.

I'm forty-one years old and my whole life has been dominated by this struggle. It's cost me everything ... all the people I've loved, my home, my freedom, the person I used to be. Samuel and I could have grown old together. Now I'm just old, hard and uncaring. For some reason I can't explain, I feel more alone and lost than I've ever known.

* * *

Samuel would have told me it's a terrible sin, yet compared to the sins of this island, mine is like a teardrop in the Clyde. It's strange to remember how broken I was by fear the day that Joseph was murdered, and now I'm about to put a noose around my neck with my own hands. I don't know why I've kept going. Better to end it than live this miserable life.

I said that to Samuel as the *Crown of London* was breaking up. Was I really ever that person? I knew such passion then ... passion and love and loyalty and friendships borne out of shared hardships and danger. We had a great cause to fight for, the religious freedom of the Church of Scotland.

Thomas was wrong in what he said all those years ago about my destiny. I've climbed up to the loft in the barn and tied a rope to a beam. It's the one that's used. Abraham once showed me how to make a noose and position the knot so that death would be instant. Slaves need to know such things and they pass on the knowledge to those who might also need it. So many have ended their existence in this building.

I hesitate, not because of doubts but just to savour the moment, for in these last minutes on earth I'm free. Everything is so intense ... the smell of the earth, the sound of a mouse rustling the straw. The motes of dust caught in the sunlight coming through the cracks in the walls explode in colour. When I slip on the noose the tiny fibres tickle the skin of my neck as though it's become unbelievably sensitive.

Samuel, my love, are you waiting for me?

I lean forward, not quite off balance, then lean a bit more. My body isn't tipping over, not yet, but it's reached a point of no return.

No going back, Violet.

Suddenly a figure appears in the entrance. He's running and shouting. I'm falling and silent.

* * *

The sight of the ceiling ... *that* ceiling ... instantly fills my mind with terrifying images, lying in this bed while Drummond rapes me, so often it should be beyond my ability to count.

I do know, though, every single detail of every single time. Have I gone to Hell?

'I've prayed for your recovery.'

I don't know the voice. A young man's. Well educated. The owner appears by the side of the bed then he sits and takes hold of one of my hands. Even in my confused state I think it's an extraordinary gesture.

'To kill yourself is a terrible sin and I know that nothing other than unbelievable despair would have driven you to attempt such a thing. God guided me to that entrance in time to save you, although I must admit I would have appreciated a bit more warning. Seeing you jump as I entered that barn almost had me fainting in fright. I only just managed to break your fall and hold you up until people answered my cries for help. I'm afraid the skin around your neck was burnt by the rope, but it should heal in time.'

He's so handsome, with a kind face and a smile that makes me think he's like a combination of Samuel and Calum.

'My name is Mathew Drummond. I'm the nephew of the previous owner.'

He lets go of my hand, picks up a nearby glass and gently lifts my head to help me drink. My throat is dry and sore.

'Don't speak. You'll be safe here. I've given instructions for one of the maids to look after you. I have much to find out, but in a few days we can talk. I want to hear your story.'

* * *

It's four days later when I'm sitting opposite the new owner in the drawing room. Tamar has brought me constant news about him and his shock as he's gone around the plantation, speaking to slaves and the few remaining servants. He's certainly not his uncle. I feel an unexpected sympathy for him. He'll not survive a month.

The only other person present is Tamar. She pours tea into a china cup and is about to give it to the young Drummond when he indicates that I should be served first. I stare at it for ages without moving.

'Violet,' she whispers eventually.

I take the saucer. She pours another. He thanks her then says she can leave and he will serve if more is needed. Tamar almost trips over the rug in surprise on her way out. Then we're alone, drinking our tea while surrounded by ridiculous wealth.

'How's your neck?'

I instinctively reach up a hand, but let it drop slowly without feeling the ring of rough skin. 'I'll live.'

'But do you *want* to live?'

I don't know how to answer.

'Perhaps I should ask, why did you want to die?'

We sit in silence for such a long time, yet he gives me the opportunity to think through my answer.

'I've never told my story, but if you want to hear it, then I will tell it.'

He nods and I do. I tell him about falling in love with Samuel when we were six years old, how we grew up as a couple destined to be married, how his father was thrown out of the parish because he was a Covenanter. I explain how all our lives were changed dramatically because of our wish to have religious freedom. He hears of the battles and the deaths, of the captures, tortures and executions; of that fateful journey kept locked in the hold of the *Crown of London* and how that night was the last time I ever saw Samuel.

Young Drummond is particularly keen to hear what happened once I arrived at his uncle's plantation, and he is the most appalled at these details. When I tell him how his uncle raped me for so many months, in the very bed that I have lain in these last few days, he drops his delicate china cup. The thickness of the rug prevents it from breaking.

I tell him about my baby, the plague and deaths, the whippings and punishments, how Calum was taken away from me, about Joseph swinging from the branch and my own terror at believing I was next. Despite the clock ticking on the mantelpiece time doesn't seem to exist in that drawing room as I relive my life to this stranger who saved my body but can never save me. When I finish, he sits without speaking, occasionally wiping away a tear. That he should cry is, well ... he'll not last a week in this godforsaken place.

'I'm sorry beyond words for the things that have happened to you. There is nothing I can do about events in the past. However, I can affect what happens in the future. The ship that brought me will leave in a few days, once its supplies have been replenished and the cargo of sugar is loaded. I will pay for your passage back to Scotland and provide papers to show you are a free woman.'

'You should also leave on the ship,' I tell him, 'for this place will destroy you, despite being an owner.' I don't call him master and he doesn't seem to expect it. 'One man alone cannot undo such evil. It's in the soil, in the sugar that sweetens the tea of European ladies and gentlemen. It's in the very air we breathe.'

He nods along, yet I see the anxious struggle in his eyes, in the way he wrings his hands.

'My future was meant to be in the Kirk, a minister like your Samuel. I fear you may be right that this is not the place for me, yet for now I'm as trapped as anyone.'

* * *

Over the following days I'm like a ghost. People rarely even acknowledge my presence. It's as if I've already left. Only Tamar and I talk. Out of sight of others we say our farewells. She sheds tears for her mother and for others. I don't cry – I'm done with that.

On the day before the ship is due to depart, I go early to the cemetery. Men, women, children, slaves, workers, masters … they rot under the soil as equals in a way that's unimaginable when walking on top of it.

I kneel by the grave of my beautiful baby boy. Conceived out of fear and loathing yet loved from the moment he drew breath. Such a short life. At least Duncan was free throughout it. I stay for a while, remembering his baby sounds, how it felt to hold his tiny body, how his fingers were so small yet so strong. I'll never know the man he would have become. Finally, I gently kiss the wooden cross and move on.

I reach Rory's grave. The cross has fallen over, so I straighten it, though it will probably fall over again in the next high wind. He once said that the only things certain to grow on Barbados were sugar canes and cemeteries. He was right. How many people lie here who I have known, sometimes loved, sometimes hated? There are so many stories buried within this earth. Even Findlay is somewhere. He was found dead in his bed one morning and for all that I despised him, he was a part of my story.

Who will know in the future what has happened here in the past? The simple wooden markers will be eaten by insects. New masters and slaves will work, live and die. The production of sugar will continue as surely as the rising of the sun. Yet nobody will know of the suffering and despair that has occurred, for this shall disappear into the shadows of the suffering and despair still to come.

I pass by other graves ... Alan, Comar, Abraham, Naomi, Thaddeus, who died young as he predicted. Then I come to Joseph's. How many times have I asked for his forgiveness? I don't go near the resting place of Drummond. Despite all our time together I never understood him and he often took me by surprise. He never understood me either, although I'm not sure I ever surprised him.

'I apologise for intruding into your privacy.' Young Drummond has approached without me realising. 'I have to ride over to Martin Bay. You'll need to get to Bridgetown today and board the *Edinburgh*. The captain will almost certainly take the morning tide.

'I wanted to give you this before I go,' he says, handing over a purse that contains coins by the feel of it. 'And these, of course.' He gives me a roll of canvas tied with twine. 'Your papers, which prove you're a free woman. Keep them safe, Violet.'

Nobody had the right to take away my freedom, but I thank him. 'When you finally leave the island,' I say, 'take Tamar. Either keep her safe with you in Britain or set her free, but don't leave her behind.'

'Why Tamar in particular?'

'Because she's your cousin.'

He stares at me for a moment. 'I see.'

'The one decent act your uncle did was to forbid any man to touch her. He wouldn't himself, so she's never been hurt physically and has also stayed ... intact.'

Reluctant or not, he nods his agreement. 'I'll make sure no one does anything inappropriate.'

'If a man raped her, would you hang him?'

He flinches at the brutality of the question and, I suspect, being asked it by a woman.

'Well ... no, I couldn't do that.'

'Then you can't protect her. The men won't fear you like they feared your uncle. Keep her in the big house.'

'All right, I will. And I promise to take her with me when I return to Britain, although only the good Lord knows when that might be.'

I can't hope to get anything more from him and feel that I've fulfilled my promise to Comar to look after her daughter. Our parting is awkward. How can two people connected as we are possibly say goodbye to each other? He wishes me well. I don't reply and in silence watch as he goes to his horse and rides away. I'm left standing in the cemetery by myself and decide to leave. I don't have any possessions to collect because I'm wearing them.

Nearly everyone is working in the fields. I pass along the track, which is too far away to call out. However, I'm spotted and several pause to stare. A few wave, including Thomas. I stop and hold up a hand. When I first arrived on the plantation poor Thomas was not much more than a boy and one of the people we thought wouldn't survive. Yet here he is these many years later. It shows how wrong we can be in judging others.

McKinnon stares across the field. He's old now and has to rely on younger thugs to terrify others and carry out punishments. He shouts at those around him to get back to work and I walk on so that I'm not a distraction.

Eventually, I leave the boundary of the plantation. Although there's no one around I feel vulnerable, as if strangers are going to jump out from behind a rock and take me to another place for it all to start again. I put my hand into the pocket containing the papers and close it around the canvas roll.

When I arrive at Bridgetown I go to the harbour and speak with a sailor on the *Edinburgh*. He confirms they will leave early in the morning. Discovering I have a few hours to spare, I head into the town itself and with almost every step my amazement increases. Apart from the day we arrived on Barbados I've never been to the island's major town. The sheer variety and number of shops, warehouses, taverns and grand buildings is beyond anything I've ever experienced.

I hear many languages I don't understand while the hugely different forms of attire reveal just how far some people have travelled. Although nobody appears to take any notice of me my hand never lets go of my purse and papers. I hunt out shops selling clothes but the first ones I encounter display ballgowns in the window, ridiculous, frilly items for the wives, or mistresses, of rich planters. Indeed, some of the women I've seen strolling along in pairs and with a large male slave behind them are dressed to show off their wealth.

I carry on until I find a shop selling clothes for women that appear suitable for what I need, yet I hesitate at the doorway. It's only at this moment I realise I've never entered a shop before, not like this one. So I wait, unsure and fearful. Did I ever really fight the king's army at Bothwell Bridge? I open the door and step inside. A woman watches me enter from behind the counter, a person who has seen something of the world. She assesses me with a single glance but speaks respectfully, nonetheless.

'How may I help?'

'I'm to sail back to Scotland tomorrow and have nothing more than what I'm wearing. I have money to pay.'

She comes around to face me and studies my body not, I feel, out of any hostility but to better gauge what is needed. 'These will certainly not do for a Scottish climate. And you also need everything else for your journey?'

'Yes, I suppose I do.'

The next instant the shop owner shouts out instructions, which initially confuses me until a young girl appears and immediately starts to fetch items.

'Come into the backroom.'

Over the next few minutes the girl fetches a selection of petticoats, waistcoats, stays, stockings, shoes, coats. All of them suitable for where I'm going and for my size. I strip off in front of the owner and she starts to hand me items. Dressing a naked woman is simply part of her job.

'This ... this ...'

I dress in the order she hands me clothes and when I'm half-dressed, she stops and goes over to a drawer to pull out what looks like a wide cloth belt with sewn sections.

'That purse which you're trying so hard to hide amongst your old clothes is too easy to steal,' she says, reaching around my waist to fit the belt. 'Split up your coins into these and they'll be safe even when you're asleep. Just keep enough in your purse to have some handy. When you entered my shop you didn't look as if you had anything worth stealing. When you walk out, thieves will look at you differently.'

I hadn't expected that anyone in this town would want to watch out for my safety. 'Thank you.'

'Excuse me for a moment.'

I appreciate the gesture for while I'm alone I distribute the coins, leaving what I hope is enough for my purchases and a little extra. She returns shortly afterwards carrying a strong, canvas bag, which she lays down nearby.

'Come, let's finish.'

When I'm dressed, with spare clothes, and a warm kerchief and blanket in my bag along with other items such as a comb and small mending kit, I assume that our business is complete. However, the owner beckons me over to a nearby cabinet.

'I wouldn't suggest this to every customer, and I hope you'll forgive my presumption …'

She unlocks a drawer and opens it. I study the contents without moving or making comment. They're all small enough to keep in a pocket, rather than hanging on a belt as a man might do. I pick one up and pull the blade out of the leather sheath. Despite its size it's potentially a lethal weapon. The handle fits well in my hand.

'I'll take this.'

'A good choice,' she says, closing and locking the drawer. 'Don't keep it in your bag or you'll never reach it quickly enough, should the need arise.'

I nod my agreement and slip it into a pocket. I have no concept of the cost of these items but rely on my instincts that she will not cheat me.

'Leave your old clothes if you want and I'll take something off the price. Let's say four pounds five shillings.'

I hand over the coins. 'Thank you, for everything.'

'My advice is free and if your ship is at harbour, I suggest going straight on board until it sails. Good luck in your new life in Scotland.'

I head in what I believe will be the most direct route to the harbour, making sure I don't take any alleyways or stray into a street or area that feels dangerous. I've not been in this part of the town and soon find myself walking past the edge of a market square. I stop.

A large crowd has gathered around a raised platform. When I arrived ten years ago there were adults being sold, this time it's naked girls of about eleven years old. The buyers are women, who walk along the line speaking to the girls and physically checking them, sometimes intimately.

Men in the crowd shout obscene comments. I've heard stories about what's happening here for these women are the owners of large brothels in Bridgetown, buying young girls who have been born on the island and destined since birth to be sold as prostitutes. I've seen enough, seen more than enough, and move on quickly, arriving soon afterwards at the harbour, where I'm allowed on board the *Edinburgh*.

I find a place on deck out of the way of everyone but from where I can sit in my respectable, sturdy clothes and watch the many activities around the quayside. As I hug the canvas bag containing all of my other new possessions, part of me wonders whether it might not have been better if young Drummond had arrived at that barn just a few seconds later.

Epilogue

4 October 1690, Stromness harbour, Orkney

A LARGE SHIP HAS BEEN SIGHTED and is expected at Stromness later this morning, so I've come to my favourite spot on a low wall to draw the vessel once it's docked. The weather is unusually fine for October and it's pleasant to sit watching the frantic activity around the harbour; men loading and unloading cargoes, people arriving and departing, families and friends waving, crying and hugging whether those they know are coming or going.

Orkney is famous for supplying sailors and they travel the world, their experience greatly valued by captains of all types of vessel. I suspect that several families waiting on the quayside are related to sailors on board the new ship.

'Don't forget dinner this evening, Samuel.'

'I won't, Alasdair,' I call back to the passing figure. 'I haven't eaten for days in anticipation!'

The invitation is from one of the wealthy ship owners who has an impressive house on the hill. I've been successful with paintings of ships, which owners and captains are willing to pay handsomely for, while crews are often keen to purchase a sketch of the vessel on which they've sailed.

Sometimes individuals ask for a likeness of themselves and in a few minutes I can create something that gives them a small degree of happiness. People would willingly buy these drawings but in memory of the Reverend Sinclair's late wife Anne, I never charge. I've probably sketched half the population of Stromness, and because of this I'm a guest in a humble dwelling as often as I am in some grand house. I consider it a privilege to sit and chat about life to the occupants in either.

So far the new ship has remained hidden from view to anyone at the harbour by the island of Hoy and I'll have to wait until it's quite close before I get my first glimpse of it.

* * *

Young Drummond was true to his word and my passage from Barbados has been uneventful. The money I spent in Bridgetown made little impact on the amount he had handed over and there's sufficient to let me travel wherever I want, with plenty left over to live on. But where? Covenanters are no longer hunted so I'm free to go anywhere in a world where there is no obvious destination.

I forgave Hamish long ago. One of the government's aims with its King's Peace, the various Indulgences and the other oaths of loyalty to the monarch was to split up those involved in the Covenanter cause. They could hardly have been more successful than with us.

I hope Hamish has found it within him to have forgiven me. He'll most likely be in Coylton. Who knows, perhaps my mother still lives, and then there's Calum's son as well? Yet despite all this I don't intend to return. I would be such a strange figure in Coylton that it can hardly be considered home any more. Better to live out my life in some quiet place where no one knows me.

* * *

The ship is new to me and as it appears around the headland I begin capturing details that I will want later, as the owner has already commissioned a painting. When it's finally docked and the gangplank run out, I stop what I'm doing to watch people coming ashore. First off are the young, single men, their wide variety of clothing indicating their wide variety of status and wealth. They're followed by the older men, then families and finally the first of the sailors unloading produce.

I've assumed that everyone has come ashore and am just about to return to my task when an old woman walks into view and stands near the top of the gangplank. Even at this distance there is an extraordinary aura about her that captivates me. I sense, rather than see, an echo of beauty. It's so faint, like words that are impossible to discern yet you know they were once spoken clearly and strong.

But her face! Here is someone who has known pain and horror and sadness beyond the measure of even the poorest of wretches I've encountered over the decades. There is also wisdom and kindness and ... greatness; a woman who has done great deeds in her life. I can't explain why I'm so sure of it. Quickly, I turn to a clean sheet.

* * *

My senses are so confounded by the sights, smells and sounds around the harbour that I'm utterly confused and stand on the ship, hesitating to put a foot on the wooden gangplank that will take me on to land as a free woman for the first time in ten years. It's hardly more than a dozen steps, yet they feel so incredibly difficult to make, so momentous, that I'm rooted to the spot.

In front of me people hug and laugh, men slap each other's backs and loudly welcome home a brother or son. How can I walk into this world knowing what I know ... having seen what I've seen ... the terrible things I've done? There are memories that will haunt me until I die. Yet they're my memories and no one else's. I haven't travelled this long journey to falter now. There is a pause in the sailors going backwards and forwards.

I take a deep breath and put a hand on the rope railing.

* * *

I'm surprised at how stooped the woman is. Standing like a statue on the ship, there was an elegance about her, but upon moving, she is bent over, hanging on to the handrail as if fearing she will fall at any moment. She looks and moves like someone who has seen too many harsh winters, though I sense she is not so old but rather ... beaten. Any joy or hope have been sucked out of her to leave only an impression of the woman she was.

I try desperately to catch on paper what I see and sense. I've never felt such an intense need to capture an image since those days when I used to draw Violet.

* * *

I've walked several yards along the quayside when the world around me fades in an instant. The years have been kind to Samuel. His beautiful hair is perhaps not so strikingly ginger, but it's thick and well-groomed and he has the appearance of a much younger man, his passion and enthusiasm for his art obvious to all those around him. How well I know those quick movements of his hand as he sketches a scene or figure that inspires him.

I stare, not far away ... near enough to call out his name. He looks up. Our eyes lock for a brief moment – for such a brief moment – then he is once more drawing. If I had believed that my heart was so broken into tiny pieces that it could never again feel emotion, I was wrong. It beats livelier within my chest than I have known for many years.

For all that he studies me with his keen artist's eye, he doesn't recognise me. How could he? There's nothing left of the woman he once loved; not in body, spirit, faith ... not in anything.

He glances over, sees I am watching him, and continues with even greater urgency, hoping to finish before his subject moves on. It would be a cruel act to reveal myself, cruel to both of us, for I couldn't bear for him to know what I've become. Let him continue to believe his Violet, who had fought and loved and lived with such zeal, died long ago still the person he knew. There is nothing I can offer. The truth is that I love him but cannot give him what he needs.

Judging by his expensive jacket and waistcoat, Samuel has prospered. He seems content, sitting on his wall amongst so many interesting potential subjects. People call out friendly greetings to him as they pass and he is so lost in his task that he is totally unaware of them. I recall that expression of his well.

I stand a while longer. He continues, glancing up, glancing down. I will let him have his picture. Perhaps he'll look at it now and again and wonder about the strange figure on the quayside. I hope he never realises. And I will remember how he made my heart beat once more.

Finally, I turn away from my past and the man I've loved since we were children. I'm grateful, for I'll take with me the knowledge that he is well and that my heart is not so broken it cannot feel love ... and if there is love, there is hope.

I will return to Coylton. I'll climb the hill and lie in the hollow where Samuel drew me so often, and maybe I'll search for the girl who was so free and bold and passionate. Perhaps she's still there ... somewhere.

* * *

I watch the old woman walk slowly past the moored vessels, stopping often to speak to a sailor as if seeking another ship to continue her journey. Following the last conversation, she walks across a nearby gangplank and disappears from view.

It's only then that I look down at the sketch and gasp, as if I've not been aware of what I've been drawing. It's the most extraordinary face I've ever recorded and I'm captivated by what's been created.

'You will be framed and hung by the fireplace, next to the only woman I have ever loved.'

The picture is so alive I almost expect an answer. Carefully, I place the paper between other sheets to keep it safe and, reluctantly, take out once more the sketches of the ship and begin to fill in more detail of the rigging.

Author's Notes

During our annual holidays in Orkney, my wife and I often passed the imposing Covenanter Memorial, erected in 1888 to commemorate around 200 people who drowned on 10 December 1679 when the *Crown of London* sank nearby. They had been banished from Scotland because of their Covenanter beliefs. The background to all this remained a mystery to me for years until I had completed *The Last Witch of Scotland* and was seeking my next project.

As soon as I started reading about the Covenanters, I was hooked by this extraordinary period of Scottish history that I knew nothing about. During the seventeenth century, a state of civil war existed in Scotland for decades as various monarchs proclaimed they were head of the Church of Scotland while much of the population – Presbyterians who believed the head of the Church was Jesus – disagreed; although the issues were, of course, much more complex than this. The violence became so great that part of this period is known as the 'Killing Times'.

Throughout *A Fire in Their Hearts*, I drop my fictitious characters into major events that occurred, where they often encounter real people from history. The novel begins in 1662 when hundreds of Church of Scotland ministers are thrown out of their manses, kirks and parishes because they won't agree to be re-ordained by bishops newly appointed by the king or acknowledge that King Charles II is the head of the Church.

The catalyst to the Pentland Rising in 1666 was the rough treatment of an old man in St John's Town of Dalry, Kirkcudbrightshire, and I've tried to follow the main sequence of actual events that led up to the Battle of Rullion Green on 28 November 1666. The execution of seven Covenanters by their former friend Cornelius Anderson is a harrowing scene. A stone marks the site of their graves in the Auld Kirk of Ayr.

Because the novel covers almost thirty years, I needed to move on the story at certain points and so I send Samuel to the staunchly Protestant Holland to train as a church minister because this is the country that many Scots went to or, indeed, fled to when things were bad.

It was in the south-west of Scotland that the Covenanter cause had its greatest support and early in 1678 the Privy Council sent what became known as the 'Highland Host or Horde' to capture leading Covenanters, collect unpaid fines and prevent field preaching known as conventicles, which were attracting thousands of people. During this period of occupation, the brutality, theft and disregard for people and property was staggering.

The encounter at Drumclog, when the famous 'Covenanter hunter' John Graham of Claverhouse (Viscount Dundee) hoped to surprise people at a field preaching, was one of the rare occasions when Covenanters defeated a Royalist force. This success set in motion events that would result in the Battle of Bothwell Bridge.

A Covenanter army of around 6,000 had based itself on the south side of the River Clyde near the village of Bothwell in Lanarkshire. The Duke of Monmouth, King Charles II's eldest illegitimate son, commanded the Royalist army. Figures for the size of this army vary enormously but there are several references to it being around 15,000 strong. They arrived on the north side of the river on the morning of 22 June 1679. The only way across was to use the bridge and for more than an hour some 300 Covenanters held back the Royalist army using one brass cannon and muskets.

The main Covenanter force watched from a short distance away, so paralysed by internal dispute and distrust amongst its different factions that they provided neither additional men nor ammunition. Eventually, the defenders ran out of powder and shot and had no choice but to rush back up the hill.

Apparently, it was only after a considerable number of Royalist soldiers had crossed to the south side that some Covenanters came down to fight them, but by then the battle was already lost. It's estimated that around 400 Covenanters were killed and 1,200 captured. Many of those who escaped were later hunted down or put on wanted lists by the government.

Those captured were held in Edinburgh at Greyfriars Kirkyard, a walled area of approximately three acres. Visitors to Greyfriars church today can look through gates at the 'Covenanters' Prison' but this is only a tiny portion of the area used and there were no graves at that time. Indeed, those gates wouldn't have existed in the seventeenth century, with the entrance into the enclosure at a different place altogether.

On 15 November 1679, the remaining Covenanters, who were in a desperate state by this time, were taken to Leith and put on board the *Crown of London*, on which they later began their fateful journey. After the ship sank, almost fifty Covenanters were recaptured and banished as intended, with most writers saying they went to Barbados. A few Covenanters survived being recaptured and are thought to have fled to Ireland, or even settled in Orkney.

The Drummond plantation and the characters on it are completely fictitious, although I have tried to be as authentic as possible in describing, in the form of a historical fiction, the lives people typically endured on sugar plantations in Barbados (the illness was yellow fever). The subject of indentured servants is absolutely fascinating. Hundreds of thousands of people left Britain's shores during the seventeenth century as indentured servants, either willingly or because they were forced to.

The appointment in 1689 of William of Orange and his wife Mary as co-monarchs of Scotland subsequently led to the Church of Scotland being officially proclaimed as Presbyterian, overseen by its own General Assembly free from outside control. Banished Covenanters could return to Scotland in safety but only if they had the money for their passage. Most remained in the countries they had been sent to and there are descendants of Covenanters around the world, particularly in North America, because of this fifty-year struggle in Scotland for religious freedom ... a struggle which is so often ignored, misunderstood or forgotten.

Acknowledgements

A Fire in Their Hearts could only have been written in the way it has with advice from experts in a huge variety of fields, from muskets to painting techniques in the seventeenth century, who helped to ensure that the background details of the novel are as authentic and accurate as possible. Some people aided me in finding those experts and I am extremely grateful to everyone for their help.

Dr Frederick E Alleyne, Nick Ball FSA, Barbados Museum and Historical Society, Dr Sandra Cardarelli, Abby Cox, Reverend James Currall, Professor Jane Dawson, Alexandra Dold, Major James Erskine, Dr Nicholas Evans, Professor John Finlay, Joseph Ford, Professor Julian Goodare, Dr Jamie Grant, Kevin Hall, Bert Hutchings, Stuart Kennedy, Dane Love, Major General Patrick C Marriott CB CBE, Dr Jim MacPherson, David McAllister, Ellen McFadzen, Susan E Millar, Orkney Library, Reverend Nigel J Robb, Reverend David Scott, Dr Joseph Wagner.

I must also thank the team at Black & White Publishing in Edinburgh, who had the faith in me and my writing all those years ago to publish my debut novel, *The Italian Chapel*, in 2009. Since then we've worked together on many different books. I was grateful to once again benefit from the sage advice of my editor, Clem Flanagan.

A special thanks must go to my darling wife Catherine for her love, wisdom, encouragement and support, without which very little would ever get written. In return I have explained in detail the difference between seventeenth-century flintlock and matchlock muskets – and for this, I am certain, she must be grateful beyond words.

Also by Philip Paris

Historical Fiction
The Last Witch of Scotland
The Italian Chapel
Effie's War

Contemporary Fiction
Men Cry Alone
Casting Off – written as P I Paris

Non-Fiction
Orkney's Italian Chapel: The True Story of an Icon
Nylon Kid of the North